In the

BORDERLANDS

death is the least of your fears!

- An inflatable love doll promises instant gratification . . . and unspeakable terrors

- A lonely woman offers her body to locusts in a gruesome carnal sacrifice

- A cabbie opens a terrifying window to the future on a blood-chilling ride to Hell and back

Praise for the first

BORDERLANDS

"One of the strongest anthologies to appear in years . . . Shows us how relentless, protean, dark, and probing horror can be."
PETER STRAUB

Other Horrific Anthologies edited by
Thomas F. Monteleone
from Avon Books

BORDERLANDS

BORDERLANDS 2

An Anthology of Imaginative Fiction

edited by
THOMAS F. MONTELEONE

AVON BOOKS ◆ NEW YORK

Additional copyright notices appear on the acknowledgments page, which serves as an extension of this copyright page.

BORDERLANDS 2 is a work of fiction. All characters and events depicted in this book are purely fictitious, and any similarity to actual persons or events is purely coincidental.

AVON BOOKS
A division of
The Hearst Corporation
1350 Avenue of the Americas
New York, New York 10019

Copyright © 1991 by Thomas F. Monteleone and individual story authors
Cover art by Philip Singer
Published by arrangement with the editor
Library of Congress Catalog Card Number: 91-92069
ISBN: 0-380-76517-9

First Avon Books Printing: December 1991

AVON TRADEMARK REG. U.S. PAT. OFF. AND IN OTHER COUNTRIES, MARCA REGISTRADA, HECHO EN U.S.A.

Printed in the U.S.A.

RA 10 9 8 7 6 5 4 3 2 1

This Is For
David F. Bischoff
and
John DeChancie,
Two Guys Who Are Writers.

ACKNOWLEDGMENTS

General introduction, acknowledgments, and author/story introductions copyright © 1991 by Thomas F. Monteleone

"Foet" copyright © 1991 by F. Paul Wilson

"The Chrysalis" copyright © 1991 by Lois Tilton

"Breeding Ground" copyright © 1991 by Francis J. Matozzo

"Love Doll: A Fable" copyright © 1991 by Joe R. Lansdale

"Apathetic Flesh" copyright © 1991 by Darren O. Godfrey

"The Potato" copyright © 1991 by Bentley Little

"Saturn" copyright © 1991 by Ian McDowell

"Androgyny" copyright © 1991 by Brian Hodge

"Stigmata" copyright © 1991 by Gary L. Raisor

"Sarah, Unbound" copyright © 1991 by Kim Antieau

"For Their Wives Are Mute" copyright © 1991 by Wayne Allen Sallee

"Dead Issue" copyright © 1991 by Rex Miller

"Down the Valley Wild" copyright © 1991 by Paul F. Olson

"Taking Care of Michael" copyright © 1991 by J. L. Comeau

"The Atonement" copyright © 1991 by Richard Rains

"Peacemaker" copyright © 1991 by Charles L. Grant

"Stress Test HR51, Case #041068" copyright © 1991 by Stanley Wiater

"Churches of Desire" copyright © 1991 by Philip Nutman

"Sweetie" copyright © 1991 by G. Wayne Miller

"Romance Unlimited" copyright © 1991 by James S. Dorr

"Slipping" copyright © 1991 by David B. Silva

CONTENTS

INTRODUCTION

In some ways, I feel like Neil Armstrong—you remember him, don't you?—after he returned from his journey into history and his first steps on the lunar surface.[1] Or maybe Edmund Hillary—after he finally made it to the top of Everest. Or maybe even *me*—after I've been running with the most beautiful, intelligent, scintillating, willing-to-experiment, hates-to-nag, accepts-me-the-way-I-am woman in the northern hemisphere . . .

Why should I feel like any of the above, you might ask?

Because I'm sitting here trying to write an introduction to this second batch of *Borderlands* stories, and I'm facing the challenge of what the ballplayers call the *sophomore jinx*. After a simply great rookie season—which is what *Borderlands 1* enjoyed—it is tough to come back and do it as well. Editing and publishing the initial volume wasn't exactly in a class with the achievements of paragraph one, but the book did turn out to be a tremendous critical success and a benchmark by which all other original anthologies of the Nineties will be measured.

Is he hyping us?—you might be asking yourselves . . .

No, not this time. The original *Borderlands* was conceived to be an anthology of fiction which pushed the limits of what was being done in darkly imaginative

---

[1] It is said by those who know that his first words were NOT that "small step, giant step" business, but actually something like "Gee, this shit's kinda powdery . . . but it looks like it'll be okay . . ."

1

fiction, which expanded the envelope, opened the gates to new territories, scorched pathways through the jagged landscape of the imagination, and all those other neat metaphors.

And the nice thing was—it actually *did* it.

Dig: the limited, signed hardcover sold out within six months; it garnered rave reviews from every major publication ranging from "best anthology of the year" to the "best anthology *ever*"; fifteen of its stories received nominations for superior achievement by the HWA, Inc.; many of the stories were selected for subsequent "best of the year" anthologies; it was nominated for the World Fantasy Award. It was so successful, in fact, that it served as the cornerstone for a specialty publishing venture I founded, called Borderlands Press, and which is doing very, very well, thank you.

So you see—I'm talking about a very tough act to follow. As the series shambles into the Nineties in earnest, I am faced with finding a continuous stream of kick-ass fiction when no one else seems to be able to do it.

Hey, that's okay. I've been married a couple of times—I like a good challenge.

But seriously, friends, what I'm trying to say here is that even though it's been tough (I figure I read about one thousand manuscripts over the six months the anthology was open), I still caught up with a high fastball and clocked one into the downtown seats. Yeah . . . you hold in your hands the second volume of in-your-face, provocative, visionary fiction—*Borderlands 2*. In keeping with the traditions established in the initial volume, I have managed to shake up the table of contents so you have more to deal with than the list of Usual Suspects (you know who they are) who manage to get their stuff in just about everybody's magazines and anthologies with stories which often strike me as less-than-inspired. Oh sure, you'll find work by some of the best and most recognizable names in the field in here. But you'll also discover, as I did, some of the most exciting and daring new fiction by writers who are still making their bones as the class acts of the Nineties.

I can't tell you what a pleasure it is to discover these newer writers and share their visions with you. Someday they're all going to be writing novels and dedicating their second books (the first ones always go to parents and wives and husbands and children . . .) to me for giving them their Big Chance and all that stuff, but for right now, they're the Young Turks, the Surly Invaders who, if they could, would take us out like assassins in the night, who would slice us with their words and watch us bleed.

And we should be glad they're here. Because they are the future of the genre of darkly imaginative fiction, and we need their new ways of seeing past the veil of the everyday, of revealing the shrouded shape beneath Steve King's sheet.

And so, welcome to *Borderlands 2*. The stories which follow don't have to be read on a dark night, with glowing embers banked in the fireplace, and a dark wind howling across the moors. You can read these tales under the clear light of day and pure reason, and they will still knock you around and dance some flamenco rhythms on your head. You won't find any of the traditional bugbears and boogymen here. No ghosts or vampires need apply. No zombies, no werewolves, no mummies, succubi, or Hitchcockian spouses planning to do in their mates. None of the tired old symbols which have defined the genre for far too long will be found here.

And that's what *Borderlands* is all about. So turn the page, and have fun with your *new* fears.

—Thomas F. Monteleone
Baltimore, MD, 1991

FOET

F. Paul Wilson

When I solicited stories for this anthology series, one of the phrases used to describe the kind of fiction I'm looking for was "stories which do not employ the usual symbols and traditional plot elements . . ." Written with a delicately satiric touch, F. Paul Wilson's "Foet" fulfills that requirement perfectly. He is the best-selling author of novels The Keep, The Tomb, *and* Black Wind, *and an extremely accomplished writer of the short story. His collection,* Soft and Others, *belongs on every HDF reader's shelf. He is also the editor of the upcoming Horror Writers of America anthology,* Freak Show. *But enough about Paul, now it's time to find out what the strange title to his story really means . . .*

Denise didn't mind the January breeze blowing against her back down Fifth Avenue as she crossed Fifty-Seventh Street. Her favorite place in the world was Manhattan, her favorite pastime was shopping, and when she was shopping in midtown, it was heaven.

At the curb Denise stopped and turned to stare at the pert blonde who'd just passed her. She couldn't believe it.

"Helene? Helene Ryder, is that you?"

The blonde turned. Her eyes lit with recognition.

"Ohmigod, Denise! Imagine meeting you here! How long has it been?"

They hugged and air-kissed.

"Oh, I don't know," Denise said. "Six months?"

"At least! What are you doing in the city?"

"Just shopping," Denise said. "Accessory hunting."

"Me, too. Where were you headed?"

"Actually, I was looking for a place to get off my feet and have a bite to eat. I skipped lunch and I'm famished."

"That sounds good." She glanced at her watch. A diamond Piaget, Denise noticed. "It's tea time at the Waldorf. Why don't we go there?"

"Wonderful!"

During the bouncy cab ride down Park Avenue, Denise gave Helene a thorough twice-over and was impressed. Her blonde hair was short and fashionably tousled; her merino wool topcoat, camel's-hair sweater, and short wool and cashmere skirt reeked of Bergdorf's and I. Magnin.

Amazing what could happen when your husband got a big promotion. You could move from Fairfield to Greenwich, and you could buy any little thing your heart desired.

Not that Helene hadn't always had style. It was just that now she could afford to dress in the manner to which she and Denise had always hoped to become accustomed.

Denise was still waiting to become accustomed. Her Brian didn't have quite the drive of Helene's Harry. He still liked to get involved in local causes and in church functions. And that was good in a way. It allowed him more time at home with her and the twins. The downside, though, was that she didn't have the budget to buy what she needed when she needed it. As a result, Denise had honed her shopping skills to the black-belt level. By keeping her eyes and ears ever open, buying judiciously, and timing her purchases to the minute— like now, for instance, in the post-holiday retail slump— she managed to keep herself looking nearly as in style as someone with a pocketbook as deep as Helene's.

And on the subject of pocketbooks, Denise could not take her eyes off Helene's. Fashioned of soft, silky, golden brown leather that seemed to glow in the afternoon sunlight streaming through the grimy windows of the cab, it perfectly offset the colors of her outfit. She

wondered if Helene had chosen the bag for the outfit, or
the outfit for the bag. She suspected the latter. The bag
was exquisite; the stitchwork was especially fascinating
in its seemingly random joining of odd-sized and odd-
shaped pieces. But it was the material itself that drew
and captured her attention. She had an urge to reach out
and touch it. But she held back.

Later. She'd ask Helene about it during tea.

Sitting here with Helene on a settee along the wall in
Peacock Alley at the Waldorf, sipping tea and nibbling
on petits fours from the tray on the table before them,
Denise felt as if she were part of the international set.
The room whispered exotic accents and strange vowels.
Almost every nationality was represented—the Far East
most strongly—and everyone was dressed to the nines.
The men's suits were either Armani or Bill Blass, and
a number of the women outshone even Helene. Denise
felt almost dowdy.

And still . . . that handbag of Helene's, sitting between them on the sofa. She couldn't escape the urge
to caress it, could not keep her eyes off it.

"Isn't it beautiful?" Helene said.

"Hmmm?" Denise said, embarrassed at being caught
staring, wondering if the envy showed in her eyes. "The
bag? Yes, it is. I don't think I've ever seen anything
like it."

"I'd be surprised if you had," Helene said. She pushed
it closer to her. "Take a look."

Soft. That was the first thing Denise noticed as she
lifted it. The leather was so soft, a mix of silk and
down as her fingers brushed over the stitched surface.
She cradled it on her lap. It stole her breath.

"Um . . . very unusual, isn't it?" she managed to say
after a moment.

"No. Not so unusual. I've spotted a few others around
the room since we arrived."

"Really?" Denise had been so entranced by Helene's
bag that the others had gone unnoticed. That wasn't like
her. "Where?"

Helene tilted her head to their left. "Right over there. Two tables down, in the navy blue sweater chemise and matching leggings."

Denise spotted her. A Japanese woman, holding the bag on the coffee table before her. Hers was black, but the stitching was unmistakable. As Denise scanned the room she noticed another, this one a deep coffee brown. And she noticed something else—they belonged to the most exquisitely dressed women in the room. Among all the beautifully dressed people here in Peacock Alley, the women who stood out, who showed exceptional flair and style in their ensembles, were the ones carrying foet bags.

Denise knew in that instant that she had to have one. It didn't matter how much they cost, this was the accessory she'd been looking for, the touch that would set her apart, lift her to a higher fashion plane.

The Japanese woman rose from her table and walked past. She glanced at Denise on her way by. Her gaze dropped to the bag on Denise's lap and she smiled and nodded. Denise managed to smile back.

What was that? It was as if the women with these bags had formed some sort of club. No matter what the dues, Denise wanted to be a member.

Helene was smiling knowingly when Denise looked back at her.

"I know what you're thinking," Helene singsonged.

"Do you?"

"Uh-huh. 'Where do I get one?' Right?"

Right. But Denise wasn't going to admit it. She hated being obvious.

"Actually I was wondering what kind of leather it is."

A cloud crossed Helene's face.

"You don't know?" She paused, then: "It's foet."

"*Feet*? Whose feet? And then Denise realized what Helene had said. "Oh . . . my . . . God!"

"Now, Denise—"

Foet! She'd heard of it but she'd never thought she'd see it or actually touch it, never *dreamed* Helene would buy any. Her gorge rose.

"I don't believe it!" Denise said, pushing the bag back onto the sofa between them and staring angrily at Helene.

"Don't look at me like that. It's not as if I committed a crime or anything."

"How could you, Helene?"

"Look at it," Helene said, lifting the bag. "How could I not?"

Denise's eyes were captured again by the golden glow of the leather. She felt her indignation begin to melt.

"But it's human skin!" she said, as much to remind herself of that hideous fact as to drag it out into the open.

"Not human . . . at least according to the Supreme Court."

"I don't care what those old farts say, it's still human skin!"

Helene shook her head. "*Fetal* skin, Denise. From abortions. And it's legal. If fetuses were legally human, you couldn't abort them. So the Supreme Court finally had to rule that their skin could be used."

"I know all about that, Helene."

Who didn't know about *Ranieri v. Verlaine*? The case had sent shock waves around the country. Around the *world!* Denise's church had formed a group to go down to Washington to protest it. As a matter of fact—

"Helene, you were out on Pennsylvania Avenue with me demonstrating against the ruling! How could you—?"

Helene shrugged. "Things change. I'm still anti-abortion, but after we moved away from Fairfield and I lost contact with our old church group, I stopped thinking about it. Our new friends aren't into that sort of stuff and so I, well, just kind of drifted into other things."

"That's fine, Helene, but how does that bring you to buying something like . . ." She pointed to the bag and, God help her, she still wanted to run her hands over it. "*This!*"

"I saw one. We went to a reception—some fund-raiser for the homeless, I think—and I met a woman who had one. I fell in love with it immediately. I hemmed and hawed, feeling guilty for wanting it, but finally I went out and bought myself one." She beamed at Denise. "And believe me, I've never regretted it."

"God, Helene."

"They're already dead, Denise. I don't condone abortion any more than you do, but it's legal and that's not likely to change. And as long as it stays legal, these poor little things are going to be killed day after day, week after week, hundreds and thousands and millions of them. We have no control over that. And buying foet accessories will not change that one way or another. They're already dead."

Denise couldn't argue with Helene on that point. Yes, they were dead, and there was nothing anyone could do about that. But . . .

"But where do they sell this stuff?" Denise said. "I've never once seen it displayed or even advertised."

"Oh, it's in all the better stores, but it's very discreet. They're not stupid. Foet may be legal but it's still controversial. Nobody wants trouble, nobody wants a scene. I mean, can you imagine a horde of the faithful hausfraus from St. Paul's marching through Bergdorf's? I mean *really*!"

Denise had to smile. Yes, that would be quite a sight.

"I guess it would be like the fur activists."

"Even worse," Helene said, leaning closer. "You know why those nuts are anti-fur? Because they've never had a fur coat. It's pure envy with them. But foet? Foet is tied up with motherhood and apple pie. It's going to take a long time for the masses to get used to foet. So until then, the market will be small and select. Very select."

Denise nodded. *Select*. Despite all her upbringing, all her beliefs, something within her yearned to be part of that small, select market. And she hated herself for it.

"Is it very expensive?"

Helene nodded. "Especially this shade," she said, caressing her bag. "It's all hand sewn. No two pieces are exactly alike."

"And where'd you buy yours?"

Helene was staring at her appraisingly. "You're not thinking of starting any trouble, are you?"

"Oh, no. No, of course not. I just want to look. I'm . . . curious."

More of that appraising stare. Denise wanted to hide behind the settee.

"You want one, don't you?"

"Absolutely not! Maybe it's morbid on my part, but I'm curious to see what else they're doing with . . . foet these days."

"Very well," Helene said, and it occurred to Denise that Helene had never said *Very well* when she'd lived in Fairfield. "Go to Blume's—it's on Fifth, a little ways up from Gucci's."

"I know it."

"Ask for Rolf. When you see him, tell him you're interested in some of his better accessories. Remember that: 'better accessories.' He'll know what you're looking for."

Denise passed Blume's three times, and each time she told herself she'd keep right on walking and find a taxi to take her down to the train and back to Fairfield. But something forced her to turn and go back for one more pass. Just one more pass. On the fourth, she ducked into a slot in the revolving door and swung into the warm, brightly lit interior.

Where was the harm in just looking?

When he appeared, Rolf reminded her of a Rudolf Valentino wannabe—stiletto thin in his black pin-striped suit, with plastered-down black hair and mechanical pencil mustache. He was a good ten years younger and barely an inch taller than Denise, and had delicate, fluttery hands, lively eyes, and a barely audible voice.

He gave Denise a careful up-and-down after she'd given him the code words, then extended his arm to the right.

"Of course. This way, please."

He led her to the back of the store, down a narrow

corridor, and then through a glass door into a small, indirectly lit showroom. Denise found herself surrounded by glass shelves lined with handbags, belts, even watch bands. All made of foet.

"The spelling is adapted from the archaic medical term," Rolf said, closing the door behind them.

"Really?" She noticed he didn't actually say the word: *foetal*.

"Now . . . what may I show you?"

"May I browse a little?"

"*Mais oui*. Take your time."

Denise wandered the pair of aisles, inspecting the tiers of shelves and all the varied items they carried. She noticed something. Almost everything was black or very dark.

"The bag my friend showed me was lighter color."

"Ah, yes. I'm sorry, but we're out of white. That goes first, you know."

"No, this wasn't white. It was more of a pale, golden brown."

"Yes. We call that white. After all, it's made from white hide. It's relatively rare."

" 'Hide'? "

He smiled. "Yes. That's what we call the . . . material."

The material: white fetal skin.

"Do you have any pieces without all the stitching? Something with a smoother look?"

"I'm afraid not. I mean, you have to understand, we're forced by the very nature of the source of the material to work with little pieces." He gestured around. "Notice, too, that there are no gloves. None of the manufacturers wants to be accused of making kid gloves."

Rolf smiled. Denise could only stare at him.

He cleared his throat. "Trade humor."

Little pieces.

Hide.

Kid gloves.

Suddenly she wanted to run, but she held on. The urge passed.

Rolf picked up a handbag from atop a nearby display case. It was a lighter brown than the others, but still considerably darker than Helene's.

"A lot of people are going for this shade. It's reasonably priced. Imported from India."

"Imported? I'd have thought there'd be plenty to go around just from the U.S."

He sighed. "There would be if people weren't so provincial in their attitudes about giving up the hides. The tanneries are offering a good price for them. I don't understand some people. Anyway, we have to import from the Third World. India is a great source."

Denise picked up another, smaller bag of similar shade. So soft, so smooth, just like Helene's.

"Indian, too?"

"Yes, but that's a little more expensive. That's male."

She looked at him questioningly.

"They hardly ever abort males in India," he said. "Only females. Two thousand-to-one."

Denise put it down and picked up a similar model, glossy ink black. This would be a perfect accent to so many of her ensembles.

"Now that's—"

"Please don't tell me anything about it," Denise said. "Just the price."

He told her. She repressed a gasp. That would just about empty her account of the money she'd put aside for all her fashion bargains. On one item. Was it worth it?

She reached into her old pocketbook, the now dowdy-looking Fendi, and pulled out her gold MasterCard. Rolf smiled and lifted it from her fingers.

Minutes later she was back among the hoi polloi in the main shopping area, but she wasn't one of them. She'd been where they couldn't go, and that gave her special feeling.

Before leaving Blume's, Denise put her Fendi in the store bag and hung the new foet bag over her arm. The doorman gave her a big smile as he passed her through to the sidewalk.

The afternoon was dying and a cold wind had sprung

up. She stood in the fading light with the wind cutting her like an icy knife and suddenly she felt horrible.

I'm toting a bag made from the skin of an unborn child.

Why? Why had she bought it? What had possessed her to spend that kind of money on such a ghoulish . . . artifact? Because that was just what it was—not an accessory, an artifact.

She opened the store bag and reached in to switch the new foet for her trusty Fendi. She didn't want to be seen with it.

And Brian! Good God, how was she going to tell Brian?

"*What?*"

Brian never talked with food in his mouth. He had better manners than that. But Denise had just told him about Helene's bag and at the moment his mouth, full of food, hung open as he stared at her with wide eyes.

"Brian, please close your mouth."

He swallowed. "*Helene*? Helene had something made of human skin?"

. . . not human . . . at least according to the Supreme Court . . .

"It's called *foet*, Brian."

"I know damn well what it's called! They could call it chocolate mousse but it would still be human skin. They give it a weird name so people won't look at them like they're a bunch of Nazis when they sell it! Helene— how could she?"

. . . they're already dead, Denise . . .

Brian's tone became increasingly caustic. Denise felt almost as if he were talking to her.

"I don't believe it! What's got into her? One person kills an unborn child and the other makes the poor thing's skin into a pocketbook! And Helene of all people! My God, is that what a big pay raise and moving to Greenwich does to you?"

Denise barely heard Brian as he ranted on. Thank God she'd had the good sense not to tell him about her own bag. He'd have been apoplectic.

No doubt about it. She was going to return that bag as soon as she could get back into the city.

Denise stood outside Blume's, dreading the thought of facing Rolf in that tiny showroom and returning her foet, her beautiful foet.

She pulled it out of the shopping bag and stared at it. Exquisite. Strange how a little extra time could turn your attitude around. The revulsion that had overwhelmed her right after she'd bought it had faded. Perhaps because every day during the past week—a number of times each day, to be honest—she'd taken it out and looked at it, held it, caressed it. Inevitably, its true beauty had shown through and captured her. Her initial beguilement had returned to the fore.

But the attraction went beyond mere beauty. This sort of accessory *said* something. Exactly what, she wasn't sure. But she knew a bold fashion statement when she saw one. This, however, was a statement she didn't have quite the nerve to make. At least not in Fairfield. So different here in the city. The cosmopolitan atmosphere allowed the elite to flash their foet—she liked the rhyme. She could be so very *in* here. But it would make her so very *out* in Fairfield—out of her home, too, most likely.

Small minds. What did they know about fashion? In a few years they'd all be buying it. Right now, only the leaders wore it. And for a few moments she'd been a member of that special club. Now she was about to resign.

As she turned to enter Blume's, a Mercedes stretch limo pulled into the curb beside her. The driver hopped out and opened the door. A shapely brunette of about Denise's age emerged. She was wearing a dark gray short wrap coat of llama and kid over a long-sleeved crepe-jersey catsuit. In her hand was a black clutch purse with the unmistakable stitching of foet. Her eyes flicked down to Denise's new handbag, then back up to her face. She smiled. Not just a polite passing-stranger smile, but a warm, we-know-we've-got-style smile.

As Denise returned the smile, all the doubts within her melted away as if they had never been. Suddenly she knew she was right. She knew what really mattered, what was important, where she had to be, fashion-wise.

And Brian? Who said Brian had to know a thing about it? What did he know about fashion anyway?

Denise turned and strode down Fifth with her new foet bag swinging from her arm for all the world to see.

Screw them all. It made her feel good, like she was *some*body. What else mattered?

She really had to make a point of getting into the city more often.

THE CHRYSALIS

Lois Tilton

The majority of stories submitted to Borderlands *are from totally unknown writers—that great, seething mass of people who send out story after story, gathering up their rejection slips as they learn their craft and hone their resolve to keep doing it till they get it right. But being unknown does not mean you can't be a good writer, nor will it exclude you from the* Contents *page of* Borderlands. *The following story by Lois Tilton, who lives in Glen Ellyn, Illinois, reached out and grabbed me from the first sentence, and now it can do the same for you.*

The morning sun came through the window and played lightly onto Mrs. Vivian's eyelids. Half-asleep, she rolled over onto her side, where her hand met something cool and damply resilient. The unpleasant sensation jolted her awake, and she opened her eyes to see her husband Gregory's discarded skin lying facedown on his side of the queen-sized bed.

He was gone, and he hadn't even made a sound, hadn't even wakened her to say good-bye.

An oily, yellowish fluid had oozed from the split in his back, staining the sheets. Mrs. Vivian got up to strip the bed, to save the mattress. She lifted up the skin by the armpits, but it was surprisingly heavy and awkward, like a damp rubber wetsuit. The limbs almost seemed to move of their own accord. Recalling her parents' passing, she had expected Gregory's husk to be somehow lighter, drier. It had split from the crown of the head down to the crack of the buttocks.

Curious, she flopped it over onto its back and stared at what had been her husband's face. It was puckered and distorted, barely recognizable. An eyelid was half-open onto the emptiness behind it, and she brushed it closed. There was a gray stubble of beard on the chin.

How ugly it was, she thought, looking down at the wrinkled, age-worn husk, the blotches of age on the skin, the sparse gray mat of hair on the chest. And at the crotch, where the flaccid member lay in shrunken mockery of its former rampant glory. She thought of it stiffening erect, plunging inside her to discharge its seed. But the time for that sort of thing was over now.

She draped the skin over the back of a chair while she stripped the bed to the mattress and put on fresh sheets. She was alone now. What was she supposed to do until her own time came?

Soaping herself in the shower when she was finished with the bed, she was intensely, distastefully aware of her aging flesh—her sagging breasts, the loose skin of her upper arms, neck, and belly. How she longed for her own metamorphosis, to emerge transformed from her hateful, cast-off husk. The wrinkled lips of her sex reminded her again of her husband's limp, shrunken organ. How they had made love in their youth, and she had borne children, the opening stretched impossibly wide by the pressure of their emerging skulls. Her children were grown now and gone, having children of their own, and her womb was useless and dried out. Like she was.

She knew she ought to call her children, to arrange for the decent disposal of Gregory's remains, but then she would truly be alone. It was easy to pretend he was still in the room, inside the husk draped over the chair. Gregory hadn't talked that much, anyway. But he had been there.

The discarded skin was stiff and dry by the time she was ready for bed that night, and in the dark it almost looked as if he was sitting on the chair at her side. He had sat there that way, she recalled, when she had the babies. Not saying much, just sometimes holding her hand, waiting. She hoped he was still waiting now.

In the middle of the night she woke, panicky and alone. There beside her was the shape of Gregory's husk in the dark, and she got up, lifted it, and brought it back to the bed. She had slept with him next to her for the past thirty years and it was too lonely without him now. The skin was light and dry, almost crisp. This wasn't Gregory, she knew, pulling the covers up over both of them, but the wrinkled shell he had discarded was a familiar thing, and she felt fond of it, in a way, as a remembrance of him, still faintly carrying his scent. It made her feel better as she fell back into sleep.

The next morning she felt strong enough to make the necessary phone call, and soon the children had gathered, sober as befits a solemn occasion, her two sons and daughter. She had made the bed and laid the husk there on its side, but at the sight of the dried-out skin they knew at once what she'd done. "Honestly, Mother," her daughter frowned in disapproval. "How long has it been?"

Her oldest son, named Gregory after his father, put a hand on his sister's arm to shut her up. "Are you all right, Mother?" he asked. "Maybe you might want to come and stay with Elenor and me for a while."

"No." Mrs. Vivian shook her head. "I want to be here, when my time comes. It can't be long now."

"But, Mother, you can't be sure."

"What more do I have to wait for? All of you are grown, and I want to move on. While your father is still waiting for me." She took a breath, gathering determination. "And I'm going to keep him with me until then."

"But, Mother—" her daughter started to protest, until her brother shook his head. "Let her keep it. There's no harm. She's right. It can't be too long, after all."

The next days were very difficult for Mrs. Vivian, even with the comforting presence of Gregory's shell. Oh, if only he hadn't gone on ahead of her! If only he'd waited so they could be renewed together! He was waiting now, in his new form, she told herself, but inwardly she had doubts. After metamorphosis, a person was changed. In his present state, Gregory would be beyond such mundane concerns as food. Or sex. She could imagine his new body, pure, smooth, and unmarred by orifices or dangling sex organs. Next to him, she knew she would appear ugly and grotesque in her wrinkled, worn-out flesh. How she longed to cast it off!

Without her husband to cook for, she had little interest in food. She lost weight, and her flesh began to sag even more. She pulled at the loose skin as if she could tear it away. Desperately, she took off her clothes and lay out naked and pallid in the sun, hoping to harden her skin, but the only result was a painful burn that made it red and tender. After a week or so, a thin layer peeled away in tissue-thin shreds, but that was all.

Late at night she would lie sleepless next to Gregory's desiccated remains and moan quietly to herself, "How long? Oh, how long?" Once, thrashing restlessly, her arm struck the husk on the other side of the bed. There was a sharp snapping sound and she sat up in alarm. A piece of the face had cracked. The husk was as thin and brittle as chitin now. She pulled the sheet away and glanced down at the fragile, shrunken remains of his penis, still intact. She wondered if he had regretted leaving this one piece of him behind to shrivel and disintegrate with the rest of his discarded flesh.

And then it happened at last, what she had waited for so long. She woke with her scalp feeling stiff and taut. It hurt to blink her eyes, and she could barely open her mouth. Now she understood why Gregory had never spoken. But, oh, it was happening, it was happening at last! She would be with him soon, wonderfully transformed. Tears of joy ran unfelt down her cheeks, the skin already going numb.

There was a sharp, tearing sensation as the back of her scalp split open. Eagerly, she reached up to pull it away. She could feel the edges starting to part, but then there came a terrible pain as it resisted, still attached to the flesh beneath. A trickle of warm blood ran down her neck. Alarmed, she realized that the process couldn't be rushed.

Impatiently, she waited while the split lengthened and widened. Soon her scalp had pulled away down to her forehead. She tore it down, stripping it away from her face, but the skin was still attached at the eyelids and it couldn't be pulled any farther.

The whole process was like reliving the births of her children, the long, slow hours of labor, the spasms as her uterus contracted and opened her cervix, wider and ever wider. There had been pain then, too, and blood. It had felt as if their emerging skulls were splitting her apart. Only now she was giving birth to her new self. She breathed in the rhythms she had learned so many years ago and waited for the next contraction. How had Gregory been able to endure it, she wondered, without the experience of childbirth to draw on?

Inside her, transformations were occurring. She could feel her organs altering, preparing for her next stage of existence. Systems would atrophy, she knew. Her womb would shrivel and disappear. She would cast off her external genitalia, her dried-up, sagging breasts, with the skin already hanging loose between them.

But why was it taking so long? What was wrong? It was past dawn already, and there hadn't been another contraction for what seemed like hours. Surely it hadn't been like this for Gregory! It was agony, crouching on her hands and knees, barely able to move. Her muscles were cramped and knotted. She shrugged her shoulders, and the split skin tore a little more along the line of her spine. How much longer did she have to wait? She moaned and wept through stiffened lips and tearless eyes.

Daylight flooded the room, the sun rose high into the sky outside the window. There was a grotesque, contorted figure on the bed. Mrs. Vivian's skin had opened from the crown of her head to just below the shoulder blades. Half of her scalp hung inverted over her forehead, the hair fallen into her face, stringy with clotting blood. She had torn away raw patches of flesh from the margins where it was still attached, desperately trying to pull it free. Her bloody fingernails had bent and broken off.

Along her spine, the edges of her split skin were stiffening and turning dry, cracking a little as she writhed feebly, still struggling. Her contracting skin, refusing to come free, was forcing her body into a fetal position, knees drawn up against her chest. Her ribs heaved shallowly as she fought to breathe. Beneath her, the broken fragments of her husband's crushed husk crackled under her weight.

Systems had altered within her. Her larynx atrophied until her groans were no longer audible. Blind and mute, she lay trapped in her shrinking, stiffening skin, still breathing, still twitching occasionally.

Her hearing alone was unimpaired. The birds sang outside her window every morning, cars passed by in the street, the bedside clock clicked as the minutes advanced, one by one, endlessly. A mosquito made its way into the room through a space in the window sash, and it hovered around her face, whining shrilly, for a long eternity before it settled on her eyelid to probe for fresh, unclotted blood. Voicelessly, unmoving, Mrs. Vivian screamed and screamed.

After a number of days, new processes of transformation began. Bacteria began to multiply within the dead tissues, producing foul-smelling gases. Her abdomen swelled, distending her brittle skin until it split and cracked. Once the gases finally escaped, her body subsided and settled in on itself. Decomposition proceeded quickly in the summer heat. Liquids oozed through the split skin, staining the mattress.

It was in that condition that her children found her, metamorphosis aborted, half remade and half unmade.

"I knew we shouldn't have let her stay here all alone," her daughter said, holding a hand over her face and averting her eyes from the remains.

But her oldest son shook his head. Nothing could have been done. If it had to be this way, it was better that she'd been here, where she wanted to be, at the end.

He picked up a shard of transparent dry skin from the floor beside the bed and identified it as part of his father's broken husk. He had known things could go wrong like this, everyone knew it. But to actually see the remains—

The fragment crumpled to dust in his hand as he considered his own approaching old age with newly awakened misgivings.

And then with dread.

BREEDING GROUND

Francis J. Matozzo

*Stories are often metaphors for larger themes or ideas.
They are most successful on this symbolic level when
they operate unconsciously—that is, without any upfront planning by their authors. The following novelette
by Frank Matozzo is a case in point. The human mind
and the human heart are the breeding grounds for most
of the things which ultimately define us, and not always
in ways that are pretty. In the following tale, Matozzo
interweaves threads of emotional stress among his characters to tell a larger story. "Breeding Ground" is a
complex, ambitious tapestry of pride and jealousy, fear
and guilt, and ultimately, pure dread.*

1

The only time the pain is gone is when I sleep at night.
The physical agony is replaced with the dream, which
only adds a new dimension to my wretched life, one of
dread and paralyzing terror.

At times, when the pain of the day climbs to new,
icy heights of glory, I believe the trade-off to be fair.
I'm a big boy—a nightmare, no matter how terrifying, is preferable to the reality of the flesh. But when
I awaken in the middle of the night, it's a different
story: the terror flows like glaciers through my veins,
oozing from my brain into the narrowest ventricles and
arteries of my nervous system. Then I would prefer to
battle the pain.

Angela does her best to cope, which is to say she does
nothing at all. Dealing with reality, with life and all its

*ugly warts, has never, in twenty years of marriage, been
her strong suit. Once she would have held me in her
fierce grip, fighting this disease with all the passion of
her being, but that was an eternity ago, when she truly
did love me.*

*Now I am an object of disgust for her. She buries
her head in the sand, denying her deceit, her betrayal,
staying with me only because of the money that keeps
her standard of living.*

*So I am alone, and the circle of my existence is
unbreakable—the pain of the day roaring into the terror
of my nights.*

2

Angela Lynch sat uncomfortably in the waiting room,
trying to shut out the droning voices of a morning talk
show buzzing from the television in the waiting room.
She wanted to turn it off, but a short, squat cleaning woman was sitting next to it, sucking on a cigarette, laughing loudly with every stupid joke from the
show's host.

Angela left the room.

She stepped out into the ugly, marble-green hall and
walked to the nearest window; leaning on the sill, she
looked down into the streets below. It was early November and the tree-lined streets outside the hospital were
vivid with changing colors. Fallen leaves rested in hap-
hazard piles, scattering along the sidewalk at the mercy
of the wind. She should be out there, enjoying the
beauty of the autumn day, not stuck in some boring,
drab hospital waiting room. Doing nothing while her
life fell to pieces.

Out of control.

She sighed, a long exhale of frustration. She had been
sitting in limbo since 6 A.M., when she last saw her
husband being wheeled into surgery.

"I love you," she had managed over the gurney,
squeezing his weak hand and planting a swift kiss on
his dry lips. He had looked at her with eyes glazed in pain

and fear and she was genuinely shocked at seeing him so helpless. He was many things—selfish, cold, brooding, and uncommunicative, but he had never been weak.

And she was shocked, too, at her own lack of feeling; what an effort it had been to simply say those three words, to kiss his lips when everything about him repulsed her. Twenty years of marriage and she couldn't work up more than a passing kernel of sympathy. It was horrible, but true, and she hated herself for feeling that way—and hated *him* for making her that way.

She began to cry.

She pulled a tissue from her handbag, dabbing her eyes; there had been no time for makeup that morning, which was just as well since she probably would have been a horror show of running mascara. Her black hair was uncurled, raining on her slender shoulders in straight lines, drawing out the thinness in her gaunt face. She was dressed in a pair of loose-fitting blue jeans and a thick green sweater that added some shape to a body ravaged by anger and endless nights spent baby-sitting for her husband. Listening to his screams as he pulled her into the madness of his nightmares.

And yet she had no one to blame but herself—hadn't she fought him to accompany her to Shelton? If she really hated him, why did she badger him to come?

Because of the same reason I've stuck with the self-centered bastard for all these years, she answered herself—*because I've no backbone, no guts to leave on my own . . .*

And what of Lee? He loved her, paid attention to her emotional needs, was gentle and passionate and kind. God, when they had started the affair two years ago she had felt reborn, beautiful again, the center of one man's life . . . she needed that so much, to be the single all important, all consuming focus of another's life. She needed that more than anything in the world.

Sure.

More than economic security? Social acceptance?

The knowledge that a beautiful home always waited

for her to crawl into, safe from the world . . . she could
never give it up.

And Lee didn't have a pot to piss in. It was horrible
to think, but money was the bottom line. And she almost
lost it all that weekend in Shelton. A stupid mistake, a
love letter she had forgotten to destroy, written at the
start of their affair. *How stupid!*

In one way, at least, Jonathan's accident was a boon—
it kept his mind off her infidelity.

Christ, I'm a mess . . .

She was so confused by her life that the world seemed
to be a madly churning whirlpool, opening into a dark
abyss that threatened to suck her down so that whatever
she was, what little insignificant part of Angela Lynch
actually existed, would be forever snuffed out, forgotten
and buried.

3

Dr. Benjamin Rossini, head neurosurgeon at Mont-
gomery Hospital, watched with quiet approval as Joseph
Moyer, a second year resident, meticulously scrubbed
over the stainless steel sinks in OR9.

Rossini liked Moyer: young and aggressive, he displayed an inherent respect for the value of careful routine. So many of the residents were ready to march
through the Hallowed Halls of Medicine while ignoring
the details, and in brain surgery to ignore the details
was to play Russian roulette—sooner or later you would
catch the bullet.

Rossini finished adjusting his blue scrub pants. Turning from the sink, he waited for the circulating nurse to
dress him with gown and surgical gloves, his soft blue
eyes surveying the room. As usual when he operated,
the place was crammed with bodies. Grouped on one
side of the tiled, windowless room was a trio of technicians who were carefully monitoring their vital signs
equipment. The technicians were overseen by a fourth
man, Dr. Philip Giovinco, the anesthesiologist Rossini
loved to hate. It was Giovinco's job to bring the patient

as close to death as possible without actually killing him, a job ideally suited for a Sicilian, Rossini decided. The pressures of an anesthetist were unique—they quite literally held life and death in their hands; a slight turn of a valve at the wrong moment could usher in fatality— and for this Rossini could excuse the arrogant, skittish behavior of most . . . as long as they did their job well. And as far as he was concerned, Giovinco was not only a lout, but a questionable man to rely on in the operating theater.

He turned his attention to Robbin Lipinski, a short spark plug of a woman, his favorite scrub nurse. She was busy taking a physical inventory of every instrument and towel that would be used for the operation. He knew that she, at least, would provide a boost for the strange sense of spiritual malaise that seemed to afflict him from the moment he woke, wincing from the arthritic pain in his back, earlier that morning. Her professionalism and energy were contagious and on this day it helped to be motivated by those around him.

Just inside the room, huddled in the background around a video screen, a half-dozen students and young residents gathered to watch the operation firsthand. To learn from the master, Rossini thought, frowning.

Finally, Rossini looked at the reason everyone had gathered—the silent shape lying behind sterile green drapes. A face, a shaved scalp, a mouth bulging with a ventilator. A body, with clear plastic tubes extending from it, carrying urine away, bringing anesthesia in. A body that would, in a very short time, be further reduced to a small red hole in a white skull.

Jonathan Lynch.

Rossini's mind drifted. A voice from the not-too-distant past rang coldly in his mind. *"What came first, Benjamin?"* his father asked. *"The chicken or the egg?"*

"Are we ready yet, Doctor?"

Giovinco's impatient voice interrupted his thoughts. Rossini slowly rested his eyes on the man; there was something predatory about him. The sharp nose, the thick black mustache, the wet, slicked-back hair glued to a pointed scalp, the deep brown eyes like black ice. The man exuded hostility.

"We have no music," said Rossini after a moment. "How can we work without music, Philip?"

The anesthesiologist glared at him. Rossini turned casually to the circulating nurse. "Judy, I'm in the mood for Vivaldi."

"*Four Seasons?*"

"Great."

Seconds later, music filtered through the OR. Rossini nodded in Moyer's direction and the two of them approached the still body on the table. Moyer positioned himself to the right of the body. Rossini gave him a thumbs-up sign, then turned to the students and began his monologue.

"Jonathan Lynch is a forty-year-old man in excellent physical condition who suffered a mild concussion from a freak accident in August. Almost immediately afterward he began to suffer from severe facial spasms of increasing duration and pain. In October he came to us after conventional treatment failed. An angiogram clearly indicated pathology of the right hemisphere in and around the area of the fifth cranial nerve. A classic case of trigeminal neuralgia."

As he spoke, Dr. Moyer cut into Jonathan Lynch's scalp, his scalpel making an elegant slice—a gleaming, satin-red zipper.

"Our job," continued Rossini, "is to isolate the pressure on the facial nerve at the base of the brain stem and through vascular decompression relieve the cause of the spasms."

"How long does an operation of this nature last?" asked one of the students.

Rossini narrowed his eyes, the displeasure evident in his voice. "What time is it now?"

"Uh . . . 8:20."

"Jot it down," he admonished. "When we're finished, look at your watch again and subtract. That's how long it will take."

Everyone laughed and the student who asked the question shrugged his shoulders, embarrassed.

Robbin Lipinski detected the cold edge in his put-down—she knew his work habits better than anyone. "How are we today, Doctor?" she asked, her lively green eyes staring a hole through him.

He forced a smile. "Fine, Robbin."

"Are you sure?"

"Positive." Rossini turned back to the student who asked the question, deciding to soften the blow. He spoke in his customary soft voice, more for Robbin's benefit than anything.

"Every operation, like every person, is different. Some go by fast, without complications. Others last an eternity. The rule, no matter what, is to make sure what you do is *right* for the patient, regardless of time."

Rossini paused, waited for more questions, and when none were forthcoming, turned his attention to the operating table. Moyer was humming along to the classical music as he peeled back the patient's scalp, revealing the muscle below.

"Have you ever read him?" asked the young resident.

"No, I haven't."

"He's really an excellent writer." Moyer rattled off titles, gave brief synopses, critical evaluations, and one last endorsement for the benefit not only of the older surgeon, but the nurses, students, technicians, and whoever else was within hearing distance. His enthusiasm, Rossini knew, would carry young Moyer far. His only drawback was his looks: apple-pie skin, freckles, frivolous red hair. Quite simply, he looked too boyish to be a neurosurgeon. The public expected old faces that reeked with experience.

His own, for instance.

All furrowed brows and thick white hair and cheeks that were creased with the weight of responsibility. At the age of sixty-two, he possessed just the right mixture of authority and knowledge that people yearned to trust.

Yet what do I really know?

He sighed. Robbin had been correct to question him—

he simply was not in the frame of mind to operate. He was thinking too much of his father. He couldn't shake the image of the old man sitting at his kitchen table, cutting paper dolls out of loose-leaf paper and carefully stuffing them into envelopes—his favorite pastime during the last pitiful months of life.

Alzheimer's . . . it had taken him at the age of eighty-six, only a few short months ago, wiping out his memory of everything and everyone along the way.

Rossini had never felt so helpless in the face of suffering. So unworthy of his success.

He glanced at his slender, delicate hands: a super-dexterous gift of nature that his profession demanded, enabling him to gracefully probe the most intricate apparatus known to man.

Brains.

Rossini had seen a Mount Everest of brains, all of them with varying capabilities, yet more or less the same. Crack open any skull, he knew, and one would find the same things over and over again: pons, cerebellum, pia arachnoid—a nuts and bolts alignment that he knew by heart.

What makes it work? What triggers the human mind to create the Vivaldi concerto filtering over the speakers, the brooding images of a Goya, the inventions of a da Vinci? What sector of the brain housed genius? Where in the gray matter of Jonathan Lynch did the ideas of his art spring from?

It was the old question that his father, in better times, always chided him with. The chicken and egg metaphor. The physical mechanics of the brain, which Rossini had mastered, versus the metaphysical consciousness of the mind. Which came first?

Rossini suddenly pinpointed the vague sense of dread he had been feeling all day. After thirty years of brain surgery, lectures, classes, and published essays, he was still, beneath the experienced surface, afraid of what he did not know.

The fear brought him back to his childhood and the memory of a book: an encyclopedia with a page of color

photos depicting reptile eggs as they hatched. How his
skin crawled as a boy, seeing the ugly, scaled heads
of alligators and crocodiles erupted through the pure
white of eggshell. It was a warning he had forgotten
over the years, now springing back into his mind along
with the nightmares of his residency, when he dreamt
of screaming patients retarded and scarred because of a
slip of *his* hand. Beware the surface, it told him; ugliness
lived below, waiting to claw into the world.

4

*A neurosurgeon promises relief. He knows my disease
and claims to have a cure for it. In my brain, he says,
there is a blood vessel (somewhere) pressing against a
facial nerve. He proposes to drill my skull open, dig into
the mess, find the recalcitrant vein, and either remove or
cushion it, thus relieving the pain.*

*Angela buys it, for all the wrong reasons. She doesn't
have to think, doesn't have to feel responsible. Let the
doctors handle me.*

*What can I expect? She is a child of thirty-eight,
grown tall and willowy (beautiful in her way) and emotionally bankrupt.*

*I wonder about her lover (the one she denies). Does
he, can he really know her?*

*How ironic that the part of me she once loved the
most, my writing . . . my emotional sensitivity, as she
used to say . . . would be the thing that drove her away.*

*How naive I was to think that she would understand
my work.*

*Yet, in those first years of our life together, did even
I understand fully the violent grip my work would have
on my life? Like a greedy mistress, it never let me stray,
the exclusion of all else.*

*Still, I thought she loved that part of me—even after all
this time. After all the hard work constructing unscaled
walls from the cold blocks of silence and non-contact
and jealousy.*

At least the pain stops me from dwelling on her

*betrayal. It begins at a fever pitch, growing by degrees
from the base of my skull, just below the ear. By midday
the entire right side of my face is contorted in a dance
of pulsating flesh.*

*Hemifacial spasms, the doctors call it . . . "spasms"
lasting ten, fifteen, twenty minutes. Until five minutes
respite every waking hour seems as peaceful and comforting as death.*

*All of my will and desire is squandered in war against
pain. Alcohol, drugs, compresses, rage, and fucking
blasphemy are my weapons. I spit in its face, scream
at it, mock it. Nothing works—except the dream.*

*The nightmare which carries a whole new dimension
of terror, becoming more vivid and real with each endless night.*

5

It was her twentieth high school reunion—Shelton
High, Class of 1970—and after much bitter arguing,
Jonathan had agreed to accompany her. On the drive
up, his deafening silence let her know what an inconvenience it was to interrupt his work on his latest novel.
Of course, she had no way of knowing then what was
truly on his mind.

Shelton was located in upstate Pennsylvania, squeezed
between a gap in the timbered ranges of the Blue
Mountains. The last curve of highway coming through
the mountains provided a perfect overview of her
hometown—from the gray water tower at the west
end, to the onion-shaped dome of the Russian Orthodox
church on the eastern fringe. Bookends that propped up
the wooden houses and vanished spirit of a community
economically impoverished since the demise of anthra-
cite. Once, Shelton had been the thriving seat of the hard
coal region. Now, the majestic woods surrounding the
town bore the ugly stamp of strip mining—black gashes of
barren soil lined the slopes like open sores, a wasteland of
blasted rocks and irregular piles of earth, interspersed
with dead trees that rose like skeletons from the ground.

Angela drank too much at the reunion on Saturday night, trying to deaden the nameless misery she felt. And Jonathan, rude and obnoxious in his aloof way, succeeded in alienating everyone—poor Angela, she could hear her old classmates thinking, what a cold bastard she married.

In the hotel that night they did not speak, but went straight to bed, taking separate positions on the strange bed like fighters in a ring, waiting for a bell that never rang.

Jonathan woke her early on Sunday. "I want to explore the old colliery before we leave," he said. "I might use it in my book."

She was too hung over to argue. After checking out, they rode to the outskirts of town where the abandoned remnants of the Shelton Mining Corporation loomed high up the slopes of Mount McKernan.

To their surprise, they were not alone—at the foot of the mountains they met a tall, thin man with glasses, apparently engaged in some sort of solo archaeological excavation. Bare-chested and sweating in the hot morning sun, he reminded Angela of the weakling in the old magazine ads who gets sand kicked in his face. He was resting when they approached him, a spade slung over one bony shoulder. He greeted them with shrill, nervous energy.

"Carrol's people, right? He sent you. Bastard. Knew he'd find out. Nosy bastard!" His beady eyes darted behind thick-lensed glasses, an inappropriate, girlish giggle punctuating his last words.

Jonathan explained who he was, and why they were there.

"Name's Grayer," said the man, after a moment of silence. "Writer?" He giggled, shaking his head, looking away, up the slope. "Don't want this in the paper. No way. It's my baby. My discovery. Those conceited twerps at the University think Carrol has all the answers. Well. Just wait. But I don't want it getting out, you understand? I have more tests. Need to be positive."

"I'm just here to research a book," said Jonathan. "I

don't write for any newspaper."

"Good. You can keep a secret. Come with me. I want to show you something remarkable."

As they followed Grayer, Jonathan glanced at her and the look on his face—the amused grin, conspiratorial sideways wink—brought her back to the old days when they were literally inseparable. So in love and in tune with each other's emotions that one of them always seemed to be able to finish the other's thoughts in words *before* they were spoken. And how she loved to hear him speak: the depth of his emotions, the passion of his feeling filtering through words to some uncharted center of her being. It was a mind-fuck like none she had ever experienced. Had it been so unrealistic, so absurd a dream to hope that she alone would always be the focus of that passion?

She stared at him, wanting to cross the chasm of years and simply feel love again, and for a moment their eyes locked. Then, like a storm cloud blotting out the sun, the light left his eyes, replaced with his own distant thoughts and dreams and the hint of something darker than rain.

Grayer led them to an exposed outcrop of shale at the base of the mountain, and in the reflection of the brilliant sunlight, Angela saw a multitude of shapes imprinted in the rock.

"My babies," said Grayer, outlining the fossils with a tender finger. "No prior record exists of creatures like this. Of course, I assumed they were among the first. An original link on the evolutionary chain. But my tests! They sang a different tune. These creatures lived in the *early quaternary!*"

He looked at them as if expecting applause, no longer suppressing his laughter.

"I don't understand," said Jonathan.

"Don't you see? These things. These creatures with their dual heads and little pincers and tiny *crowds* of legs were *contemporaries* of man!"

Grayer beamed, running his hand over the rock, beads of sweat sparkling on his forehead. His words, to Angela, seemed weightless. She could see nothing but spherical lines and twisted circles, so tiny that they looked like the letters from some ancient alphabet.

Jonathan exchanged a few more words with the man, and then the two of them started up the slope. As they did, the man called a warning: "I wouldn't go poking around. Not by the old mines."

"Why?" asked Angela.

"Ground's bad. Underneath it's on fire. Been burning for years. State's supposed to put it out some day. You'll see the steam coming out of holes. But I wouldn't go walking up there. That ground will give way and eat you."

"Thanks for the warning," said Jonathan. "We'll be careful."

We'll be careful . . . we'll only kill each other.

She couldn't think of that day any longer. Biting her lower lip, she stared out the hospital window at the awakening world below. It was best to forget all about Shelton and what happened at the old mine—thinking about it was like swallowing poison.

Angela turned away from the window just in time to see a young nurse approaching her down the hall, and immediately she heard the words in her mind: *"I'm sorry, Mrs. Lynch, but there were complications. Your husband is dead."*

And then her own emotions. Sadness. Pity. Undeniable relief.

"Mrs. Lynch?"

"Yes."

"I have a message from your husband. He said he had to leave, but he'll meet you later."

"I don't understand."

"It's what he told me."

"But my husband's being operated on."

The nurse looked confused. "Oh. I just assumed he was your husband."

"Who are you talking about?" asked Angela, growing impatient.

"The man you've been sitting with in the waiting room."

"But I've been alone all morning."

"No you haven't," said the nurse bluntly. "I saw the two of you earlier. He was sitting right next to you."

"No one's been in that room except myself and a cleaning woman."

The nurse shrugged. "Well, maybe I'm seeing things, but this man kind of stood out. Dressed in black from head to toe. Like an undertaker. Wore a funny black hat. And he *most definitely* was sitting next to you. But—whatever. I have to get moving now."

She turned and walked quickly away from Angela, who wanted to reach out and stop her, but instead did nothing. The nurse disappeared around the corner and Angela was left with the empty green corridor.

She thought of her husband's night terrors: once, during a rare moment of shared thought, he told her about the dark figure that haunted his dreams. A man dressed in black, wearing a black bowler hat. And as she recalled the fear behind his eyes, the look of mindless dread, her breath began to quicken and her chest felt tight.

I need to calm down.

She thought of breakfast. She would find the cafeteria, order some orange juice and biscuits and a cup of tea, then come back and wait. It was the most reasonable thing she had thought of all day. It would give her a chance to get her mind off of Shelton and the recent past. And more importantly, it would get her away from the waiting room.

6

"Someone's been here before us."

Joseph Moyer stopped working and glanced up at Rossini, who was staring intently at the square patch of exposed muscle beneath the peeled scalp of Jonathan Lynch.

"There's too much blood," he said quietly.

Moyer nodded. "Bipolar."

Lipinski handed him the two-pronged instrument. Using the electrical current that ran through the bipolar coagulator, he sealed off the offending blood vessels that had been severed in his efforts to reach the skull. When he finished, the scrub nurse squirted a thick stream of saline solution over the area, irrigating the wound and removing the excess fluid with a suction device. For a few seconds this was the only sound in the room, the gurgling suction momentarily overriding the blips of Giovinco's monitors. The Vivaldi had blended into the white, scrubbed walls.

"Can you see what I mean?" asked Moyer finally.

Rossini could see it clearly now—the muscle beneath the scalp normally resembled red, raw meat. That was not the case with Lynch; gray, gristle-like trails laced the muscle. Scar tissue, as if someone had sliced a road map in the tissue. It shouldn't have been there, and Rossini's earlier sensation of dread was exacerbated by that fact.

"He wasn't opened before," said Moyer, roughly probing. "But this is clearly scar tissue."

A shrill voice cut the room neatly in half: "I don't believe this, Ben."

Both doctors turned and saw Giovinco standing away from the sterile screen that hid his instruments and technicians, his head tilted back, nose sharp and uplifted as if sniffing the incompetence in the room. "I want to see the file again."

"I'll handle it, Phil," said Rossini.

Giovinco ignored him and addressed the circulating nurse. "I want it *now*."

Avoiding everyone's eyes, the young nurse moved off her chair to retrieve the file.

"Wait." Rossini raised his voice slightly, stepping away from the operating table. "I've been through the file a half-dozen times. Jonathan Lynch has never had brain surgery."

"Then why the scar tissue?"

"I don't know. Not yet, anyway."

"Well, you better find out," snapped Giovinco, tilting his head aggressively forward. "It's all fine and well to tell these students not to worry about time when they're in surgery, but in my profession a few seconds either way can mean the difference between life and death."

Rossini tried to speak calmly, conscious of the stares from the students, but he could not entirely resist the urge to bite back. "No one's trying to denigrate your job, Phil," he said. "I was merely trying to point out that brain surgery is not like a ten-minute lube job. Now, if you need to refresh your memory on the patient's file, by all means do so. I've memorized it."

"I'm through now," interrupted Moyer. "Time to drill for oil."

Rossini stared at Giovinco. Despite his age, the older surgeon was in superb condition, possessing the squared-off shoulders and stocky build of a middleweight boxer, and though he knew a physical reaction to Giovinco's pompous remarks was highly unprofessional, nothing would have delighted him more than to take the anesthesiologist into the next room and pound some humility into him.

"Let's continue," said Rossini. Giovinco—perhaps reading his mind—grunted his disapproval and vanished behind the screen.

The harsh sound of Moyer's cranitone drill filled the room. The skull was thick and resistant and the drill bit revolved fiercely into the white bone as chips of skull misted the air.

"That's it," said Moyer, ten minutes later. He stood back and surveyed his work: a hole in the skull gaped back at him, three-quarters of an inch in diameter, an opening that revealed the dura, a leathery membrane that was the brain's last defense. As a resident, this was as far as Moyer's experience and knowledge allowed him to go.

"Fine," said Rossini, moving into position. "I'll take over from here."

Moments later, he was back in control, where he needed to be—working, cutting into the dura, his previous anxiety fading—nothing was better for his soul than work. Moving gracefully, he hit his marks without any wasted motion. Peeling back the protective membrane, he had a clear view of the cerebellum—*nice ass*, he thought lewdly as he used the shining retractor to lift the twin halves, exposing the nerves at the base of the brain.

"Microscope, please."

The circulating nurse moved behind him, struggling with the massive surgical microscope that loomed above her like an eight-foot metallic giant. "Let me give you a hand," said Moyer. "This is like trying to roll a box-car."

The microscope was moved into position behind Lynch's head. Through its twin lens, both men would have a clear view of the brain. "Hit the lights," said Rossini.

A blanket of darkness fell over the room, accentuated by the oasis of light around the operating table. As Rossini leaned into the eyepiece, the students in the darkened OR gathered closer around their video monitor. A recorded image of the brain greeted them as they watched—a white mass of spongy tissue intersected with hundreds of thin red blood vessels.

Rossini sat like a jeweler, arms lifted, eyes glued to the lens. What he saw was infinitely more vivid than what any video monitor could pick up: the redness of the blood vessels had a deep, thick texture, like freshly cut rose petals; a redness that he could almost *smell*. And the brilliance of their crimson light was prodded by the eggshell whiteness of gelatinous brain tissue. Gently now, he could proceed.

   . . . *what came first, son, the chicken or the egg* . . .

His father's mocking voice flickered in his mind, just before Moyer spoke.

"The patient moved."

Rossini froze. His arms hung in the air. Without moving his eyes from the microscope, he called to Giovinco: "Damnit, Phil. What's happening?"

"We're stable," replied Giovinco irritably.

"But I *see* movement."

"There *is* movement," reiterated Moyer.

"Are you telling me how to do my job?"

"I'm telling you . . ."

"Wait!"

Rossini's body had tensed like a car accident victim just before the brick wall.

"It's not *the brain* that's moving!"

Moyer quickly was on the lens again. "Jesus," he hissed.

"Are you seeing what I'm seeing?"

"It can't be."

"It is."

"What the hell *is* it?"

" . . . don't know . . . never seen anything . . ."

"Doctor?"

" . . . but it's alive . . ."

"Jesus fucking Christ!"

" . . . and moving."

The circulating nurse suddenly burst out laughing. "This is a joke, right?"

Giovinco pushed his way up to Rossini. "Just what the hell is going on?"

Cries of horror and disgust rose from around the video monitor—the students were seeing what no textbook in the world described.

And through the noise, all Rossini could think of was alligators.

7

Why struggle on?

It's not the quality of my life. God knows, it's not Angela.

No, what I fight to keep alive for is a sense of responsibility born more from guilt than any moral imperative.

Something dreadful has happened to me and I doubt if any surgeon can cure it. Within the closed doors of my unconscious mind, a creature lives, a man who longs to be free.

I have dreamt him into existence. Night after night he comes to me, always the same: dressed in a black suit, tall and thin, wearing a black bowler, his face a canvas without features, a void of bone-white flesh.

I call him the Walker, because in my dreams he walks endlessly—through cities and towns, across oceans, circling the globe. Growing larger as more people see him, until he rises above buildings, his head lost in the clouds, his shoulders blotting out the sun. And his eyes, as large as two black planets, stare down into the panic and terror below.

With every dream I bring him closer to reality, forming him bit by bit, only to contain him within the borderlands of my dreams.

If I should die under the surgeon's knife, I am afraid that he will live on without me.

He is so vivid in my mind that when I awake in the morning (or in the middle of the eternal night) my eyes scatter round the room, anticipating that pale face grinning down at me, free at last, for he is everyone's secret nightmare.

He is the unknown hand of fear that clutches men and women around the throat as they sit alone on cold winter nights, consumed with the knowledge of their lonely existence. He is the nameless dread that thickens the air of abandoned buildings, avatar of the incomprehensible void that lies just beneath the surface of reality. He is the demon in the pit, the monster at the center of the maze. His face is blank, until gazed upon; then he becomes a mirror, for he is nothing less than ourselves. Naked and hairy—exposed—our evil and guilt, our betrayals and ravenous egos. He is the hidden reality of the beast.

8

Angela sat in the cafeteria, trying desperately to keep her mind on the tangible reality before her, but nothing worked. Her mind kept rushing back to Shelton . . .

. . . ascending the rocky trail up the mountain to the old mines.

The slope above the fossil site was littered with the husks of dead trees leaning above a raging ocean of wild brush. She had worn a pair of khaki shorts and the bramble that encroached upon the path scratched her bare legs. Sweating and sore, she reached the plateau where the decaying wood buildings stood, a few yards behind Jonathan. Stopping to catch her breath, she stood in the shadows of a moldy breaker.

Her husband kept walking. He moved parallel to the old rail tracks that led to the rotting gangways down to the mine. Piles of rotted lumber and old railroad ties lay in clumps along the tracks, supporting the twisting growth of vines and weeds.

Then she saw the smoke, rising from fissures along the ground—dozens of them—the pillars of vapor snaking upward toward the blue sky. There was an odor of sulfur in the air and, combined with the heat, it made breathing difficult. She felt like she was standing in the lair of some ancient, fire-breathing dragon.

"I want to leave," she called out.

Jonathan stopped with his back facing her.

"No."

"Why can't you listen?" she complained loudly, venting her frustration. "The man said it was dangerous here. You could *see* that for yourself if you just opened your eyes. You won't be happy until you kill yourself."

"You would like that, wouldn't you?"

He was standing on a mound; a few feet to the left was one of the smoking fissures. She could only see half his body, the rising steam from the underground mine fire obscuring his figure. He turned to her, the sunlight diffused through the gray fog, making a wavering silhouette with dark eyes that shone like hard nuggets of coal. His voice rang clearly when he spoke: "We have to talk about something."

The rising smoke billowed around him, floating over his shoulders, encircling his legs, moving across his stiff face like the fingers of a lover.

"Explain this."

His arm appeared out of the vapor. In his hand, he held a creased note.

Automatically, she shook her head and laughed, denying the gleaming fact of the note's existence. Denial filled her like a flood of water forced into a narrow-lipped jar, spilling over the top.

"Explain," he repeated, jabbing the note at her like a prod, stepping off the mound of dirt. His broad, wide face was flushed crimson, a red fist of anger.

"Explain what?"

"This note, that's what!"

"How do I know what it is?"

"It's addressed to you. '*Dear Angela . . .*' Read it to me. *Loud, to refresh your memory!* I want to hear his words come out of your mouth."

"*Whose* words?"

"Your lover . . . I want to hear if he's a better writer than I am."

"I don't know what you're talking about."

"Yeah? Does he fuck you good?"

"You're an asshole!" she shouted in utter disgust.

He moved for her. She could see every muscle and nerve in his body trembling. "WHY? HOW COULD YOU?"

Then he was in her face, his harsh breath blowing wetly over her cheeks. He gripped her shoulders.

"*You fucking whore! Who is he?*"

"Stop it," she cried, feeling real pain from his violent grip. "There's no one else."

"*Bullshit!*" He began to shake her, his face a clenched mask of animal fury.

"What the hell do you care?" she screamed through her tears. "You self-absorbed prick! You're not there for me! You don't even know I exist. You don't talk to me, don't touch me . . . I'm not even *human* to you. I don't matter . . . the only thing that matters is your work."

"Yeah, my work and my royalty checks . . . you sure exist when they come in, don't you? DON'T YOU? PARASITE!"

Angela shrieked. The hatred snapped through her bones like a brittle, white-hot wire. She twisted one of her arms free and slapped him viciously across the mouth. The jarring impact shot to her elbow, inciting her rage. She flung herself at him with all of her strength.

"*Bastard! Bastard!*" she cursed him as he was driven back, tripping over the railroad tracks. She delighted in watching him fall, a graceless drunk. The back of his head thumped dully against the ungiving rail. His face squeezed out a silent moan of pain. A pool of copper blood seeped into his light brown hair.

Time stopped.

I killed him, she thought. *I betrayed him and then I killed him.*

And then the dragon opened its mouth and swallowed him.

A burst of gas-scented smoke poured out of the soil as a hole opened beneath him. With a look of almost comical amazement, her husband tumbled down into the earth, his desperately clawing hands trying to reach for support.

"*Jonathan!*"

Angela rushed forward, reaching through the dust and smoke for a grip on his hands, but they had vanished. "Jonathan? Jonathan!"

The dust cleared in silence.

"Angela!"

His voice was a ghost, filtering up through the black hole.

She scrambled down onto her stomach and brought her face to the brink of the opening. The hole was no more than four feet in diameter, sealing off the penetrating rays of sunlight at the very top.

"Help me!"

She stared at the impenetrable murk. "I can hear you, but I can't see you. Are you all right?"

"I'm right here . . . wedged in . . . I can see you . . . help me out."

"I don't know what to do," she cried in desperation. "I'm sorry."

"Find something I can hold . . . hurry . . . there's things down here."

"Things?"

"For God's sake, hurry! Get a piece of that old lumber that's piled up!"

Angela ran from the hole, grateful for the sense of direction. At the old woodpile she swiftly began to sort the lumber—most were so rotten with age that they crumbled in her hand—but toward the center she found a solid two-by-four and raced back to her husband.

"I have it," she called, kneeling over the hole.

"Good! Angle it in . . . hurry."

Angela moved the board into the hole until the front end struck against the earthen wall below. She pushed the opposite end tightly against the partially exposed railroad tie that rimmed the opening.

"There! It's done!"

Almost immediately she saw his right hand grab the board. There was a loud grunt and his other hand followed. "Come on," she urged.

Slowly and painfully, he pulled himself up out of the blackness, his face streaked with blood and dirt. She was surprised at how close he actually was—she had a vision of him tumbling and screaming to the center of the earth—but he had only fallen about six feet. Using the wood as a hoist, he moved toward her outstretched hands. The need to touch him sliced her heart like a razor.

She remembered the exact feeling as she sat drinking her tea and staring through the nearly empty cafeteria—for that one brief instant, on a desolate slope in a forgotten town, she *could* have brought him back. Across years of silence, betrayals, lost dreams. Pulled him back from the blackness of her own guilt and anger, into her safe arms. But time had run out and whatever control they had on the fate of their relationship had been taken from them like toys from naughty children by an unseen force greater than any hope she could possibly summon. She remembered the look in his eyes as he reached the top of the hole; there was a riot going on behind them, fueled by terror and panic. Using his upper body strength, he planted the palms of his hands on the wooden tie, swung himself completely out of the hole, rolled once, then jumped to his feet, shouting: *"There's something in my hair!"*

And that's when she saw it, through his clawing fingers at the back of his head—it was like seeing the door shut on her future.

At first she thought the wind was lifting his straight brown hair, but the atmosphere was dead with humidity, and there wasn't a sliver of breeze around them.

She realized it wasn't his hair that was moving, but something alive, clinging to the back of his head like moss on a cypress tree. Something with dark gray tentacles that danced in the air with liquid grace. She thought absurdly of a wig that had sprung to life, transformed into a large, bristling oval of horror, multi-dimensional, a chaotic brew of evolutionary stages. Part water creature, part insect—the shiny, stiff center reminded her of the hard shell of a beetle—and when she saw, briefly, a lizard jaw lined with needle-point teeth snap up from the tufts of hair, she thought of reptiles . . . and Grayer's old fossils at the base of the mountain.

Jonathan reached back with his right hand, shouting like a madman. He grasped the wriggling mass and tore it away from his head, hurling it back into the steamy, dark pit. Out of sight forever . . . gone in an instant, so that Angela doubted whether or not she had actually seen it. The only trace of its existence was the fear left in her husband's wild eyes, the revulsion she felt in her own crawling skin, and the small puncture wound at the base of her husband's neck.

An opening that healed within two days, just before the nightmares and the pain began.

Angela shook her head, trying to dislodge the images of that day and return to the present. She searched the cafeteria, staring at the people around her—a group of nurses laughing at one table, an old janitor emptying trash, a father and a young boy silently eating breakfast.

She had never told anyone what she had seen that day, not even Jonathan (who only knew that *something* had gotten into his hair), because she knew they would have thought that she was crazy. And maybe she was. Either way, she was responsible for what happened. Everyone in the cafeteria seemed to reflect that guilt in their eyes when they looked at her. There was no end to it. No matter where she ran to, or where she tried to hide, the reality followed her, hounding her like a criminal, accusing her of the failures of her dreams. All she ever wanted was to be taken care of. She was weak and she was selfish, and she wanted—*no, demanded*—someone to love her who didn't care about her faults. Someone who was blind to everything but love for *her*; who did not reflect in their own selfish pursuits and cold silences her own weaknesses. She wanted the White Knight to take her forever.

9

Robbin brought him back, squeezing his hand, shaking his trembling arm.

"Ben, get control. If you can't continue, I'll call someone."

"Get someone now!" ordered Giovinco.

Rossini whirled around, his eyes circling the room, trying to find an opening, an escape from the madness, but he was trapped—nurses, students, doctors— they surrounded him, waiting for him to fail, or succeed, or lead them back into the hellhole he had opened.

"I want quiet in here!" he screamed, sucking up every last ounce of willpower he could muster. "Get back on the lens, Moyer. I need forceps, Robbin. Giovinco, you mealy-mouthed son-of-a-bitch, *get back to work!*"

And to himself he said, *I'll show you what comes first, Pop.*

He went back to the microscope. His hands were shaking, a betrayal. He wanted to scream at them, command them, hurl them against the wall until they obeyed. A vicious rage possessed him—he was tired of looking into the unknown like a newborn babe.

"Dr. Moyer? Are you with me?" The young resident was hovering above his lens. His eyes were glazed with tears and when he spoke, the words sounded as if they had been stretched like rubber bands, about to snap and backfire.

"What the hell is it?" he kept asking.

Rossini didn't know. He had seen many parasitical diseases of the brain in his time; he'd relieved the pain of cutaneous larva migrans on more than one occasion. He had found tapeworms, roundworms, and even fly maggots in the brain. But he had never seen anything like the thing in Jonathan Lynch's head.

It was about four inches in diameter, with numerous tentacles that entwined in the folds of the pulpy brain matter. Its body was alternately flat and bulging. Parts of it adhered to the living tissue like a second layer of skin; other sections bulged with undigested brain matter. The head was the most remarkable thing—long and narrow, eyeless, scaly, and possessing a mouth lined with numerous pointed teeth. It was something out of a nightmare.

"I'm going in for it," said Rossini. "I don't know what the hell it is or how it got there, but the principle has to be the same . . . relieve the pressure, relieve the pain."

Lipinski handed him the forceps as silence fell over the room once again—a quiet alive with unspoken fear.

As Rossini entered the skull, the creature moved, sensing danger, but the surgeon was precise and swift. He clamped down on the twisting creature. The thin tentacles lifted protectively, wrapping around the forceps as the angry head reared back, biting into the steel. But Rossini was not to be denied. With a single brutal, inelegant move, he tore the thing out of the skull.

And as he did, Jonathan Lynch tried to open his eyes.

"Goddamnit, Giovinco! You've lost him!" shouted Rossini, holding the forceps, and the wriggling creature caught between the prongs, as far away from his body as possible.

"Get his hands!" Lipinski cried. The circulating nurse sprang forward, reaching for Lynch's flopping hands. A deep, raw gurgling issued from his throat and his head shook in the vise.

"Shit! He's tearing arteries!"

A powerful fount of blood spurted from the skull, spattering onto the gleaming tiled floor.

"Get another unit of blood," ordered Rossini. Whirling in the opposite direction he shouted at Giovinco, who was frantically turning the valve to increase the flow of anesthesia. "GET HIM UNDER CONTROL!"

"I can't . . . he's dropping *too* fast," yelled Giovinco in desperation. "Jesus Christ . . . I'm going to *lose him!*"

Rossini cursed in disgust, turning to Moyer; in his left hand he held the forceps. "Take this from me."

Moyer hesitated, staring at the revolting creature as it struggled to escape.

"*Move it, man!* I have to stop that bleeding!"

Rossini held the forceps out for Moyer to take, and as he did, out of the corner of his eye he saw Lipinski rushing forward with a clear plastic bag of blood. Then she was falling, slipping on the wet red tiles, colliding into him. The impact knocked him back. His arm shot up, releasing the forceps high into the air. The unit of blood fell and burst like a water balloon. The forceps clattered next to it.

"Get another unit," gasped Rossini to the other nurse, helping Lipinski to her feet. Everything around him seemed to be moving.

And now there was screaming.

The thing from Jonathan Lynch's skull had fallen through the air and—like a slapstick scene from an obscene comedy—landed directly on Moyer's cheek, flattening itself and instantaneously burrowing its razor mouth into his flesh.

"*Get it off me,*" screeched the young resident, ripping his surgical mask off and clawing at his face with mind-less dread.

"Stop it!" Robbin cried.

"*I can't get it off! It stuck something in me!*"

Lipinski ran to help him, but Moyer violently pushed her away. He pulled off a scalpel from the instrument tray and began to flay at his cheek. A shower of blood ran down the side of his face as he sliced his cheek, and the creature, into scarlet ribbons.

And as he hacked away, he kept screaming: "IT'S GOING FOR MY BRAIN!"

"Stop him," shouted Rossini, motioning to the students.

Two of the young males rushed forward and grappled with Moyer from behind. Lipinski sprang forward again, reaching for his arm. The dead thing dripped off his face in damp pieces, along with chunks of his own flesh.

"Stop it, Joe!" shouted Lipinski. "It's dead! You killed it!"

"It's still on me! I can feel it crawling inside my head!"

Another student joined the little scrub nurse and together they wrestled the scalpel from his hand. The second he was disarmed, Moyer went limp and collapsed to the floor.

"Get him out of here," said Rossini, fighting the maelstrom of insanity that was brewing in his head.

"Doctor?"

Rossini looked up. Giovinco was standing next to him, perfectly still. "I lost him."

"No!"

Rossini lunged for Giovinco. Fiercely, he grabbed the lapels of the man's white lab coat and almost lifted him off the ground.

"It wasn't *my* fault," croaked Giovinco, feebly trying to stare the older man down.

"Doctor Rossini!" shouted Nurse Lipinski. "The patient is gone!"

Rossini stared bitterly at the cowed anesthesiologist, a rational portion of his mind trying to gain a foothold in the ocean of blind rage that had swept him away. He had done battle with his old arch-enemy—death—and he had lost again. Yet his pride would not accept that. He had to show them that he could overcome defeat. Had to prove to himself that he was more than just a skilled mechanic, that he truly did understand that unknown spark of life that was housed in the brain. He could make miracles happen, he was certain.

He released Giovinco and returned to the table. "Coagulator," he called. He waited with his right hand outstretched. The spritzing blood from Lynch's torn arteries had been reduced to a faint trickle.

"Doctor, he's dead. There's nothing you can do."

"*Coagulator.*"

Lipinski handed him the instrument without further comment.

Rossini looked in the lens. After a few minutes, he began to cry.

The creature had laid eggs—a mound of larvae concealed in a gaping cavity below the cerebellum. Some of the eggs were partially hatched, and he could see, quite clearly, the tiny reptilian heads snapping blindly at the airy space around them, longing to be fed.

10

It was dark when Angela returned from the hospital. She parked her car in the garage and entered through the kitchen door. Simon, their affable cat, rushed to greet her, brushing against her ankles. She crouched down and patted the animal, gently lifting him to her cheek. "Just us now," she said, and the cat purred.

She went through the daily routine of switching on lights, feeding Simon, checking the mail. Over a cup of tea, she sat in the kitchen, her weary legs propped on a chair. The mail was mostly for Jonathan (as usual). After finishing her tea, she gathered his mail and placed it on his desk in the first floor den. Just as if he would be coming home from some book promotion tour to go through it.

In bed, later, she lay with her eyes open and Simon curled at her feet, exhausted to the point where she could not sleep. The empty bed seemed enormous, the house hollow. Sleep was out of the question. She left the bedroom and went back down to the kitchen, where she poured herself a glass of wine. Deciding that the cool night air would help her sleep, she stepped out into the quiet autumn night.

She wanted desperately to cry, but every emotion had been wrung out of her. She was as dry as the desert.

The glass of wine went quickly and she was about to return to the kitchen for a refill when a shadow at the edge of the driveway coalesced into a human shape that stood, stiff and tall, in the full rays of the moon.

The man in black nodded his head and she thought she heard her name called. Fear rose like boiling water, scalding every nerve in her body. For a moment the pale, nebulous face took on the shape and lines of Jonathan. But then it changed, like a whisper, to other faces—her lover's, Rossini's, finally her own face, trembling and scared.

"Who are you?" she managed to ask, not really wanting to know.

The silent black shape nodded once more, tipping his hat. The face returned to a pale, expressionless mask.

The man in black turned away from her and started walking down the driveway, toward the twinkling lights of the city.

LOVE DOLL: A FABLE

Joe R. Lansdale

Moving right along, we continue to consider the notion that a short story can be a marvelous metaphor for larger concerns. But let's make the additional observation that nothing can add a little hot sauce to your basic metaphor any better than equal amounts of humor and satire. East Texas writer Joe R. Lansdale has known this for a long while now; and that's one of the reasons he's considered such an excellent craftsman of the short fiction form. His latest contribution to Borderlands *explores the territory of such diverse writers as—believe it or not—Donald Barthelme and Joe Bob Briggs.*

I buy a plastic love doll because I want something to fuck that I don't have to talk to. Right on the box it says Love Doll. I take her home and blow her up. She looks pretty and sexy and innocent.

I fuck her. I sit with her on the couch and watch TV and put an arm around her plastic shoulders and hold my dick with my other hand.

I fuck her some more. In the morning I let the air out of her and fold her up and put her in a drawer.

When I come home from work at night, I give her a blow job and she is full and stiff again. I take her into the bedroom and fuck her. I watch TV with my arm around her, one hand on my dick.

This goes on for a while.

I start to talk to the doll. I never wanted to talk to a woman, but I talk to the doll. I name her Madge. I had a dog named Madge that I liked.

I stop letting the air out of her in the mornings. I leave

her in bed. I fix breakfast on a tray, enough for two. I come in and eat beside her on the bed. There's plenty of food left when I stop and get ready for work.

When I come home the tray is where it was and the doll is gone. There's no food left on the tray.

I find Madge in the shower. She smiles at me when I slide the shower door back.

"I was going to clean up for you," she said. "Be sexy. I'm sorry the house isn't clean and dinner isn't ready. It won't happen again."

I get in the shower with her. We have sex and soap each other. We dry off and go to bed and have sex again. We lie in bed and talk afterward. She talks some about girl things. She talks about me mostly. She has good things to say about my sexual prowess. We have sex again.

Next day she drives me to work, picks me up at the end of the day. All the fellas are jealous when they see her, she's such a good-looking piece.

She always looks nice. Wears frilly things, short skirts. For bop-around she wears tight sweaters and T-shirts and jeans. She smells good. She puts her hands on me a lot. The house is clean when I get home. Dinner is ready in a jiffy.

A year passes. Quite happily. Life couldn't be better. Lots of sex. A clean house. Food when I need it. Conversation. She tells me I'm a real man when I mount her, that she needs me, calls me her stallion, makes good noises beneath me and scratches at my back, she makes a lalala noise when she comes. She likes my muscles, the scruffiness of my beard. We watch movies on the couch, my arm around her. She holds my dick in her hand. When I tell her to, she gives me a blow job while I watch the movie. She always swallows my load.

One night we're laying in bed and she says, "I think maybe I should go to school."

"What for?" I ask.

"To bring in more money. We could buy some things."

"I make enough money."

"I know. You're a hard-working man. But I want to help."

"You help enough. You be here for me at night, keep the house clean and the meals ready. That's a woman's place."

"Whatever you want, dear."

But she doesn't mean it. It comes up now and again, her going to school. Finally I think, so what? She goes off to school. The house isn't quite so clean. The meals aren't always ready on time. I drive myself to work. Some nights she doesn't feel like sex. I jack off in the bathroom a lot. We sit on the couch and watch movies. She sits on one end, I sit on the other. We wear our clothes. I have a beer in one hand, the remote control in the other. We argue about little things. She doesn't like the way I spend my money.

She gets a degree. She gets a job in business. She wears suits. For bop-around the stuff she wears is less tight. She doesn't wear makeup or perfume around the house. She keeps her hands to herself. No kissing good-bye and hello anymore. We have sex less. When we have it, she seems distracted. She doesn't call me her King, her Big Man like she used to. After sex she'll sometimes stay up late reading books by people called Sartre or Camus. She's writing something she calls a business manifesto. She sits at the typewriter for hours. She goes to business parties, and I go with her, but I can tell they think I'm boring. I don't know what they're talking about. They talk about business and books and ideas. I hear Madge say a woman has to make her own way in the world. That she shouldn't depend on a man, even if she has one. Thing to do is to be your own person. She tells a man that. Guy in a three-piece blue suit with hairspray on his hair. He agrees with her. I feel sick.

I tell her so in the car on the way home. She calls me a prick. We don't fuck that night.

I watch a lot of movies alone. She yells from the bedroom for me to turn them down, and why don't I watch something else other than car chase movies, and why don't I read a book, even a stupid one?

I feel small these days. I go to the store and look at the love dolls. They all look so sexy and innocent. I think I might buy one, but find I can't. I don't feel man enough. I can't control the one I have. I get a new one, she might change, too. Course, a new one I could let the air out of when I finished fucking her, never let her have a day alone full blown.

I go home. Madge is there. She's writing her book. I get angry. I tell her I've been patient long enough. I'm the man around here. I tell her to stop that typing, get her clothes off, and get in bed and grab her ankles. I'm going to fuck her unconscious.

She laughs. "You skinny, little, stupid pencil-dick, you couldn't fuck a gnat unconscious. You're about as manly as a Kotex."

I feel as if I've been hit in the face with a fist. I go into the bedroom and close the door. I sit on the edge of the bed. I can hear her typing in there. I get up and go over to the dresser and open the bottom drawer. I take off all my clothes and find the air spigot on the head of my dick and pull it open and listen to the air go out of me. I crumple into the open drawer, and lay there like a used prophalactic.

An hour or so later the typing stops. I hear her come into the room. She looks in the drawer. No expression. I try to say something manly, but nothing will come. I have no air and no voice. She moves away.

I hear the water running while she takes a shower. She comes out naked. I can see her pubic hair above me. I note how firm and full of air her thighs are. She opens the top drawer. She takes out panties. She puts them on. She goes away. I hear her sit on the bed. She dials the phone. She tells someone to come on over, that her thing with me is finished.

Time passes. The doorbell rings. Madge gets up and goes past me. I get a glimpse of her, her hair combed out long and pretty, a robe on.

I hear her laugh in the other room. She comes back with a man. As they go by the drawer I see it's the man in the business suit from the party. I hear them sit on the bed. They laugh a lot. She says something rude about me and my sexual abilities. I can tell she has his dick out of his pants because they're laughing about something. I realize they're laughing about sex. He's making fun of his equipment. I never like being laughed at when it's about sex. I don't like being laughed at at all, especially by a woman.

The bathrobe flies across the room and lands in the drawer on top of me and everything is dark. I hear the bedsprings squeak. They squeak for hours. They talk while they screw. After a while they stop talking. He grunts like a hog. She sings like a lark. Afterward I hear them talking. He asks her if she came. She says only a little. He says let me help you. I can't be sure, but I think he's doing something to her with his hand. I can't believe it. She doesn't seem to mind this at all.

I hear her sing again, this time louder than ever. Then they talk again. She tells him she never really came for me, that she always faked it. That I was a lousy fuck. That I didn't care if she came. That I got on and did it and got off.

A little air caught at the top of my head floats down and out of my open mouth.

They talk some more. They don't talk about him. She doesn't talk girl things. They talk about ideas. Politics. History. The office. Movies—films they call them—and books.

In the middle of the night the robe is lifted off of me. It's Madge. She's down on her knees looking in the drawer. She smiles at me. She picks me up and folds me gently. She has a box with her. It's the box she came in. The one that says Love Doll on it. The words Love Doll have been marked through with a magic marker and Fuck Toy has been written in above it. She puts me in the box and seals the lid and puts me back in the drawer and closes it.

APATHETIC FLESH

Darren O. Godfrey

Another way a story can become part of the Borderlands
*canon is if it is truly disturbing. Provocative, innova-
tive, stylish, and stuff like that are all good, but it is
the occasional story that really bothers you on some
elemental level that's most rare. After reading thousands
of submissions, believe me—I know of what I speak on
this. That's why "Apathetic Flesh" is the next thing
you'll read. I finished it and couldn't get some of its
more central images out of my mind. Darren Godfrey
is a new writer from Pocatello, Idaho; he's thirty years
old, married, and has a strong dislike for professional
wrestling. The story which follows is his first appearance
in a major anthology, and if this thing doesn't get you
by the short hairs, I don't know—maybe you ain't got
any . . .*

If you were to stop and think about it, you wouldn't
really be able to say why it is you watch these films;
though, as a child, you enjoyed being frightened, and
some of the movies did that; and as a teenager you
enjoyed being shocked (and perhaps a little revolted)
and the "splatter" films fit that bill nicely. But now, at
an ancient and creaking twenty-seven years of age, the
movies—horror, splatter, or otherwise—no longer seem
to have any effect on you. Nil.

But still you watch them, every one.

And *think* about it is something you never do anyway,
so, tonight, you merely chew stale popcorn and gawk
at the silver screen where the lead zombie (nicknamed
Harley) effortlessly tears a young woman's head from

her quivering white shoulders, delicately tongues one of her eyeballs, sucks it from its socket. Harley chews it, apparently savoring the taste, and the only discomfort you feel is the rock-hard lump against the small of your back, a special feature of all the seats in the Chief Theater. No point in moving. So you don't.

Until it's over (completely over; every last credit read and recorded in your junkshop mind), at which time you stand and brush salt and popcorn bits from your jeans.

"Well, that was fun," you say to no one as you step into the aisle and make for the glowing green EXIT.

Outside, the air is somewhat cooler than you expected it to be. You gaze up at the clouds gathering fast in the night sky and wish you'd brought along a jacket. You walk.

Midway across the gloomy parking lot a hump of shadow swells in your peripheral vision. It extends, detaches itself from the side of a parked car, and speaks in a well-mannered voice: "Sir, did you enjoy the film?"

Your feet stop dead in their tracks. You think of your home, a mere three blocks away, and you wonder if you can outrun this person; then you suddenly realize that this shadow is only a child; a young boy with a stocking cap pulled tightly down over his ears.

You say, "Sure. It was great," and walk passively on. You hear the shadow-child follow you.

"I very much wanted to see it," he informs your back, "but they would not let me in. They said that I am underage."

The boy has an accent, you notice, an odd one; but you only shrug the shoulder over which you speak: "That's too bad, kid. Now why don't you run along home now, huh?"

"Was there much blood?"

Again, you stop. You turn and face this inquisitive youngster. You notice that he, too, is wearing insufficient clothing against the chill, aside from the stocking cap. His arms are wrapped round himself and he bounces up and down on his heels. You notice a shiny black ribbon tied round his goose-pimpled left arm, just below the short sleeve. You wonder who died.

"Listen, kid. Didn't your mother ever tell you not to talk to strangers?"

An expression of hurt spreads over the boy's face as he turns away. You watch him for a moment, curious, and then turn homeward.

Once on the porch of your home, you flip through the tangled mess you call keys. You jump when lightning flashes over the sky. It is closely followed by loud thunder.

Rain begins to fall.

Should you watch TV or go to bed? You know that if you watch television all night you'll end up sleeping most of the day away tomorrow and then the weekend will be over before you know it. On the other hand, if you go to bed now you'll lie awake for hours staring at the wall, and then the late-night-dreads will set in. You don't want that.

The crack of another, closer, thunderbolt threatens to throw a tingle up your spine. Is such a thing still possible? A real shiver . . . how long's it been?

Okay: TV it is.

Beer or soda? In the tiny kitchen, you open the refrigerator door and your mind is made up for you: beer. Out of soda.

Then you are in the recliner, shoes off, cold can of beer in one hand, remote control in the other. Stations are flipping by, the light strobes on your face; all other lights are out now.

There.

You think you've seen this one before but that's all right because it's black-and-white (you like black-and-white) and has practically just begun. Outside: cold and stormy. Inside: warm and cozy. Perfect.

In five minutes you are snoring.

With a start, you are fully awake without knowing what it was that woke you. Still here, in the recliner, in the living room. You see that a different film is playing on the TV screen now, this one in color. You squint at the glowing numerals on the VCR: 3:33. Still, the sound of rain slapping the pavement outside.

You lift the can of beer from the table next to your chair, find that it has warmed, drink from it anyway.

A knock at the door sends dribbles of foam into your lap. *Damn*. Who can that be?

On your feet, you set the can down and head for the door. It couldn't be anyone from work, no one there speaks to you. A neighbor perhaps? Doubtful. They, too, avoid you. Everyone avoids you.

Another knock greets you as you reach the door and open it, a little.

It is the shadow-child. He is facing away from you and you see that his clothing is completely soaked, clinging wetly to his back. He is shivering, still wrapped in his own goose-pimpled arms.

"What is it you want from me, kid?"

He turns, one thin shoulder moving up in a tight shrug. "A bowl of soup would be nice," he says.

You weren't going to let him in—a trick, he's tricking you—but his soggy state compelled you to relent. His shirt and cap are slung over the back of a chair as he slurps chicken noodle soup at the kitchen table. His dark hair is pasted flat against his skull. He has your favorite beach towel wrapped around his shoulders, one corner of which he uses as a napkin.

"Here," you say. "Try this." You tear a sheet of paper towel from the roll above the sink and hand it to him. He takes it with a nod.

"Where do you live, Vaughn Meadows?" you ask, shaking your head again at the name he gave as his.

"It's hard for me to remember, but I know it's far away from here."

"And your parents? What about them?"

Spoon poised before his lips, he looks at you. He shakes his head, then takes in the soup

"You don't know, or you won't tell me?"

"I don't know."

"Why do you wear that thing around your arm?"

Again, he shakes his head back and forth.

So: ask more questions or shut up? Would you get any answers? The clock on the wall tells you that it is nearly 4:00 A.M.

"There's a couple of blankets on the couch," you say to the boy. "You can sleep there."

He lifts the bowl and drinks the remainder of the soup. "Thank you."

Very near sleep. Your bedroom wall sinks back into a fog bank as your body slowly relaxes itself, your respiration deepening. When you hear the muffled, close-yet-far-away sound of gunshots you believe that it is the beginning of a dream.

Voices. Rapid-fire gunshots. Screams.

Not a dream.

You lift your head from the pillow and the suppressed sounds of violence become more distinct. It is the television in the next room you hear. The boy, Vaughn.

Your bedroom door opens directly onto the living room. From the doorway, you see the blanket-wrapped child seated on the floor, expressionless oval face turned up to the screen.

"What are you watching?" you ask, half expecting him to jump at the intrusion. He doesn't.

"One of your videotapes."

"Oh? Which one?"

"*Dawn of the Dead*. Just starting."

You move into the center of the room and plop into the recliner. "You shouldn't be watching that, you know."

"Don't worry. I've seen it before."

On the screen, a man with a shotgun kicks open a door and blows the head off another man. No reaction from the boy. Searching for the remote control, you see that the open can of beer is missing from the table. You ask Vaughn Meadows what happened to it.

"Right here," he says, and one hand emerges from the folds of the blanket. The sides of the can have been squeezed together. "I drank it." His eyes never leave the screen.

"Where's the remote?"

His other hand appears, gripping the flat, black box.

"Turn it off and go to sleep."

"I can't sleep."

You rise, step around him, push the power buttons of both the TV and the VCR. The room falls into near-total darkness. "It'll be light soon. Try to get some sleep."

"Does anyone ever visit you here?"

"Why? What do you mean?"

No answer.

"Go to sleep."

"All right. I'll try."

You hear him scoot over to the couch. As you reach the bedroom door, his voice floats out to you: "The ribbon?"

Nonplussed, you respond, "Yeah, what about it?"

"If I take it off . . . I will stop."

You don't know what to say to that, so you say nothing.

"Do you want me to take it off?"

"I want you to go to sleep."

7:30 A.M. In the kitchen, Vaughn Meadows is devouring his third bowl of cold cereal. As you don a fresh pair of jeans and a sweatshirt you peer out your bedroom window at the small, sodden patch of backyard. No lawn mowing today. So: what to do on a rainy-day Sunday? See another movie? Go to the mall? Find the kid's parents?

You enter the kitchen, pour yourself a cup of coffee, and take up a chair opposite Vaughn Meadows. You blow across the top of your cup. With a short, distracted laugh, you decide it's question time again.

"You're not American are you? Where are you from?"

"I think I am American."

"From where?"

"I don't know."

"Where were you before you went to the movie theater last night?"

"Here."

"Here, where?"

He points a finger at the front door.

"Did you follow me?"

He nods.

"Why?"

"Do you have more of this? It's good."

"Tell me first why you're here."

He smiles then. A very knowing smile. "Take me to your leader."

You shake your head, rub a hand over your eyes, look at him again. His dark hair is neatly combed, his face clean, his smile widening.

You sip your coffee. You ask, "Vaughn, is there something you want from me?"

Now a giggle comes out. "Today is the first day of the rest of your life."

"Oh, forget it."

The books you purchased—or at least their covers—seem to amuse Vaughn Meadows. "Are they very disgusting?" he asks, his face glowing.

"Sometimes."

From the cashier's stand, you move out into the shopping mall, half expecting someone to approach and ask about the child. Did you kidnap him? What's going on here? Let's see some identification, buddy.

But no one looks at you or the boy. Everyday business.

"Will you let me read one of them?" he asks.

You say no and then ask him if he wants pizza, burgers, or fast Chinese.

The question: "How come you haven't told anyone?" He looks pointedly at you.

Driving out of the parking lot, your books and a couple of rented videotapes (G-rated Disney films) rest in the boy's lap. The car smells faintly of pepperoni. The question startles you. "What?"

"Why haven't you told people—the authorities, or anyone—about me?"

You slip on an expression that says: *Don't bother the driver while he's driving*, as your brain mulls this question over, tasting it.

Finding it flavorless.

No tears were shed for Bambi's mother, though there was much giggling and head-shaking at Thumper's antics. Now, as the tape rewinds, you turn to your visitor. "Have you ever seen that movie before?"

"Yes."

"Where?"

"I don't know."

"How long ago? Do you remember that?"

His head shakes. Back, forth.

"It couldn't have been very long ago—how old are you? Eight? Nine?"

"Yes."

"Which one?"

"Eight."

You pick up the other cassette. *The Cat from Outer Space*. "Have you seen this one before?"

"Yes," is Vaughn Meadows's reply, and he grins. "Take me to your leader."

Monday afternoon leaves you tired, worn out, wanting only to recline.

"Hello!" At the door, Vaughn Meadows's voice is bright and cheery. "We have to return the videos and you are in need of groceries. I watched a lot of commercials today, they're funny. Oh, and the telephone rang."

"Who was it?"

"I don't know. I didn't pick it up." He follows you into the living room, his hands on his hips. "*Should* I have, do you think?"

You fall into your chair, stretch, sigh greatly. "Doesn't matter. I don't care, I don't care, I don't care. Why don't you go home now?"

You close your eyes—the sting somehow pleasurable—and let your muscles relax, loosen, a notch at a time, until you feel as though you're ready to melt right through to the floor. The room is silent. You unstick your eyelids to see Vaughn Meadows staring back at you. He stands perfectly still, hands glued to hips: a statue in your living room. "What?" comes from your lips.

"Do you want me to leave?"

You would shrug at him if you didn't feel so drained, so permanently *in place*. You raise your eyebrows to him instead.

"Do you care?" he asks, and his small head with combed hair tilts to one side.

"I don't know," you respond, and your voice sounds strange in your ears, as if changing altitudes. "I don't know if it's a good idea to care, you know?"

Then the very air in the room seems to change, turn gray. No. Only your eyes, your tired mind playing tricks on you.

"I want to show you something," says the boy.

"What."

"You. I want to show you *you*."

Vaugh Meadows moves out of your view and out of the room. You hear the bathroom door quietly close . . . and your eyelids close, too. So comfortable. No aches, no pains. Only sweet nothingness.

Time has passed; the last vestiges of light coat the windows. How much time? It seems it has only been a minute, maybe two, but your mind plays tricks. You try to stir, yet from the neck down your muscles apparently have no intention of complying.

Vaughn Meadows is in the room. He is completely bare but for the black band round his arm; his skin is pale and somehow flat. A cardboard cutout, you think. He grips a small, shiny square in the fingers of one hand. There is a large pan (the one you use for stews and spaghetti) on the floor at his feet.

Of course, this is a dream.

"Don't worry," the cardboard Vaughn says, "you won't feel a thing." Then he half-steps forward, placing a foot on either side of the pan, knees apart. He brings the fingers holding the razor blade up and makes a five-inch vertical incision in the center of his chest. Blood spills, bubbles, courses downward, slowing only briefly at the navel, then drips from the boy's tiny penis, making *ponk-ponk* sounds in the pan. Not cardboard, then.

"You know how it feels not to feel," states Vaughn Meadows, conversationally. He drops the blade into the pan with one careless hand and looks at you, and the look is unmistakable. Joy. Your muscles persist in their mutiny; you can't lift a finger.

"What?"

"Absence. The total absence of sensation, pain, *feeling* . . . you are familiar with it, am I right?" His slender fingers move to the wound and pull at it, widen it, make the red flow faster. His eyes are still upon you. The *plonk-plonk*s are becoming *drip-drip*s and then—

—*PAIN IN THE EXTREME, SUNBURSTS OF BRIGHT AGONY IN THE CENTER OF YOUR CHEST, SPASMS THAT WILL KILL YOU IF—*

—but, so stupidly, so incredibly stupidly, you find yourself nodding your head. Viciously nodding your head.

Vaughn Meadows's own little head nods slowly as he grins. "Uh-oh," he says, nearly laughing now. "I lied. Sue me."

Up-down-up-down, idiotic is your head, and there's no use trying to stop it.

"Aaaaand, when one ceases to feel," he continues, "one ceases to live. Isn't that also correct?"

Chin thumps chest, hair rats itself between head and headrest. Your face is growing hot.

"Of course it is."

Nails of the fingers tug the sides of the slit, pull it even wider. The hot stream is rapid, completely missing the pan now—

—*FLESH, HEART RIPPED OUT, BODY TORN IN TWO—*

—and your mouth, suddenly operable, shouts, "Stop!" and you are startled by the voice, as if it came from somewhere else, somewhere *not of you*. There are tears on your face, tears, you think, of shock. But the pain is gone now . . . but from the boy, so much—

" . . . blood . . ." The word is a croak, it still doesn't sound like you.

"Yes." Laugh. "This blood's for you."

" . . . die . . ."

"Oh, yes. I will die, but not from this." His glowing eyes move from your face to his own narrow chest. Smooth skin parts further. "I can't even feel this . . . which . . . is the point . . ."

His body sways a little, he has to move a foot forward quickly to keep his balance. Weakening.

"I can't feel it, I have never felt it." His head comes up again, his half-lidded eyes fixed back upon yours. "But this, *this* . . ."—grin becomes grimace, pallid lips stretch—" . . . is the first day . . . of the rest . . . of your . . . stupid . . . *life* . . ."

One hand exits the spouting slit, slides beneath the ribbon colored awful midnight—" . . . the tie that binds . . ."—and pulls.

Break.

And the boy falls flat on his still-smiling face as one pale, impossibly white foot nudges over the pan before coming to rest in a widening crimson pool.

You now are able to move.

But you don't.

Dark outside; a punctuation of faraway lightning, thunder.

Somewhere, sometime, between lifting the boy's slight corpse to your shoulder and gently depositing it into a shallow backyard grave, the midnight ribbon somehow finds its way to your arm. Wrapped.

Where it pretends to be secure.

THE POTATO

Bentley Little

*There are only several repeat offenders in Borderlands
2. This is not by design, even though I'm always looking
for new talent; it just worked out like that. But Bentley
Little is a California writer who seems to have tapped
into Borderlands's line very well. He writes the kind of
story that employs a singular image or takes a surreal
turn that demands the reader do some work on his or her
own. He is the author many short stories and his second
novel,* The Mailman, *is currently available. His latest
effort is a thought-provoking tale of obsession, desire,
and something a bit more troublesome . . .*

The farmer stared down at the . . . thing . . . which
lay at his feet. It was a potato. No doubt about that.
It had been connected to an ordinary potato plant, and
it had the irregular contours of a tuber. But that was
where the resemblance to an ordinary potato ended.
For the thing at his feet was white and gelatinous, well
over three feet long. It pulsed rhythmically, and when
he touched it tentatively with his shovel, it seemed to
shrink back, withdrawing in upon itself.

A living potato.

It was an unnatural sight, wrong somehow, and his
first thought was that he should destroy it, chop it up
with his shovel, run it over with the tractor. Nature did
not usually let such abominations survive, and he knew
that he would be doing the right thing in destroying
it. Such an aberration was obviously not meant to be.
But he took no action. Instead he stared down at the
potato, unable to move, hypnotized almost, watching

69

the even ebb and flow of its pulsations, fascinated by its methodical movement. It made no noise, showed no sign of having a mind, but he could not help feeling that the thing was conscious, that it was watching him as he watched it, that, in some strange way, it even knew what he was thinking.

The farmer forced himself to look up from the hole and stared across his field. There were still several more rows to be dug, and there was feeding and watering to do, but he could not seem to rouse in himself any of his usual responsibility or sense of duty. He should be working at this moment—his time was structured very specifically, and even a slight glitch could throw off his schedule for a week—but he knew that he was not going to return to his ordinary chores for the rest of the day. They were no longer important to him. Their value had diminished, their necessity had become moot. Those things could wait.

He looked again at the potato. He had here something spectacular. This was something he could show at the fair. Like the giant steer he had seen last year, or the two-headed lamb that had been exhibited a few years back. He shook his head. He had never had anything worth showing at the fair, had not even had any vegetables or livestock worth entering in competition. Now, all of a sudden, he had an item worthy of its own booth. A genuine star attraction.

But the fair was not for another four months.

Hell, he thought. He could set up his own exhibit here. Put a little fence around the potato and charge people to look at it. Maybe he'd invite Jack Phelps, Jim Lowry, and some of his closest friends to see it first. Then they'd spread the word, and pretty soon people from miles around would be flocking to see his find.

The potato pulsed in its hole, white flesh quivering rhythmically, sending shivers of dirt falling around it. The farmer wiped a band of sweat from his forehead with a handkerchief, and he realized that he no longer felt repulsed by the sight before him.

He felt proud of it.

* * *

The farmer awoke from an unremembered dream, retaining nothing but the sense of loss he had experienced within the dream's reality. Though it was only three o'clock, halfway between midnight and dawn, he knew he would not be able to fall back asleep, and he got out of bed, slipping into his Levi's. He went into the kitchen, poured himself some stale orange juice from the refrigerator, and stood by the screen door, staring out across the field toward the spot where he'd unearthed the living potato. Moonlight shone down upon the field, creating strange shadows, giving the land a new topography. Although he could not see the potato from this vantage point, he could imagine how it looked in the moonlight, and he shivered, thinking of the cold, pulsing, gelatinous flesh.

He should have killed it, he thought. He should have stabbed it with the shovel, chopped it into bits, gone over it with the plow.

He finished his orange juice, placing the empty glass on the counter next to the door. He couldn't go back to sleep, and he didn't feel like watching TV, so he stared out at the field, listening to the silence. It was moments like these, when he wasn't working, wasn't eating, wasn't sleeping, when his body wasn't occupied with something else, that he felt Murial's absence the most acutely. It was always there—a dull ache that wouldn't go away—but when he was by himself like this, with nothing to do, he felt the true breadth and depth of his loneliness, felt the futility and pointlessness of his existence.

The despair building within him, he walked outside onto the porch. The wooden boards were cold and rough on his bare feet. He found himself, unthinkingly, walking down the porch steps, past the front yard, into the field. Here, the blackness of night was tempered into a bluish-purple by the moon, and he had no trouble seeing where he was going.

He walked, almost instinctively, to the spot where the living potato lay in the dirt. He had, in the afternoon,

gingerly moved it out of the hole, with the help of Jack
Phelps, burying the hole, and had gathered together the
materials for a box to be placed around it. The potato
had felt cold and slimy and greasy, and both of them had
washed their hands immediately afterward, scrubbing
hard with Lava. Now the boards lay in scattered disarray
in the dirt, like something that had been torn apart rather
than something which had not yet been built.

He looked down at the bluish-white form, pulsing
slowly and evenly, and the despair he had felt, the
loneliness, left him, dissipating outward in an almost
physical way. He stood rooted in place, too stunned to
move, wondering at the change that had come instantly
over him. In the darkness of night, the potato appeared
phosphorescent, and it seemed to him somehow magi-
cal. Once again, he was glad he had not destroyed his
discovery, and he felt good that other people would be
able to see and experience the strange phenomenon. He
stood there for awhile, not thinking, not doing anything,
and then he went back to the house, stepping slowly and
carefully over rocks and weeds this time. He knew that
he would have no trouble falling asleep.

In the morning it had moved. He did not know how
it had moved—it had no arms or legs or other means
of locomotion—but it was now definitely closer to the
house. It was also bigger. Whereas yesterday it had been
on the south side of his assembled boards, it was now
well to the north, and it had increased its size by half.
He was not sure he would be able to lift it now, even
with Jack's help.

He stared at the potato for awhile, looking for some
sort of trail in the dirt, some sign that the potato had
moved itself, but he saw nothing.

He went into the barn to get his tools.

He had finished the box and gate for the potato,
putting it in place, well before seven o'clock. It was
eight o'clock before the first carload of people arrived.
He was in the living room, making signs to post on
telephone poles around town and on the highway, when

a station wagon pulled into the drive. He walked out onto the porch and squinted against the sun.

"This where y'got that monster tater?" a man called out. Several people laughed.

"This is it," the farmer said. "It's a buck a head to see it, though."

"A buck?" The man got out of the car. He looked vaguely familiar, but the farmer didn't know his name. "Jim Lowry said it was fifty cents."

"Nope." The farmer turned as if to go in to the house.

"We'll still see it, though," the man said. "We came all this way, we might as well see what it's about."

The farmer smiled. He came off the porch, took a dollar each from the man, his brother, and three women, and led them out to the field. He should have come up with some kind of pitch, he thought, some sort of story to tell, like they did with that steer at the fair. He didn't want to just take the people's money, let them look at the potato and leave. He didn't want them to feel cheated. But he couldn't think of anything to say.

He opened the top of the box, swinging open the gate, and explained in a stilted, halting manner how he had found the potato. He might as well have saved his breath. None of the customers gave a damn about what he was saying. They didn't even pay any attention to him. They simply stared at the huge potato in awe, struck dumb by this marvel of nature. For that's how he referred to it. It was no longer an abomination, it was a marvel. A marvel of nature. A miracle. And the people treated it as such.

Two more cars pulled up soon after, and the farmer left the first group staring while he collected money from the newcomers.

After that, he stayed in the drive, collecting money as people arrived, pointing them in the right direction and allowing them to stay as long as they wanted. Customers came and went with regularity, but the spot next to the box was crowded all day, and by the time he hung a "Closed" sign on the gate before dark, he had over a hundred dollars in his pocket.

He went out to the field, repositioned the box, closed the gate, and retreated into the house.

It had been a profitable day.

Whispers. Low moans. Barely audible sounds of despair so forlorn that they brought upon him a deep, dark depression, a loneliness so complete that he wept like a baby in his bed, staining the pillows with his tears.

He stood up after awhile and wandered around the house. Every room seemed cheap and shabby, the wasted effort of a wasted life, and he fell into his chair before the TV, filled with utter hopelessness, lacking the energy to do anything but stare into the darkness.

In the morning, everything was fine. In the festive, almost carnival-like atmosphere of his exhibition, he felt rejuvenated, almost happy. Farmers who had not been out of their overalls in ten years showed up in their Sunday best, families in tow. Little Jimmy Hardsworth's lemonade stand, set up by the road at the head of the drive, was doing a thriving business, and there were more than a few repeat customers from the day before.

The strange sounds of the night before, the dark emotions, receded into the distance of memory.

He was kept busy all morning, taking money, talking to people with questions. The police came by with a town official, warning him that if this went on another day he would have to buy a business license, but he let them look at the potato and they were quiet after that. There was a lull around noon, and he left his spot near the head of the drive and walked across the field to the small crowd gathered around the potato. Many of his crops had been trampled, he noticed. His rows had been flattened by scores of spectator feet. He'd have to take a day off tomorrow and take care of the farm before it went completely to hell.

Take a day off.

It was strange how he'd come to think of the exhibition as his work, of his farm as merely an annoyance he had to contend with. His former devotion to duty was gone, as were his plans for the farm.

He looked down at the potato. It had changed. It was bigger than it had been before, more misshapen. Had it looked like this the last time he'd seen it? He hadn't noticed. The potato was still pulsing, and its white skin looked shiny and slimy. He remembered the way it had felt when he'd lifted it, and he unconsciously wiped his hands on his jeans.

Why was it that he felt either repulsed or exhilarated when he was around the potato?

"It's sum'in, ain't it?" the man next to him said.

The farmer nodded. "Yeah, it is."

He could not sleep that night. He lay in bed, staring up at the cracks in the ceiling, listening to the silence of the farm. It was some time before he noticed that it was not silence he was hearing—there was a strange, high-pitched keening sound riding upon the low breeze which fluttered the curtains.

He sat up in bed, back flat against the headboard. It was an unearthly sound, unlike anything he had ever heard, and he listened carefully. The noise rose and fell in even cadences, in a rhythm not unlike that of the pulsations of the potato. He turned his head to look out the window. He thought he could see a rounded object in the field, bluish-white in the moonlight, and he remembered that he could not see it at all the night before.

It was getting closer.

He shivered, and he closed his eyes against the fear.

But the high-pitched whines were soothing, comforting, and they lulled him gently to sleep.

When he awoke, he went outside before showering or eating breakfast, walking out to the field. Was it closer to the house? He couldn't be sure. But he remembered the keening sounds of the night before, and a field of goose bumps popped up on his arms. The potato definitely looked more misshapen than it had before, its boundaries more irregular. If it was closer, he thought, so was the box he had built around it. Everything had been moved.

But that wasn't possible.

He walked back to the house, ate, showered, dressed, and went to the foot of the drive, where he put up a chain between the two flanking trees and hung a sign which read: "Closed for the Day."

There were chores to be done, crops to water, animals to be fed, work to be completed.

But he did none of these things. He sat alone on a small bucket, next to the potato, staring at it, hypnotized by its pulsations, as the sun rose slowly to its peak, then dipped into the west.

Murial was lying beside him, not moving, not talking, not even touching him, but he could feel her warm body next to his and it felt right and good. He was happy, and he reached over and laid a hand on her breast. "Murial," he said. "I love you."

And then he knew it was a dream, even though he was still in it, because he had never said those words to her, not in the entire thirty-three years they had been married. It was not that he had not loved her, it was that he didn't know how to tell her. The dream faded into reality, the room around him growing dark and old, the bed growing large and cold. He was left with only a memory of that momentary happiness, a memory which taunted him and tortured him and made the reality of the present seem lonelier and emptier than even he had thought it could seem.

Something had happened to him recently. Depression had graduated to despair, and the tentative peace he had made with his life had all but vanished. The utter hopelessness which had been gradually pressing in on him since Murial's death had enveloped him, and he no longer had the strength to fight it.

His mind sought out the potato, though he lacked even the energy to look out the window to where it lay in the field. He thought of its strangely shifting form, of its white, slimy skin, of its even pulsations, and he realized that just thinking of the object made him feel a little better.

What was it?

That was the question he had been asking himself ever since he'd found the potato. He wasn't stupid. He knew it wasn't a normal tuber. But neither did he believe that it was a monster or a being from outer space or some other such movie nonsense.

He didn't know what it was, but he knew that it had been affecting his life ever since he'd discovered it, and he was almost certain that it had been responsible for the emotional roller coaster he'd been riding the past few days.

He pushed aside the covers and stood up, looking out the window toward the field. Residual bad feelings fled from him, and he could almost see them flying toward the potato as if they were tangible, being absorbed by that slimy white skin. The potato offered no warmth, but it was a vacuum for the cold. He received no good feelings from it, but it seemed to absorb his negative feelings, leaving him free from depression, hopelessness, despair.

He stared out the window and thought he saw something moving out in the field, blue in the light of the moon.

The box was still in the field, but the potato was lying on the gravel in front of the house. In the open, freed from the box, freed from shoots and other encumbrances, it had an almost oval shape, and its pulsing movements were quicker, more lively.

The farmer stared at the potato, unsure of what to do. Somewhere in the back of his mind, he had been half-hoping that the potato would die, that his life would return to normal. He enjoyed the celebrity, but the potato scared him.

He should have killed it the first day.

Now he knew that he would not be able to do it, no matter what happened.

"Hey!" Jack Phelps came around the side of the house from the back. "You open today? I saw some potential customers driving back and forth along the road, waiting."

The farmer nodded tiredly. "I'm open."

Jack invited him to dinner, and the farmer accepted. It had been a long time since he'd had a real meal, a meal cooked by a woman, and it sounded good. He also felt that he could use some company tonight.

But none of the talk was about crops or weather or neighbors the way it used to be. The only thing Jack and Myra wanted to talk about was the potato. The farmer tried to steer the conversation in another direction, but he soon gave it up, and they talked about the strange object. Myra called it a creature from Hell, and though Jack tried to laugh it off and turn it into a joke, he did not disagree with her.

When he returned from the Phelpses' it was after midnight. The farmer pulled into the dirt yard in front of the house and cut the headlights, turning off the ignition. With the lights off, the house was little more than a dark, hulking shape blocking out a portion of the starlit sky. He sat unmoving, hearing nothing save the ticking of the pickup's engine as it cooled. He stared at the dark house for a few moments longer, then got out of the pickup and clomped up the porch steps, walking through the open door into the house.

The open door?

There was a trail of dirt on the floor, winding in a meandering arc through the living room into the hall, but he hardly noticed it. He was filled with an unfamiliar emotion, an almost pleasant feeling he had not experienced since Murial died. He did not bother to turn on the house lights but went into the dark bathroom, washed his face, brushed his teeth, and got into his pajamas.

The potato was waiting in his bed.

He had known it would be there, and he felt neither panic nor exhilaration. There was only a calm acceptance. In the dark, the blanketed form looked almost like

Murial, and he saw two lumps protruding upward which looked remarkably like breasts.

He got into bed and pulled the other half of the blanket over himself, snuggling close to the potato. The pulsations of the object mirrored the beating of his own heart.

He put his arms around the potato. "I love you," he said.

He hugged the potato tighter, crawling on top of it, and as his arms and legs sank into the soft, slimy flesh, he realized that the potato was not cold at all.

SATURN

Ian McDowell

Not every story in this anthology has to be dealing from the bottom of a new deck. Sometimes a more traditionally executed tale can work its way in simply by being well-written and cleanly plotted—as long as it's not some tired old idea. The next tale is a good example of what I'm talking about. Its author, Ian McDowell, lives in Greensboro, North Carolina, where he earned a master's degree in English Literature. He's had several stories in magazines such as F&SF *and* Asimov's, *plus an appearance in Karl Wagner's* Year's Best Horror *anthology, and his latest offering is a grim little love story . . . kind of.*

Returning with the Sunday *New York Times,* he found Jan gone and Michael's skull resting on the coffee table, next to Jan's half-empty *Far Side* mug. It was smaller than he remembered it, no bigger than a squeezed orange. The left orbit and much of the zygomatic arch were gone, and dark soil spilled out of the tiny brain pan onto the varnished table top. He could smell the garden through the open French doors, and when he walked across the room to see if Jan was outside, he saw more dirt on the stoop, as well as several fragments of bone. Jan's Fiat was gone, and Bodger was curled up asleep in a fresh hole in the geranium bed. It wasn't hard to figure out what had happened.

He should never have gotten her the dog. *Terrier* comes from the French word meaning "to dig," and that's what the little Jack Russel's did, incessantly, though in the past, beatings had convinced him to confine his efforts to the neighbors' property. He was always unearthing things and leaving them on the back stoop, dismal offerings to the household gods. Last time, it had been the dead gerbil the McNaughten kids had buried in their backyard. Jan had more than once laughingly said she should take the dog along on her next dig; he was certainly more industrious at it than her current gaggle of grad students.

And now he'd been in the geranium bed, and had thoughtfully disinterred Michael's skull for Jan to find when she came downstairs for her coffee. With clinical detachment, she must have carried it inside to examine more closely, as though it were a relic from the Hopi mound she'd excavated last summer and not the cranium of her infant son. And where was she now?

At the police station, most likely. When one's eight-month-old child disappears and, four years later, the dog finds a baby's skull in the flower bed, one generally goes to the authorities. She was probably being very cool about it, too, puffing calmly on her cigarette as she explained her suspicions to a nonplussed desk sergeant. None of his other wives had had such *sang froid*. Was that very lack of sentiment the reason he'd stayed with this one, the reason he actually loved her?

Despite her cold academic facade, she was sure to be in Hell right now. He tried to shut out pain and guilt by wondering if she'd cooperate with the producers of the inevitable TV docudrama. Who'd end up playing her, Farrah Fawcett? God, and who might get his role? Someone cast against type, probably, like Ted Danson.

Enough of this, he had little time left. He knew, immediately knew, that he didn't want to live without her, though he didn't know why. After more than two hundred years, had it taken such an ice queen to get a real hold on him, or was he just tired of it all? Regardless of that, he owed her an explanation.

Walking quickly to his study, the *Times* still under his arm, he switched on the Mac and threw the paper on the floor. Opening the MicroSoft Word file, he sat and wrote for what seemed an improbably long time,

listening all the while for a car in the driveway. When
he was done, he opened the wall safe and got out his
World War I service revolver. He hadn't fired it since
the Somme, but kept it loaded and in good condition.
Moving the computer table against the wall, he cleared
the center of the room and spread out the *Times*. Sitting
cross-legged on the "Week in Review" section, he put
the gun to his temple. With luck, a cop would find him,
not Jan, though he was sure she could handle it if she
did. As his finger tightened on the trigger, it occurred to
him that it would have been better to have put the barrel
in his mouth.

Dear Jan,

Yes, I killed Michael. And buried his head, hands,
feet, and bones in the geranium bed, after eating the
rest. I can't even honestly say I regret it, although I'm
sorry you had to find out. I want to be very blunt about
this. It will probably be better for you if you manage to
hate me.

A word of advice. Cooperate with the hack bestseller
writers and the TV producers who come sniffing around.
You won't be able to stop them, and you might as well
get some money out of it.

I do love you. That's why I'm going to tell you the
whole truth. I want, perversely perhaps, someone with
whom I've been intimate to know precisely what I am
and what I've done. I've had sixteen wives, if you
count the common-law ones, but you're the only one
I've felt close to, in spite, or perhaps because, of the
way we've always held sentiment at arm's length. At
best, the wisdom of the heart remains obscure.

I may be selfish in my intentions here. It's possible
that knowing me, my intimate truth, will blight the rest
of your life. But would it have been any easier on you to
believe me UNCG's sociopath-in-residence, an Ed Gein
with tenure? I'm egocentric enough to think myself more
interesting than that.

Hell, forget about cooperating with the people who
want to crank out another *Fatal Vision*; write the book

yourself. You can do a better job of it than any hack.

Here's some corroboration for what I'm about to tell you. In the locked drawer of the file cabinet in my departmental office, you'll find a few items of interest. There's a 1941 Duke yearbook, for one thing. Look at the class portrait on page 239. That's me, third from the right. Yes, the picture was taken more than fifty years ago, and yes, the man whose name is listed as "Jacob Cranshaw" looks a good decade older than "Bill Fields" did when we met in '78, but it's me, just the same. You'll also find a clipping from the society column of the March 21, 1908 *Omaha Herald*. That photo is quite faded, but you should be able to recognize me, despite the heavy mustache, and the fact that my name is given as "James O'Keefe." There'll be a few other items of interest, too, assorted mementoes of past lives. Not much, though; I haven't saved much. Almost nothing from my pre-academic days, and those were the first hundred and sixty years of my existence.

The earliest corroboration is rather more difficult (literally) to dig up. Do you know where Qualla Hollow is, up on the eastern border of Cherokee, NC? There was a dig there, ten years back, before the Tribal Council called in A.I.M. to protest the desecration of sacred ground. On the rise above the hollow is a ridge that marks the western boundary of Trencher's Farm. There's one structure atop the ridge, a dilapidated one-room shack, as well as an old well. Actually, neither the shack nor the well are all that old; they weren't in existence when I first saw the area.

About ten feet from the shack, in a straight line to the well, is where a small cabin stood, two hundred and six years ago. Nothing remains on the surface, but excavation should yield various Colonial-era pots, pans, and cutlery, as well as the bones of my first wife and child. I came to be what I am now in the harsh winter of 1784, when I lived in that cabin with Nundalyee, my Cherokee wife, and my half-breed daughter, who never lived long enough to have a name.

Just try to absorb the blunt facts right now. Worry about believing them later. God, I sound like those two body builders on *Saturday Night Live*.

I was born Jamie MacComber, in Aberdeen, in 1748. Came over with my father and three surviving brothers (the rest died at Culloden) in 1774, to the Scots settlement at Cross Creek, where Fayetteville is now. Like all our kin, we'd been forced to swear fealty to the crown, and ended up fighting for Allan MacDonald and the Loyalists. The real reason my left knee pains me sometimes is the musket ball I took at Moore's Creek Bridge, where the Colonists slaughtered the Highlanders in '76. My father and brothers were not as lucky as I was.

That soured me, and when the Treaty of '77 pacified the Cherokee, I headed west to the mountains. After seven years of trading and trapping, I had a Cherokee wife, and the cabin on Qualla Ridge I've already mentioned.

Nundalyee was a strong, impassive woman, not unattractive in her dark, squatty way. Although I spoke some Cherokee, and she picked up a slight smattering of English, I can't remember us ever exchanging more than a dozen words at a time. But then, the man I was wasn't much for conversation. She was a functional enough wife, and I loved her as much as most men loved their wives back then. Strange, but I don't think I've thought about this, my first life, in over fifty years.

Things were fine until the winter of '84. Nundalyee's health declined after the baby came, a great, huge, squalling thing that seemed to be sucking the life out of her through her tit. A less sturdy woman would have died sooner; as it was, she never lived to see it weaned. As for me, I managed to get my ankle savaged by a trapped raccoon that had seemed dead but wasn't, and the wound got infected. By the time Nundalyee was dying, I could barely walk.

And then the snow came, whiteness everywhere, piling up against the door like heavy wet laundry, like bags of white cement.

There I was, crippled, snowbound, with a dead woman and the starving infant that had killed her, and nothing to eat. So I ate the baby. Raw mostly, although she was actually big enough that some of her ended up as cured jerky, and the bones went into soup.

You might want to pause a moment here, pour yourself a drink. It does get worse.

Food brought strength, more strength than a few pounds of meat and bone should have brought. I immediately started to get better, and could walk fine by the time the snow had melted. I tried to continue my dealings with the tribe, and forget what I had done, but things didn't work out that way. The small cabin had too many ghosts, and at night my dreams echoed with the cries of a starving baby. So I went back to civilization. And that's where I saw my reflection, for the first time in several years.

I looked at least ten years younger, with all the gray gone from my hair and the lines smoothed out of my face. I didn't know what I was yet, but I knew something impossible had happened, somehow.

I have to keep this short; the police should be here soon. Can't allow myself to be tried as a criminal or institutionalized as a psychopath. You wouldn't visit me, I'm sure.

An aside. Several months before your pregnancy began to show, I was walking down the hall of Graham Building, and passed your classroom. I don't remember what you were lecturing about, or what class it was. I just remember how the blinds let in the afternoon sun, highlighting your long, strong face and very black hair. I don't want to give this up, I thought. Not this time. She's not really beautiful, not even at her best, and certainly not now. Yet I would rather feel one of her fingers on the back of my hand than fuck any other woman in the world. How does it feel to be thought of that way, by someone who is, quite literally, an ogre?

But back to my history. I've no time for anything but the barest synopsis. You'll have to hunt up your own details, if you do decide to research and document my life.

Skipping ahead, then, to 1794. I had settled in Boston, and remarried, and eventually owned my own smithy. In due course, my wife—her name, I think, was Anne—gave birth to twin boys. They were three years old when I felt the hunger.

The signs of age came first—crow's-feet literally overnight, wrinkles in a week, hair all gone gray in a month. Fortunately, it didn't continue at that rate, or I would have been senile and dying before I'd figured out what I must do. As it was, though, I aged over a decade in less than a year. And with the aging came the gnawing emptiness in my gut, the consuming void nothing seemed to fill. The smithy had prospered and food was plentiful on our table, but none of it did any good, not pork or mince pies or salt cod or chicken or corn or strawberries or fresh crabs from the harbor. By the time I knew what I had to do, I weighed less than a hundred and thirty pounds, and I'm big-boned for this century, much less that one.

I held off for a while, held off so long, in fact, that when I gave in, I ended up killing and eating both my plump young boys—what *were* their names? I'm afraid I recall how they tasted better than I can recall what they were called, or even what they looked like. The flavor isn't as much like pork as you might expect. More like mutton, really, or fresh young goat. Is that why we call children *kids,* now? What a thought. Perhaps I'm not unique.

Of course, I had to kill Anne, too (if that was her name), although I didn't eat her. I've never eaten any human being I didn't help to conceive. I give them life, then take it away—it used to seem a fair trade. Well, that's one way of reconciling myself to an existence punctuated by the deaths of my children. What's the line the Jeff Goldblum character says in *The Big Chill,* about rationalizations?

Another aside. It will be your birthday, soon, an occasion you generally find quite traumatic enough, without the coloring of this new revelation. Don't be so terrified of getting old, Jan. There are worse things.

Or maybe not. Look which alternative I chose.

Don't worry, though; I never planned to kill you. Other than Anne, or whatever her name was, I've only had to kill two wives in as many centuries. Once things were all sorted out, and I fully understood my new existence, I began perfecting all the techniques that have brought me this far. Of course, the slave trade helped immensely, although it was some time before I was prosperous enough to buy mothers for my children. Still, a big, strapping, industrious man who never got sick and who'd long since lost all scruples found plenty of opportunities to make money, and I eventually had the necessary capital to buy breeding stock. That particular affront to their enlightened sensibilities might be the one thing our colleagues would find most unforgivable about me, don't you think? If it's any defense, I must say I never tried to assuage my guilt by pretending my slaves were subhuman.

Emancipation required me to learn the skills I've maintained to this day. By the end of the nineteenth century, I was proficient in all the dodges, all the ways a man can stage the abduction or disappearance of his children, then slip out of the marriage and into a new life somewhere else.

You're the first I've stayed with. Rather pointless, really; I mean, it could only have lasted so much longer. The hunger comes back approximately every ten years, so we only had six left. I would have had to move on, rather sooner than that, or face your watching me die. God knows what modern medicine would make of my case. I haven't allowed myself to suffer "withdrawal pains" in nearly a hundred years.

What does what I am say about the Way the World Really Works, about all the assumptions rationalists like you and most of our colleagues base their lives upon? I don't know. It was only with the birth of this century that I decided to cultivate my mind. Scholarship came to me rather late in life, and it wasn't until after the First

World War that my academic career really flourished. This new direction in my life is what brought me back, ultimately, to North Carolina. Before returning here, I'd earned degrees in History and Anthropology from Emory and Berkeley. At Duke, I even made an abortive foray in Medicine, but didn't really have the knack for it.

I tried one experiment, though. I fed rats their own newborn offspring. Their lifespans were not appreciably increased. Perhaps this ability is something unique to humans. Could there be a ruling cabal somewhere, immortal Masters who know the Secret and control it, pulling the strings of puppet nations? Are the Illuminati or the Masons real, and actually anthropophagous infanticides? What a wonderfully melodramatic thought. If such a brotherhood exists, I've never stumbled across it. Yet, surely, I cannot be unique.

Or perhaps I can. I leave that for you to determine. Think of the vistas—medical, biological, anthropological, historical, philosophical—I have opened up for you.

I am amazed that the police have not arrived yet. I've had more time here than I expected. If I am not interrupted in the next few minutes, I intend to append to this letter a list of every name I've ever had, and every place in which I've ever lived. That should be enough, I think, to start you on your search. That and the things you'll find in the file drawer in my office, and in my safety deposit box at First Union. The diary that I intermittently kept from 1894 to 1953 should be a help; unfortunately, it's the only documentation of that sort that I've held on to. It contains the details on how my scholarly career began, and how I established new identities in the academic community.

I expect they'll dissect me, if they believe this testament (if you believe it). They'll find part of a musket ball in my knee, and at least one bullet. My wounds have always healed well. And I've never been sick since my transformation, or had a cold, not even when I was suffering "withdrawal pains." What internal differences I may have from the average mortal man, I do not know. Still, forensics should yield some evidence of my unique condition. I hope it does. I don't know why, but I very much want to be believed. Fame would have hampered me while I was alive, but I don't object to having it posthumously. Even if it's really infamy.

So write a book, if you wish, and in it make me a monster for all seasons. In an age where child abuse is more widely acknowledged and decried than ever before, where missing children are pictured on milk cartons, where tabloid journalists rave about child-sacrificing Satanists, I can be everyone's official ogre. For the Religious Right, I will be selfish, Godless secularism run rampant, the perfect symbol of how the intelligentsia are anti-family. No doubt the Right-to-Lifers will make of me a particularly Horrible Example. And the feminists will see me as the ultimate exploitative male, victimizing women solely for the fruit of their wombs.

Cannibalism and infanticide are among our oldest taboos; what can be said of one who has repeatedly violated both? How have I lived with myself, with the knowledge that I am one with Sawney Beane and Goddard Oxenbridge and Mumpoker, all the child-devouring bogies of my Highlands youth, or kin to the Manitou and Wendigo of the folk I once called savages? I'm worse, really; none of those fabled ogres ever ate their *own* progeny. I have become rapacious Saturn, staving off entropy by devouring my children. How have I borne that stain?

Easily enough, really. I was born in a simpler era, when survival was all, and babies died all the time, in birth and soon after. Nobody in my field or yours really understands just how common infanticide was in that pre-contraceptive age. I am nothing like Jamie MacComber anymore, but I would not be anything at all if he had not been the man he was.

Lifeboat Ethics, the precepts that women and (most particularly) children come first, arise from nothing nobler than communal self-interest, the knowledge that our offspring are a vicarious investment in immortality. But what if everyone knew the next generation can yield a far more direct bounty, that birth is a miracle indeed, creating some vital essence that for a time infuses nascent flesh? How many, if offered, would forsake the communion of that flesh? The *elixir vitae* is a tempting draught, even if it runs only in the veins of our own children.

That was once all the rationale I needed. Now, having forsaken everything in favor of survival, I find survival no longer quite sufficient. I have become too moored in this moment to prepare for the next one. This particular life, however dry and academic and circumscribed, has become more important than Life itself.

Bullshit and romantic maundering. If the truth be known, it is hard to imagine prolonging this peculiar existence into the next century. In our increasingly cybernetic, cross-indexed, triple-documented world, the constant fuss of new lives and identities is increasingly difficult. I think they'd eventually catch me no matter what I did. Maybe blowing my brains out is no act of romantic despair; I'm just quiting the game while I'm ahead.

I wish I could end on a pithy aphorism. Unfortunately, I've only learned two really interesting things in as many centuries. One is that, no matter what, you can always start over again. The other is that the liver of a newborn girl is delicious with red wine and wild onions.

So, I close with a bland truism and a tasteless grotesquerie. Do remember one thing, though. If I didn't love you, I wouldn't be writing this at all.

> Best,
> Bill

Yes, he should have put the barrel in his mouth, he thought on his second or third awakening. During the building of the Union Pacific, he'd seen dynamite blast a crowbar into a man's head, and the man had lived to see his grandchildren. He'd later (much later) read that the man's skull and the crowbar were somewhere in the Smithsonian, although that might be a myth, like Dillinger's penis.

For a while, all he knew was tubes and medication and concerned nurses, rather too concerned looking, considering they must know *something* of what he'd done. The expected detectives never came, though, not even after the tube was out of his nose and he could talk. Just a therapist of some sort, a big man who looked disconcertingly like Oliver Hardy in horn-rimmed glasses. The therapist spoke of depression and stress, but never a word about infanticide.

Finally, Jan came.

He awoke to find her sitting there, puffing on a cigarette, her unwashed hair tied back with a rubber band. She'd switched to Camel Filters, he saw. Wasn't smoking against the rules? Well, it had been in the faculty lounge, too, and she'd always made that room fumid enough.

There were new lines around her eyes, or old ones he'd not noticed before. When she cocked her head, and the sun caught her hair, he saw the gray. When had she stopped using the rinse?

"I've been through your things. I believe your story." Her voice was quite hoarse, but uninflected.

"Do the police?"

She put out the cigarette in a Styrofoam hospital cup. "They don't know about Michael. I dug up the rest of him, triple-bagged it, and pounded it all flat with a hammer. Then I replanted the flakes, rather deeper than you did."

"Why?"

She wouldn't meet his eyes. "I love you, too, goddamn you."

For a while, neither of them spoke. Finally, she broke the silence.

"I didn't want him, you knew that. Couldn't understand why you insisted we allow the pregnancy to come to term. You never struck me as the fatherly type. I guess I understand your motivations now, but it was certainly a mystery at the time. Anyway, I didn't want him at all.

Mothers tend to become grandmothers."

He looked at the ceiling. "Better than spinsters, I should think. Grandchildren are supposed to be a comfort." He knew how stupid that must sound, coming from him.

"I don't want to get old, either, Bill."

He waited for her to say the rest.

"I've been off the Pill for a while now. And I've made plans to go on sabbatical. I'll be as secluded as a nun. If I were to get pregnant again, no one need ever know."

He certainly didn't feel horrified. But he wasn't sure what he did feel. "I don't know if it would work for you. I mean, it can't be a purely biological process, can it? As I said in my suicide note, other people would have discovered the secret by now."

"Perhaps they have. And never let the rest of us in on it. You weren't thinking very clearly when you wrote your note, Bill. Can you imagine the effect upon human society if your story had been believed, if I had parlayed the book and TV rights into fame and fortune? No, if eating our own children is the secret to immortality, we'd better keep it just between ourselves."

He said nothing, and she kept talking, in the same quick monotone.

"Do you have to wait until your ten-year cycle is nearer the end, or could you 'renew' yourself now?"

Their eyes met. "I don't have to wait."

"If I take fertility pills, there should be enough for both of us."

They talked for a while longer, mostly of inconsequential things. Finally, she left, pausing to kiss him on the forehead. Before the nurse came to check on him, he was sleeping like a baby.

ANDROGYNY

Brian Hodge

If there is any discernible trend in the genre of the darkly imaginative tale, it might be a looking inward, not as much at the unconscious clockworks of our minds as the prison which keeps our minds forever captive—our bodies. Over the last year or so, I've seen a definite rise in the number of stories which investigate human biology as a new source of mystery, fear, and even true repulsion. Brian Hodge is a youngish writer from the midwest with short story appearances in some very prestigious, anthologies with names like Book of the Dead, Final Shadows, *and* Under the Fang. *His most recent novel is* Nightlife, *to be followed by* Deathgrip *and* The Darker Saints. *His work for* Borderlands *is an emotional journey into a strange and ultimately absorbing subculture.*

The afterglow fades, always.

The quicker it happens, the more ardently you're left to wonder about the origins. Even if the focal point of earlier affections is still lying beside you, dozing, maybe even cuddled in the crook of your arm, it doesn't matter. The afterglow fades, and the questions rear their heads . . .

How did this happen? What twist of fate and chemistry turned us from strangers into lovers in a few hours?

Gary knew it would probably happen all over again the moment he saw her. Some bar on Basin Street, the outer fringe of the French Quarter, well-removed from the mainstream. Less than a dozen drinkers, more than half of them hard-core, beyond redemption. Lights were

93

low, smoke was thick, exotically resilient bacteria likely grew on the floor.

Look at her clothes and you wouldn't think she belonged here; look in her eyes and you quickly reconsidered. Slumming, like Gary, for the thrill of it.

It took a full twenty minutes of flirtatious eye contact through the smokebank before she came his way, took the stool next to him. This he took as a good sign: she was no hooker. No hooker with her looks would work this stretch, and even if she did, she wouldn't have wasted twenty minutes before moving in. Gary may have been new to New Orleans, but knew that some games were universal.

"What are you?" was the first thing she said.

"Career? Astrologically? What do you mean?"

She smiled, traced a lacquered fingernail around the rim of her glass, some fruity concoction, sweet contrast to his whiskey sour. "I see you sitting here, like you know the lay of the land. You're not a tourist, I can tell that right off, no tourist ever comes around here unless he's some conventioneer drunk out of his mind. But you're not a native, either. Are you?"

"Long-term transient," Gary said, and clinked his glass to hers. "Seeker of non-conformist Americana."

Her face lit up hopefully. "Jack Kerouac for the Nineties?"

He mused this with cocked head, then shrugged. For the first time he smiled, which he did not do often, but when he did it was always genuine.

"I like that," he said. "I'd never have thought of it, but I like it. A lot."

Talk progressed, easy and loose and non-binding. Names were traded, Gary for Lana. Libidos simmered during the seductive ballet. He liked best these encounters where the traditional roles were blurred. Who was the predator, and who the prey? A toss-up, one answer as valid as the other. In the end, he supposed it didn't matter, so long as the orgasms were mutual.

Six years of high-ticket vagrancy had shuffled him through a streetwise succession of primary, secondary, and graduate schools of one-night stands and short-term loves. Money was no problem, not so long as the plastic credit umbilical card kept him linked to the New England bank account. He never had to stick around when it no longer seemed wise, and that seemed important. He didn't want to leave behind a legacy of pain any more than he wanted to lug one around with him.

"You like riddles?" she asked after four rounds of drinks had gone by, maybe five.

"Usually. Let's hear it."

"It's not easy." Lana smiled mischievously. "But. Do you know what the worst part of being *me* is?"

"The worst thing, let me see." He studied her a moment, the fine-boned face, the tall straight posture, the so-black hair, shoulder length. She didn't look to have lived *too* harsh a life thus far. Her eyes knew pain, though, and her soul was evidently as on display as her small cleavage. "You don't know how to love."

A coy shake of her head. "Wrong. Very wrong."

"You . . . you've never been *in* love."

Another shake. She was enjoying this immensely. Then, sometimes this was the most fun game of all, opening yourself up like a maze to a stranger, escorting them into blind alleys.

"You don't think," he tried slowly, "you'll ever find the *right* one to love."

Lana arched an eyebrow, half conciliatory. "You're still off, but that's a little warmer."

He offered a few more stabs at it, then gave up. Lifted his drink and swirled it, watched it in near-hypnosis. "I can think straighter later."

"Love and friendship," Lana mused, obliquely avoiding coughing up the answer. "They're opposites, in a way, you know."

"Bullshit," he grinned.

"Really. Joseph Roux, in *Meditations of a Parish Priest*, said, 'What is love? Two souls and one flesh. Friendship? Two bodies and one soul.' " Lana nodded.

"I believe that, with all my heart and soul." She dropped her hand to his thigh; that thrilling heart rush of first contact. "How 'bout you? Do you believe it?"

"I might. Give me time to think it over."

And what's it going to be for us? he wondered. *Love, or friendship? Two bodies . . . or one?*

Snap judgments were risky, but he thought he'd be agreeable to either. Something about her eyes, her manner, her tip-of-iceberg hint that—for the right person—she was far more than someone who merely wanted compatible flesh to sustain her until morning light. A needle-in-haystack find among French Quarter sin, someone with depths of fascination and arcane philosophy worth diving for.

"Well, if you can believe that," she said, leaning in close to whisper, "then I have *so* many secrets to share with you."

Gary watched, listened, with dual personae: The Romantic longed to believe her. And the Cynic thought it mere puffery; worse yet, sweet bait so she could lure him to a partner in hiding, and they would mug him.

He would bite; he would swallow. Have a little faith for once.

Soon they danced, pressed close as they leaned together and slow-shuffled about the floor, glowing with neon bleed-through from the street. They were watched by the dismal eyes of other drinkers, weary survivors clinging to desperate rafts of Jim Beam and Seagram's. The jukebox scratched out the mournful alcoholic laments of Tom Waits, the original Skid Row troubadour.

She later led him out back, to an alley with too little light, and for just a moment he was sure his judgment had failed him at the worst of all possible moments. But no gun was drawn, no lead pipe fell from shadows.

Lana drew down his zipper and, her dress forgotten, dropped to her knees before him in the grime. Overhead, the moon looked sickly, the color of whiskey.

Yet finally he knew that, for awhile, at least, he had found a home.

The afterglow faded. As always.

To his credit, it had taken a good deal longer than usual, four months of cohabitation in Lana's apartment. Contact with the seductive unknown usually had that effect.

Lana had shared her most intimate secrets a couple of days after that first night. Shockingly unexpected though they had been, they hadn't been enough to send him packing. He was, by then, head over heels in . . . well, fascination, he supposed. This was too . . . *different* . . . to turn away from just yet. Without exploration.

Scratch the mundane surface of conventional normality, and the underground of counterculture was revealed, rich and teeming. It was now far more diverse than in the days of Kerouac, and this was the landscape Gary had long been traveling, making up for the loveless stultification of his first twenty-one years.

Next: scratch the underground and peel it back, and there was the land where Lana lived.

But the afterglow fades. He had bitten, he had swallowed. Best to move on before the emotional hooks barbed him any deeper.

April, the warmth and renewal of spring after a winter of oddities. The famous final scene, lovers at bittersweet poles, opposites that once attracted and now repelled. Gary had played it out a number of times. Never pleasant, just seemingly inevitable.

"How can you do this to me *now*?" Lana wailed. "My operation is just a week away!" Her eyes were dazed and wide, glassy with psycho-sexual trauma. Tears were abundant.

In the center of the living room, Gary held her tightly. That desperate agony of final contact. "I'm sorry," he whispered. "You knew what I was like before . . ."

Lana, snuffling and huge-eyed. "I . . . I just wish I could have children with you, that might make all the difference in the world . . . wouldn't it? *Wouldn't it?*"

He bit his lip, hating it when she talked this way. Blind to her own limitations. It wasn't healthy.

"Don't live in a fantasy world, Lana," he said. Gently, so gently. "Climb out, *please*."

He crushed his eyes shut a moment. When he reopened, Lana seized him by the shoulders, a peculiar fire having ignited within her. One last, savage kiss from her lips, and when she tore away it was not without disdain.

"*Then go.*" Her voice had grown uncharacteristically husky.

Gary retrieved his two bags; a tendency to travel light. *What is love? Two souls and one flesh.* The rending of one back into two was always painful.

Out the door, then into a musty corridor whose air generally seemed yellow. It led him to the elevator, an ancient suicidal machine, an open cage that clanked and shuddered down a gloomy open shaft. An iron rehearsal for death, condemnation, descent.

The gunshot clutched him, head to toe.

Hand shaking, Gary levered the elevator to a grinding halt and reversed directions. Dust sifted from the cage's upper framework. He knew precisely what he would find back upstairs. It had been no ruse, no shot of frantic urgency fired into a pillow or a wall to plead for attention.

Strange. Mode of suicide had usually been a great divider between the sexes. Major bodily damage—gunshot, or intentional car crash, and the like—were the general province of men. Women tended to opt for more passive methods. Pills. Carbon monoxide. Neat incisions of wrists in the bathtub.

Gary was too shocked to weep just yet. It was the most masculine thing Lana had ever done. He stood in her opened doorway a long while, one albino-knuckled hand clenched on the iron knob.

The tableau before him was grisly, one of legendary scandal had it occurred in a small town. Here, though, few would care at all, back-page news. The only stomachs and sensibilities which would get a jolly twist were those of the police.

Lana, half-sprawled onto the sofa, legs askew at odd angles. One small breast bared. Smoking gun in hand, an oral fixation with its barrel having left a crimson fan on the wall behind her. Eyes open, bulging violently. Adam's apple absurdly prominent. Her skirt was bunched messily around her hips, showing small silken panties.

And that unmistakable bulge of male genitalia.

"What you've got to keep remembering is that you are *not* responsible for anyone else's happiness but your own."

Gary nodded. "It's not the happiness aspect I have a problem with. It's the responsibility for her killing herself."

Across the desk, pristine and uncluttered and orderly, Dr. Thatcher laced her fingers. "But it was Lana's decision, fully. You didn't put the gun in her hand. You never even knew she owned it."

Gary slumped back in the chair, glanced about the office. For a psychiatrist's office, it appeared remarkably non-academic. The furniture was shiny and modern, the plants more in keeping with a corporate reception lobby. The diplomas, wall-mounted along with a framed picture of Carl Jung, were the giveaway. Even the couch was out of the way, in a corner. A nod to tradition—in case someone felt therapy mandated the horizontal—but only grudging. Of this, Gary approved. He was no respecter of tradition. Tradition was all too often a mask worn by regression.

"She was an adult who made her own decisions. And as painful as it may be to come to terms with, she lived and died according to those decisions. *Her own*. Not yours."

"God knows I've never been the most reliable guy to get involved with. I've always tried to make that understood upfront, at least." Gary had been giving his hands a workout, tugging fingers and knuckles. "But Lana . . . I have *never* had anybody place such importance on me. I wasn't used to that. Almost like she idealized our relationship."

Dr. Thatcher nodded. Her hair was trimmed into a short blond helmet, and it wavered as one distinct mass. "That's fairly common among transsexuals. When a relationship is going well, there's no greater person on earth than their partner. If it's going badly . . . then their partner is just this side of an ogre."

Gary rose from his chair and paced to the window. Three floors down, Spanish moss swayed from willow branches in warm spring winds, like tattered flags on the masts of rotting ships.

Painful business, this visitation of Lana's therapist. Catharsis, purging the guilt, whatever. Lana was two days gone, and on a whim Gary had phoned Thatcher to ask if he could take the slot Lana would never honor this week. There had been no mutual friends to speak of, not that he could truly open up to. Family? Laughable. He wasn't even sure he could have opened up to Lana's shrink had it been a man. That bedrock shame of admitting the masquerade's success, the outcry of having been duped into getting horny for a *guy in drag* . . . and after he found out, *it didn't matter*. Difficult to own up to that before another man. When he had entered Thatcher's office, first met her, he'd had the brief impulse to request she hoist her skirt. Double-checking.

"It might also help you to realize that transsexuals can be suicidal over a long timespan. Convinced they're trapped in the wrong body, it's not a problem they can resolve as easily as a job they dislike. They're constantly at war with themselves, and with the perceptions of what their families and society expect them to be. Not all of them can shoulder that kind of burden for long."

Gary leaned against the window. "Lana didn't much care what anybody on the outside thought. She had her friends in the same subculture, these people she hung out with at some underground club called The Fringe. That seemed all the acceptance she needed."

"I know. She was very stable in that respect."

Gary turned from the window to glare. "Lana wanted to have children with me. Does that sound very stable to you? The biggest miracle since the Immaculate Conception?" He shook his head, his voice hoarse. "How could you approve her final surgery under those conditions?"

Dr. Thatcher smiled gently. She was good at that, years of practice, he reasoned. "Because it wasn't a delusion. She wanted it desperately, but I never felt she for a moment believed it possible. Other than that, she was one of the most psychologically sound candidates for complete gender reassignment I've ever counseled."

Gary slid along the wall, idly stopping to tinker with the fronds of a fern. To straighten a Willem de Kooning print, level to begin with. Gradually easing back to the chair.

"She had this dream of perfection. Once she was healed from the surgery, everything was going to be perfect. Kept saying, 'We'll be wonderful, everything'll be perfect, as soon as I get my pussy everything'll be perfect.' "

"That's another thing, Gary. Transsexuals often have an unattainable ideal of perfection. Just as an anorexic sees herself as continually too heavy. Transsexuals are sometimes never satisfied with the results, particularly with the male-to-female procedure. They can go through years of cosmetic operations trying to reach a pinnacle of femininity. That hope can be all that keeps them going."

"What happens if the hope runs out?"

Thatcher flexed her fingers, rested composed hands atop her desk. "Sometimes they kill themselves *then*." A pause. "You have to realize that Lana's emotions would not necessarily have stabilized after the vaginoplasty. That perfection might've been one more operation away. Or another. Or the next. Your continued presence in her life would not have been her salvation . . . because it had no bearing on her self-image."

Gary rummaged his hands through his hair until it stuck out in mad winglets. Maybe he could shave it off, buzz it to stubble, the rudely bared head a sign of penance. He was finding absolution tough to come by here. This was like a hydra. Hack off the head of one source of guilt, and another one or two would sprout to take its place. Timing, maybe it had all been horrid timing . . .

Dr. Thatcher shifted in her chair, seeming to sense his reluctance to forgive himself. "Why don't we go back, focus on the beginning of your relationship and see what it was founded on? Because you say you made no promises of permanence. How did you meet her?"

Gary frowned. "I'd have thought she would've told you that."

"She did. I'm interested in seeing how *you* perceive it."

Gary settled back, absently scratching at his chest, stomach. Itchy under his shirt. Maybe a rash, guilt surfacing in somatic symptoms. His nipples ached. There, Dr. Thatcher, rethink your rejection of traditional Freudian symbolism in light of *that*.

"I met her in a bar near the French Quarter, four months ago. A straight bar, not one of the places where the transvestites and the sex-changers usually hang out." He wet his lips; drymouth was coming on. "Hell, how does anybody meet in a bar? We made eye contact, started talking. I thought she was gorgeous. Sure, there was something different about her, something exotic, but I never would've guessed. Later I found out she'd been on daily estrogen for over a year, had her breasts and the smooth skin. Her voice seemed natural enough. She'd been living totally inside her female identity all that time. Already gotten rid of facial and body hair with electrolysis. How could I have known?"

Dr. Thatcher nodded. "She *was* extremely convincing."

"We danced, and started fooling around. Pretty soon we went out back, into this alley doorway, and she . . . she performed oral sex on me."

For no more reaction than Thatcher showed, he might as well have been describing a trick knee. "And did you initiate sexual contact with her?"

"I tried to. She said it was her period. We went our separate ways that night. But I . . . I went back the next night, same place, hoping she'd be there. And she was." Gary smiled, bittersweet. "We got drunk, and she went home to my hotel with me. The sex was the same, though, she said it was still her period."

"When did you find out the truth?"

"The next morning. We were taking a shower. See, she had this *trick*. She'd push each ball up into her pelvic cavity, then stretch her cock back between her legs and sort of keep it wedged between the bottom of her ass muscles. We were in bed, naked . . . *and I didn't know*."

"Until the shower. The act of coming clean."

"The shower." Only now did he start to flush. "Lana said she had a secret to share with me, and she thought I was ready. She squatted down and it all sort of . . . *popped* out into place. I think she just wanted to see what I'd do."

"And what *did* you do?"

"I gagged. Dry heaved."

"And then?"

"And then . . . ? I rinsed out my mouth, and I . . . I blew her."

Thatcher and her amazing clinical nod.

"It wasn't like I was thinking of her as a man, even though she told me her name was legally Alan, still, and she just scrambled the letters. To me she wasn't a man, she was . . . was . . ."

"A woman with a penis?" Dr. Thatcher prompted.

"Exactly. I'd never had a homosexual experience before, and I still didn't think I had. I mean . . . look. I've spent the last six years living off a trust fund I got the day I turned twenty-one."

He backtracked for several moments, describing his earlier life, so vastly different from the path he had chosen. The son of a family of Massachusetts real estate barons. Where mother and father advocated a hands-off policy of parenting, turning over such domesticities to the hired help, while advocating stoicism and scandal-free civility for the good of the family name. Prep school uniforms were de rigueur, and polite conformity was the norm.

"Twenty-one years was enough. I saw too many kids I'd grown up with turn into neurotic assholes. Sure, they'd end up in the highest tax brackets and still find the loopholes, but I just knew that none of them would really, truly . . . *live*. I *had* to do a one-eighty away from all of that. And so . . . I've spent the last six years trying everything I felt like I missed out on while growing up, no matter even if it was bad for me. *And* I've taken a special delight in things I know my family would hate. So, this, Lana . . . ? This was just so intriguing, I couldn't leave it be." Gary spread wide his hands. "I don't mean this to sound callous . . . but I went into my relationship with Lana like another new experience. Mostly decadent, but at the same time, there was something hallucinatory about it. Sometimes even spiritual."

"Is that why you wouldn't have made any promises of something more permanent?"

"It was a fantasy. Something forbidden. You can't live a fantasy every day of your life, it loses power then."

"What about love? Did you love her?"

The toughest question of all. The two souls/one flesh proposition. He wandered back to the window, forehead to glass.

"I suppose I did. Yes . . . *yes*. I did love her." He shook his head, sighed. Scratched that nagging itch. "That was the problem, wasn't it? Somewhere along the way I think I got scared of feeling too close to someone else."

Wasn't it just the irony of human nature, he decided without voicing it. Mankind viewed monogamy as good and proper, yet so very many went to great lengths to sneak around it. While those who decried it from the outset eventually succumbed to jealousies and that need to bond. Only to later betray.

We never learn, he thought. *That's the only constant*.

Lana was buried the next day, ushered into the afterlife by a minister who looked more befuddled than grieved. The square pegs of the world are always more difficult to eulogize.

The turnout was small, little more than a dozen who paid their respects under a sky which couldn't make up its mind between bright and overcast. The sun played masquerades with clouds, and the air was gravidly thick with the damp of a southern spring.

Beneath his shirt, the itch nagged merrily. Heat rash, maybe. Probably have to go to a doctor. He wasn't used to this humid climate.

He knew at a glance they were Lana's nighttime friends, a peculiar trio in dark clothes who oversaw the sendoff with a melancholic brooding. Beneath overcoats worn against the unpredictably hostile sky, they were of indeterminate gender, somewhere between the poles of male and female. Straddlers of the gender fence.

While circumstances may not have been the norm, the emotions of grief were universal. That longing to connect with others who had shared the now-dead.

Once the service was concluded and the mourners began to straggle home, he paced toward them over moist ground. Their gazes ranged from guarded to inimical.

"Oh look," said one of the trio. Long blond hair, full red mouth, mascaraed eyes. A square jaw belied male origins. "I bet I know who *this* is."

The tallest of the three nodded. Dark hair cropped close, sparse stubble on the jaw. The hands were too delicate, though. This one was traveling the opposite road of change. "You're Gary, aren't you?" The voice fell between alto and tenor, a vocal netherland.

He said he was, and while there was little warmth, the introductions were civil. The blond was Alexis, the short-haired one Gabriel. The third of their group—small and pale, hostile eyes red from weeping—was Megan.

Ringlets of brown hair fell into a blotchy face, and were pushed back with incongruously large hands, veined and muscular.

"Let me guess," Gabriel said. He? She? *He*, Gary decided, conceding to their chosen gender identities. Gabriel appeared far less accusatory than analytical. "You're feeling guilty because you dumped her, and think that's why she did it."

Gary frowned. "How do *you* know what happened between us?" This was either scary insight or an unerringly accurate guess. "Lana did it . . . immediately."

Gabriel shrugged, stared at the dead sky a moment. "I've seen it happen before."

"I'm sorry," Gary said. It sounded lame, but at least it was heartfelt. "I never meant to hurt her."

"No, no, of course not," Megan snapped. "*She* didn't have feelings, did she? Just a new kind of kick, until the new wore off."

Gary stared her down until she closed her angry mouth. "Look, I'm not planning on standing here to trade arguments with you." Then, to all three: "I can't claim I was perfect. But I never, *ever*, intended anything like to this to happen. I did care for her."

Alexis nodded. "But you didn't truly understand her world, did you?"

"The best I could."

"No." Gabriel shook his head. "If you did that, you would've already met us. We . . . didn't see much of Lana the past four months. *Those* belonged to you. She subjugated herself for you. All so you wouldn't be hit with too much at once, and go running."

Gary took a step back. This was too much to hear at once, too raw an implication he was ignorant of the *real* Lana, as opposed to the Lana she had chosen to reveal. He'd thought all along she simply preferred being alone with him.

"I should go," he whispered. Another step.

"Why don't you join us tonight?" Gabriel said. "At The Fringe. You know that much about Lana, don't you?

How much she liked that place?"

He nodded, hesitant. "I know of it."

"Then join us. It'd be a far better tribute to Lana than watching her get lowered into some hole in the ground." Gabriel looked distastefully toward the grave. "I'd think you owe her that much."

"At least," he said softly, then thought for a moment, then told them he'd be there.

He carried the memory of Lana's spiritual brothers and sisters throughout the rest of the afternoon and into the night, along the gauntlet of French Quarter bars he ran. Smoothing down the rough edges of remorse and responsibility.

Mardi Gras was over by two months, but revelers still choked the Quarter's streets, furiously bent on good times. The South had always seemed so fundamentally more sensuous than New England, its passions ignited by a crueler sun, and allowed to boil out and flow and cool like sweat. Here the food was rich and spicy and full of delicious venoms that the body embraced. Here Dixieland rubbed uneasy shoulders with punk. Here an empty glass was intolerable.

Gary had lied, of course. There had been precious little intention of meeting them at The Fringe. To say otherwise was simply the best way to save face for the moment, avoid conflict. But he felt low enough as it was. Sitting there baring his head and soul for them to whack on would do no one any good. He'd get along better on his own. Never been the type to crumble into a drunken crying jag and beg sympathetic strangers to listen to his woes. Let the drinks settle inside, then, and glaze him over with brooding silence.

The French Quarter: strip shows and black jazz bands both modern and traditional. He watched from the shadows while numbness crept in. Absently scratching his chest, fighting that damned persistent itch. It took a deliberate effort to stop and realize just how long he'd been at it. Enough to make it second nature.

He rubbed again, tenderly probing with his fingers.

Swelling. There was *swelling* going on inside his shirt.

Gary rose to tread the sea of drunkenness into the bathroom, which might have been clean back when Louis Armstrong played. He stopped before the cracked mirror and parted his shirt.

And stared at the two very feminine nipples staring back from his chest. Protuberant and erect, the areolae as large as silver dollars.

His reflection, staring. Cracked in the middle, two jagged halves, incongruent at their juncture.

"She was contagious," he muttered in cold shock.

And quickly reconsidered the lie.

Through a light spitting rain, he found it an hour later, twice stopping street-level locals to point him in the right direction. The Fringe, built within a renovated warehouse near the river, just off the beaten path of mainstream French Quarter. Night seemed deeper here, the air ageless. No one would ever come here by mistake.

The Fringe. Though Lana had spoken of it several times, he had never accompanied her here. Somehow, he supposed she alone had been enough to sate his curiosity about her particular breed of counterculture. The Fringe, haven of acceptance for all species of gender benders, and those who sought them out of fetishistic impulse.

Gary found within its dark and hallowed walls an alternative world. Alternative music, alternative clothing, alternative anatomy. A maze of multiple levels in architecture, just as Lana had described, each dimly lit and an enclave in its own right. There was supposed to be some sort of garden atop the roof, where ephemeral couples could retreat for whatever liaisons their bodies, lacerated or whole, would allow.

Gary bought a bottle of wine at the main bar, weaved through the open center where dancers writhed beneath black light and strobes to music that sounded like the roar of a techno-industrial Armageddon. The volume could peel skin.

Here he was groped endlessly, and let it happen, drunken enjoyment of sliding hands. All sensory delight despite the known world of his flesh falling about him. Here, pretensions were few, the common denominator libidinous. The real effort lay in pulling back from the brink, pushing on, remembering why he was here.

Eventually he found them near the upper level, Gabriel and Alexis and Megan, tucked into a dim booth. One noticed him, then all watched as he approached their table and slammed the wine bottle down.

"You finally came." Gabriel looked vaguely pleased.

"We're mourning the way Lana would have wanted us to," said Alexis, the blonde, tipping a highball at the table. A forest of bottles and glasses, hours worth of bereavement. "Sit, sit."

He glared down at them while fumbling with shirt buttons.

Megan perked up, brushed ringlets of hair from her face. "I don't want this fucker sitting at our table."

"Megan," Alexis chided. "Don't be a bitch."

Gary sat beside Gabriel, tense as a coiled spring. Left the shirt unbuttoned but draped shut, feeling the steam build inside. He would wait a moment before boiling into this last of all confrontations.

"After what he did to Lana?" Megan continued the squabble. "Are you that callous? Lana was fragile."

Alexis reached across the table, intimately touched Gary's arm. "Lana was like a . . . a goddess to our little clique. She was the first to get the actual go-ahead for her final surgery."

building

Megan wiped her eyes, smeared mascara. "It should've been me. But my therapist? That asshole says I'm not stable enough yet." She gulped her drink in desperation. "He's not satisfied with my reasons for the change. Says I'm doing it because, as a boy, I was so threatened by the thought of wanting to make it with my mother." Hysterical laughter. "Freudian asshole."

critical mass

"Answer me one thing," Gary said, low and even and electric. He yanked open his shirt to bare his chest. "*What the hell is happening to me?*"

They stared at his nipples, now in full nursing deployment. By now an arrangement of eight or ten red welts had erupted beneath them, down his ribs, like especially prominent mosquito bites.

Alexis smiled broadly. Mischievously. "You empathized with Lana after all! How sweet."

"You think I'm fucking around here?" Gary roared. In that moment, he wanted to hit Alexis, woman-in-the-making or not.

"It *must've* been love." Gabriel leaned in to dart his once-feminine tongue onto a nipple. An unexpectedly intense pleasure trilled through Gary. Horrifyingly intense. For a moment, he wanted only to feel it again, ever the hedonist. He snapped his shirt closed.

"But I didn't take any hormones!" he cried, head swimming.

"When two people love each other," said Gabriel, "a little bit of each one stays inside the other. From you, Lana took a certain amount of independence, I think."

"And what did I get from her? *Tits?*" His laughter rivaled Megan's in hysteria.

"Oh, it's much more than that, Gary, surely you can feel that by now," Gabriel said.

Gary peered down his torso, suffering a mental duststorm. With a clearer head, maybe he could make sense of this, pinpoint some allergic reaction as the culprit. But no, he'd had to pollute himself once again.

"I don't want this, don't understand it . . ."

Gabriel propped his head atop a loose fist, leaned in. "Do you know what the very worst part of being us is? The very worst aspect?"

The question sounded familiar, but he couldn't place it. Try for an answer, any answer, try to work this through . . .

"Your body is wrong, a prison, what? *What?*"

"Oh, that's it, all right," Megan said.

Gabriel cocked his head. "Not quite."

"*Isn't it?*" she shrieked, then stood and whirled on Gary. "Do you know what it's like to wake up every morning with something like *cancer* hanging between your legs? Because that's what these are like to me!" Megan clumsily hitched up the tight black dress she wore. Her penis and scrotum were framed within a garter belt and stockings. "They're *wrong!* I DON'T WANT THEM AND NOBODY WANTS TO TAKE THEM AWAY FROM ME!"

Alexis rolled her eyes. "I hate it when she's like this. You'd think she was on her period or something."

Gary watched, mortified, as Megan sufficiently lowered herself to plop her genitals onto the tabletop. Flaccid from estrogen intake, limp and sexually useless. Something in her eyes, though, foaming drunken madness, accelerated by grief.

"Nobody cares," Megan muttered, then seized Gary's wine bottle and smashed it against the table's edge. She held the dripping, jagged remnant with the same reverence lavished on surgical steel.

"I know how *this* is done," she said . . .

And smiled while bringing the glass slicing down. Blood was drawn at the first firm stroke. As Megan's face twisted into a beatific mask of agonized rapture, liberation, Alexis screeched and pushed herself away in the booth. Gabriel reacted more out of surprise than revulsion, shutting his eyes sadly as Megan sawed away.

New sights, sounds, tastes, sensations, experiences . . . damn them all. This was too, too much. Gary bolted to his feet and reeled away from the booth. Fixed his eyes on the way he'd come up and lurched toward it. A moment later a firm hand gripped his upper arm, steering him another way.

"Let me help you," said Gabriel.

He tried to wrest free. "I just want *out of here!*"

Gabriel remained firm. "This way's quicker. I promise."

Gary struggled another moment, then saw the exit sign glowing where Gabriel pointed. Surrender. Gabriel knows best.

Gabriel hustled him through the gathering crowd like a master guide. When they burst through the exit, Gabriel released his arm. The roof; Gary recalled Lana's tales of the garden. The fresh air hit him like smelling salts, vibrant and tainted with the brown scent of Mississippi mud. It drew him on, and he lurched past greenery, shrubs and bushes and small trees in planters. Within, shadows moved to the rhythms of breathless moans, and he saw them . . . face to face, head to lap, groin to buttocks.

Help. He needed help. Medical help.

Near the far edge of the roof, Gary collapsed, spent and shaking. He rolled onto his back, beginning to weep at the night sky while distant thunder rolled. The desultory rains were moving on, leaving darkly blue and violet clouds in their wake, boiling past the face of the moon.

Gabriel knelt beside him, set a comforting hand on his traitorous chest. Beneath the hand, Gary's flesh throbbed tenderly. Pleasantly. Rebellion by carnality, for part of him was intrigued.

"Poor Gary." Whispered, soft.

"What's wrong with me?" Choking on tears.

"Megan." Gabriel shook his head. "Sometimes she's so gothic. I'm sorry you had to see that. I knew she'd do it someday, she was so obsessive."

Gary's shoulders shuddered.

"I never got to answer my own question. About what the worst part of being *us* is. Can you guess?"

Again, that nudge of familiarity. Further this time, nudging all the way to recollection. Lana had asked him nearly the same question, that first night on Basin Street before he had even known the truth about her. A riddle which had gone unanswered, forgotten.

"No . . . I don't . . ."

"I'll tell you in a minute." Gabriel looked fondly down at him, that androgynous face at once strong and tender.

And calculating. "We can't go all the way across, you know. We never will make it one hundred percent."

His hand stroked Gary's lap, popped the button of his slacks, drew the zipper down. Massaged him, bared him. And, Heaven help him, against all wishes he was growing erect.

"If you're going man-to-woman, the surgery's pretty successful, but the hormonal changes are lacking. If you're moving the other way, like me? The hormone change is better, but not the surgery. They can build me something that *looks* like a cock . . . but it won't much act like one." Gabriel gave him a squeeze. "This hard-on? It's a miracle I'll never, ever know. At least . . . *their* way."

Gabriel paused long enough to peel away his own clothes. Behold, the hybrid. Still on his back, Gary saw moonlight glint off the shiny healing scars of a double mastectomy, amid sprouting hair. Lower, the wonders of the pubic triangle still hid within a thatch of hair.

"You've known Lana's half, now why don't you try my point of view?" Gabriel murmured, then straddled him. Mounting firm.

Raped. The thought was murky, surreal. *I'm being raped.* But his hips surged upward all the same. Tomorrow had always been soon enough for self-reproach.

"But the very worst part of being us?" Gabriel stared down, sheened in sweat. "We're made, not born. *We can't procreate.* But . . . I think maybe we can change that."

This was more than fucking, Gary knew that when he saw the others gather round to watch. This was tranquilizer. This was anesthesia. Bribery and reward and homage. Total manipulation. Oddly, humiliation never entered his mind.

"A friend once told me . . . the land of Dixie is the land of ghosts." Gabriel's breath was deepening with the rhythm, voice growing huskier. "I believe that. And I believe that New Orleans is a magic place. There're people here, they know things that others think they have no business knowing at all. Maybe they're right. But Lana didn't think so."

When Gabriel stripped Gary's shirt away, he saw the twin rows of nipples aligned down his torso. Erect and straining, like those of a sow with a farrow of piglets.

Gabriel bent low, placed his lips to one. And sucked.

Gary gasped, shaking his head, but feeling a flow of transient warmth, and an emotional glow he could label only as maternity.

"Lana looked for someone like you for a long time. I never saw her any happier than after she met you. Someone open-minded . . . interested in new experiences . . . who wanted no part of his past life." Gabriel touched a quieting finger to Gary's lips when he started to speak. "But let your conscience off the hook. She didn't kill herself over you . . . *she did it for us*."

Once content to observe, the others now started forward.

"It was the one sacrifice she wanted to make, to thank the rest of us for making her feel like she belonged somewhere. It . . . didn't take long to make up her mind once she decided you were the one."

Gabriel raised to kiss him, and the others closed in. Half-men, half-women, these walking techno-miracles of endocrines, scalpels, and silicon. Taking positions at the nipples, tenderly joining to him with suckling mouths. They were very gentle, did not bite.

"Lana was spiritual . . . and she was carnal . . . and she was maternal. Just like a goddess should be." Again, Gabriel shushed him with fingertips. Still grinding with muscled hips. "Reproduction is more than working body parts. It's spiritual, too. I think Lana knew that better than anyone else. And now? She's closer to you than she could ever have gotten with her body. Can't you *feel* her inside . . . yet?"

He searched hesitantly, tentatively. Thinking maybe, maybe, there was another light, another warmth, pulsing within.

"No matter what, though," Gabriel whispered, "don't ever think she didn't love you. Oh, she did. She *does*."

Of course she would. How could she ever have done this to someone whom she hated? For, *What is love? Two souls and one flesh.*

Gary writhed, the eye in an emotional hurricane. Tears, love, revulsion. But fighting would accomplish precious little. And he was needed. So he lay back amid this roof-bound Eden, beneath the roiling sky, and let them nurse, while still more found their way to the roof to take their place in line. And within—*from* within—the juices flowed. Testosterone, estrogen, androgen; spiritual and hormonal mother's milk. To nurture and nourish miracles greater still.

Gabriel cupped his cheek. "You are truly honored. You're the madonna of an entirely new gender."

Gary surrendered, fully, the pleasure and contentment swamping even the staunchest denial. He stretched wide his arms, satisfied he and Lana would forever be as one, and reached to embrace their children.

STIGMATA

Gary L. Raisor

Spare, hard-edged, merciless. These words all fit the following offering from Gary L. Raisor, a tall, basso-voiced writer from the heart of basketball country— Louisville, Kentucky. The editor of the well-received anthology, Obsessions, *Gary has been quietly gaining a reputation as a short story writer who pulls no punches as he bolts together tales of not-always-likeable characters and hermetically sealed plots. His writing reminds me of Jim Thompson, Rod Serling, and James Cain. We should all be so lucky . . .*

An arrow flashed off and on across the street, red neon humping the night as it pointed the way to Ray's Package Liquor. Raindrops whispered against the neon-lit window, ran down it like congealing blood in the strobing light. Above Ray's, inside a room, a music box played the last notes of the "Anniversary Waltz." It was muted and soft, a little scratchy, a little melancholy. The porcelain bride and groom ceased their measured dance across red velvet and drew apart.

They seemed to be listening—

—as Douglas Mercheson raised a pistol to his fore-head and eased the hammer back. Once. Twice. It made a distinct click each time. His finger tightened around the trigger.

It edged back ever so slightly, metal sliding on metal.

The odor of the oil he had used on the revolver was very strong, the barrel of the gun was cold as it pressed into his skin. This was going to make one hell of a mess. He wondered if he would hear the shot before he died. He wondered if he had enough guts to pull the trigger.

A sound penetrated, buzzing around like a gnat in the silence of the room, causing Mercheson to fall back on the sweat-soaked bed and listen.

His phone was ringing. Or maybe it was the d.t.'s again.

Too much Scotch had screwed up his head and he couldn't tell what was real anymore. Earlier tonight, an old drinking buddy, Vince Dougherty, had dropped by with some fresh razor blades so he could shave. When Vince had handed them over, Mercheson saw the thin gaping wounds on Vince's wrists, saw the blood on the blades. He had yelled at Vince, but Vince had only smiled and shrugged apologetically. "Sorry, Doug," he said, "you know how I am when it comes to new razor blades."

But Vince's visit hadn't been real because Vince had been dead five years now. Mercheson had been the one who had found him, both wrists slashed, staring up through a tub full of blood. He wouldn't have believed a skinny little guy like Vince could have held so much blood.

The jangling of the phone tugged at Mercheson, yanking him back into the present. The ringing continued while he rubbed the sweat from his eyes and tried to focus on the clock. 3:27 A.M.

The .32 fell onto his chest, a cold hard fist.

Mercheson stared at the phone. Willed it to stop.

The ringing wouldn't go away and it was causing a hot wire to thrash around behind his eyes. The last of the thin, watery Scotch slid down his throat before he lifted the receiver. He forced his hands to be steady and the effort cost him more than he could afford. "Mercheson," he managed.

"It's Russell. I found her, I goddamn found her," the voice on the other end said.

"Where?"

"9311 Hemdale, over by the park."

Mercheson hung up and his hands were shaking so badly it took him three tries to call a taxi. He slumped on the edge of the bed, taking in this shithole of a room, knowing full well he might never see it again. There was furniture, scratched and worn by time, a piano that his wife, Anna, used to play sometimes before she had . . . left. The keys were covered with dust, now.

The silver music box he'd given her on their wedding night twenty-one years ago.

Possessions were all he had left and now they were what his life was all about. Anna used to laugh, half in jest, half in despair, when she said he was physically incapable of turning loose of anything.

That wasn't quite true; he'd had to turn loose of his most prized possession, Anna.

Her last letter lay on the dresser beside the music box that he played every night while he acted out the cliché his life had become, as he drank himself into oblivion. The letter had once smelled of roses, now it smelled of Scotch and sweat and sadness. It said that Anna had found someone else.

It said that she could no longer be one of his—

(*The hot wire began thrashing again.*)

—possessions.

Downstairs, tires slushed to a halt and the taxi honked its horn twice. Time to go. He scanned the room, found the music box. It went into his coat pocket. He wasn't a man who would ever part with something that was his. Even though his wife was a faithless whore who had left him for another man, he would give her a chance to come back. One last chance.

If she refused . . .

The gun went into the other pocket.

The cab sitting at the curb was old, rusted, held together by a thin layer of paint and hope, and it wasn't from the company Mercheson had called. It was some independent pirating a fare. Rheumy exhaust wheezed into the night air, making Mercheson wonder if this urinal on wheels would leave him stranded.

"She'll take you anywhere you wanna go," a voice said from the darkened interior as though reading his mind. "You coming, pal? I ain't got all night here."

Despite his better judgment Mercheson climbed in, and was surprised to find the interior spotless. From the dash a plastic glow-in-the-dark Jesus stared out over the backseat with huge sorrowful eyes that seemed to have seen all the suffering in the world. Strings and strings of rosary beads were wrapped around the figure, chains to prevent it from escaping? Beneath Jesus, a picture of a large-breasted nude was taped to the glove box, legs opened invitingly.

Mercheson tried to look away, couldn't.

"Where to, pal?"

Mercheson recited the address and the ancient vehicle lurched into motion.

"Lotta people ask me how come I have Jesus standing over a naked whore," the driver said, noticing his passenger's stare. The man behind the wheel had a soft, weary voice. "Hell, Jesus didn't have nothin' against whores. He forgave them for their sins, so who am I to judge them?"

Mercheson snorted, tried to make out the ID on the visor.

"Eddie Angelotti," the driver supplied. "It's a hundred percent Italian in case you couldn't tell." The driver had short crewcut hair streaked with gray and his old leather bomber jacket had the collar turned up over a scarf against the cold.

"Doug Mercheson. It's Irish, in case you couldn't tell."

"Smells more like Scotch from where I'm sitting. Ninety proof." Eddie tried to laugh but the sound dropped to a liquid, guttural cough.

Mercheson's mouth tightened in disapproval.

"Sorry pal, just joking around," Eddie said, getting his voice under control. "I spent most of my life in one of these things and I guess I talk too much sometimes. My old man, God rest his soul, swore I was talking two minutes after I was born. Which, incidentally, was in the backseat of a cab." The cabby only smiled this time. "Of course my old man was a fucking drunk, so you couldn't believe everything he said."

Angelotti. Eddie Angelotti. That name was familiar, only Mercheson's Scotch-soaked mind refused to yield why.

Mercheson saw the driver studying him. "You act like you know me."

The cabby smiled again, shook his head no.

Outside the cab window, darkened tenements drifted by like cliffs on some distant shore. Patches of fog clung low to the ground, obscuring the street.

The cab dodged a pothole and the slewing motion made Mercheson bite back a gagging noise as Scotch slide up his throat and pressed against his teeth.

"Sorry about that." The cabby looked back, saw the sheen of sweat of his passenger's face. "Mister, you don't look so hot. You want maybe I should pull over or something?"

"No, I'm fine, just got a lot on my mind lately. My wife and I had a fight—sometimes I drink too much."

"Know what you mean," Eddie commiserated. "I used to be married, myself."

Before the driver could turn away, oncoming headlights lit up the cab, and Mercheson saw the scars that encircled Eddie Angelotti's neck. Beneath the scarf they looked like some kind of pale, bloodless snakes that had melted into the skin.

The cabby saw the disgust on his passenger's face because his fingers strayed from the steering wheel to the colorless ridges of tissue.

Mercheson looked away, embarrassed that he'd been staring.

Eddie swallowed and the snakes wriggled as though trying to slither off his neck. "Got these from a fare. Guy had one of those silver crosses with a crucified Jesus hanging from his left ear, long dark hair tied up in a ponytail. Crazy, spooky eyes. Shoulda never picked him up, but hell, I was on the tail end of a fourteen-hour shift. Guess I got a little careless."

"It happens to us all," Mercheson said, wishing he'd brought some Scotch with him.

"Ain't it the God's own truth. Anyway, there I was, driving along, the next thing I know I got an eight-inch switchblade under my chin. This punk is saying that I gotta hand over all my money. Like Hell, I busted my ass for that money!"

The cab veered across the center line and a horn blared, dissolving into the night.

Eddie leisurely guided the cab back into the right lane without missing a beat. "I saw those crazy eyes in the rearview, and when you been driving as long as me, you've seen lotsa eyes looking back at you. You get so you know what they're thinking." The mist had given way to rain and Eddie reached out to turn the wipers up another notch. "My gut told me this guy was gonna kill me whether I gave him the money or not."

Something about Eddie Angelotti came back to Mercheson.

Something that made Mercheson glad he had the gun.

"Mister," Eddie said, indignant, "I told him to go fuck himself and I stood on the brakes with both feet. The little bastard was quick, I have to give him that. He cut me good. When all that blood started gushing out, I thought, Eddie, you're a dead wop for sure. But I got these around his throat"—Eddie raised huge, powerful hands—"then I dragged his ass up here in the front seat, and I started squeezing."

Eddie's eyes went hazy as his hands gripped the steering wheel. "He thrashed around for a while and he got me a couple more times with the knife. In a few minutes all the fight went out of him." Eddie's huge fingers kept squeezing. *Squeezing* as though they had a life of their own. "Right then he reminded me of this scrawny old tomcat that my old man hadda drown."

Mercheson put his hands over his ears and pressed himself into the seat, trying to escape the whispery voice.

There was no escape.

Eddie continued, "That tomcat was always coming around our house every morning and breaking our milk bottles. My old man knew what to do. He took that cat into the bathroom and held him under the water until all the meanness oozed out of him, until his mouth opened up wide and you could see how pink his tongue was. It looked like, I swear to God, like he was trying to say how sorry he was for breaking all those milk bottles. Only my old man didn't give a shit."

The rain was falling harder now, pounding the roof of the cab. Pounding Mercheson's skull.

"He just kept on holding that old cat under," Eddie said. "Holding him, until all you saw was his pink tongue sticking out and two eyes staring back at you, all peaceful, all the meanness gone, until he was dead . . . like that bastard who cut me."

The mangled voice became thick, trailed off, and Mercheson realized the driver was crying. "I work nights now," Eddie said, "that way nobody has to see these." His hands touched the scars on his throat, caressed them, as though they were old friends he hadn't seen in a while. "Long as I wear this scarf, people don't treat me like some kinda freak."

"Let me out here. Right now!" Once again Mercheson saw his friend, Vince Dougherty, floating dead in a bathtub of blood. Vince's mouth had been open, his tongue protruding.

"You sure, pal? You got two blocks to go and it's awful nasty out there."

"Let me out, goddamn it." The Scotch boiled up behind his teeth. "I'm going to be sick."

The cab stopped and Mercheson staggered out, no longer able to control his roiling stomach. The Scotch he had fought so hard to hold back spewed out onto the sidewalk in a steaming geyser. His legs buckled and he fell to his knees in his own puke. When the cramps at last passed, he struggled up and pulled money from his pocket. He threw it at the driver.

"You sure you gonna be all right?" Eddie asked, ignoring the money.

"I'm fine. Too much to drink." Mercheson straightened up and wiped his mouth with the back of his hand. "Fresh air is what I need."

Eddie looked skeptical when he leaned out the cab window and called after his passenger. "Is it? I know what you're doing here, Doug." The watery voice carried after Mercheson in the predawn stillness. Eddie put the cab in gear and slowly pulled alongside, keeping pace with the walking man. "It ain't none of my business what you do, I just take people where they wanna go, tell 'em a story or two. But I'm telling you, you can't get her back. Take my advice, pal, don't go up there. Let me take you home."

"Go to Hell." Mercheson touched the .32.

Eddie's eyes followed. "Where you're going, that gun ain't gonna do you a damn bit of good."

Mercheson kept walking.

"Listen, Doug, most of my fares act like I don't even exist, but you listened to me. I wanna say I appreciate that, so I want you should listen to me. Don't go up there. You do what I think you're gonna do, there ain't no going back. Not ever."

"Get away from me, you crazy son of a bitch." Mercheson pulled the .32 from his pocket. "How do you know what I'm going to do?"

The cabby looked at the gun, at the man holding it, and spat on the sidewalk. There was only sadness in the seamed, worn face when he put the cab in gear and drove away.

9311 Hemdale was a crumbling old brownstone covered over with obscenely green ivy that seemed to be sucking the life from the house to feed itself. All the other houses on the street were dark, silent, except for this one. The rain drummed the roof, thousands of impatient fingers that beckoned Mercheson nearer. In the light from the window, the house looked on the verge of collapse.

Several rosebushes stood sentry duty in Anna's flower garden. A lone impossible flower clung to one, dark as dried blood in the rain. When the wind eddied, the rosebushes began swaying back and forth in agitation, and some of the petals peeled away. To Mercheson's eyes they looked like tiny, scarlet, disembodied mouths mocking him.

As he pushed through the wrought iron gate, walked up the sidewalk, he wondered if anyone at all lived here, or if this was some kind of hoax. Still he forced himself to climb the steps. They groaned beneath his weight in the voice of a tired, scared old man. It had been so very long since he had last seen Anna. He wondered what he would say to her.

Unable to bring himself to knock, he leaned his head on the cool wetness of the door and listened.

Voices were coming from inside. Laughter.

One voice belonged to Anna.

The other was that of a stranger.

He peered in a window and all of the empty drunken nights were forgotten. There was Anna, beautiful, desirable, just like he remembered, and though he only saw her for a second before she turned out the light and climbed into bed, an image of white silk and dark hair lingered in his mind. He felt heat building in the pit of his stomach.

A man's voice came out of the darkness of the bedroom.

She laughed again, playful.

Teasing. The way she used to laugh for him.

More talk, low and urgent. Soon words were replaced by the rhythmic squeaking of bedsprings.

Mercheson stood in the cold rain and listened to his wife make love to another man.

It seemed to go on forever.

Mercheson burned with shame, outrage, and God help him . . . desire. The odor of roses mixed with musky sex floated on the night air. Her scent. Real or imagined, he couldn't tell. He felt himself growing hard and he wanted desperately to plunge himself into her, to lose the pain that had consumed his life. Maybe it was the only way he could find himself again.

The bedsprings quieted and there was more talk between the lovers, lazy, muffled words too low to hear.

Anna pulled away and turned on a small bedside lamp. Her expression was troubled, and slowly, almost imperceptibly, the conversation began shifting away from the small talk of lovers, edging toward something unknown. She was staring at the window, so Mercheson could only gauge what was said by her face. She shook her head no. No again. Agitated now, dark hair flying. Her expression was stern, unyielding, despite the sudden tears that tracked down her cheeks.

Mercheson strained to get a look at the man who had stolen his wife away. He caught a partial glimpse of the stranger in Anna's bed. But what he saw, couldn't be.

The hot wire began thrashing in his brain as memories tugged at him. Painful memories.

Pulling him along, taking him toward something he didn't want to face. Long before Anna's lover entered the light, Mercheson knew who the man was.

Mercheson knew it was—

Himself.

He should have been shocked, yet the only thing he felt was weary resignation. The window held him captive as it played out his meeting with Anna like some cheap melodrama with a bad soundtrack.

The man in the room sat a music box on the piano and opened it. The familiar silvery tinkle of the "Anniversary Waltz" seemed lost in the silence.

Anna softly closed the music box. Handed it back.

The man on the other side of the window walked across the bedroom and pulled something from his coat pocket. Mercheson knew it was a gun.

The man pointed it at Anna. Cocked it.

Her eyes held no fear, only pity.

The man's face was stricken with remorse and seemed to fold in upon itself. The gun wavered, fell to the side. The man who looked like Mercheson smiled a sad little smile, then calmly raised it to his own head. There was a flat crack and the back of his head simply disappeared.

Blood splattered the window, ran down it, giving everything inside a reddish and oddly soft glow.

The music box spilled to the floor, opened, and once more the tune Doug and Anna Mercheson had danced to on their wedding night filled the room. The tiny porcelain bride and groom spun and twirled with mechanical perfection across their velvet dance floor. Cold and aloof. Oblivious of the vagaries of the human heart. *Unable to feel pain.*

Mercheson stumbled away from the blood-smeared window, still numb as he pushed through the wrought iron gate and ran past the rosebushes that were now bare of any flowers. He pounded on the door of house after house, scraping his knuckles raw, trying to raise someone. Anyone.

But no one answered.

The houses all remained dark, empty.

Finally he ventured into the street and began walking back the way he'd come. He fell, got up, kept on going. Fell again. The seventh time he fell he couldn't get up. Headlights pinned him in their glare, blinding him, and he hoped the car would run over him, but it didn't. The car rolled to a stop and a vague, shadowy bulk leaned out the window. The sound of a door opening came to Mercheson, followed by footsteps.

"There you are, pal," the familiar watery voice of Eddie Angelotti called out. "Thought you could maybe use a ride back home. Looks like I was right, too."

Mercheson tried to pull away as the huge driver eased him into the back of the cab, but he was too weak to resist.

"Sorry about scaring you back there earlier, Doug. I was only trying to help." The seamed face was filled with concern. "I guess I got a little carried away."

"It's all right, just take me home." Mercheson hid his face in his hands. "Please."

"Sure thing." Eddie adjusted his scarf and clicked off the cab's meter. "You just take it easy, I'll get you home safe and sound."

Mercheson looked up and caught sight of his own

waxen face in the rearview mirror, saw there was now a scar on his forehead, a perfectly round little scar that resembled a bullet hole. It was bleeding slightly. His eyes returned to the ID on the cab's visor, sought out the driver's face. Eddie Angelotti's name was familiar. It had been front page news a couple of years back in connection with a brutal death.

Only Eddie had told the story wrong.

The truth was—

The truth was Eddie had been the one found dead in his cab, his throat cut. No, *more than cut*.

His head had been completely severed from his body.

But that couldn't be right, it was someone else. It had to be. Mercheson's mind was playing tricks on him, the d.t.'s again, and somehow he had gotten Eddie Angelotti confused with the dead cab driver in the newspaper.

Then why was the cab suddenly ankle deep in blood? He felt it, smelled it, coppery, warm, dark, sticky, covering everything, the dash, the seats, even the windshield. It was dripping from the roof like a gentle spring rain, and the odor of it was thick and cloying.

Overpowering.

Eddie Angelotti's sightless eyes stared back at him from a severed head, a jack-o'-lantern carved by an enraged child.

Dangling beneath the rearview mirror.

Tied there by his own rosary beads.

The plastic Jesus sitting on the dash looked at the carnage with his huge sorrowful eyes, and when the blood from Eddie's head landed on the plastic head, it seemed to seep from the crown of thorns. A plastic stigmata, Mercheson thought, on a plastic Jesus. Just an illusion. Not real. *Not real.*

None of this was real.

The blood trickled down to Jesus's glowing eyes, filled them to overflowing before continuing on. It splattered onto the picture of the nude girl and trailed over her breasts, sliding between her legs, soaking into her pubic hair.

In the front seat someone was going through Eddie's

pockets and he was the guy Eddie had described earlier. He had long dark hair in a ponytail, a silver crucifix in his ear that twinkled in the light, and the meanest eyes Mercheson had ever seen. The guy must not have liked what he found because he took the switchblade and began ripping savagely at Eddie's decapitated body slumped over the steering wheel.

Slashing at it in fury.

Over and over. "Shouldn't have fucked with me, you old bastard." He began cutting off Eddie's hands.

Eddie's severed, mutilated head began rocking beneath the rearview mirror, banging the windshield in agreement.

Thump Thump.

"I hear you knocking," Mercheson whispered. "But you can't come in." His mind backed into a dark corner. "*You can't come in.*"

Eddie's head continued banging against the windshield. *Thump Thump. Thump Thump.*

Mercheson kept on telling himself that none of this was real and finally he was able to see beneath the illusion. It was like a slide projected onto reality and for a moment the slide had become reality. He closed his eyes, listened to the slap of the windshield wipers until he realized how much they sounded like a severed head beating against the window.

There was no place to hide. Behind his eyes he had his own slide show going on, and it always ended the same way. With him dead.

After an interminable time the cab came to a stop in front of Mercheson's apartment.

"Here you go, pal," Eddie said. "Home safe and sound just like I promised."

Mercheson stepped out into the steady drizzle and looked toward the east. The sky showed no signs of becoming lighter. It was as if the sun had become a distant memory. He looked at his watch and saw it still said 3:27.

"Eddie, where are we, what is this place?" He sounded like a lost child.

The cabbie looked thoughtful for a moment and then laughed his watery soft laugh. "1930 Browder Street, your apartment. You really tied one on tonight, didn't you?"

"I saw something back there," Mercheson said.

"Oh yeah, like what?"

Mercheson struggled with the words, couldn't say them.

Eddie started to roll up the cab window, but he paused, his face torn between anger and pity. "This was your first trip, wasn't it? Doug, I like you, so let me give you a little piece of advice, no charge. Give up on getting your wife back or you ain't ever gonna leave here."

Mercheson was about to ask where here was when he heard the sound of footsteps coming down the street. A figure was walking toward them. Alone, coming steadily closer out of the darkness as though it had all the time in the world.

Passing streetlight after streetlight.

Coming toward them.

The figure drew closer and Mercheson saw it was a guy in an Army field jacket, with long dark hair in a ponytail, a crucifix in his ear. Something was wrong with his eyes. They were crazy. Spooky.

"Don't pick him up, Eddie, please." Mercheson's voice was desperate. "Let this one go." He laid his hand on the cold leather of Eddie's jacket, held on to it, began tugging.

"Thanks Doug, I appreciate it, but I can't leave a fare on the streets in this kind of weather," Eddie answered. "Besides, what makes you think I've got a choice?" He touched the awful scars on his neck and sighed. "What makes you think *any* of us have a choice."

"He's going to kill you. I saw it."

Eddie wearily shook his head. "No, we're past that now. All we can do is watch what's already happened." He winked. "I guess you could say that makes us Peeping Toms for the dead, doesn't it?"

The guy with the ponytail climbed in the cab, closed the door.

"You take care of yourself, pal," Eddie Angelotti said. "I gotta go now, gotta take my date here to the late show. I hear we're starring tonight."

Mercheson touched the indentation on his forehead. "When I first got in the cab, you were looking at me. You were looking for my scar, weren't you?"

"Yeah, I thought you were hiding it."

"What about the scars, Eddie, how come they bleed?"

"Don't know. One thing's for sure, long as you're bleeding you won't ever leave this place."

"You know anybody who ever made it out?" Mercheson asked. The red neon arrow in front of Ray's Package Liquor turned the rain on the cab into blood, back into rain.

"I hear there've been a few."

"Did you know any of them?"

Eddie shrugged, looked away. "No, I can't say I did."

Mercheson nodded, took his hand away. "You take care, Eddie."

The cabbie rolled up the window and drove off into the night with his sad Jesus chained to the dash.

Mercheson was halfway up the steps when someone called out to him. Over on the stoop was his old drinking buddy, Vince Dougherty, with a bottle of Scotch and a package of fresh razor blades beside him. "Just had me a little bath," Vince said, "and I feel a lot better now." He smiled, then tucked his protruding tongue back in. "Stop by later for a drink if you get a chance." Vince smiled and raised the bottle of Scotch to his lips, showing fresh red slashes beneath the cuff of his shirt.

Mercheson paused and touched the tiny round scar on his own forehead, looked down at his fingertips.

He went inside and waited for the phone to ring.

For David Hinchberger, a musical story for a music man.

SARAH, UNBOUND

Kim Antieau

Kim Antieau is quietly creating a reputation as a short story writer of finely pointed, emotionally charged fiction. Living in the state of Washington, she has seen her work published in most of the major magazines and anthologies. Her contribution to Borderlands 2 *is a subtle, sensitive journey into the mind and imagination of a small boy. It is also a poignant examination of one of our society's most gut-wrenching problems.*

"Sarah," Paul whispered, his breath warm on her ear. His lips brushed the small of her back and then kissed the tiny rose that bloomed from the dimple above her left buttock. "My tattooed lady," he said. She turned and drew him toward her, inside her. She saw stars in his eyes. "I will give you whatever you need," he whispered. Sarah gasped with pleasure.

Suddenly, she was eight years old. Her father's footsteps were quiet outside her bedroom door. Then he was in the room, pulling up her nightgown, groping for her in the darkness. He pushed the pillow over her mouth as he rammed himself into her.

The phone rang, and Sarah opened her eyes. Morning. She was alone. She sighed. The dream was all wrong. She didn't know a man named Paul and her father hadn't raped her until she was eleven. The phone rang again. She answered it.

"Sarah? It's Nancy. Did I wake you?" Her sister's voice did not sound two thousand miles away.

"Sarah?"

"No, I was awake," Sarah said. "What's going on?"

"Sarah . . ." Nancy's voice broke.

"What's happened?" Sarah's stomach was suddenly in a knot.

"It's Carl." Their brother. "He and Katie have split. Apparently he's been molesting his daughter."

The room shifted slightly, and Sarah drifted. Who was that in the distance talking on the phone, her face white, her lips turning red where she bit them?

Sarah tasted blood, and she was on the phone again, listening to her sister cry. Molest. What a stupid word. He had *raped* his daughter. He had *assaulted* her. He had taken her body away from her.

"That bastard," Sarah said.

"Sarah!" her sister cried. "He needs our support." Easy for her to say. Their father never touched her.

"Like father, like son," Sarah said. There was silence on the other end of the phone.

Finally her sister said, "I'll talk to you later when you're calmer about all this."

Sarah set down the phone. When she got her degree a year ago, she had moved as far away from her family as she could—without leaving the country. It hadn't been far enough.

Suddenly she realized she did know someone named Paul. He came to her office once a week for counselling. Only he wasn't an adult. He was eight years old. Sarah grabbed her stomach. "My God," she whispered. She was having wet dreams about her young clients! "Like father, like son. Like daughter." She bit her lip until she tasted blood again.

Sarah's office seemed grayer than usual as April clouds covered Mount Hood in the distance and dropped down to become fog in the Columbia Gorge. She knelt on the floor and pulled out the toy box. Often children who had been molested became molesters. A learned behavior. Which meant she, too, could molest some innocent. She pulled out a black plastic horse from the box. Paul loved this horse. She smiled. He called him Caesar. He was a mature child; only when they played together did he act like an eight-year-old. Sarah dropped the horse into the box. She felt too deeply for the children. She dreamed of them, and their wounds were open sores she could not heal. Children were too fragile; it was too easy to damage them permanently.

She closed her eyes. She heard her nightgown ripping, felt the pillow cover her mouth. How could her brother do what her father had done to her for countless nights?

Sarah pushed away the toy box and stood up and went to her desk. She thought about talking to Henry, the head of the counselling and resource center. She would ask to be taken off any cases which involved children. She knew what he would say. He would want to know if she had ever touched or talked to her clients in a sexual manner. Of course she hadn't. Then he would remind her that dreams were only symbolic representations of other things. He would also tell her that she was very good with children. They seemed to instinctively trust her.

She rubbed her face and sighed. She had gone to counselling herself while completing her degree. They had talked about her childhood experiences with her father. She thought she had dealt with it all. So had the counsellor. Now the memories were resurfacing. Like some kind of toxic waste.

She looked at her desk calendar. Paul was her first client this morning. He had been coming to her for two months, ever since his mother committed suicide by driving into the Columbia River as Paul watched. The mother had left behind a boy with little self-esteem. At each session, Sarah worked on making him feel important and loved. Later, she would help him feel anger. Today, they would play, as they often did. It was good for him to be a child for a little while each week.

Sarah went into the waiting room. Paul sat quietly, reading a *National Geographic*. He was alone as usual. His grandparents didn't think he should be coming to these sessions, but the court had insisted. He looked up when she entered the room and smiled.

"Hello, Sarah, whose name is like a sigh," he said. His fine blond hair fell down across one blue eye. He put the magazine down and got up. Then he went to her and grasped her hand in his and said, "How are you today?"

"I'm good," she lied. "How are you?"

"Fine," he said.

They walked together into her office. Paul let go of her hand and went to the toy box. Sarah closed the door and then sat on the floor next to Paul.

"Caesar!" he cried, pulling out the horse. He laughed and galloped the horse across the carpet. Sarah took out another horse, a palomino with a purple saddle and golden mane and tail.

"I've been coming here for two months," he said. "I looked on the calendar. I like it here."

"I'm glad."

"It's safe here," he said. "Sarah, whose name is like a sigh, I'm going to marry you someday."

Sarah laughed. "Are you?"

He nodded. "And I'll give you whatever you need."

Sarah stiffened. The man in her dream had said that. Her heart raced. How had Paul known? No, no, he didn't know. He had probably said it to her before, and she had incorporated it into her dream. Yes, that was what had happened.

"And what do I need?" she asked.

He looked at her. "To be safe."

That was the second time he had mentioned being safe.

"What do you need?" she asked.

"I need to go away," he said. He rocked the horse back and forth.

"Why?"

"Because she told me to go away. She said she needed to be alone. Then she pushed me out of the car and drove into the river."

At last, he spoke of her death.

"Maybe that was what your mother needed. What do you need?"

He reached out and touched her hand lightly. Then he smiled.

"Are you going to leave me?" he asked.

"No, I'm not going to leave you."

He crawled up onto her lap, as he often did, and Sarah held him close. She rocked him gently and felt his tiny heart beating next to hers. His mother had killed herself, his father had left when Paul was three, after putting out a cigarette on his son's buttocks. Now Paul put his small arms around Sarah. He smelled clean and fresh, like Tide. Like the pillow her father had used to press against her mouth until she felt as though she was going to suffocate, and when she couldn't get her breath, she floated out of her body. She went higher and higher until it seemed as though she was on the ceiling. Below, her father grunted, his pants down at his knees. She couldn't see herself beneath him. It was as though he was pushing himself into nothing. She floated to the stars and watched them twinkle. When she came back, her father was gone. She wiped up the blood and semen and wished she could go away forever.

Paul pulled away and looked up at Sarah. There were stars in his eyes. She smiled at him. She would not hurt him; she was sure of it. Not like she had been hurt. Not ever.

"There are stars in your eyes," she said.

"There are roses in yours," he answered.

"That's because you're seeing your reflection. And you're like a rose, a beautiful little flower!"

"Then that means you are a star," he said.

He kissed her cheek and then slid off her lap. They began playing with the horses again.

Sarah's mother called when she got home from work. She talked vaguely about Carl being in trouble.

"I know he's been raping his daughter," Sarah said, interrupting her mother.

"Sarah! That's nonsense. He's been accused of molesting his daughter. He's innocent until—"

"Until you can ignore it long enough to forget it?" Sarah said. She wanted to slam down the phone and be rid of her mother.

"You shouldn't dress that way," she had told Sarah once. "It only provokes men." Sarah had been thirteen and the loose, peach-colored dress was a birthday gift from an aunt. Sarah hugged herself. She knew her mother was talking about provoking her father.

"You shouldn't be so angry," her mother said now. "You'll die an old, bitter woman."

"Good-bye, Mother," Sarah said. She dropped the phone into its cradle. Why did her mother bother to call? She had never admitted that her husband had raped her daughter on a regular basis, even after Sarah told a school counsellor when she was sixteen. When confronted, her father had denied it, and her mother refused to discuss it. She stayed with Sarah's father, and he stopped coming to Sarah's bedroom.

Sarah unplugged the phone and went to the bathroom and took off her clothes. The day had seemed endless. Paul was the only bright spot. She had been nauseated all day, like she had been when she was eight and her father first came into her room and roughly fondled her. After that, she had always felt nauseated, until she was nineteen. She was in her second year of college when she found a tattoo place and had an illustrated man scratch a rose tattoo in her dimple. Her way of reclaiming her body.

She twisted her neck to look at the tattoo. It was a tiny blossom, barely visible. She had been proud of it; now she wanted to cover it up. She didn't want to think of her body and what her father had done to it.

She stepped into the shower and turned on the water. She closed her eyes and thought of Paul. Today he had spoken of his mother's death. Maybe soon he would cry. He needed to. She wished she would cry. She hadn't since she was eight years old.

That night, Sarah dreamed she stood at one end of the Hood River Bridge. The Columbia River flowed beneath her. She was wrapped in gauze like a modern day mummy. On the other side, Paul stood, his child's arms held out to her. Between them was darkness. Sarah couldn't move. She couldn't breathe.

She woke up gasping for air. She lay still for several minutes until her heartbeat went back to normal. Then she wrapped the blanket tightly around her. She was frightened and alone, a child again with no safe place left in the world. She hoped morning would come quickly.

She felt tired and lost at work the next day. She told the secretary that she wasn't in if anyone related to her called. The secretary laughed and said she understood.

Sarah went into her office and closed the door. She wished she understood. She should have dealt with all of this by now. She had moved to the West Coast to get away from her family and the memories, yet here they all were again. When she was younger, she had thought the only way to escape it all was by dying. But she didn't want to die, so she had just gone away. She had floated above it all. A living ghost. She couldn't stop her father, but she didn't have to participate. She left and wished she never had to return to her damaged little body. Sometimes, she felt as though she had never really completely returned.

Sarah stayed in the office long after everyone had left. Near nine, she went outside to eat a sandwich. She sat on the steps and turned her back to the lights of the Hood River and stared up at the stars.

"Hello, Sarah, whose name is like a sigh."

"Paul," Sarah said. "Where did you come from? Isn't it late for you to be out?" He sat next to her on the steps.

"I was watching the stars. I followed one and it led me here." He smiled. "Tomorrow's Saturday, so I can stay up late."

"Do your grandparents know you're gone?" Sarah asked.

He shook his head. "They're asleep."

They were drunk, Sarah supposed.

"Look, there's the Big Dipper," he said, pointing to the sky.

"And there's the little one," she said.

Paul laughed. "You and me."

"Two dips?" Sarah said.

"Two dippers! You're silly!"

She laughed. They watched the stars for a time.

"How are your grandparents? Do you like living with them?"

He shrugged. "They don't notice me much. I go away sometimes."

"What do you mean?" Sarah held out half of the sandwich to him. He took it.

"Sometimes, when my mother was screaming or my father was around, I'd go away. You've done it before. I remember."

"What are you talking about?" she asked. He had never spoken of this before.

"I float away. I did it the first time when my father put out his cigarette on me. Called me an ashtray. Grandpa says I was too young to remember, but I do. I was three. I floated away to the stars. I met them all. They were my friends. You were up there, too. You breathed your name like a sigh."

Sarah remembered one night when her father raped her, one of the last times, nearly six years ago; she had left her body and floated above the house, the street, the town. For a moment, she had sensed other souls pressing up against hers. Now she looked at Paul and wondered if those souls had been other abandoned or abused children trying to find a safe place in the world.

He smiled. "You were a rose blooming across the sky," he said. He looked at his feet. "My grandparents say I can't come here anymore."

"Here to see me?" Sarah asked.

He nodded.

"Do you want to keep coming?"

He looked surprised. "Yes. I like playing together. I can teach you all about the stars and you can teach me about playing horses."

"You are a wonderful child," Sarah said. She rubbed the top of his head. "Don't worry about your grandparents. I'll talk to them. It'll be all right."

"I better go now," he said. He started down the drive and then he stopped and looked at her. "I'm glad you came down out of the stars. I like you here."

She watched him disappear into the darkness. She stood until she saw him under a streetlight again, and then she watched until he reached his grandparents' house. She finished her sandwich and then she went home.

Sarah dreamed about Paul. This time, they walked across the bridge together, hand in hand. Whenever the darkness started to close in around them, they laughed at it and it drifted away like smoke. The sky was filled with stars which blossomed into white roses.

Sarah drove to her office first thing the next morning. She sat in the middle of the floor and pulled the toys from the toy box. She galloped Caesar and the palomino across the carpet and laughed. This was why she enjoyed her sessions with Paul so much. She was a child during their fifty minutes. They were growing up together. Her only real childhood.

She pushed the toys away and looked around. She shuddered. She felt afraid so much of the time. Like the darkness was just around the corner waiting for her. A darkness her father had brought into her life when she was eight.

Sarah stood and got a piece of construction paper and a box of crayons from her desk. She often had the children draw, another way to express themselves. She pulled out a brown crayon. At first, it felt fat and awkward in her fingers as she drew an outline of a man. Then she wrote "Daddy" across his torso. She picked up the blunted children's scissors and cut out the figure. She took a matchbook from a candle holder on her desk and then went to the bathroom. She lit a match and held Daddy's foot to the flame until it caught. The fire ate his feet. The pillow pressed harder against her face. She gasped for air. She was thirteen and she put her hand between her legs and gently rubbed the place where it hurt. The fire licked her father's crotch. He was always so hard and hurtful, disgusting as his penis rammed up against her. She was too tiny. The flames ate his buttocks and started up his back. Sarah began to cry.

And always as he pushed into her he whispered that he loved her, loved her, loved her. His body spasmed and shuddered and he did not see her. The fire severed his body from his head. The ashes floated into the sink. Sarah choked on her sobs. Then she screamed. She hated him so much. She had loved him. Why had he done it? The fire ate his mouth, his eyes. Sarah's scream became a wail. She dropped the last bit of paper into the sink before the flames touched her fingers. "Good-bye," she whispered.

She wiped her tears and turned on the water and washed the ashes down the drain. There went her father. Her brother. Her mother. All the bad memories. She looked around. Everything appeared fresh and new, as if all had been out of focus and now it was clear and sharp. Perhaps all these years, parts of her had been scattered across the universe. Now she had come home to her body. Or almost. It would take time. But she was safe. She was whole again. Now she was ready to protect herself and Paul. She would make certain he was safe and happy.

She turned off the water, went to the front door, and opened it. The darkness was gone. She thought of the stars in Paul's eyes, and she smiled and stepped out into the morning.

FOR THEIR WIVES ARE MUTE

Wayne Allen Sallee

What can you say about Wayne Allen Sallee after making the observation that he is a very remarkable guy? Well, I guess I could tell you why I think of him in such a way: for starters, he's published more than 700 (yes, you read that right) poems, and probably close to one hundred short stories in the small press magazines and several major publications and anthologies. He has written a grim, hard-edged look at himself—a novella entitled Pain-Grin—*which details his life with cerebral palsy, and also a strange, surreal novel called* The Holy Terror. *He is soft-spoken, courteous, and just the other side of brilliant. He sent me lots of stories before I finally selected the one which follows—an odd mix of obsession, fear, and ultimately, a unique brand of passion.*

She had been glad that the damp, cold spring had kept them from burrowing through her skin and into her world again. It had been seventeen years. It had been a lifetime.

"Jen, how can you say you like this weather?" Vonnie would say to her over egg and cheese croissants at Warburton's. "It's the middle of May and we haven't reached sixty degrees yet! Don't you want to go to the beach?"

"Why, so I could look like a little nymph?" she retorted and instantly regretted using that word. It made her think of the cicadas just beneath the surface of the ground outside. She knew all there was to know about cicada nymphs—seventeen-year locusts in Chicago—and had read and reread the information in her daughter's *World Book* until she was ready to puke.

"Happy are the cicadas, for their wives are mute." Some Greek man named Xenarchos had written that in Rhodes. Wherever that was. In Greece, she supposed. "Jennifer Spano, you can't be expected to know everything," she would look in the mirror and say to her reflection. Then she would examine her scalp for gray hairs and wonder where all the time had gone. Contrary to the popular saying, it hadn't flown because she was having fun.

She had fun for awhile. A senior in high school who maybe could have been visited by the titty fairy, she had had her fair share of dates. And a lesser share of meaningless trysts in AMC Gremlins and Chevy Caprices. A teenager who thought she was in love each time. Not a tease or a sex fiend, and there were plenty of nymphomaniacs to go around in Wagner High's class of 1973, oh no. Yet she never argued when she had been denied the final word in the consummation of the act.

A lifetime ago. Her daughter's lifetime.

The largest of the bugs of the order Homoptera, *special organs on the male cicada's abdomen produce the long shrill sound associated with its name*.

And oh, how the young boys would stroke away. Like they were on borrowed time. Thursday night, May 31. The cicadas were out there now, the temperature rising these past few days into the eighties away from the lake, high sixties inland. "Vic Solvig always said I could be a great weathergirl on TV," she said to the mirror.

They were loud, very loud, making sounds like the giant ants in that fifties movie. Vic Solvig had said that the cicadas sounded like a lot of miniscule Shemps. Shemp, the forgotten Stooge, whose trademark was his almost lamentable *eeb-eebbee-eebbee-ebe-ebe-ebe*. Vic Solvig had told her that and made her laugh the night she became pregnant.

He had folded his four limbs over her body like a roof and let his drumlike membrane do its dirty deed. She hadn't been a nymph like the others in her class.

But the cicadas wouldn't be around when autumn closed in, no sir. The big blue city trucks would come and spray the trees. Her heroes, the Streets and Sanitation. "I don't know what kind of poison they use," she spoke now to the gray hair she had plucked from her scalp.

With dozens of red eyes staring in at her from the trees.

The cicada female has a chisel-like ovipositor beneath its abdomen which is used to slice openings into twigs. Eggs are laid, which then hatch and fall to the ground to enter the soil and feed on the tree roots.

And now they were back. Her forearms prickled and she thought that if she looked, she might see a young female again burrowing out of her to shed its skin. She hadn't wanted to get pregnant, and now, why she was almost thirty-five. Who would have her now?

She listened, every day it seemed, but there were no men making keening noises or singing antiphonal songs.

The male produces his chirping sounds by oscillating an arched plate, the tymbal, which is stiffened by parallel ribs. This produces up to 600 rasping noises per second; they sound like the clicks made by depressing and releasing the arched lid of a metal box.

Or my computer beeping when I type a word wrong, she thought. Were there computers seventeen years ago? She had gone to the school's ten-year reunion in 1983, amazed that eight of her classmates had died in that deacade following graduation. Tony Chiarmonte had been shot in a bar fight in Tallow Lake, Wisconsin. Chestine Diedzek had gotten drunk and fallen off the bleachers at Poplar Creek during an AC/DC concert. Jen couldn't read past that.

Three years ago, and she hadn't gone to the reunion with anyone. Thinking, what kind of world were we born into that eight children couldn't live to their ten-year high school reunion?

She hadn't given her unborn baby ten weeks.

The Magicicada septendecim, *or periodical cicada, are among the most striking of insects, owing to their grotesque shape. Their forelegs are modified digging tools, the shovels being formed particularly by the femora. The imago, in the four to six weeks of its existence, does not eat.*

And the wives remain mute, Jennifer thought.

She couldn't watch the news or read the papers because it seemed that every day another clinic was being bombed or another march was taking place around City Hall. That was the only time the women did the talking, the men who did the dirty deed cowering mute in the shadows of the County Building or their male-bonding get-togethers.

I don't want to say that I was an unwanted child, but I was born with a coat hanger sticking out of my forehead. She hated that joke more than she hated the rustling of their skins on the trees outside her window.

She stared back at them just the same.

Not much later, she was standing in front of the biggest tree. "Look at me," she said to the rustling shadows. There were hundreds of them, covering the tree the way army ants would converge over a wounded animal. She wondered what they saw. Even when her hair was not pulled back into a tight bun, she had a pronounced widow's peak. And crow's-feet visible and magnified beneath her wire frame glasses.

She looked down at her almost non-existent breasts, like two little nubs poking at her T-shirt, which read PEPSI: THE CHOICE OF A NEW GENERATION. She had gained a secretary's ass from her days at the comput-er. Her mother, if she were alive today, would have said that Jennifer had hips for good breeding. Once, she had. And maybe it had driven her crazy. Just a little.

* * *

The other day, Vonnie had met her for lunch at Old-Timer's. She had a longer lunch hour and always got there first to reserve a table in the non-smoking section. When Jen had finally gotten across Michigan Avenue and rushed breathless into the restaurant, the first thing she saw was the engagement ring on her friend's finger.

She made an excuse for not staying, turned west down Lake Street in her confusion, and heard their voices. The cicadas.

She went down Garland Court, one of the Loop's glorified alleys, and came across an old brick storage house. They were in there somewhere. In the brick. She was mesmerized. A man with a briefcase asked her if she was okay and she was embarrassed. Maybe the cicadas had been on the roof.

But for seventeen years? Vonnie had been wearing an engagement ring . . .

She was mesmerized again. Looking at their eyes as they shifted and she did as well, moving the weight from one foot to the other, their forms were a fractal image. Always changing. What was so terrible about these creatures?

Did they find her beautiful, as well?

She hadn't gone back to work since seeing them downtown.

She pulled the T-shirt up over her head, feeling self-conscious of how pale she must look where her ribs pressed against her skin. The temperature had dropped down to the fifties by ten that night, and her nipples were tiny, hard bullets. What did they see in her?

In some neighborhoods, the sounds of the males' chirping is enough that people standing next to each other would have to shout to be heard.

There was nobody there for Jennifer to talk to.

Her jeans and panties off now, the skin on her buttocks prickled in the chill. She had to do this.

The cicada would not be back until she was fifty-one.

Jennifer rushed forward and pressed her body into their thousands. She clenched her fists, mashing the bodies together and hearing the skins break softly, like a nacho in melted cheese might.

Those cicadas that were pressed up against the lenses of her glasses writhed as if they were on a microscope slide. Some squeezed free of their gray skins like Vic Solvig had liberated himself from his condom. Others wriggled around the edges of the wire frames with brown and red and green legs and antennae. She did not blink or wince.

Many of the cicadas had red veins in the membranes of their wings.

Jennifer breathed through clenched teeth in tight, prolonged gasps. She ground her hips into the pulp on the tree. The male cicadas screamed in her ears.

She did not say a word.

DEAD ISSUE

Rex Miller

Writers have a problem with their readers attributing the traits of their characters to the writers personally. This is especially troublesome for writers with dark imaginations. You know the shtick—you write about serial killers or child molesters and some donut in Paducah immediately thinks you're a serial killer or child molester yourself, and he writes you a dumb letter and reports your name to the FBI. This can also be a problem for spouses who read our twisted scenarios and wonder who it really is they are sleeping with each night. It is usually not an issue for writers amongst themselves. We understand the creative process and know we're able to create characters of abject darkness that are nothing like us. Right. But after reading Rex Miller's utterly convincing "Dead Issue," I started having my own doubts about this guy who lives in the midwest and sounds so normal and nice on the phone . . .

Inside the big car it smelled of booze, weed, new car smells, and musk, and she slid across the slick, cold seat letting it all hit her at once. She was high and saw no danger signs.

"Hi, baby," he said, leaning into her.

"Hello, darling," she breathed, and he kissed her very lightly and turned the ignition key, pulling away from the curb and heading out toward the highway. She was hot stuff.

"It was fun, wasn't it?" Foxy Roxy. Twenty-two. Unmarried.

"Uh huh." Her live-in lover.

147

"I love to party," she said sexily, leaning into the solidness of him beside her.

"I know you do, honey."

"You had a good time—huh?" She looked at him.

"Sure."

The woman started to reach over and turn on the radio and then remembered, caught herself in time, and asked:

"Want some music?"

"Pass," he said softly, smiling, pulling her tightly up against him. She smelled womanly, he imagined he could smell her pussy scent through the other fragrances in his nose, and he looked over at her chest. It was a black cocktail dress under the coat and he slipped his hand inside. Her body felt warm. He stiffened, imagining what it would be like later to stuff his maleness into her mouth, choke her with his masculinity. He smiled, feeling the heat and growing hardness as he touched her, thinking about her taking him in her mouth later. How he'd make her swallow it. Her pale, smooth, alabaster skin, so soft and sleek and unblemished. She looked like a teenybopper when she was naked. Little flat tits and a young girl's high, firm ass.

At the stop sign he pulled her to him, kissing her roughly, kissing her closed mouth as hard as he could.

"You make me hot for you," he breathed.

"Good," she said, startled. He looked back and pulled out onto the highway.

"Yeah," he said and suddenly pulled over again, right on the shoulder of the road in front of all the traffic and started making out with her like he was about to take her clothes off right there and put it to her in the middle of traffic.

"Somebody got horny," she laughed into his mouth sexily and he squeezed her breast very hard and said:

"Tongue." She obliged him.

"Let's go home," she purred.

"Tongue. Stick that fucking tongue in my mouth." They kissed some more. He imagined what her wet, red mouth would look like later, the look of that long, white throat as she licked and sucked.

"I'm going to make you eat a beautiful girl's cunt while I fuck you in the ass," he told her. He was always threatening to make her do it with another woman, but she realized it was just pillow talk. She went along with it as usual.

"Okay. I'll go down on Linda for you," she told him. She knew he fantasized about her and their next door neighbor: a vacuous, somewhat overweight slut whom she wouldn't touch on a bet.

"Yeah. That'd make you hot, wouldn't it?" He pinched her breast through the thin fabric of the cocktail dress and the bra, really hurting her.

"Ouch. Oh—honey. Don't."

"Get yourself all wet down there thinking about eating Linda's hot cunt while I ream out your ass."

"Umm."

"Little whore." He grabbed her long hair in back and twisted it savagely as he forced her mouth to his.

"Let—don't—"

"Will you put that cunt TONGUE in my mouth, god-damn you, you fucking hot little tramp? Do I have to tell you every time when I kiss your little whore mouth? Now stick that bitch out as far as you can." She did and he kissed her brutally, sucking her tongue. Then he eased up a bit and started kissing her gently and tenderly, but still with her hair in his hand. Getting very dangerous now and oddly she began to smell it before she sensed his mood. It was like he was turning into an animal.

"Let's go home, darling. Come on," she said, looking around as if people would see them. And he relaxed the lock on her hair and she pulled away in the moment when he checked the rearview mirror and pulled back onto the highway.

"You're nothing but a fucking cunt, you know that?" he asked her in a soft, lilting, pleasant tone. His love-making voice.

"I'm your cunt, baby," she said. She had a splitting headache now and her breast was sore and her tongue hurt. She wanted to get him home and they'd do it and then he'd leave her alone. It was amazing. He'd come in about a minute and then go right to sleep like a baby. She knew him like a book.

"Slide back over here, you fucking bitch." She came back.

"That's right." She felt his large right hand reach over and caress her left knee, sliding up the leg under the short skirt.

"I hate fucking pantyhose," he said. "I wish I knew who the pussy was who invented the sons of bitches, I'd like to kick the living crap out of them."

"They're wonderful, baby. Don't say that." She was trying to snap him out of it a little till they got home.

"Did I just tell you they suck? I oughta get you a pair of crotchless pantyhose so that twat would always be open for me—eh?"

"That's a good idea," she said.

"You fucking had your legs open tonight," he said dangerously.

"Huh?"

"HUH? You heard me, bitch. Every time that prick Joel smiled at you, you'd spread those fucking legs a lit- tle more. You're nothing but a cheap fucking cooze."

"Darling, don't talk silly."

"Bullshit. If you want to suck Joel's dick so badly, why don't I invite him over and we'll take turns with you? Is that what you'd like, you fucking bitch?"

"I just want you," she said as he bore down, squeezing her soft inner thigh in his vise-grip. She cried out and he laughed.

"Oh, yeah." He let go of her momentarily, inflamed now. And he waited quietly at the stop sign. She tried to figure the best way to handle him now. She knew what he was like when he started his fantasy games.

"Linda sounds better to me," she said. "Maybe we could get her over and you could watch us together. Would you like that?" But he was gone. He didn't bite and as soon as the traffic moved out he hung a right on an unfamiliar county road and she said, "Let's not go this way, honey. Come on. Let's go home and make love."

"Yeah," he said, driving.

"Are you mad at me or just playing?"

"Yeah. I'm playing."

"You know I would never even look at anybody else. You're all I want."

"Yeah. You're—" He didn't even bother to finish. Suddenly she felt a chill in the car. She was starting to become afraid, and she realized that was ridiculous.

"I love you," she said.

"I love you, too," he said, surprisingly. She slid back to him and he kissed her. In a moment he pulled over again, but this time he cut the engine, putting it in Park and killing the lights. It was a heavily traveled but dark stretch of county road. A truck came by. He began kissing her very gently and she responded. "I can't wait to get home with you. I want to make it with you here. Please, baby?"

"Let's go home, darling, it isn't that far. We'll be so much more comfortable." He kept kissing her. "I'm cold."

"You need something hot." He unbuckled his belt and undid his pants. By the time he'd moved down in the seat and repositioned himself, his trousers down, he was limp. He took her by the hair again and pushed her down on top of him, saying:

"Make it WET," as he started jacking himself off into her mouth. She licked the head of it. He was hard almost instantly, and she put a cold hand under his balls as she started going back and forth on him with her mouth. He had to fight not to explode.

"Squeeze, you goddamn shit fuck, SQUEEZE MY BALLS." He had her hair with his left hand, ramming it into her throat, slamming her back and forth on him, choking her with the fullness of his penis, and when she squeezed him he began shooting into her.

"Come on, come on, COME ON. Ohhh." He let go. And he kept her down on him.

"Don't stop licking, fuck shit, oh, oh please, OOOOOOOH!" She knew he couldn't come again that soon but he made the noise he made when he came. It must have really gotten him off. He pulled his pants back up.

"Was that good?" she asked, mischievously.

But all he could think about was the way she'd looked, close to Joel, the two of them almost SNUGGLING right there in the living room. That fucking whore. He'd seen her once reach over and pat his arm when they were laughing about something. Flirting with him like some goddamn tramp.

"You really like to flirt in front of me, don't you, you scummy bitch?" he said, out of nowhere. She looked at him sharply.

"I don't flirt." Her voice had a hard, surprised edge. He reached out and took her hair like a handle and cracked her head forward on the padded dash.

"OHHHHHH!" She cried out, she couldn't see. Blue and red and yellow stars exploded.

"Yeah. You like to flirt so well. See if this teaches you something," he said, the car still moving, but him turning and with a big, mean fist punching her as hard as he could, aiming at nothing, but catching her a hard, grazing shot in the kidneys as she jerked farther forward, the blow knocking her down into a heap on the floorboard of the car.

"Goddamn shit bitch," he fumed.

Nothing. She was still.

"How's THAT feel, you whore?" She didn't say anything but he could see her moving, breathing hard. He pulled over again, braking but keeping the car running. He touched her arm.

"I'm hurt."

"You're not hurt, cunt. Get up."

"(something)—the hospital."

"Speak up. What'd you say?"

"Better get me to the hospital, honey."

"What's wrong?"

"I'm bleeding inside."

"That's no big deal. You'll be all right. I didn't even hit you that hard. Get up."

"Better get me to a hospital, fast." It was her serious

voice and it snapped him out of it.

"Really?"

"Yeah, babe. I'm hurt. I'm bleeding inside. I can feel it. It's—real bad." She cried.

"Shit," he said, but he pulled out and decided he'd run her by the emergency ward.

"Where's Memorial?"

"On Grand."

"You mean MacArthur."

"It's on Grand. Good Samaritan's on MacArthur."

"You'll be all right. Fuck."

"It's the baby," she told him.

"Bullshit."

"I can feel it."

"That's crap," he said, but his tone lacked conviction.

"I think you hurt the baby," she said softly.

"Bull. You don't know that." He exhaled. Always something.

"I can feel—OH!" She screamed twice, as sharp pains hit her.

"Take it easy," he said, gently.

"Hurry."

"Listen. You tell 'em you fell down the stairs. Don't say anything about me or—who the fuck knows? I might get some heat on it. Just say you fell."

"I fell on my back?"

"Yeah. You could be coming up the stairs, you slip, go over backward, and land on your back. Whatever."

"No." She'd worked as a candy striper. "They'll never buy it. They know from the way somebody has an injury. I better say somebody did it to me. You know, some drunk guy on the street or something."

"Don't be stupid. They INVESTIGATE that kind of crap. You don't want the goddamn police. Use your brain. You fell down the back stairs."

"OHHHHHHHHH! Jesus!"

"Come on. Shit. You'll be okay. I'll be there in three minutes."

"We don't have time."

"HUH?" He was worried now, worried for the first time since he'd hit her.

"We won't make the hospital."

"What do you mean we won't make—"

"It's bad. Stop at a gas station or something. Blood's comin' out of me fast." She could feel herself hemorrhaging.

"Aw, shit. Take it easy. Hold on, now."

"STOP! Come on. NOW!"

"Okay, okay." He wheeled into a gas station and convenience store. Got out and tried the door marked Ladies, to see if he'd need to go in and get a key for her, but it was open. He turned to go get her but she'd managed to get out of the vehicle and was standing right behind him, clutching herself, moaning. He was beginning to worry now.

"AH!" It was almost a scream. She burst into the women's john and slammed the door. He went back to the car and waited, pissed at the inconvenience.

Five minutes. Enough already. He got out and banged on the door of the toilet. Nothing. He tried it and it was locked. Fucking bitch.

"Open this, goddamn it. Come—" He felt it click open and turned the knob as she staggered back in, collapsing onto the commode in a stall. He followed her.

"Let's go."

"I passed it."

"Huh?"

"I passed tissue. The baby. I passed the baby. YOU KILLED OUR BABY, YOU FUCKER."

"BULLSHIT!"

"I passed the baby."

He was very still. Watching.

"I'm messed up inside. I need a doctor."

"Fuck the doctor, all right?"

"Please. You've already killed my baby. Do you want me to die, too?"

"Don't be stupid."

"You mean bastard," she sobbed, letting it all pour out.

"I'm sorry, baby," he said in his gentlest tones. Trying to hold her in his arms, inhaling disinfectant, listening to her weep. "I'll make it up to you, I swear. And a couple of—you know, six, eight weeks. It's not really a baby yet anyway, it's just—" He felt her stiffen as she cried and tried to pull away from him. He changed tactics and cooed to her and stroked her and finally she let him hold her.

Foxy Roxy eventually cried herself out. He kept holding her. Figuring what would be the coolest move. No way was he taking her to a hospital where the heat could get their nose into it. Get some haired-off social worker on his case. Fuck that shit.

"Come on, doll." He whispered, and very gently he eased her up, and they made their way to the car, him practically carrying her.

He was extremely tender and solicitous all the way home. She assured him she could go under her own power but he supported her from the car into the apartment building, and all the way up in the elevator.

He carried her in, tenderly, lovingly, like a newlywed husband, and gently deposited her on the bed. She curled up into a fetal ball and hugged a pillow.

He went into the next room and built himself a stiff one at their wet bar, and came back in the bedroom.

The little black cocktail dress had hiked up on her and the back of her beautiful, sexy legs, and that great butt looked so good to him. He told her:

"You never looked so fuckable, baby."

"Get real," she moaned, hugging her pillow.

"Is this real enough for you?" he asked, unzipping and guiding himself into her mouth. "I love you baby," he said. "You know I do, don't you?"

She tried to push him away but when he was like this it was better to just go along with him. She'd learned the hard way.

It was over pretty quickly, and she was getting lightheaded from the blood loss so she knew if she was going to do something she'd better be doing it. He was snoring, the bastard. Really sawing those logs. Passed out, dead to the world.

She went in the kitchen and got what she needed and came back and took care of business. When she was through she forced herself to take a fast shower, then called for a Yellow Cab and got dressed. She was waiting for it, in front, when the taxi pulled up to take her to the hospital.

It was the next day before she told the cops about him and four guys let themselves in and found him.

"Forty-one, I make it," the M.E. told the ranking officer in charge. He'd counted forty-one stab wounds in the decedent's bod. "Somebody was truly pissed," he said.

DOWN THE VALLEY WILD

Paul F. Olson

Paul F. Olson is a tall, friendly-looking fellow from Illinois who made his mark in publishing as one of the founders of Horrorstruck *magazine—a popular periodical of essays, articles, and columns about the HDF genres. Published on a bi-monthly schedule, the magazine became a controlling factor in Paul's existence, taking time away from his family and his own writing, and so it came to pass that* Horrorstruck *folded its mighty tents and went the way of the Great Auk. Paul has since written several novels and an ever-growing corpus of short stories, the most recent of which is "Down the Valley Wild," a journey across the scarred landscapes of childhood, guilt, and the possibility of its expiation.*

You ran screaming for your father, because there had been a terrible accident . . .

Very little had changed. The terrain was more weathered, the undergrowth wilder, the cabin sadly rundown—but it was still there, and nearly forty years had not altered any of it beyond recognition or repair.

Stewart arrived in the early afternoon. Of course there was no longer a family Jeep and he had not trusted his Mazda to negotiate the roads that linked the property to Highway 41, so he had parked at the Amoco in Patterson Falls and had asked the pump jockey, a man by the name of Larry Allison, to run him out in his pickup.

"Hey, I know that place," Allison said. "Used to hunt out there when I was a kid. Ain't nobody lived there long as I been alive. What, you buy it from the fambly or somethin?"

Stewart shook his head. "I *am* the family. Name's Don Stewart. The land and cabin belonged to my father. He died a few months ago."

"Sorry to hear that," Allison said, and Stewart nodded to show he appreciated the thought.

Now he used the tarnished key that had been in the lawyer's envelope to unlock the front door. He hefted his suitcases and went inside, immediately staggering from the overpowering odors of age and decay. He gulped and blinked rapidly, but his eyes began to water and his stomach uttered a threatening groan.

There was no trace, no lingering evidence whatsoever, of his mother's fanatical housekeeping or the slightly less effective but still dedicated cleaning his father had done after her death. Everything was coated with dust and a greasy, almost jellylike slime. Cobwebs dangled from the ceiling and decorated the few remaining sticks of furniture. Newspapers, which had once been tacked over the windows to combat sun fading, now lay on the floor, yellow and faded themselves. Rodent droppings were scattered across table tops and windowsills. A black and white photograph of two young boys with their arms around each other withered alongside a 1952 issue of *Life* on top of the woodstove.

Stewart swallowed hard and went in the rest of the way. It was going to take work—Jesus, was *that* an understatement—but it could be done. He figured that by tonight the place could be sleepable, in two or three days it would be livable, and by the end of his vacation it might actually be comfortable again.

He set the suitcases in the corner and returned to the edge of the road, where he and Allison had piled the things he'd purchased in town: cartons of food, boxes of cleaning supplies, mops and brooms and buckets. It took three trips to get everything into the cabin. After that, feeling old, Stewart forced himself to go out again for a quick tour.

The yard had been consumed by saplings and weeds.

A shame, but clearing it would have to wait for his next trip north. He had neither the proper equipment nor the ambition, and he knew that the cabin would keep him busy enough, thank you.

The woodlot to the east had succumbed to chaos as well. Deadfalls and scrub growth were everywhere. Windstorms had toppled the best of the older maples and ironwoods, while others were ravaged by age and disease. He would eventually need the chain saw he had put off buying, he supposed, for someday he'd have to come in here and salvage what he could. But luckily there was still some firewood already cut, split, and stacked under the overhang on the cabin's eastern wall. Because of his father's superior craftsmanship, the overhang was still weather- and waterproof. Mostly, anyway. There was at least half a cord of ironwood that was nicely seasoned, unrotted.

He saved the worst of the tour for last, but finally could put it off no longer. He strolled around the back of the cabin, his hands jammed casually in his pockets, a strained but still lighthearted whistle on his lips. With his boyhood summer home squarely at his back, he ventured to the far southern edge of the property.

The ravine was still there.

Of course that was a bit like saying that the pyramids were still standing in the desert or that Niagara Falls was still roiling and rumbling. Ravines simply didn't disappear. You didn't have to be a geologist to know that they *grew* with time, but still . . . still . . . seeing those sloping, canyonlike walls for the first time in so very many years, laying eyes on the tangled thickets that ran downward into seeming oblivion . . . the very sight of those things made him forget about breathing for a moment or two and kicked his heart into a crude, jittery tap dance.

An image of the faded photograph in the cabin rose in his mind.

You ran screaming for your father . . .

No.

It was too early. He would deal with it. Of course he

would. Dealing with it had been one of the prime reasons
(or to save a lie for a rainy day, *the* prime reason) that he
had accepted the key from the lawyer in the first place.
But not now, not yet.

You ran screaming—

He turned angrily and stomped back to the cabin, the
gloom of the ravine and its quietly rustling trees shut
off, closed off, blocked out of his thoughts.

For the first time he was grateful that such great untold
quantities of work were waiting for him inside.

By nine that night Stewart felt that he could spend the
night in the cabin without contracting a dread illness or
falling prey to the March of the Marauding Mice. He
had worked without a break until twilight, stopping then
only long enough to fire up the woodstove, eat a quick
sandwich, and down two beers. Then he had gone back
to work, sticking with it until the mild complaints being
offered by his body had progressed to grumbles, and
from grumbles to an outright yammering bitch.

He closed the windows he had opened to air the place
out and sat down by the stove with a package of Fritos
and another beer. An hour ago it had begun to rain. The
sound of it on the roof merged with the crackling snap
of burning logs to bring back a flood of memories:

The time he and his father had driven to Conley Lake
to go fishing and had somehow managed to overturn the
rowboat not once but twice . . .

. . . the time he and Dale had rigged a high jump
in the side yard, complete with a cross-pole made from
a birch whippet and a landing area that consisted of
rat-eaten mattresses from the county dump . . .

. . . the time Dale had challenged him to climb to
the cabin roof and leap to the branches of the cedar tree
seven feet away (little Donnie had accepted that challenge and had tumbled gracelessly to earth, fracturing
his wrist and spending the remainder of the summer in
an awkward, joy-spoiling cast) . . .

. . . the time when his mother had still been alive and
all of them had driven into the Falls to attend a movie

at the newly opened theater. The locals had called it a "picture house." They saw a double feature with shorts, and they'd had a fine time—except, perhaps, when Dale stole all his popcorn and *he* had gotten in trouble for trying to snatch it back.

Memories could be a good thing, but too many memories (or the *wrong kind* of memories) were not. He told himself that it was for that reason more than any other he had tossed the photo of the two young boys into the woodstove first thing, before the old newspapers and magazines, before the kindling twigs, before the logs. Even still, picture or no, he seemed to have little control over the things that came to mind. They came, the good and the bad, at random, in bits and pieces, some cloudy, some clear, each demanding in its own quietly insistent way to be heard. He guessed he could have sat there by the stove for his entire vacation, listening to the fire and helplessly reflecting, letting in whatever might come (with one exception, of course), and still not touch on half the things that lurked back there in those first eight years of his life.

That night he dreamed of Dale. Not Dale on the last day, but he and Dale high-jumping in the yard. He had been terrible at it. He had knocked the whippet from its supports every single time. But not Dale. Dale could fly. Dale would run and leap and sail upward, his body arched in a triumphant parabola, soaring. And then he would thud onto the pile of moldy mattresses and look up to ascertain that the pole was still in position, his grin dazzling, his eyes glistening and alive.

He awoke from that dream with the beginnings of a sob locked in his throat and the certainty that someone was tapping on the window next to the bed. He rolled over, expecting to see a gaggle of drunken teenagers, a lost camper, perhaps even a wilderness hobo.

But there was no one there. The tapping was just the sound of rain pattering on the glass.

Stewart sighed and lay down. Ten minutes later he was asleep again, tossing, muttering.

Dreaming.

* * *

On the third day he took a noontime break, laid down his scrub brush, and went out. The time had come. He knew that. He *felt* it, although it had not been a conscious decision. The idea had simply come to him, unbidden, almost as casually as a man might decide at one in the morning that it is time to get out of bed and make a sandwich.

He waded through the tidal sea of grass and stopped at the edge of the ravine, trying to remember where the path had been. He shuffled slowly back and forth along the edge of the slope, but finally abandoned the search and picked the clearest spot he could find to start down.

It was steeper than he remembered. He was forced to move from tree to tree, struggling to keep his balance. Brambles caught at his jeans. The gravelly soil beneath his boots gave way again and again. Several times, when there were no trees large enough to support his weight, he had to go it alone, slipping and skidding and sliding on the edge of disaster down to the next handhold.

It took nearly ten minutes to reach bottom. Once there he paused, gazing at the junglelike lay of the land. For the first time since Allison had dropped him off at the edge of the property he could hear the river, although it didn't sound nearly as ferocious as it once had.

He supposed it had been a dry spring.

He forged ahead, moving cautiously into the heart of the ravine. The ground was booby-trapped with the hidden corpses of trees and frost-heaved rocks. Overhead branches groped for his face and snapped viciously as he passed, cutting him off from everything behind.

"Jesus," he murmured, partially in surprise at just how wild the ravine had become, partially in response to the whole new rush of memories that cascaded over him as he moved along.

Good Lord, but they had spent the time down here. He and Dale, he and his father, Dale and his father, all three of them. Sometimes he would come alone, but not often; even in those days it had not been a good place

for a child to play by himself, and little Donnie Stewart
had never been a courageous sort of kid. So they had
come together, inventing games of Jungle Scout, River
Guide, African Explorer, and bizarre permutations of tag
or hide-and-seek. Of course Dale always won. Whatever
the game, Dale came out on top. But little Donnie, far
from brave yet stubborn to a fault, had always gone back
for more.

Their summer hideaway. Their summer playground.

The growth began to thin a little and he broke out at
the edge of the river. It was as disappointing as he had
guessed from the sound. Its banks were still rocky, still
wide, but the flow of water couldn't properly be called
a river at all. It was, in fact, not much more than a
muddy creek. He knew he hadn't been looking forward
to seeing it the way it had been that final summer, but
still he felt a curious pang, an unaccountable frustration,
a sense of being let down. It was as if he had traveled
a great distance only to find—

He whirled suddenly, staring at the wall of trees
behind him.

There had been a noise back there, a crisp snapping of
branches and a slow dragging sound, as though someone
was pulling something very heavy through the scrub.

He tried to remember if there had ever been any
animals down here. There had, yes, but only squirrels,
chipmunks, and the occasional jackrabbit. If there had
been anything large enough to make a noise like that,
they would have known about it, and they probably
wouldn't have played down here as often as they had.

Was it a bear, he wondered.

But whatever it was, it was gone now. There was
nothing but the gentle sough of wind and the pitiful
gurgle of the river. He listened a little longer and finally
lifted his gaze to the sheer rock wall across the water.
The sight chilled him. He was seized with a sense of
pure, uncut sorrow more powerful than he had felt in
years. Remorse he recognized. Guilt he knew well. But
this . . . this was an agonizing sensation of burning loss.
He felt as though someone had seared the inside of his

chest with a blowtorch, making every heartbeat a weeping cry of pain, every breath a stinging jolt of misery.

He shook his head slowly.

"I'm back, Dale," he whispered. "I finally came back."

He stayed there for a long time, staring at the wall. He wasn't sure if he still wanted to keep the memory at bay or not, but it was too late for such distinctions. Choice was not a factor. Free will, if it had ever existed, was gone. The memory had arrived and there was no stopping it as it played itself over and over in a vivid loop. The game that had soured. Little Donnie's anger rising. Dale on the edge and Dale going down. The mighty, almost mystical roaring of the river. It was very hot that summer, he remembered, but there had not been a dry spring, oh no, not that year, not by a long shot.

You ran screaming for your father . . .

Oh yes, you ran screaming, didn't you? You wailed and wept and wet your pants and kept thinking it couldn't be true. You wished it were you, wished you were the one and not Dale. You wanted to go back and do it again and have it all turn out differently, have the beginning and the ending magically alter themselves until—

Stewart left the riverbank, his steps quicker now that a path had been made. He was almost running, *was* running, as though the shadows and phantoms and wicked creatures thundering through his brain were actually things that could be left behind.

But they followed him.

And something else followed him, too.

He stumbled along, pushing branches aside, trampling the underbrush, making enough noise to completely smother the heavy dragging sound that dogged him like a nightmare from the past.

He drank a great deal of beer that night, fell asleep early, but awoke sometime later in the middle of a foggy, troubling dream. He sat up in bed, gulping air, rubbing his eyes, trying to rein in his wildly galloping senses.

The tapping was at the window again, only this time the night was dry, the sound not the whisper of black rain but something else. He looked out and saw the kind of darkness that was only possible in places like this, miles from civilization . . . except that *this* darkness was marred in the center by two distinct pinpoints of light.

Stewart blinked. The pinpoints didn't waver. He drew a breath and fought back the irrational fear that was stirring within him. Those pinpoints, those dots of light— they were glowing eyes.

"Kids," he muttered drunkenly, and struggled out of bed. He found his pants and pulled them on without bothering to zip them. He wobbled out into the main room and yanked open the back door, finally sobering a degree as the chill of the summer night struck his skin and made it tingle.

"Hey! You kids! You get outta here right now! This is private property!"

There was a brief silence, but then he heard the tapping again, still at the bedroom window around the corner from where he stood.

"I told you to get outta here! You're trespassing, and I've got a gun inside." That was a lie, but he didn't intend to give the little sneaks a chance to find out.

The tapping continued, increased, grew louder. It was fast becoming a sound of angry insistence.

"Well, goddamnit."

Stewart went back inside to grab whatever weapon he could find. It took him awhile, but when he reemerged he was brandishing the scrub mop he had purchased in the Falls. He held it in both hands, like a bat, and stepped into the yard.

"You got one more chance!" he yelled, moving gingerly through the long and dewy grass. "I want you kids outta here—*right now!*"

The tapping had become a banging. It seemed impossible that the intruder would not break the glass.

"You asked for it!"

He raised the mop and rounded the corner.

And then he stopped, the anger drying and dying within. In its place was an instant of stark confusion, followed by a dark, crawling sensation in the pit of his stomach.

Whoever had been at the window was running away, into the forest, but in the dark what he saw didn't look anything like a kid. Actually, it looked only vaguely human, rather more like a gnarled woodland animal, its body pale and twisted. It scuttled into the underbrush on skinny, bowed legs, its arms swinging spastically, apelike.

"What the hell . . . ?"

He put out a hand and steadied himself against the cabin wall. His Adam's apple bobbed up and down. His mouth opened and closed in convulsive silence. He finally managed to force something out—"*You stay away from here, damnit! Next time I'll shoot you for a thief!*"—but he felt ashamed even as he uttered it, well aware of the hollow force behind the words.

Then he began to tremble violently, uncontrollably, his body wracked with great, quaking sobs. He told himself he was shivering because of the unseasonable temperature, but he knew that wasn't true. It was because of something else, oh yes, because of that moment just before the thing had scurried off into the wilderness, when it had turned toward him for one brief breath of a moment and he had seen its face. It was because of that, and it was because of the four words that had risen to his lips as he gazed at that face, the four words he had barely choked back in time.

Those words were: *Dale? Is that you?*

He wanted to laugh at that now—oh God, he wanted it so *badly*. But a laugh would be wrong. It would be misguided. It would be fraudulent, worse than a lie. Because even a mild laugh would not in any way change what, for that one instant, he was certain he had seen.

That year a fierce, rainy spring had finally surrendered to a summer of almost unheard-of heat. Temperatures in the nineties day after blistering day had driven them to the ravine more than ever before. It was better down there in that wild valley, sheltered at least a little from the merciless, unblinking eye of the sun and the brain-busting humidity.

On that particular day the game had been a northwoods variation on the old cowboys-and-Indians theme. True to form, it had started on a free and happy note, but had plummeted downhill rapidly.

The problem, of course, was Dale.

(*Dale, whom Donnie loved.*)

Dale who was tall and athletic.

(*Dale, whom Donnie respected.*)

Dale who could play baseball with the high school boys, despite the fact that he was only eleven, and who did better in school on his bad days than Donnie could ever hope to do.

(*Dale, whom Donnie idolized.*)

Dale who had been his mother's largest joy, who was still his father's pride.

(*Dale, whom Donnie envied.*)

Dale who could never do any wrong.

(*Dale, whom Donnie feared.*)

Dale who always seemed to find the quickest way to spoil a good game, whether by obstinate bickering or by developing new rules in midstream or just by simple dictatorial domination.

Dale whom Donnie loved, and respected, and idolized, and envied, and feared.

And hated.

Dale.

He could not remember now precisely what had gone wrong that day. He *could*, however, remember the important parts—the two of them playing well together, wading across the river like true scouts from the John Wayne school, racing through the wilderness, and then later, finally, standing on the crest of the far slope, above the sharp rock wall and the water, screaming at each other.

"Your fault!" he yelled at Dale. "You always ruin it! You always mess things up!"

Dale only smiled, that infuriating smile that was an unmistakable feature of the patented Dale Stewart up-your-ass-kid-I'm-better-than-you expression. He reached down and gave Donnie a condescending pat on the head.

"Poor, misguided, demented little brat."

"But you cheated! We had rules, pus bag! You're a creep, you know it? You're a snot-faced, nose-picking creep! I hope you die! I hope you rot! I hope you—"

Dale reached out with a lightning-stroke hand and slapped him across the face. His head rocked back and came forward sharply. His chin struck his chest. He began to cry.

"I'm gonna tell Dad! You hit me! I'm gonna tell on you!"

"Be my guest, brat. Dad won't do anything to me. Jesus, you *know* that. He'll blame it on you. He'll say it was your fault. So go on, I'd like to see it. Run and cry to him, blow your nose all over his shirt. We'll see what happens. Go on."

And that was when the weakening thread of Donnie's self-control snapped. It might have been the prosaic fact that yet another enjoyable game had been spoiled. Perhaps the humidity was working its dark, heavy magic on him. Most likely, it was the unavoidable realization that every single word Dale had just said was true. He didn't know. He was beyond reasoning then, didn't stop to question why, and later he could never be quite sure. The thread stretched . . . and stretched . . . and snapped. That was the only thing that really mattered.

He bent down and dragged a hand across the rocky hillside, coming back up with his fingers curled around a sharp and jagged stone that was roughly the size of the grapefruit their father favored for breakfast. Dale stared at the stone as though it were a cheap toy. He began to laugh. The laugh had a taunting, frustrating ring to it, a horrible touch of mockery, an air of irrepressible snottiness.

"You cheated!" Donnie's voice was high and hoarse and bitterly triumphant as he pronounced that verdict.

And then it was time for the sentencing.

He raised the rock and with one smooth motion leapt at his older brother. Dale's eyes grew suddenly wide, comically startled. It was an expression Donnie cherished—but the moment was dreadfully short.

The rock in his hand came down. Hard. Oh Jesus, oh God, there was no denying that it came down hard.

Dale's comical eyes rolled up in his head, the lids snapping shut like shades on a roller. And then he was gone, slumping, leaning, teetering, and tumbling down the rocky hillside, body crashing through the brambles like a sack filled with dead, very heavy weight.

Donnie stared in dawning horror as his brother's body reached the bottom of the hill and the lip of the rock wall. It seemed to pause there for a heartbeat, but then it took flight, soaring up and out . . . up . . . and out.

It was that moment more than any other he would never forget—Dale in the air for an impossibly long time, completely limp, utterly out of control, sailing up and out . . . and then dropping.

He hit the river with a mighty splash.

Donnie screamed, "DAAAAAAAAAAAAALLE!" and took off down the side of the ravine, stumbling and sliding, scrabbling for handholds and footholds, almost out of control himself. His brother's name broke out of his throat over and over, becoming one long, uninterrupted syllable, a wailing siren of pure panic.

He reached the rock wall and peered down, but Dale was not in sight. Running parallel to the rushing water, he came to their well-worn footpath, the one that bypassed the wall and zigzagged down a shallower embankment until it reached the shore. He raced down it, falling repeatedly, skinning his hands and knees, bloodying his nose, heedless of everything but getting to the river in time. He hit bottom and charged headlong into the water.

"Dale!" he cried again. "*DALE!*"

He struggled against the current and waded back to shore, then ran frantically up and down the bank like a frightened rabbit searching for a way across. His eyes darted left and right, searching, scanning. His older brother was nowhere. There was nothing there but an old log being churned downstream. There was just that, the log, swept along in the endless, furious flow.

The log.

The flow.

The tremendous rushing noise in Donnie's ears.

The empty river and his own bald panic.

After an unknowable time he forded across and ran for the cabin, ran screaming for his father to tell him there had been a terrible accident. They had been playing atop the far side of the ravine and somehow Dale had lost his balance. One slip and Dale was gone.

The underbrush flogged and flayed him as he charged homeward, but he ignored everything, kept running, kept screaming.

Oh Christ, he ran screaming . . .

Stewart blinked and stared at the trickling river and the rock wall behind. For a second there he had seen it all again, that picture of his older brother's body suspended in the air, then dropping, crashing into the water and vanishing from sight forever.

He shuddered.

There had been many volunteers from the Falls and the neighboring town of Kelly's Corners. They had searched the ravine and surrounding woods for days. (Twenty days? It might have been that long, perhaps even longer.) They had dragged the river all the way to the county line and beyond. No body had been found.

They were told to blame it on the current. The current could carry something for weeks and weeks, miles and miles. The current could trap an object against an underwater obstruction and pin it there until it decomposed. The current was a powerful, usually unbeatable force, especially when there had been such a rainy spring and the water on this branch of the Little Spruce River was so high, so wickedly swift.

No body had been found.

That had been their last summer at the cabin. His father, barely recovered from the natural death of his wife two years before, could no longer cope with the summer place. The cabin had been locked, the yard left to go wild, the woodlot left to grow and die and slowly rot.

Stewart turned away, suddenly wishing he had never taken the key from the lawyer and yet knowing that, all the same, it made no difference. The memory was there anyway. It always was. Unacknowledged, it waited. Patiently it lingered. And in weak moments of drink or exhaustion or sleep or just plain boredom, it pounced— that stark mind-picture of Dale in the air.

He took a step in the direction of the cabin but hesitated almost immediately. There was something up ahead, at the verge of the trees. Somebody, staring at him.

This time there was no mistake.

"Dale," he breathed.

The trees rustled. The somebody turned away.

"Dale, Jesus, don't run! Don't go—"

But he stopped himself, because he was getting carried away again. Call it a guilt fantasy. Call it a mind ghost created by the long-buried, long-hidden, long-unadmitted, long-kept-inside. Whatever the case, it hadn't been Dale, any more than the thing outside the cabin had been. Oh, it had his brother's face, but that face was pale and broken, lumpish, freakishly grotesque. It was his brother's size, but the body was bent and twisted, cruelly deformed. And forty years had gone by . . . yes . . . his brother had been dead for almost forty years.

But there was something else that silenced him, too, that kept him from giving chase. It was the sound the thing had made, that weak, whimpering noise it had uttered as it turned away, like an old dog that was very, very sick, like something ancient and weary, drowning in despair.

He stood there, hugging himself but unaware that he was doing so, listening to its hasty retreat, catching glimpses of its white and naked form scrambling away through the brush.

There were glimpses of something else, as well, glimpses of the wild forest animals that scuttled along after the creature. It was a virtual parade of squirrels and rabbits, foxes and woodchucks and coyotes, waddling porcupines, wriggling badgers—fifteen or twenty wild things in all, following the leader.

Stewart groaned.

Then the thing was gone; the thing and its followers had vanished.

He stood there, catching his breath, dying inside, and finally left the ravine as quickly as he could.

He was almost running.

That afternoon he walked the three miles to the highway and hitched a ride into town. He returned several hours later with three purchases: more beer, a cheap plastic lawn chair from the Ben Franklin, and a shotgun with birdshot from one of the local sporting goods stores. As evening fell he took the chair and the beer and the shotgun out into the backyard and planted himself in the middle of the grassy sea, midway between the cabin and the rim of the ravine. He drank beer, watched the sun go down, kept the weapon across his lap, and waited.

Night came, the moon rose, yet he saw and heard nothing. He wasn't deterred. Despite the beer coursing through his system, he felt sharply and wildly alert. He knew what he had to do. For his own good, his own safety, his own protection, his own sanity, he had to get the thing that was trying to fool him, trying to con him into believing it was his brother. You betcha, he thought. You've got to get that liar, that trickster, that false sibling. That's the answer.

He waited.

It came at last, one hour past midnight.

He heard it first, grappling up the slope, coming through the brambles. He straightened, every muscle and shred of tendon in his body stiffly complaining.

It finally appeared—a moonish face peering at him over the edge.

He raised the shotgun.

"C'mon out!" he called.

The face didn't move.

"Hey, now! Come out where I can see you! Your game's over!"

Something in the face seemed to twitch slightly.

Stewart's hands twitched on the shotgun.

And then the thing spoke to him, saying just a handful of indecipherable word-sounds in a voice that was thick and crusty, dirty and old, gravel-filled.

Stewart gulped and choked. The shotgun slipped from his grasp and fell to the ground, clanking against a half-full beer can and overturning it. His hands opened and closed, as though trying to wrap around the weapon he no longer held. He never bent to retrieve it. His eyes never left the white and gleaming face.

The thing gargled out something else. Stewart felt his chest constrict around a heart that was on fire with rushing blood and raging emotion.

"Dale," he whispered.

The thing was silent, staring at him.

"Dale, oh God, I don't . . . I mean I never—"

The thing's hands suddenly appeared from below the rim, ghostly claws darting forward and back so quickly that Stewart thought he must have imagined the movement. There was something lying at the edge of the grass now, something the thing had put there for him, although he could not tell what it was.

"Dale—"

The thing grunted and turned to go.

"No, wait! Dale . . . please . . . you've got to listen to me."

The thing hesitated.

"Jesus . . . aw, Jesus, Dale, it's been so long since I could talk to somebody about this. I never . . . actually, I never talked to anyone. I've never been *able* to talk to anyone. How *could* I? And you . . . oh, Dale. I didn't mean to . . . I never meant to—"

The thing cocked its head slightly to one side, listening as though it didn't understand the words, *couldn't* understand them. Stewart groped for something else, some way to bridge the gulf between them. He thought he saw (hoped he saw, *prayed* he saw) the creature's eyes sparkling in the moonlight, a single bright drop highlighted on its misshapen cheek.

His own eyes filled with tears.

This time when the thing turned its back to him, it vanished quickly, dropping out of sight as though it had never existed at all. Stewart held his breath, distantly aware of that now familiar sound, those clumsy, blundering movements fading in the distance.

His mouth opened. No sound came out.

When the night was silent once more, he rose from the chair and walked slowly over to the ravine, stooping to retrieve whatever the thing had left there for him. His hands touched it and he felt a sharp jolt.

A photograph. An old black and white picture.

For a moment he thought it was the same photo he'd found when he'd arrived at the cabin, somehow, impossibly, risen phoenix-like from the ashes. He quaked with equal parts sorrow and terror before realizing that it was not the same picture at all. Close. The same subject. The same year. But not the same photograph. This one was faded, crusted with dirt, parts of it torn or eaten away by time and dampness and, he thought, the touch of malformed hands that had taken it out often for study and remembrance.

"Oh God, Dale," he breathed to the silent night and dark ravine. "Dale, believe me, I'm so sorry . . ."

But it was not enough.

At five minutes past sunrise Stewart walked again to the edge of the ravine. He was freshly showered and shaved, dressed in the last change of clean clothes he had brought with him. A hundred yards behind, the cabin that had once belonged to his father and now belonged to him was engulfed in hungry, greedy flames. The sky above was choked with clouds of smoke. It would bring people from town eventually, he supposed, but by that time it would be over. The cabin would be gone and all the memories would be dead.

He looked down and saw them waiting for him, his escort, the small cluster of forest animals. They seemed possessed of perfect patience, complete and utter calm. He smiled at them, a pure expression of acceptance and peaceful satisfaction.

It was time, that voice had said to him. *He had hidden for too long. He had stayed away. He had kept the truth inside, denying it. He had let their father die without knowing. He had let the world go on without hearing. Forty years. Four decades. Two score. Too long. He was overdue, so very long overdue, but now it was time. All secrets must be confronted. All truths must be spoken. All debts must be paid.*

That's what his brother had said to him, and of course he had really said none of those things, or if he had, they had been spoken in a dead language, in words beyond Stewart's comprehension. But still he had heard them, and he had somehow translated them in his heart. He had understood.

The memories will be dead. The debt must be paid.

He looked to his right, toward an ancient, gnarled maple that grew at the edge of the hillside. There, high up the trunk, he had spiked a certain photograph on a bent and rusty nail. It was the photograph that he remembered Dale carrying with him everywhere in the pocket of his jeans—two boys, brothers, grinning brightly at the camera, the cabin in the background, and beyond that, two upright poles crossed with a willow branch above a pile of ancient mattresses.

The photograph, beyond the reach of the flames, fluttered in the breeze. The maple leaves rustled their secret messages around it.

For one last time Stewart saw a picture of Dale in the air—but not as he had been on that final day. Oh, no. This was a picture of Dale as he *should* be, Dale on the day they had high-jumped in the side yard. Dale soaring upward, almost flying, his back arched and his smile eternal, unbeatably dazzling, a thing of the gods.

Dale.

Reaching for the sky.

They were perfect, the memory and the remembering.

All debts must be paid.

A moment later he started down into the ravine.

TAKING CARE OF MICHAEL

J. L. Comeau

The "J" in J. L. Comeau stands for Judy. She is a newer writer from Falls Church, Virginia whose short stories have appeared in many small press magazines. She writes in a clear voice with a relentless eye for the grimmest details. "Taking Care of Michael" is another take on the whole sibling rivalry theme. It is also one of those stories that creeps up on you and takes a bite before you even realize you've been violated.

Michael's ear falls into the bathwater with a loud plunk and I have to remember not to scrub so hard when I wash him. Momma would've had a fit before she got so quiet, but Michael doesn't seem to mind. I blow a sweaty strand of hair away from my forehead and fish around the bottom of the tub with one hand for the lost part. I need my other hand to hold on to Michael. Wouldn't want him to fall under the water, too! I find his ear soon enough and stick it back onto the hole in the side of his head where it came from, but it keeps sliding off back into the water. Finally, I give up and lift Michael into his roller chair where I wipe him dry real good with a big fluffy towel nice and hot from the clothes dryer.

Just think what Momma would say about that ear! She thinks I never do anything right. Michael, he was always the smart one. He made good grades in school and always had lots of friends. Popular, you know? And Michael was always good to me, too, sticking up for me when the other kids laughed at me or called me ugly names and ran away. One time, the kids left me out in the woods holding an empty pillowcase. They said they were going to fan out and drive some kind of animals called "snipes" toward me so I could catch them in the pillowcase. I was real happy that the kids let me play with them and I waited and waited, but the snipes never came and neither did the kids. I found out later that they all laughed and went home. I don't see what was so funny, do you?

Anyway, Michael came into the woods the next day and found me still holding the pillowcase and waiting. He never said a word about the way I'd peed and messed my pants. That's Michael for you. A real prince of a young man, like Momma always used to say.

One day Momma came in my room crying and told me Michael crashed his little red car and was hurt real bad; broke his neck, she said. When they brought him home from the hospital, Michael was in a chair with wheels and couldn't move his arms or legs or talk or anything. He could move his mouth a little, and his eyes, that's all. So Momma took care of Michael, feeding him and bathing him and shaving him and everything. It's too bad about Michael, Momma said all the time. We've got to take care of your brother now.

But then a couple of weeks ago, Momma never got up from the couch after watching *Jeopardy*. She's still there in the front room, sitting on the sofa in front of the television set. She watches the television all day and all night, even when there's nothing on but fuzz and static. Momma never blinks, even though her eyeballs got all dried and crusty. I guess she just got tired from taking care of Michael all the time.

I don't mind taking care of Michael while Momma rests. He's my brother and I'd do anything for him. He's always been good to me and now it's my turn to be good to him.

I'm going to shave Michael's face now. Momma always said she hated whiskers on a man, even before we took Daddy out to the big green park with trees and rocks and buried him in a long box in the ground. I like the sound Daddy's straight razor makes on the leather strop hooked to the bathroom wall. *Whop, whop, whop,* it goes. It doesn't take long until the blade's sharp enough to split a long black hair I pull out of my own head.

I turn to Michael with a smile, but Michael doesn't smile back because I accidentally slipped and cut off his lips the last time I shaved his face. But I can tell by the way his eyes roll around that he's ready for Daddy's big, sharp razor. This time I'll try not to slice off anything by mistake.

Like Momma always says, "Practice makes perfect." And I'm getting better all the time.

THE ATONEMENT

Richard Rains

From Fort Worth, Texas we get a story written in the style and mood of Rod Serling—in fact as I read "The Atonement" I kept thinking old Mr. Zone himself would have loved this story. Its author, Richard Rains, has sold his work to several Texas newspapers and magazines, co-edited a cookbook, and (by dint of a Cavalier *fiction contest) co-authored with Stephen King one of three published versions of "The Cat From Hell." Although more traditional than the usual* Borderlands *tale, this story made the cut because of its keen attention to detail, crisp sensory images, and seamless narrative.*

It was already snowing when Vogel stepped out of the post office and into the raw, unrelenting winter that had come unseasonably early to Mannheim. As he reached out to close the steel-plated service door, a sudden gust of icy wind swept through the alleyway, slamming it shut for him. He checked to make sure that the door was secure; satisfied that it was, he pushed his wire-rimmed glasses firmly against his nose and pulled the collar of his overcoat snugly about his neck. Clenching and unclenching his gloved hands in an effort to loosen the stiffened joints, he walked down the alleyway and into the street.

He had worked a long day, several hours extra, and now only primal thoughts occupied his mind: he wanted warmth, companionship, shelter; he wanted surcease from the arthritic pain that he suffered. With a refilled prescription, some schnapps with friends at his favorite bar, the company of a whore, perhaps, followed by a good night's sleep, Vogel's immediate needs would be satisfied.

When he came upon The Apothecary, the only drug shop in his neighborhood that kept late hours, he instinctively turned the doorknob. Locked. Puzzled, Vogel peered through the plate glass window. Only a single pale light burned at the back of the store. He looked around the room until noticing the clock above the prescription counter. 19:40. Glancing at his wristwatch, he verified that the time was accurate.

Vogel knew that something was wrong. The drug shop never closed before 21:00. He tried the door again. Still locked. Then he noticed the calendar hanging on the wall. Today's date had been circled in red. Then it struck him: today was Yom Kippur, the most sacred of Hebrew holy days.

Yom Kippur, the Day of Atonement. Vogel laughed to himself. What do these goddamn Jews feel they have to atone for? For being themselves? For being who and what they are, what they always will be?

Vogel shook his head at the inanity of it all, slid his aching hands back into his pockets, and walked on. As he walked, a thought insinuated itself into his mind. A thought which had recurred often of late. Death. He thought of death. It had been seven years since he had brought death to anyone. Seven years since anyone had died as a result of his . . . ministrations. His curiosities. Seven years, too, of living under a name not his own, of living a life that he detested, in a world not of his choosing, while so many of his comrades were discovered, tried, and unjustly punished.

Seven years. Without death.

The death of a Jew.

Ein underer tote Jude.

Another dead Jew.

That was what Vogel sought after all of these impotent, frustrating years: another dead Jew. That was the thought that oozed, worm-like, through his mind, that bloomed darkly within him like a blood-red flower.

Death: he could almost taste its bitter, ashen blossom on his tongue.

Hurriedly, Vogel walked on . . .

As the minutes passed, the chill reality of snow, of bitter-cold wind, of frozen bricks beneath his shoes reestablished itself in his mind.

Soon he rounded a corner onto Müllenstrasse, where he could see, through the falling snow, the lights of *Das Alta Bierhaus*, a half-block down. Cheers, laughter, and the boisterous melody of a polka echoed toward him, urging him on, urging him to join his friends—Hans, Jurgen, Dietrich, Karl-Georg. They would all be there by now for their nightly fellowship. But theirs was more than a mere gathering of cronies for the purpose of eating and drinking and singing themselves into a stupor. Theirs was a meeting of true comrades. Men who shared the same past, loathed the same present, and were working diligently and in secret—like thousands of others like them—to create the same perfect, orderly future.

Vogel continued on . . .

As he was about to enter the bar, he saw the woman.

She was standing across the street, leaning against the side of a building, her blonde hair and white gloves stark, even in the falling snow, against her dark fur coat. She was smoking a cigarette; and she was watching him.

Vogel studied her. He was waiting for the whore's signal: a lingering look, an averting of the eyes, a return look of confirmation. When he got it, a smile of recognition formed on his lips. His heart fluttering in anticipation, he approached her.

She was tall and slim, and a plumed hat tilted stylishly across the side of her face, a strikingly beautiful face framed by flowing ash-blonde hair.

Vogel looked into her eyes: they were light blue, almost gray, and they stared back at him without blinking. The eyes of a professional: cool and indifferent, adept at sizing up a potential customer.

This one has class, Vogel thought. In the days of triumph, during the war, she might well have commanded a luxury suite at the Hotel Anderberg in Berlin, servicing an exclusive clientele of high-ranking military personnel, industrialists and bankers. Perhaps even *Der Führer* himself. Now, in these wretched times, she was reduced to selling herself in the street like a common prostitute. Or so Vogel imagined . . .

As the whore brushed back an errant lock of hair from the side of her face, Vogel looked at the white gloves that she wore: gloves that only a lady of substance or a first-class prostitute could afford; gloves filled with hands that were narrow and fine-boned, fingers that were long and tapering and steady.

The fur coat and the white gloves.

The blonde hair and the cool blue eyes.

Vogel felt himself becoming aroused.

The whore lifted the cigarette to her lips, drawing off it slowly, self-assuredly; then she exhaled a deliberate, lazy stream of smoke out into the cold snowy air.

Vogel found himself intrigued by the whore's poise, her aloofness. He felt his knees begin to weaken.

"Well?" she asked.

"Drink?" he said, indicating the bar.

The woman shook her head no.

Vogel looked at her a moment, then said, "How much?"

"Three marks."

Expensive, he thought. Especially in these times when so many things—including sex—were bartered. Vogel remembered once acquiring the services of a whore in exchange for a half-full pack of cigarettes. Three marks was one-fourth of his weekly salary. But Vogel knew the depth of his hunger, and so quickly nodded agreement.

The whore took a final draw from her cigarette and ground it out with the toe of one of her dark, spike-heeled shoes. Then she motioned for Vogel to follow her.

They walked for some time. Through a frozen, deserted park; across the rubbled backlot of a burned-out synagogue; down narrow, darkened streets. The extended walking allowed Vogel's thoughts to shift and refocus:

again he thought of death, of murder. He thought of killing with his own bare hands. Killing a Jew. Such pleasure, he thought. Such exquisite delight!

The woman strode on swiftly, purposefully, always maintaining a steady pace, always a step ahead of him. Vogel knew that she was in control and it made him feel powerless. A feeling he feared and hated, a feeling he would not have tolerated during the war.

But because Vogel wanted and needed what this beautiful and strangely silent woman had to offer, he let himself be let deeper into the maze of unfamiliar streets and alleyways.

Finally, though, deciding that he had been delayed enough, he grabbed the whore's arm, stopping her. "How much farther?" he demanded.

She looked at him with those penetrating blue eyes. Her gaze was steady, controlled.

Vogel had rarely encountered such directness in a woman; it both disconcerted and fascinated him.

"*Sind sie angstig?*" she said.

"No. Of course I'm not frightened," Vogel replied. "I only—"

It was her smile that silenced him; a faint, knowing smile that teased the corners of her mouth.

Vogel had the distinct feeling that something had been stolen from him.

"It's not much farther," she said softly, revealing a trace of tenderness.

Vogel watched her for a moment: so difficult to break away from her gaze, from those enticing blue eyes.

Then he nodded and they walked on.

Some of the areas they passed through had been rebuilt, though many still lay in disrepair. Financed by the Americans, the rebuilding helped to create the so-called German Federal Republic—risen from the ashes of the old. But the Americans were fools, Vogel thought. They were helping us back onto our feet—and that was their mistake. For soon we would rule again, and for the next thousand years . . .

Finally they came to the mouth of a dark alley, between

two buildings. The whore walked in, motioned for him to follow, but Vogel was unable to move. Muscles tensed, he stared into the darkness. A sudden intuitive fear of entrapment told him not to enter, told him to end this venture now, to turn around and go back.

But Vogel did not believe in intuition; he was a practical man who believed only in what he could see, what was real. So when the whore stepped from the mouth of the alley and walked up to him, peering deeply into his eyes and touching his cheek gently, so gently, with her white-gloved fingers, and said to him, "Don't you want me?"—Vogel felt his heart flutter and, ignoring his intuition, followed her into the alley.

Immediately they were shrouded in darkness. Moist, rotting things squished under Vogel's feet; even in the frosty air the stench was nauseating. What must have been sheets from old newspapers and clumps of oily discarded rags reached out like hands to grasp at his ankles. Vogel felt the sweat of fear breaking out on his face and neck, felt his heart hammering in his chest. And yet he continued to follow her, blindly stumbling over the garbage-strewn floor of the alley.

Then he heard a voice. Or thought he did.

A plaintive, mournful voice that seemed to echo toward him from out of the darkness . . .

And then . . . footsteps? Footsteps coming up swiftly behind him?

Vogel felt the first risings of panic. He was too frightened to turn around. He speeded up until he was practically tripping over the whore's spiked heels . . .

Finally, after what seemed like a grueling eternity, he and the whore reached the end of the alley, which was faintly illuminated by a nearby streetlight.

Vogel turned quickly around.

Nothing. Nothing at all.

No one had followed them. It had been only his imagination.

Vogel sighed in relief. Using the back of his glove, he wiped the cold sweat from his brow. Then he looked at the whore, nodding for her to walk on.

Before he could take a single step, though, a hand shot out from the darkness at the edge of the alley, clasping his ankle.

Vogel cried out in horror—

The crack of machine-gun fire rent the air.

Bundled warmly in his heavy officer's coat and hat and gloves, Obermann stood and watched as another line of Jews was swiftly eliminated by the gunnery crews. After being shot, most of the corpses toppled backward into the long, deep trench behind them. The remaining ones, those which fell forward or to the side, were shoved over the edge by kommandos *of prisoner-workers.*

Obermann enjoyed watching this little display; each morning, during his constitutional, before assuming his own special duties, he made a point of stopping here. There were many ways to kill at Strassenberg, and Obermann knew this was one of the most efficient.

A new batch of Jews was being lined up now: sickly, ashen, frail-looking creatures lost within gray pajama-like fatigues. Perhaps two dozen in all: men, women, and a pair of young girls, possibly sisters, who clung to each other in tearful desperation. A few moans were heard, a few cries for mercy issued forth, but most of the prisoners stood there in silence, stoically accepting their fate.

The twin Mausers spit fire.

The prisoners fell.

Again and again, until several hundred had fallen into the trench. Until there were no more. Today's quota had been filled. Tomorrow, like clockwork, the killing would begin again.

Obermann smiled. He walked up to the trench, which was nearly full now, following days of exterminations. The horizon of corpses began only six or seven feet beneath his dark spit-shined boots. Obermann watched as armed guards circled the perimeter of the trench, scanning the bloody, tangled sea of bodies for survivors, and occasionally picking one off. After they had finished, the kommandos *began their task of shovelling the powdered quicklime onto the corpses. The quicklime would commence to eat through the flesh, hair, and organs, all the way down to the skulls and bones, a precaution against plague.*

Obermann stepped all the way up to the edge of the trench, until the toes of his boots were just inching out into the air. Closing his eyes, he drew in a deep breath, feeling the searing tang of quicklime gently tease his nostrils, causing them to prickle pleasurably. Ahh. The smell of death.

Then he felt a strange, sudden pressure on his legs. Startled, he opened his eyes and looked down to see a spindly, skull-faced Jew, dusted with quicklime, with a bloody bullet hole in his side, clutching frantically to his ankles. Recoiling in shock, Obermann tried to move but couldn't: the little, half-dead Jew would not let go. He tried to kick his way free, but the Jew's grip was tenacious: like powerful wiry talons cutting through his boots into his flesh. Obermann bent over to try and break the grip with his hands, but in so doing shifted his center of balance and suddenly found himself pitching head over heels into the trench.

He shrieked in terror.

Landing with a sodden thud, he began to sink down immediately between several corpses. A sickening miasma of urine, feces, and putrefying flesh assailed his nostrils. Quicklime rubbed off on Obermann's face and neck, crept into his nose and ears and mouth, and he imagined it beginning to eat through his skin. He gagged. He screamed again. Suddenly hands were pulling him back to the surface, and then hands were encircling his throat, choking him.

Obermann looked up into the mad, wrathful eyes of the skull-faced Jew.

Then a shot rang out, followed by several more.

Obermann felt the pressure on his throat cease. Suddenly he could breathe again.

The guards pulled him to his feet, then lifted him out of the trench. He was staggered, shaken. They removed his coat and shirt and quickly washed him down with soap and water. They told him that he would be all right, that the quicklime had not had time to do any damage to his skin. And they apologized, profusely.

But Obermann could only stare.

He was staring into the trench.

He was looking at the skull-faced Jew, lying there on his back, limbs splayed, with a bloody, fist-sized hole in his forehead. The Jew appeared to be looking back at Obermann, the incandescent madness in his eyes only faintly diminished by death's embrace.

And he was smiling. Yes, smiling.

Obermann could feel it start then, at the back of his mind. Could feel it building, growing, moving forward and gathering momentum, like white-hot magma under million-ton pressure, desperate for release; could feel his entire body begin to quake uncontrollably as a force of sheer, primal terror unlike anything he had ever before experienced burned a fiery trail through his mind, causing him to throw back his head and cry out in utter horror—

Vogel cried out in horror.

But the old wino clung to him desperately.

"*Bitte, Mein Herr!*" he pleaded. "Please . . . a few coins . . . I'm a good Catholic!"

Vogel struggled furiously with the man, dragging him halfway into the street before finally breaking his grip.

The pathetic old bum lay there on his side, sobbing.

His heart racing, his breath coming in painful, convulsive gulps, Vogel tried to steady himself. He was still rattled by the memory of the skull-faced Jew. The image of that deathly apparition . . . and all that choking sulfurous quicklime . . . sent a chill through him.

Vogel turned to look at the whore. She stared back at him coldly, silently, her face an unreadable mask. Vogel tried to peer behind that mask, tried to grasp something of this strangely private woman's essence. Yet he found nothing, sensed nothing, understood nothing at all.

Vogel looked back down at the wino, at the wasted scarecrow of what was once a man, possibly a good man, a good German, before those filthy Russian beasts stormed in, with the sanctimonious, Jew-loving Americans in their wake.

"*Bitte . . . helfen sie mir . . .*" the old bum pleaded. *Please . . . help me.* The cry of thousands—millions—of Vogel's countrymen. Displaced, homeless, hungry, and sick, they wandered the cities and the countryside from Munich to Hamburg in search of themselves, their lost identities, and their lost Fatherland.

We will give them back their Fatherland, Vogel thought determinedly. We will give them back their pride, their hope, their dignity. The Plan shall succeed. The Will shall triumph. The Great German Nation shall rise again in glory!

Vogel reached under his topcoat, withdrew a mark from his wallet, and shoved the bill into the wino's decrepit, outstretched hand. Then he look at the whore. "Now," he ordered her. "Go!"

For the first time the woman truly smiled at him.

After a short while they entered a residential district unknown to Vogel. None of the street names were familiar to him. He thought they had been moving to the northeast, but he couldn't be sure. With his naturally poor sense of direction, Vogel had long since lost track of where he was.

Snow fell heavily now and it seemed to have grown colder, grayer as the night deepened. Vogel shivered as he felt the chill seeping into his bones. His arthritic hands felt stiff and cold: he rubbed them, flexed them, trying to keep them warm and loose, but to little avail.

Tired and aching, Vogel felt himself nearing the end of his patience. Despite how beautiful, how sensuously intriguing the whore was, he was ready now to simply fuck the bitch and be done with it. Then he could return to his friends at the beer house. Provided, of course, he could find his way back—

"Stop!" he commanded.

The whore came to an abrupt halt, turning on spiked heels to face him.

"I'm tired of walking," he said. "I want to know where we're going!"

The whore smiled at him and said, "We're here."

They were standing at the edge of a wide courtyard flanked by a pair of brownstone apartment buildings. Four stories tall, with darkened windows—many of which had been broken out, Vogel noted—the buildings appeared to be vacant. At the rear of the courtyard, beyond a small fountain and perhaps thirty yards from where they stood, perched a smaller, three-story building, with walkways on either side leading to an alley in back.

The whore nodded toward the smaller building, then led Vogel into the courtyard. As they walked, Vogel noticed scattered about them, sheathed in a fine covering of snow, the detritus of people's lives: a rusted bicycle lying on its side without any tires; a worm-eaten feather mattress with the stuffing yanked out; three empty bottles of Beck's beer; an old splintered crutch (Where, Vogel wondered in passing, was its mate?); a child's doll with its head and arms torn off.

As they passed by the disused stone fountain Vogel could see a layer of ice at the bottom, embedded in which was a child's plastic ball, crushed and deflated, with a swastika emblazoned on its side.

A moment later they arrived at the front steps of the smaller building. In the snow-covered bushes off to the side lay an old, fat, derelict woman bundled up in what appeared to be several layers of threadbare sweaters. Her skirt was grayish, nondescript; her single-strap shoes were faded and scuffed, and one of the heels was missing. Within her torn stockings her ankles looked thick and swollen. A spoor of whitish, crusted vomit trailed from the side of her mouth and onto the outstretched arm which served as her pillow. Within hand's reach lay an empty bottle of Scheiner's schnapps.

For a moment Vogel thought the woman was dead. But looking closer he saw the faint rising and falling of her chest, and realized that she was still alive.

She is tough, Vogel thought. A survivor. Like the old bum back in the alley. Like all good Germans. Survivors.

The whore touched his arm and Vogel looked up. They ascended the steps and entered the building.

The foyer was poorly lit. A single light fixture, depending from a long wire in the ceiling, provided the only illumination.

Vogel knew the place immediately; he had been here before, many times, with many different women. Not *here*, in this particular apartment building, but in others like it: crumbling old tenements with fallen plaster and cracked paint, scarred by graffiti, reeking of sweat and urine and piled-up garbage. Vogel knew the terrain well. He was at home here.

As he followed the whore up the warped and creaking stairs leading to the second floor, he savored this feeling of *déjà vu*, let it comfort him, and soon he began to relax.

By the time they had come to the whore's room, Vogel felt himself in control of the situation: now *he* would lead and *she* would follow. When she opened the door, he stepped in ahead of her.

The room was sparsely furnished with a bed, a dresser, a chair, a table with a candle on it beside the bed, and a rug on the floor. In the dim light emitted by the unshaded bulb in the ceiling, Vogel could see a door which he assumed led to a closet, and a single window that looked out onto the taller building across from it. Another door opened onto the bathroom.

No pictures graced the walls, he noticed; no potted plants nestled on the windowsill; there were no personal adornments.

The ascetic simplicity of the room confirmed what Vogel had already concluded: the whore did not live here, it was merely the place where she conducted her business.

Smiling assuredly, he took off his coat.

The woman did the same, removing her plumed hat and fluffing up her thick, wavy mass of blonde hair. She wore a blue satin dress, cinched tightly at the waist, with a slit up the side revealing a long, slender thigh.

Vogel found it difficult to take his eyes off her. She was so distant, so self-possessed; so unlike the fawning, drunken sluts he usually picked up. There was about her an almost lunar coldness which infused her beauty with a special magnetism he could not resist.

But Vogel was in control now, and wasn't about to reveal the ache, the need he had for her.

As he removed his shirt, she said to him, "You can wash in there"—pointing to the bathroom.

Vogel nodded. Draping his shirt over a chair, he went into the tiny room, shutting the door behind him. He took off his clothes and started the water in the sink; it grew hot slowly. He found some soap and began washing himself, feeling the warmth spreading through him, feeling himself grow erect. Then, after rinsing and towelling off, he turned and opened the door.

The room was quite still. The overhead light had been turned out, the only illumination the faint glow from the candle on the bedside table.

In the flickering golden light the whore lay on the bed, propped on an elbow, sheet up to her shoulder, watching him.

Vogel lay beside her. He smiled greedily. And pulled her face close to his, moving his mouth roughly against hers. He liked the way she tasted: tart, almost citruslike, leaving a not unpleasant tingling sensation on his tongue. Then he pushed her back and looked at her.

She looked back at him with cold blue eyes.

That same look: challenging, inscrutable, mysterious.

And something else, something Vogel could not quite apprehend, flaring behind the cold.

Her icy composure unsettled him: he felt his confidence begin to falter and feared he was losing control again. In an effort to reassert his dominance he reached out and took her nipple, squeezed it sharply and twisted, watching her lips part in sudden pain. Ah. He smiled at that: still in control. It was going to be easy after all.

Vogel touched her skin: so pale and smooth and flawless. He trailed his fingers over the exquisite architecture of her face: the prominent cheekbones; the taut, angular jawline; the full, sensuous lips and that delicious cleft chin. He felt the firmness of her breasts, the gooseflesh running beneath his fingers. He caressed the rounded softness of her shoulders and ran his fingers down the long slender muscles of her arm . . .

And then the sheet fell away.

Vogel's eyes widened in shock as he stared at the place where her hand should have been.

His mind whirled as he tried to comprehend the polished-steel nub depending from her wrist.

Feeling a sudden spasm of revulsion, he turned away, and as he did, his gaze chanced upon the dresser beside the window. Two white gloves were lying there. One was flat, limp; the other was filled with something—difficult to tell with what, in the dim light. But when Vogel peered closer, he could see the firm outline of an artificial hand, a hint of flesh color at the glove's mouth, and the locking attachment at the wrist.

Now he understood. And was embarrassed for having reacted so childishly to her handicap. Turning to her, he said, "I'm sorry. I didn't realize—"

Her eyes fixed him with a fierce, hypnotic intensity. Her lips contorted into a strange, misshapen smile and Vogel felt a shiver of fear run up his spine. Fear mingled with pure unrestrained lust for this sensuous female enigma.

The woman then sat up on the bed and, beginning at the soft hollow of his throat, ran her forefinger lightly down his chest, through the tangle of salt and pepper hair, over the slightly knobby sternum, teasingly, tantalizingly, all the way down to the still-firm flesh of his belly.

At first Vogel found her touch ticklishly pleasurable, but then, in a sort of curious delayed reaction, he felt his skin begin to grow hot. Uncomfortably hot. Looking down, he saw an ugly red welt rising up where her finger had passed, as if he had been singed by a burning trail of quicklime . . .

Suddenly Vogel looked up at the woman. Her eyes shimmered with hatred. Then, with a surgeon's precision, she calmly inserted the tip of her finger into his navel and pushed it *all the way through* to his stomach.

Vogel shrieked as the sudden explosion of pain racked him, curling him fetally; unbearable, excruciating pain, as if someone had rammed a red-hot poker into his guts. His body trembled convulsively and a wave of nausea swept over him: he could taste bile at the back of his throat. As he clutched himself and felt the warm blood oozing onto his hands, the sharp, piercing pain in his abdomen expanded swiftly outward, searing each cell of his body.

Vogel fought to remain conscious. With great difficulty he half-opened his eyes and through a blur of tears struggled to comprehend the images before him.

The whore was moving slowly, as if through a dark dream, across the room. Lifting her artificial hand off the dresser; reattaching her hand to her wrist . . . grasping her hair . . . blonde hair . . . pulling it loose: dark hair beneath . . . slipping on her dress and shoes . . . then turning and moving toward him again . . .

Vogel looked up, his eyes filled with fear and confusion.

Who was she? *What* was she? Why was this happening to him?

Slowly the woman lowered her left arm to his face. When her artificial hand rested but inches from his eyes, she twisted her arm suddenly inward, forcing him to see the inside of her wrist. Burned into the skin was a blue tattoo. Her concentration camp identification number. As Vogel watched, the tattoo suddenly began to blur, to shimmer, to change and multiply, until there were thousands of tattoos, millions, driven out of the depths of memory by a cold wind from the past . . .

A woman . . . *this* woman . . . men, women, and children . . . prisoners at Strassenberg . . . guinea pigs in Doctor Franz Obermann's experiments . . . Obermann: the Nazis' pioneer researcher in the field of cryogenics . . . the prisoners—their arms and legs and hands—*her* hand—frozen, to study the effects of freezing temperatures on living tissue . . . and the gangrene, the dead and blackened limbs, the amputations . . . the Jews, the Gypsies, the Slavs, the homosexuals, the mentally defective, the politically undesirable, the Jews . . .

The Jews . . .

The Jews . . .

Hundreds. Thousands. Millions. Dead.

Doctor Franz Obermann looked up at the woman, his executioner. There were tears on his cheeks. In the cold blue depths of her eyes he saw sleep, eternal sleep.

In his mind he watched a flower open, a blood-red flower with a bitter bloom . . .

He knew who she was now. *What* she was. She had come to claim him. She, and all the others whom she represented. She was the instrument of his punishment, the witness to his atonement. The darkness that would enshroud him.

The woman moved in close, covering Obermann's mouth with her artificial hand. She spread the first two fingers of her real hand into a broad "V," and brought the tips close to his face. Obermann could feel their heat, could imagine them burning like hot coals through the moist yielding flesh of his eyes, down the optic nerves, to the soft gray jelly of his brain.

She brought them an inch from his eyes—

Then Obermann reared back and punched her hard in the temple.

Stunned, the woman toppled off the bed and onto the floor.

Naked, bleeding from the wound in his stomach, Obermann rolled out of bed and kicked her in the face before she could get up. Feeling a soft crunch under his foot, he knew that her nose was broken.

But the woman refused to quit. She tried to rise again—

This time Obermann kicked her in the chest, just below the sternum.

The woman fell back with a hoarse, rasping moan.

Breathing heavily, trying to stave off the pain ripping through his guts, Obermann looked down at the woman. She was still alive, this Lilith-like apparition, still clinging to life. Obermann fell on her, his hands closing tightly around her throat. The woman struggled against him, but her energy was diminishing, her spirit fading. Obermann could feel it: going, going . . . with her good hand she tried to break his grip, tried to burn him, but the Promethean fire her fingers had once possessed had dissipated, leaving only flickering embers of warmth.

Then her muscles relaxed and a glassy look came into her eyes. Her hand fell away.

Obermann slowly removed his hands from her throat. He drew in a deep breath. Then he found himself opening her dress, gently touching her bare breasts, running his fingers over the pink nipples. He took her hand, admiring it, a lovely slim-fingered hand—deadly, but beautiful . . .

But she was no longer beautiful.

Dead, Obermann thought. *Ein underer tote Jude*.

Another dead Jew.

Exposed. Naked to the world.

Another dead Jew.

In an exquisite moment of pristine clarity it struck him that the past had somehow looped back to join the present, that this woman's death was an extension of—a continuation of—all the other deaths for which Obermann had been responsible. The gnawing hunger within him, the burning desire to kill, to bring death with his own bare hands, had been fulfilled.

And *he* had survived.

He had defeated them all—all of them.

He had defeated Death: brought death *to* Death.

Feeling an exhilarating rush of energy course through his body, Obermann shivered in pleasure. He felt invincible, exalted, triumphant. He felt that he could live forever.

Then he heard something, or thought he did: a haunting strain of music, a gentle distant threnody, which seemed to slip beyond the threshold of his hearing as suddenly as it had begun . . .

Obermann looked down. The woman had begun to dissolve, to grow insubstantial. He was not surprised: it seemed part of the pattern. Though he was a practical man who believed only in what he could see, what was real, what he had *seen* tonight, what he had *experienced* in the flesh, *had been* real, as real as Death incarnate come to claim him.

But now Death, having failed, fled.

The woman grew vague. Her body continued to discorporate, to fade, along with her clothes and her artificial hand.

Then she was gone. The only trace left of her was a fine layer of powdery ash along the hardwood floor.

Obermann became aware again of the pain in his stomach. It was growing worse. It throbbed and burned and he feared that an intestine might have been punctured. If so, fluid rife with fecal matter was leaking out, building up a major infection.

But Obermann knew that if he could get out of this forsaken building and find a telephone, Klarsfeld would come pick him up and take him to his clinic. He could operate tonight, if necessary. With comrade Klarsfeld's help, Obermann knew that he would survive.

He grabbed a pillow from the bed, pulled off the case, and folded it lengthwise, like a large bandage. He let out a brief cry as he secured the cloth tightly around his midsection.

He dressed quickly, stopping now and then to breathe deeply when the pain became too great.

Then he went to the window. From the angle he was at, Obermann could see only the walkway below and the building directly behind it. He could not see the front courtyard, could not see the back alley.

He had to move carefully. It was imperative that he get out of this building without being seen and find a phone. If the police were to pick him up, wounded and wandering through an unfamiliar neighborhood, he might be questioned, his past dug into, his Nazi affiliations discovered, and that could endanger the lives of many others.

As for the woman, she no longer existed. But someone might have seen them enter the building together. Where is she now, the police might ask. Whose blood is on the sheets? What went on up there? What did you do with the body?

No. No. He could never afford such interrogations. He *had* to reach Klarsfeld.

Moving away from the window, he went to the door, opening it enough to stick his head out into the hallway. All was quiet, still. He had reason to believe that the building was deserted, but he couldn't be sure. There might still be a few tenants left, playing out their lonely lives in these wretched, cramped cubbyholes. He had to watch himself.

With his left arm cradled against his stomach, he stepped out into the hallway, shutting the door quietly behind him. Stepping lightly down the hall, he passed by several doors, all of which were closed, with no lights showing beneath them.

So far so good.

After a moment he arrived at the top of the stairs which led down to the ground floor. Slowly he descended, occasionally glancing back to make sure that no one had seen him. When he reached the bottom of the stairs the final step cracked loudly under his foot, breaking off. Startled, Obermann virtually flung himself against the wall, away from the twin windows that looked out onto the courtyard. The impact jogged his wound, causing him to cry out. But he quickly bit back the pain, silencing himself. He had to take several deep breaths before the pain became manageable again.

Then he looked about, searching for the light switch. After a moment he located it, on the other side of the foyer. Ducking down below the level of the windows, he crouch-walked across the floor, flattening himself against the opposite wall. He reached up and flipped the switch. The light went off.

In the darkness of the foyer he moved to peer out the window. The courtyard was a desolate expanse of purest white. Nothing moved. All was still. Looking up, Obermann saw that it had stopped snowing and widening patches of starlit sky showed through the marblish clouds scudding past.

Obermann was delighted. He felt his pulse quickening, felt his confidence grow with each breath he took.

He clasped the door handle and gently turned it. A muffled click, and the door creaked open. He stepped out onto the landing, again surveying his surroundings. All was motionless, serene.

Obermann smiled.

Inhaling the frosty, invigorating air, he pulled his coat snugly about him and descended the steps to the footpath. The old derelict woman who had been sleeping in the bushes was gone. Obermann decided that she must have roused herself and hobbled off. A survivor: like him.

Obermann limped forward, feeling the snow crunching pleasantly under his shoes, until coming to a stop before the small fountain. The child's ball emblazoned with the swastika was still there, lodged in the ice. He leaned over, wincing from the burning pain in his stomach, and jerked the ball out of the ice.

Then he looked up, to the brilliant starry firmament. Smiling, he hurled the ball into the sky: it went up, up, disappearing among the stars.

Then Obermann turned and walked on, a happy man.

Until the first sound came.

Obermann halted. He looked around.

Silence.

He took another step.

Again came the sound: like wood crashing into wood.

Obermann was suddenly confused, afraid. He didn't know what the sound was or where it was coming from. He didn't know whether to run or to stand stock-still.

He decided to run—

But the *sounds* stopped him. Not *one* this time, but *many*, a staccato arrhythmic cacophony of sounds, hammering at him, hammering at his mind like machine-gun fire, forcing him to put his hands to his ears in an effort to blot out the sound—and then he looked up and saw the windows, windows from the twin buildings overlooking the courtyard, windows being flung open—*they* were the source of the sound—and the glass shattering, shattering like a trillion coruscating shards filling the night, a night of broken glass—and the lights suddenly blazing in the windows, all of the windows, blazing with a solar intensity, illuminating the snowy courtyard below with a clear implacable radiance—

And then silence.

Sudden. Abrupt. Silence.

Obermann crouched there in the snow, quaking, terrified, shielding his eyes from the merciless light. Peering fearfully between his fingers, he looked up to see people standing at each of the broken-out windows—sick, ashen-looking people—behind rows and rows of windows, an impossible succession of windows extending to infinity . . .

They were watching him. All of them. Men, women, and children.

Watching, witnessing, judging.

Obermann felt exposed, revealed. Naked to the world.

Then the people began to mutilate themselves. They tore off hunks of their own bodies—arms, legs, hands—and began tossing them down at him. Obermann was horrified. He tried to run, but he slipped on the moist gray body parts. He tried to get up, but the parts kept falling, driving him to the ground, weighing him down.

Then Obermann watched in disbelief as the buildings flanking the courtyard appeared to grow upward, to extend themselves into the sky. But then he realized that it was not the buildings that were thrusting up, but *he* who was sinking down.

He was in the trench again, trapped in a tangle of body parts, inhaling the fetid stink of putrefying flesh, of urine, feces, vomit. His skin began to burn, terribly, his face and eyes and mouth scorched by the acidic quicklime shoveled down on him from above.

Obermann cried out in horror as the trench sank down into the darkness of the earth. And the last thing he saw, looking up, was the skull-faced Jew with the hole in his head, looking down.

Looking down at Obermann. And laughing triumphantly.

PEACEMAKER

Charles L. Grant

Speaking of traditionalist (we were, weren't we?), perhaps the most popular of my generation is Charles L. Grant. A prolific author with more stories and novels than I can keep up with, Charlie was also the editor of the venerable anthology series Shadows, *which served as the launching pad for many new writers in the Eighties. To say he has been a serious influence upon the literature of dark fantasy over the last twenty years is a cruel understatement. Some would say he has sustained an entire sub-genre which he has termed "quiet horror." I've known Charlie during the majority of his career and we've had more than one barroom discussion about style and substance and the direction of the HDF genre, and we often disagree on what is good and what is not (and we've rejected plenty of each other's stories—just in case you were starting to think this is some nepotistic club we've got here), but I think Charlie has stepped out of his usual mode with his latest* Borderlands *story. For me, it resonates with a lot of Shirley Jackson's best short fiction. But enough already. Check out "Peacemaker" for yourself.*

In the darklight; a moment in late October between dusk and night, when the birds aren't quite sleeping and the wind has stopped blowing and the edges of the shadows don't blend with the black; when the houses are caves and the windows reflect nothing and the streetlamps are hazed by a colorless mist; when perspective is missing and all roads lead to nothing, when the silence is complete and nothing breathes, nothing moves.

In the darklight, before midnight, the air touched with ice.

And he sat on the porch, in an old wooden rocker, his hands resting lightly on the flat of his thighs. The old sheepskin jacket granted protection from the chill, and on his head an old western hat, its brim and crown time-worn to a shape that would have seemed ludicrous on another, rain-stained and snow-pocked and darker than its color; on his feet, western boots that a shine would only ruin.

Behind him, in the house, he could hear the furnace kicking on. The foyer clock chiming. A board creaking.

In the yard a nightbird chirped, a rustling, and nothing.

Immediately to his left, on the corner, the streetlamp dropped a stage of faded white onto the pavement, and he watched it for signs of shadow, for signs of shape, and his left hand drummed his leg while his right hand curled as if lightly gripping the air.

He knew what it was, had known it was coming, had been waiting for it ever since the sun had gone down— it was excitement. The faraway and getting closer kind that didn't prod action, only prodded the senses. The sound of unseen horsemen, the chuff of a tired locomotive slowing for a mountain curve, the lazy crack of a harmless whip over the heads of buckboard horses.

He puffed his cheeks, he blew a breath, he glanced at a dark form beneath the yard's black oak branches.

One more time, he thought then, less a prayer than a command; one more time before I get too old to count.

He shifted. With a tightening of his lips to anticipate pain, and cursing the twinge that stiffened his calves, he lifted his legs until his boots were on the railing and he could see between his feet across the street to Grandy's house. The downstairs lights were on, and a spotlight hidden in the grass that was aimed at the front door, pinning a cob of dried maize to the white-curtained pane. On either side of the steps were jack-o'-lanterns Grandy carved himself every year, and in each of the windows were cardboard witches and black cats and full orange moons with comic scowling faces.

The air drifted, wind coming.

Still watching the house, he allowed himself a brief smile for the nights when Grandy would grumble about the kids roving the street, about their vandalism, their lack of respect, their general cussed attitude for things that ought not to be mocked, ought to be remembered, ought to be revered. Yet every year, every holiday, the window invitations were dragged out of his closet, taped up, and accepted.

But he never asked Rusty for the once-a-year favor.

Unlike the others, Grandy still had a hope.

Far down the street the brittle sound of voices—young voices laughing and giggling and calling. A door slamming. A car starting. Tires slowly crunching dead leaves and acorns. He glanced down at the floor to be sure the canvas sack was still there, let his left hand swing down to touch it, to be sure his eyes hadn't lied.

Shadows then on the sidewalk, and low voices, one wondering about the dark house, the other saying, "Hush!"

He shifted his attention to a hunched shape paused at the gate, and to another running up the street, ghost-sheet flapping, a large shopping bag slapping at its legs.

"Evening, Rusty," a man's voice said.

"Evening, Mr. Paretti. Having a good time?"

The man laughed and lifted one hand in a *you know how it is*. "The kid's going to wear me out if he keeps up like this."

Rusty nodded.

"Maybe I'm just getting too old, you know? The kid's got more energy than Oklahoma."

Rusty nodded again. "Know what you mean."

A car backfired in the distance, several times, then just once.

In a sudden rise of wind the man sighed loudly. "And would you believe that just yesterday afternoon I was going to ground him forever because he busted a cellar window and didn't tell me about it? Softball right through it, damn near knocked it off the hinges. I tell you, I don't know how he does it, Rusty. He always picks the days he knows I'm gonna be soft, you know what I mean?"

"I do."

"It's like he reads my mind or something."

Rusty said nothing.

The moon lay silver patterns.

"Well," Paretti said with a half-hearted chuckle, "I suppose I ought to catch up. I'm going to freeze before too long, I think."

"You keep moving, you keep warm."

"Right," the man agreed, and followed his ghost. "You moving tonight yourself?" he called back, voice oddly high.

"Soon enough," Rusty answered softly, knowing he would be heard, and watched the man reach the corner and grab hold of the ghost's shoulders, pull it close for a moment, and shake a gentle warning finger before shooing it onward, across the street to the next well-lit house.

The rocking chair creaked as he smiled and shook his head, creaked again when he brought one of his boots to the floor, then the other, before he put his hands on the railing and pulled himself up in a single heave. A deep breath. A swallow. A slight tug at his hat to pull the brim down.

He stepped away from the rocker, damning the cramp he felt stirring in his left calf. He kicked out and it was gone, but he didn't feel much better. He was getting old. Every year a little older, every year a little slower. The fingers of his right hand brushed over his palm. Again. And again, harder. Until a faint burning cautioned him to stop and he slipped the hand into his pocket and moved to the top of the steps, leaned against the post, and watched the night.

Under the oak perhaps a plume of fog.

Not acknowledging the woman and four youngsters who hurried past the peeling white fence. Not breathing when one of them tugged at her coat and asked in a shrill voice why they didn't stop at Mr. Long's. She didn't answer. But he could see the fearful white of her cheek when she glanced in his direction before rushing on.

Not yet, he told her without moving his lips; not yet, ma'am, not yet. Maybe sometime we'll talk, but it's not your time yet. Have a good evening. We'll meet another year.

The wind steadied as he waited, just enough to ruffle the fall of white over his collar, just enough to tease the weakest leaves off their branches, into the gutter.

A station wagon, lights glaring, radio thumping, parked in front of a house three doors down. He couldn't count how many costumes piled out and raced up the walk, and turned away from them when he saw they were only demons and comic book characters and one in a box painted silver, a robot.

He didn't know them.

He waited.

Someone would come, the evening wasn't done.

There was plenty of time. There had always been time, it seemed, and patience a damning virtue.

Too old.

I'm getting too old, he thought, nearly bitter, not quite resigned, and for the first time that night wondered why he bothered. Nobody cared but those he served, nobody thanked him, nobody gave him gifts or shook his hand. And sooner or later someone was going to take his place. He knew it. As sure as he knew the sun would rise in the morning and he'd have another year to wait, and watch, and listen, and think, someone was going to come along and try to take his place.

Why the hell didn't he just take Grandy's advice? Just a few weeks ago, Vell had said, "Tell you something, Rusty, this damned house is getting too damned big, and I'm getting too damned old for this stuff. I got half a mind to sell it and live in one of them condo things. They got guards there, you know, and elevators. The one I saw, I took a ride over to Harley the other day, it's got a swimming pool I could sit by and watch the ladies go around half naked." He'd shaken his bald head and pulled out his pipe to stare unseeing at the bowl. "Trouble is, I leave it now and those kids'll tear it apart."

Rusty had said nothing, and Grandy Vell reached for the pouch that held his tobacco.

"Maybe," Vell said without looking at him, "someday we'll talk."

"You know where I live."

Grandy only lit a match, and blinked when it blew out.

The wind a bit stronger, the sounds of children more fragile, and he took the steps down slowly, letting his heels crack, letting the spurs sound their warning. His arms were easy at his sides, his fingers slightly curled, and by the time he reached the gate the rhythm was set, senses alert, and it was a smooth and silent motion when he slapped at his leg and whirled, snapping up his hand to point a gun-finger at the porch.

"Bang," he said. And laughed. And made a slight sideways bow to the shape beneath the tree. "Don't lose many, do I?" he said, and laughed again and wondered if maybe he wasn't going crazy.

Someone giggled behind him.

He whirled again effortlessly and said, "Bang!" to Wendy Chambers, easily recognizable behind her burnt-cork hobo's face by the thick glasses she had to wear, and the gleaming braces on her teeth, and the stub of her nose that invited fingers to touch.

"You're funny," she said, one tiny hand clamped to a battered fedora the wind tried to take.

"Just doing my job, little lady," he told her with a grin. "Gotta keep this street safe from the bad guys, y'know. Don't want 'em bothering good folks like you."

"Then shoot my brother," she said, a hateful look over her shoulder. "He won't let me walk with him. He says I'm too little."

Rusty pushed back his hat and leaned on the gate. "What about your momma?"

"She yells a lot, but he still won't listen. She said I should to talk to you. You gonna spank him, Mr. Long?

My daddy used to before he died."

He rubbed his chin thoughtfully, finally nodded, and touched her shoulder. "He ever hit you? Your big brother, I mean, not your daddy."

"Teddy always hits me," she grumbled, one finger pushing her glasses back up her nose. "I don't like him."

He stared at her for a long time, watching the anger in her eyes, and the hurt, and the hope. Then he reached out and touched the tip of a finger to the tip of her nose.

She giggled again, and shivered, but she didn't back away.

"All right," he said. "You tell him I say he has to watch for you tonight, okay? You tell him I said that, or there'll be trouble at the OK Corral."

Wendy frowned. "What's that?"

He almost laughed. "Never mind, little miss. You just tell him what I said."

She puckered her lips in determination, set her chin, and started off. And stopped and looked around. "What if he doesn't?"

"Oh, he will," Rusty promised, and watched her break into a run, shrieking her brother's name as she swept around the corner, dropped her bag, snatched it up, and disappeared. He watched the space she left behind for several long seconds, imagining himself as she had seen him—a cowboy having a shoot-out with his porch, with no gun, and no horse at the fence.

"Jesus," he whispered, and pulled up his collar when the wind found his neck, found the run of his spine, and curled around him like a belt.

He decided then that he wasn't too old at all, he was just not old enough. Born too late to ride the range, be the hero, herd the cattle, play cards and drink raw whiskey and take the painted women upstairs for a slap and a tickle and a release for a dollar; too late to ride shotgun, to ride the Pony Express, to ride the Conestogas across the prairie to the mountains in the always better west.

Just an old man dreaming young man's notions of what it was like to be a god.

He looked up at the sky, at the moon, and wondered what the hell had gotten into him tonight.

His hand jumped on the gate.

Astonishment made him frown.

Afraid?

Good Lord, was he afraid? After all this time, was he scared?

He snorted in disgust, at himself and the idea, and turned back to the porch. Whatever the reason he was moody tonight, he would have to think about it later.

And as he took the steps, cracking heels, sounding spurs, he felt a change in the autumn air—a vague dampness on the wind, a faint smell, a spectral touch on his cheek that made him stop with one hand on the post, one foot still on a step. A sideways look without turning his head, and he saw white shapes and dark shapes hurrying under the trees, veering like schools of startled fish into front yards, onto walks, up on porches where they gathered in ragged crescents, a demon choir.

They were here.

"Hey, anything for Halloween?"

In force at last, they were here.

"Trick or treat," it seemed, had died.

By the way they were moving, and stopping on the pavement to compare prizes and duds, he gave the first bunch fifteen minutes before they reached him. Unless they stopped at Grandy's first, where they'd be invited inside for apple cider or hot chocolate. Usually they went. No one in the Station feared razors in candy and poison in gum; not anymore. And only those in the towns farther east locked their doors at night and had alarms wired to the windows.

"You should go over there and talk to them," Bill Paretti had once suggested. "Maybe they don't know. I mean, we're kind of isolated out here, you know what I mean?"

"They know," he had answered softly, and Paretti never spoke of it again.

He stood on the porch, always alone, and heard the furnace that gave him no warmth, glancing up at the sky and closing his eyes before filling his lungs with air and letting it out slowly.

Too old.

You're going to die.

At last reaching down to pick up the bag, resting it on the railing, dipping in a hand and pulling out a belt he strapped around his waist.

Old man. Stupid old man playing stupid children's games.

Reaching in again and pulling out the gun with the carved ivory grip and the long polished barrel.

He opened the chamber and filled each position, leaving one empty for the hammer to rest on when he closed it and spun it and dropped it into his holster.

Under the black oak, something heavy moved.

Despite the watch of the moon, light snow began to fall, and the silence that followed was ringed by the keening wind. On Grandy's porch a devil saw him and told the others in a whisper; Paretti was on the corner, holding the ghost to his chest; and Wendy was at the fence, her brother behind her.

She was crying.

Her broken glasses clutched in one hand.

And they watched him as he stepped off the porch and took the walk, heels and spurs, opened the gate, patted her on the head, and stepped into the street.

The snow and the silence.

The moon, and the rising wind.

"Mr. Long?" Wendy said, sniffing. "He thinks you're a jerk."

He smiled without mirth and turned toward the sidewalk, watching, not staring, until the hobo moved away and the boy standing beside her arrogantly straightened the bandanna at his throat.

"Old man," the kid said, with more a smirk than a smile. "You don't scare nobody, you know that? You're too damn old."

"Not that old," said Rusty, drew and fired in a single motion, the gun back in its holster before the boy finished dying.

The devil on Grandy's porch cheered; Mr. Paretti clapped his hands.

Wendy looked at her brother lying on his back and shook her head. "He didn't listen," she said. "He never listened at all, you know what I mean?" Then she walked into the street and opened her bag of candy. "You want some gum or something?"

He winked at her. "No thanks, little miss."

Then he walked into the shadow of the oak by the gate, took hold of the reins, and walked his black to the street. And once in the saddle, he looked around and nodded to the voices that sang his name.

"Mr. Long?"

He looked down.

It was Paretti.

"The window. You know, he never even said he was sorry?"

The black began walking, hooves with no echoes.

"Mr. Long?"

"Next year," Rusty told him. "Next year we'll talk."

Into the darklight, the color of blood.

STRESS TEST HR51,
CASE #041068

Transcribed by Stanley Wiater

*Stanley Wiater is probably best-known as the compiler of
some truly wonderful books of interviews he's conducted
with just about all of the best directors and writers of
dark fantasy and horror. (In fact I think he's talked to
just about everybody but me, right Stan?) He is editing
an anthology,* After The Darkness, *which combines his
interview skills with the fictional offerings of his con-
tributors, and he is also writing his own fiction—the
story enclosed herewith being his latest. His conversation is punctuated by a wry sense of humor and a
clever wit. He lives in western Massachusetts with his
wife, Iris, where he is hard at work on several large
projects for Tundra Publishing, and looking forward to
the day he might look as good as me in a tuxedo.*

INTERVIEWER RAYMOND T. JACOBS: You understand that this—test HR51—is the final psychological
test to be completed before any application for a staff
position is ultimately approved.
APPLICANT GINA A. GARCIA: I understand.
JACOBS: You understand that you are expected, as
in previous tests, to give completely honest responses.
Honesty is crucial to the satisfactory completion of this
test. Less than truthful and spontaneous answers will
be detected in the specially designed polygraph chair
you've agreed to sit in. You understand that this procedure is being recorded, and the level of stress in
your voice will later be measured and graded. You are
strongly advised to answer any and all questions within
five seconds.

GARCIA: I understand. [chuckles] This can't be any more nerve-wracking than the previous ones.

JACOBS: Personal opinions are not required. The test now begins. [sound of buttons being pressed] Your name?

GARCIA: Gina Anita Garcia.

JACOBS: Age?

GARCIA: Twenty-eight.

JACOBS: Marital status?

GARCIA: Divorced.

JACOBS: You are fully aware that this is a long-term, psychiatric facility for career officers and operatives associated with the Company. Many, if not all, of the patients you will be dealing with may not readily obey a woman who appears to be in a position of authority. Can you deal with that?

GARCIA: Certainly.

JACOBS: Explain. How will you deal with that?

GARCIA: As I've stated before, having been a police-woman before becoming a nurse for the Veterans Admin-istration, I can protect myself physically. From what I've already been told, I am fully aware of the risks involved in working in a severe trauma facility like this. In any case, I realize how special many of the patients are, why they had to come here.

JACOBS: Physical danger can manifest itself in many ways. Are you prone to debilitating mood-swings when having your period?

GARCIA: [startled] Excuse me?

JACOBS: You have five seconds to answer or the test will be terminated.

GARCIA: No.

JACOBS: No what?

GARCIA: No. No mood swings when I'm having my period.

JACOBS: Remember, these patients will ask you many embarrassing questions. Can you deal with even that minor form of harassment without being so easily shocked?

GARCIA: Yes. Of course. I don't like to be insulted . . .

but yes, I fully realize most of these men may not really know what they're saying. They're sick, that's why they're here. That's why I'm here. Or wish to be. To try and help.

JACOBS: Regardless of their reasons for being here, nearly all of them will still know you're a female. The question is: do you know what most career military men think of women?

GARCIA: I know what they *should* think. But you're asking about military personnel who are here because of major psychological disorders, right?

JACOBS: That is not a reply to the question. Tell me exactly what you're thinking the correct response should be.

GARCIA: I imagine they think we're just sex objects to be found, fondled, fucked, and forgotten. Honest enough?

JACOBS: What is your height?

GARCIA: Five feet, six inches.

JACOBS: Weight?

GARCIA: One hundred and twenty-two pounds.

JACOBS: Do you intend to wear a brassiere when you're on duty?

GARCIA: I . . . of course.

JACOBS: Are you wearing a brassiere now?

GARCIA: Yes . . . of course. I just don't see how—

JACOBS: Personal opinions are not part of this test. What size do you wear?

GARCIA: I don't really—I wear a size 42, D cup.

JACOBS: Ever wear a minimizer?

GARCIA: [slightly angry] No.

JACOBS: What type of brassiere *do* you usually wear?

GARCIA: An underwire, for whatever the hell that's worth.

JACOBS: It's worth something if a patient was able to remove the garment to try and physically restrain or harm you in some way.

GARCIA: Oh. Well, that's . . . different. I guess.

JACOBS: Just answer the questions. Do you buy underwear so that the panties match the brassiere?

GARCIA: Sometimes. I . . . I usually can't find garments that match because of my . . . bust size.

JACOBS: Are you wearing matching underwear now?

GARCIA: I don't know. [pauses] That was the last thing on my mind this morning. Jesus.

JACOBS: Do you ever wear edible underwear on the job?

GARCIA: Fuck, no! [pauses] Excuse me. No, I don't.

JACOBS: If a patient asked you to check or face the threat of possible physical violence, what would be your response?

GARCIA: I would immediately signal for assistance from another caretaker.

JACOBS: What if one wasn't near, and it appeared that a major incident would occur if you didn't respond accordingly to immediately defuse the situation?

GARCIA: Then I would make up a stalling response and do my best to placate that patient until assistance had arrived. [pauses] I realize that physical force is to be avoided whenever possible, though I seriously doubt if they're *all* that obsessed with sex when a woman is on the wards.

JACOBS: I will not remind you again that only satisfactory answers are required to pass this test, not personal opinions. The question remains, would you disrobe if it would possibly prevent a patient from going out of control?

GARCIA: With all due respect, if I took off any of my clothes before a patient, then I don't see how they *wouldn't* go out of control. Your scenario just doesn't make any sense.

JACOBS: Logic is not always a matter of concern in a test such as this. It's a hypothetical situation. Please answer the question as it would pertain to you personally.

GARCIA: No, I would not disrobe. I'd take my chances, right or wrong an answer as that may be.

JACOBS: Next question: if patients discussed their sexual fantasies openly with you, could you deal with such discussions?

GARCIA: I can listen to anybody talk about anything. Obviously.

JACOBS: What if a patient had a fantasy that he was able to impersonate a doctor, and wished to have sex with you as a patient?

GARCIA: I'm sure it's not uncommon for disturbed patients to believe they're doctors and project themselves into that role. And I could deal with that since, from what I've seen, this is a very secure institution, even though the only difference in dress between the staff and the patients are the photo-ID badges.

JACOBS: Would you take off your clothes then for one of the staff?

GARCIA: No. Of course not.

JACOBS: Would you dispense sexual favors if it were to ensure your obtaining this position? Well? Your responses are being recorded and evaluated for speed and directness of reply.

GARCIA: [shaking her head] No way. I've been propositioned by experts, remember? Even when I was a cop, there were always assholes who thought they could do a number on me, in or out of uniform.

JACOBS: So you can take direct verbal abuse, even if it is openly lewd and sexual in nature?

GARCIA: When it goes with the territory, yes, I can. And I think I understand this test a little more clearly now.

JACOBS: Question: if a patient was to tell you that he had been able to appropriate the photo-ID of a staff member, and then pass himself off as that staff member to a person who had never seen him before as a patient, should you have sex with him then to prevent a major crisis in security?

GARCIA: Look, I don't do anything with anybody I don't know or like. I'm neither crazy nor stupid. Unlike these questions.

JACOBS: Question: would you at least get down on your knees and perform an oral sex act upon a man who has in fact succeeded at such a brilliant masquerade, and has also been able to steal a knife from the main kitchen and smuggle it past the present staff of caretakers? And who was ready to use that knife to have his demands met?

GARCIA: [pauses] I can take verbal threats all day. I've got a very long fuse, though I respond better to actions. Like the saying goes, bullshit stinks, but the smell can't hurt you. So keep it coming, if that's the point of all this.

JACOBS: Very good. Now, tell me what this is.

GARCIA: Jesus! What the hell—

JACOBS: You have five seconds to respond or the test will be terminated.

GARCIA: Hey, I'm not blind. It's a knife. It looks like a butter knife . . . but somehow it's been sharpened on the edge. [pauses] How . . . how very interesting.

JACOBS: Just honest answers, please. If you know what's good for you. If you really want this goddamn mind-fuck of a job.

GARCIA: Right! [laughs nervously] I bet some people get pretty stressed out by this point.

JACOBS: [angrily] Just answer the questions. You're well aware that some of our patients can become quite violent in their delusions. That they would go to any lengths to find an outlet for their fantasies. This is a place where not everyone knows the difference.

GARCIA: Excuse me, but what's the question? I just said that I appreciate the point you're trying to make. Everything's cool.

JACOBS: Question: would you agree to be royally fucked by a staff member who might threaten you with this knife if you didn't immediately respond to his advances? Would you let him stick his cock inside every hole in your body if it meant saving your life?

GARCIA: [angrily] Look, this is one hell of a stress test, but I can't see the point of it, not when I know what you're really try—

JACOBS: This is a *crucial* test, Miss Garcia. So please answer the questions until it's completed. You will not be hired if you fail to complete this test. I repeat, *not* hired.

GARCIA: [long pause] I won't lay down for anybody.

Understand? Nobody had better even consider such an idea. My ex-husband learned that, so did the assholes on the force when they thought of me as just boobs and legs. [sighs] With all due respect, this is—

JACOBS: Question: do you know which symbolic metaphor should be employed when a big long knife is jammed up inside a dripping wet pussy?

GARCIA: Look, test or no test, this is complete *bullshit*!

JACOBS: That is not an acceptable response. Like another old saying goes, the patients here may be crazy, but they're not dumb. Or without balls. They get laid, you get paid.

GARCIA: Look, Mr. Jacobs, this has gone far enough. Put down that knife. This isn't funny. [pushes back chair along floor] I mean, Christ! Let me out of this room; this can't be acceptable—

JACOBS: Do you know what *this* is?

GARCIA: Oh, my God . . .

JACOBS: You have less than five seconds. Answer now!

GARCIA: It's your dick, you goddamn pervert. Jesus . . .

JACOBS: Actually, it's my secret weapon. And it's going to split you in two if you don't start giving the right answers, you stupid little ball-busting bitch. Do you know how long it's been?

GARCIA: [shouting] Put down that knife. I don't care if it's part of some crazy test, you don't know know who you're fucking with—

JACOBS: That's the real test, see? To be able to instinctively realize who is crazy and who is not. [chuckles] So where are your instincts now? What will happen next if you don't do as I ask? You have less than five seconds. Answer!

GARCIA: The same thing that got me knocked off the force when I found my old man cheating on me. [laughs] So use it or lose it!

JACOBS: What are you looking for in your purse? How'd you get that in here! My God, *you* are the crazy one! I'll call—

GARCIA: Go shove your test, you asshole! Next thing you'll claim is that this is actually stress test HR52! The one that separates the high-risk security crazies from the just wanna-be crazies! Isn't that what I'm here to prove?

JACOBS: No! [shouts] Don't *you* get it? It's an act! Miss Garcia, I swear this really *is* the way we see if—

GARCIA: —I pass the test! [laughs] Final question is, are these real bullets going through your face or just . . . test blanks? [sound of apparent gunshots, then silence as machine is abruptly disconnected]

STRESS TEST HR5I, CASE #041074

INTERVIEWER GINA A. GARCIA: What would you do if a patient demanded that you go down on him or he would initiate an act of serious physical violence?

APPLICANT GORDON M. WILLIAMS: Well, I'd see if he was just trying to get me angry or he if was really serious. You can't always tell right off. [pauses] Excuse me, are you sure these questions are supposed to mean something other than to try and raise my blood pressure? I mean, you sound pretty off the wall yourself, asking such things.

GARCIA: Your personal opinions are not relevant here. You have five seconds to answer the question satisfactorily or this test will be terminated.

CHURCHES OF DESIRE

Philip Nutman

I know this has nothing to do with the fiction at hand, but if you've seen John Malkovich in the film Dangerous Liaisons, then you've seen Philip Nutman. The resemblance is more than similar—it's frightening. In fact, the only major difference between the actor and the writer is their accents. Born in England, Phil Nutman speaks the language the way the guys doing voice-overs in American television commercials do when they're trying to sell something classy. He moved to the States several years ago and plans to be a permanent resident and become a Yank. After many years as a journalist, Phil started selling his fiction to some of the major anthologies in the field (such as Book of the Dead and this one) and is currently working on several novels. Of "Churches of Desire," I can only prepare you by saying it's a brooding, richly textured tale which turns upon the classic theme of a man's search for identity.

"What the twentieth century needed was eroticism; what it got was pornography . . ."

—Henry Miller

Meredith shivered in his brown leather jacket as he stood before the porno cinema. The wind was rising, the streets devoid of life, yet his body shook not from the chill factor but from a deep, sudden sense of dread. After hours walking the Eternal City's empty thoroughfares in search of a fellow soul with whom he could share a moment of sexual warmth, his journey ended here.

It was once said all roads lead to Rome; all the Roman roads he had travelled in his nocturnal hunt for release seemed to lead here. And as he stood before the building profound desperation pulsed through his tired, alcohol-soaked body. Just looking at the place made him feel sick.

The facade of the Passion Pussycat cinema was an affront to good taste. Green and purple neon mixed to create an emetic spill of light that washed over the marquee to luridly shower the pavement. Its curved front was segmented by electric signs depicting nubile sixties-style go-go dancers with cat ears and tiny tails. There was no indication of what was screening inside.

A newspaper scuttled against his legs making him jump, then performed a dervish dance to the gutter. He ran his hands over the week's growth of stubble that covered his face to massage his tired eyes. He guessed the program would consist of typical Scandinavian, German, and American hetero hardcore, par for the course and boring. But whatever was playing there would at least be some buggery to keep him entertained, although he hoped if there were German movies unspooling, the footage would not be as extreme as one he'd caught in a Parisian theatre.

The loop had started mundanely with a domestic scenario involving a couple, the man going to take a bath. The scene soon turned into a laughable water-sports sequence when the woman rinsed his hair with her urine after he had shampooed it, but this was succeeded by an anal scene with a surgical device that had been clinical in its presentation, almost abstract in its relentless close-up, and even to Meredith's jaded sensibilities, offensive.

He stood hesitantly like a schoolboy on a first date, the promise of a sexual encounter almost unreal after the endless hours he had obsessed over the subject. Yet it was more than nervousness; a primal instinct made his balls contract painfully to the point of groaning. Still, there was no turning back. Not now. Not after the day's hollow promises had faded as breath to the wind. All Rome had to offer was vague hopes of financial gain and a cold, dirty room at the *pensione*. That thought in mind, he walked up the steps to the door and opened it.

. . . and the world of concrete and glass, stone and slate, garbage, and dog shit disappeared, broken by a surging synaptic fracture . . . and what lay before him was in one instant an apocalyptic flash of total destruction, an unrelenting holocaust, a subliminal flash frame instantly replaced by the stronger all-encompassing vision of a Void: black, unforgiving.

He turned from the doorway to vomit his dinner of spaghetti carbonara, several glasses of mediocre *frascati*, on the grime-encrusted steps. He stumbled with a second heave, grabbing the incongruously fake Doric columns of the facade for support, easing himself into a sitting position a few feet away from the puddle of bile. He looked up the street in an attempt to clear his rolling vision. In the distance were two faint figures, one tall and painfully thin, the other short and squat. With the final wave of surreal nausea he wouldn't have been surprised if they turned out to be the Walrus and the Carpenter. A coughing fit disrupted his eyeline, his mind rolling vertiginously, and a distant voice questioned how he had come to this, reached such a state of dissolution.

He knew the answer.

As the telephone rang for the seventh time a sense of hopelesness descended on Meredith like a carrion bird swooping to a corpse in an arid landscape.

Come on! Answer the damn phone!

The tension in his stomach tightened another notch. Since arriving in Rome two days ago he'd been feeling a sense of trepidation so strong he could almost smell it, an aroma that churned his gut and diminished his appetite. Thinking of stomach ulcers, he clutched the call box receiver so tightly his arm trembled, jarring loose a length of ash from his cigarette. His mouth was dry and he badly wanted to take a pull from the bottle of Johnnie Walker in his bag.

The tone buzzed for the eleventh time and he hung up, running a hand through his thick, black hair, pushing back the stray strands from his forehead, then threw the cigarette to the floor. On the opposite side of Via

Paisello trees moved with the early evening breeze. It was 5:45 P.M. He would try Masullo one more time. After he took a quick pull from the bottle.

Where the hell was the producer, or his secretary for that matter? There was no reason why she should be ignoring the phone; he'd called each day at the same time in a frustrating attempt to get Masullo to fix a time for the proposed interview, already rescheduled four times in the past week. With the way things were going, it looked like *Film Comment* wasn't going to get the definitive story of Italian exploitation movies. This was Masullo's chance to gain some mainstream respectability, which, for a producer of over thirty cheap horror movies and soft-core skin flicks, was hard to come by, and Meredith couldn't understand why he was being given the runaround. Still, the producer of such bad-taste gems as *Emanuel and the Satanists, The Sex Crimes of Doctor Crespi*, and pseudo-documentaries like *Savage Africa*, complete with scenes of clitoral circumcision, probably didn't care about anything other than money. Sex, maybe, but Meredith could relate to both areas.

A sharp knock on the glass of the booth cracked him from his reverie. A large woman in a sickly green raincoat was rapid-firing unintelligible Italian through the glass that kept the chill of the Roman night at bay. Her face was a sour rictus, the corners downturned over cheeks the color of dough, like a bloated tragedy mask, and the coat fabric taut over the huge breasts.

Meredith vacated the booth as the woman pushed past him into the cubicle.

"Fuck you," he said with a smile. *On second thought, don't.*

The woman was truly gross. A dried shitty substance stained the back of her coat and legs, and her black hair hung in greasy rat's tails.

As far as he could make out, all Italian women belonged to one of two groups: over twenty-five and overweight, like the whores at the hotel, or under that age and curvaceous. He'd seen one Dachau-thin woman in, he surmised, her late thirties, a walking skeleton who served in the cafe near the station. But she had to be the least attractive woman he had ever laid eyes on, a woman who seemed thinner each time he saw her. Still, the opposite sex wasn't on his list of priorities.

He lit another cigarette while the woman dialed. The brown stain disgusted him. Rome was potentially the dirtiest city he had ever visited, the buildings heavily blackened from the cancer of carbon monoxide. And as soon as he stepped off the airport bus he'd trodden in a sizable turd—human, not animal. *Great*. Dirty. Smelly. Winos in the gutters near the *pensione*, rubbish spilling from the bins by the Villa Borghese. Shit in the Tiber. Meredith had had enough.

He had, however, much more to worry about than shit and magazine articles. More to the point were screenplays and movie deals. If Masullo would agree to read one or two of Meredith's novels he felt certain they could get a deal going. *Film Comment* would have to make do with what he sent them. At least he'd interviewed Dario Argento, Joe D'Amato, and Ruggero Deodato. But he had a lot riding on the idea of selling Masullo the rights to at least *Blood Stunt*, if not *A Killing for Christmas*. Throwaway thrillers deserved to be made into movies by hack producers, and Meredith was under no illusions about art: all he wanted was money. And soon. If he could get Masullo hooked he could be out of debt for the first time in seven years.

A grunting noise made him look up. The green blob vacated the phone booth, bustling past with a florish of body odor. Meredith belched in response as he fished in his pocket for a *getone* and re-entered the cubicle.

The phone buzzed against his right ear.

One . . . two . . . three . . . four . . .

Jesus! Answer the bloody thing!

. . . six . . . seven . . .

A click.

"Pronto?" said a woman's voice.

"Zebrafilm?"

"Yes."

"This is Bruce Meredith. I'm calling again about the interview with Signore Masullo."

"I have bad news, Signore Meredith. Signore Masullo asks me to apologize for not being able to see you this evening, as was suggested. He has to go to Milan for a meeting. But he can see you at 10:30 A.M. Monday."

"What? Oh, I have to return to London this weekend. Is there any chan—"

"In that case, Signore Meredith," the voice interjected, "I'm sorry. Signore Masullo has been very busy. Perhaps you will be in Rome again soon?"

Meredith threw down his cigarette. "No, that's out of the question. The magazine deadline is in two weeks. Would it be possible to see him this weekend—say Saturday?"

Please say yes!

"No, Signore Meredith. That's out of the question. Thank you."

The line went dead.

Bitch!

Monday! Damn Masullo. Damn Rome. Damn the whole shitty country.

He stepped from the booth and stood awhile, worrying his bottom lip before fumbling in his shoulder bag for the bottle. He took a large pull, the Scotch hitting instantly, burning his gut in a fiery rush. Without further thought he began to walk.

A light breeze rustled the trees, which whispered their secrets in return. What could he do? He couldn't really afford to come here in the first place and had only managed to do so by conning his sister out of five hundred quid under the pretense of repairing his car, conveniently neglecting to tell her he'd sold it. He couldn't cancel the return flight, as he didn't have enough to purchase another ticket. If he'd thought the situation through before coming he could have anticipated delays, made provisions for an alternative course of action, but as usual he had done everything in a rush. It was too much to think about, the decision requiring a ruthlessly objective look at his position, so he did the usual; procrastinated for several minutes while he paced up and down, neither thinking or acting, lit another cigarette. He looked vacantly at the trees, the pavement, the walls. He would decide tomorrow. He needed to rest, relax. And that meant one thing: sex. Yes, a night of fucking would burn out the cloud of depression that was already filling his system like ink in water. If he could get laid he'd awaken refreshed in the morning, be able to take the situation in hand. Sex always provided peace of mind.

He turned into Via Piciano, moving along the northeastern edge of the Villa Borghese. Each step he took, however, increased his sense of steadily deepening depression. His mind performed cartwheels. Images from the past appeared in a montage of disillusionment: Vanessa stating she'd need the money back by early November as it was for Christmas; Michael crying after a violent argument; Alison, his agent, informing him he had to cut back on the sex scenes, especially the rape of the pregnant woman in *Dead Dogs and Englishmen*, because every publisher she showed it to found the book gratuitous; Wilmott, his bank manager, turning down his request for a loan; Michael leaving, bags hurriedly packed, tension charging the smoky air of the flat.

"You selfish, self-pitying bastard!" his lover threw at him as he gathered his things in the hallway. "I'll be back for the rest of my stuff."

Meredith was silent, a contrite expression on his face, a bottle of Scotch still in his hand. Michael was so angry they had come to blows over the damn thing. Embarrassed, he tried to hide it behind him but Michael saw him.

"Put the bloody bottle down! Stop pissing your life away."

"Sorry," he mumbled.

Michael fiddled with the straps of his baggage as Meredith watched him, not sure what to say or do.

"I'm sorry," he said again.

No response.

Michael looked up, tears in his eyes.

"You're always sorry afterward. But words aren't enough. When you drink you're like a little kid—*and that's all the bloody time.*"

Meredith looked at the carpet.

"This is it. *Over. Dead.* You killed it."

And with that, Michael was gone, the door slamming like a gunshot in the heavy air.

Although he'd felt a tremendous sense of relief after the last of Michael's things had gone, the first few nights without him to hold had been an empty, cold time. But there were always other bodies to be found, and since the split his sex life had been a calm sea dotted with occasional faces floating like driftwood through a perpetual twilight. It was easier that way. But the immediate problem was how to find someone in this godforsaken place. The local cruising scene, if one existed, was nowhere to be found and the only form of night time sexuality he'd seen was transvestism, which held no appeal. The only possible place he could think of was the Spanish Steps.

While passing them the previous night he had been surprised by the number of people spread out on the impressive monument and the relaxed atmosphere. Couples entwined passionately, all but copulating, locked into their own romantic universes. Cigarette smoke drifted on the breeze, mingling with the sweeter aroma of hash as a guitarist had strummed old songs. The Steps were a short walk away and would be a good starting point. Failing that, the main railway station would almost certainly provide what he was looking for.

He'd gone but a few yards and had turned into Via Veneto when he came across the first gaggle of transvestites he'd seen that night. One, a blonde wearing an awful wig, tried to waylay him but he continued without stopping, scowling. When he reached Piazza Barberini he paused to scan the headlines of English newspapers on sale at a cramped news cabin. Try as he might to focus on the front pages of *The Sun* and *The Star*, his attention was drawn to the cheap colors of the hardcore magazines on sale.

Teenage Lolitas promised all girls under sixteen with text in English, German, and Italian. Who, he mused, cared about text? He'd always smiled at the French slang for such publications—books to be read with one hand. But what he found most interesting was the plethora of *fumetti*, pocket-sized, crude, explicit comics filled with a staple diet of black magic, murder, sadomasochism, rape, and mutilation. There were dozens of titles ranging from entrail-eating zombie stories to tales of futuristic sex and violence and more mundane tales of adultery and wife swapping. Nothing was left to the imagination, atrocities bursting forth on each page like rotten foliage. he'd found one in his room at the *pensione*. After skimming thirty pages of semi-literate dialog he could not translate his eyes had widened at a sudden explosion of brutal sex and degredation—close-ups of fellatio, sodomy, and a young man having his skull smashed open after orgasm by the husband of the woman he'd just serviced. Somehow, he felt these popular comics told him more about the Italian cultural psyche than he wished to know, a world view consisting of naked lust and commonplace violence. But this, after all, was the country that had made throwing people to wild animals the main form of entertainment. He laughed aloud as a black vision eclipsed all else; so this is what it all comes down to—two thousand years of civilization and it's the same as it ever was. This is where it ends.

A soberly suited businessman examining *S & M Sextacula* looked intently at him over his glasses and Meredith walked away with the bitter laugh still on his lips.

As if submitting to the dark reality was his only means of finding hope, he felt a strange sense of correctness in his situation and he suddenly saw it all for the killing joke it was, a long, hollow laugh in the face of nothingness. He continued to chuckle to himself until he came to the junction, his attention shifting to the pleasing smells coming from a restaurant on the corner. His stomach growled in appreciation. He entered without further thought, drawing the aromas from the kitchen deep into his lungs.

Like the previous night the Spanish Steps were littered with people. Small groups and couples. The lone guitarist, now surrounded by a small crowd. Here and there were boys on their own or in twos or threes. At the bottom he turned left under the pretense of looking at the Keats house, allowing his gaze to wander in the hope of making eye contact.

Directly in front of him two teenagers spoke softly, the taller of the two nodding toward a pair of giggling girls seated a few feet above them. To Meredith's left, near the bottom, sat a lone handsome youth dressed in brogues, tapered trousers, and a red pullover. The writer walked toward him.

"*Buona sera,*" Meredith said as he sat beside him. The boy—no older than seventeen, he judged—nodded.

"Do you speak English?" The boy nodded. "Perhaps you can help me," he continued slowly. "This is my first time in Rome. Can you recommend a good nightclub?" The boy did not turn to face him for several seconds, then looked in his direction. Above them the guitarist started murdering "Ticket to Ride."

"There are some." He spoke softly, trying to ennunciate correctly.

"Something to suit a man my age," he said, holding eye contact with the boy longer than was polite. He lit a cigarette.

"There is a place. Not a nightclub."

Meredith waited for him to continue but the boy was not forthcoming.

"Would you show me where? Is it far?"

The boy remained silent, then: "Pardon, I have to meet my girl," he said crisply, standing. "I have to go."

The boy began to trot toward the fountain at the base of the Steps. A blonde girl was heading in his direction. She smiled, waved, opened her arms. The boy ran to her. They embraced. Meredith watched them walk away arm in arm.

"Bitch," he muttered under his breath. The boy was nice-looking and had a good mouth. "I bet you're going to suck his little dick until it's as dry as a twig," he added before a coughing spasm cut off his words. He ground out the cigarette.

It was nine o'clock.

The entrance hall of Stazione Termini was largely deserted as Meredith entered the doors opposite the huge clock that hung above the electronic information board. It was 9:27, the display informed him mutely. His feet had started to hurt. It looked like coming here was a bad decision. There was no one around except a Gypsy woman with small child in her arms and a comatose wino sprawled beside the photobooth near track seven. The woman saw him and started in his direction.

As he turned to go, the woman grabbed hold of his left arm, pulling frantically at his jacket. Like other cities the world over, Rome had its underclass. New York had its legion of homeless, London its alcoholics, Paris its migrant work force of Moroccans. Rome, however, was infested with Gypsies such as this wretch clutching at his clothes, beseeching him for money in whatever dialect she spoke.

He jerked away. She continued to claw at him undeterred.

"Get off!"

She paused for a beat, then continued her litany of despair, and his temper erupted.

"*Fuck off!*" He pushed her away. She stumbled, nearly dropping the child.

With a screech she flew at him, pounding his back with her free arm, her tone now abusive. The child started to cry loudly. Meredith strode toward the nearest exit, but she was persistent and the blows continued to rain down on his back.

He stopped suddenly, stepped to the right, and turned, slapping away her hand, glaring at her, his eyes enflamed with rage.

"I said *get the fuck off me,* you diseased cunt!"

Like a slap his words silenced the woman for an instant, then she started to coo as she placed her arms protectively around the child, a calm expression of total hatred directed at him. The child was silenced by its mother's soft sounds and she turned, moving away at a measured pace. He watched her go, unnerved by the sudden outburst. Then the Gypsy stopped, turned again to face him. He took a step back as if pushed by the force of her expression, an expression that went beyond loathing, beyond hate. But there was something there he could not read. A glimmer of fear was apparent, and . . . revulsion? She began to babble, then spat two words at him.

"*Il morto*."

Even with his limited command of Italian he understood.

Dead man.

She spat at her feet, then ran toward the nearest exit, the words hanging in the air.

Dead man.

The frozen moment was broken by a coughing fit that swept up from his gut to constrict his throat, his heart shuddering in response, legs rubbery as gravity increased its pull, making him stumble to the nearest wall for support, the hundred yards elongating as his sense of space expanded, rolled, a wave of nausea hitting his system in a huge spasm. He closed his eyes to halt the roller coaster motion and took a deep breath, counting slowly to ten. He opened them, coughed, and tried to focus, blinking rapidly.

Go. Get out of Rome, his instincts screamed, *return to London*. To familiar territory. But he would be lonely there, too. Lonely. Lost. As he always had been.

No. No, he would find a kindred spirit to ease the emptiness with, someone with whom he could forget his troubles, albeit temporarily. There was one other place he could try; the porno cinema near the *pensione*. There he was certain he would find what he was looking for; there among the other lost souls would be a fellow spirit in search of release, of fulfillment.

He forced himself to smile, smile and regain his former optimism. His consciousness pirouetted with the slapstick grace of a clown. It worked. A ray of optimistic sunlight penetrated the storm clouds of depression that approached, breaking the darkness up into jagged shards as he pulled the bottle from his bag, and his internal horizon lightened further as he took a deep pull, coughing as the Scotch caught at the back of his throat. He needed to sit down. The cafe where the Dachau woman served was opposite, its light an island in the darkness pushing against the glass wall of the exit. He lurched away on shaky legs. He had to keep it together. One step at a time. He negotiated the revolving door and made it over the tram tracks to the cafe without falling flat on his face.

The bar that dominated the room was long and thin like the woman who served behind it. She stood looking down at the wood, a ghost of a time not so long past, her thinness painful to observe. The Dachau woman. What, he questioned, had caused her to resemble a victim of the Final Solution? She was white as a sheet, her cheeks deprived of the faintest hint of pink, her eyes the color of bruised mushrooms. If she heard him enter she did not acknowledge his presence. Neither did the three locals huddled around a TV set in the far corner, their attention consumed by *Magnum P.I.*

The woman—surely she was thinner than the previous day, but no, that wasn't possible—continued to look at the counter as Meredith ordered an espresso in his halting command of the language. As she turned to the coffee machine he noticed the spinal defect which pushed her head forward, explaining her limited movements. She handed him a steaming cup of black liquid with a trembling hand as he slapped down his money and shuffled to the nearest seat, turning his back so he wouldn't have to look at her funereal visage.

Meredith continued to tremble on the steps of the cinema, his stomach raw from its expulsion. The figures were closer now and he could see it was the Dachau woman and the fattest of the bar's occupants. The man was absently rubbing his crotch as he escorted the emaciated woman, though as they drew nearer Meredith realized the man was not holding her by the arm but caressing her arse. The thought of those two in a sweaty sexual embrace did nothing for his nausea. Yet it had been the atmosphere in the bar—or rather the invasion of the whores—that had finalized his resolve to come here. He looked up. The couple stopped by a dimly lit doorway and entered.

Doors. Opening and closing.

They seemed to punctuate every aspect of his life.

A sudden cold draught and explosion of noise from behind pulled Meredith from his thoughts as two of the whores who plied their trade outside the *pensione* entered the cafe. They cheerfully stepped to the counter, laughing and joking in a torrent of sound and broad gestures. One lifted her ample bosom to the other and broke into a loud cackle, the other echoing her movements, then joining her friend's laughter with a deep chuckle.

Each night these women had fractured his sleep with their nonstop chatter and bargaining outside his window. The Three Weird Sisters: Miss Piggy, the Vacuum Cleaner—because her mouth, a perfect, puckered circle, reminded him of the line "nothing sucks like an Electrolux" from a blatantly sexual advertisement for domestic appliances—and Mother Mary, as he'd dubbed them. They stood on the corner by the *pensione* for over twelve hours at a stretch, gossiping, joking, smoking, spitting, and scratching their fat arses.

The first night he had not been able to sleep before three A.M. with the noise coming from the street. Initially the wailed hymns of the drunks stumbling from the bar down the street, then from the endless chattering of the whores. Periodically a car had drawn up and he'd heard doors opening, then slamming shut, each vehicle pulling away fast only to return a while later as the cycle of copulation continued throughout the night.

Miss Piggy made a masturbatory motion to the Vacuum Cleaner, who laughed again, then whispered to her companion, who giggled in reply, pointing at Meredith. The Vacuum Cleaner blew him a kiss, then returned to her conversation. The Dachau woman was pouring two shots of rum without request, obviously a ritual for the whores, who toasted each other, swallowed as one, threw their money down, and departed as they had arrived: loudly.

Although his feet still ached, his legs were regaining their strength and he felt restless, the appearance of the whores once again bringing thoughts of sex to the fore. He started to luxuriate in a sense of inevitability and, as if lured by an invisible Ariadne's Thread of lust cast by the streetwalkers, stood from the table and departed the lifeless cafe.

So here he was, tired, queasy, and shaken. But the thought of returning to the grim confines of the *pensione* stirred his resolve. He'd check the place out. What he'd felt a few moments ago was the culmination of days of heavy drinking and a poor diet. No wonder his stomach had rebelled.

He stood.

And entered.

A dry, dusty smell hit his nose, the smell of a place not inhabited by man but rodents. The interior was red, tidy and functional though, not an abandoned place. The only decoration was two wilting potted palms standing sentinel on either side of the doors he assumed led to the screening room beyond. Inside the ticket booth sat an overweight, middle-aged man with black hair slicked back in an attempt to cover his large bald patch. His complexion was sallow, waxen under the spotlights illuminating the booth. Meredith placed a 20,000 lira note on the counter. The cashier continued to concentrate on his cuticles. By one pillar to the right lounged a swarthy youth with a sneer, his body language aggressive, his jeans taut over muscular thighs as he reclined, his rough trade gaze passing through Meredith's flesh as if he could see into his soul. He knew then he had come to the right place.

Click.

He turned to face the cashier. A ticket protruded from the metal counter like a small pink tongue. He took it and his change, stepping to the left of the booth to enter the inner sanctum.

For an instant blindness caressed his eyes, total, eternal. Then some distance in front a scrambled rainbow of light jumped and he made out a fuzzy rectangle of video-generated imagery with the sound of muted voices. He stood against the rear wall, mentally counting to ten as his eyes grew accustomed to the darkness. The light from the enlarged video image cast meager illumination on the aisles before him. A nigrescent sea of seats dotted with heads bobbing in the blackness like buoys came into focus. Here and there tiny beacons of cigarettes, clusters and constellations of red points, produced trails of smoke that hovered like ground fog above the body of men that composed the congregation in this church of desire. The majority of heads were separated by empty seats, the fractured symmetry of which was disrupted by occasional groups of twos and threes. But these couplings were in the minority. This was the refuge of the lonely, the lost, not a place for comradeship, yet paradoxically a vessel for communion with the flesh.

Meredith strategically took a seat in the back row to survey the audience. On screen a girl with hair the color of rotting wheat swallowed a penis.

Reverential silence blanketed the cinema. Not even the sound of bodies repositioning themselves interfered with the litany of lust coming from the screen. He lit a cigarette.

Behind the miasma of tobacco smoke lay the unmistakable musk of dust and damp. Yet there was more, and his nose wrinkled in reaction. There was a slight excremental aroma; this appeared to sweeten until a rich trace of hash rolled past his face; then this, too, changed, making him think of rotting orchids. This persisted for a

while, then faded. One moment the atmosphere appeared
damp, the next chalk dry. Suffocating. Then from somewhere in the auditorium came the unmistakable copper
tang of blood. That, too, retreated. As he inhaled the
cigarette the conflicting smells made his mind spin and
he ground out the Marlboro as he tried to stifle another
coughing fit.

*The girl continues to deep throat the long, thin phal-
lus. Suddenly it twitches spastically and a dribble of
sperm leaks from the girl's lips as she continues to eat
it, then two jets of semen shoot from her nose.*

The image jumped, faltered, faded. There was no discernible movement in the audience and the house lights
remained off. On screen a rectangle of dots and wave
patterns writhed, reminding him of the opening to *The
Outer Limits*, but no Control Voice sounded from the
speakers, no new picture took the previous one's place
for what seemed minutes. Finally, a smeared visual
flicked onto the screen. Music with too much treble
tinkled along in accompaniment.

On the left side of the auditorium a figure rose to
use the exit, the movement prompting Meredith to try
contact with a fellow lost soul. Sticking to the row he
was in, he picked his way along to the other end where
a man of similar age sat. Meredith selected the seat
next to him, opening his legs so his right knee brushed
the other's left thigh, yet the man remained immobile,
even when Meredith let his hand fall to his crotch as
he watched out of the corners of his eyes. The man
continued to stare dispassionately at the screen.

*A white Rolls Royce cruises an Alpine road. Inside
sits a big man sipping champagne, a woman on either
side of him. One is a short blonde with her hair up in
a bun, giggling as she drinks and caresses her naked
breasts.*

Meredith turned to his neighbor, smiled, and held his
gaze. The man ignored him.

Lost in your own little fantasy, aren't you? Probably
about the blonde and what you'd like to do to her. What
a waste.

The girl pours champagne over her breasts. The other woman—a brunette—leans over the man to lick at the liquid, the blonde's nipples erecting.

Meredith stood, walked back along the row of seats to cross the aisle. Three rows in front sat another man. Balding, overweight.

No, too old.

The man, the blonde, and the brunette enter a large room. In the center a group of nine people surround a young woman laid out on a table, silk cushions holding her off hard wood. She has a phallus in her mouth. Another thrusts in and out of her vagina. The crowd kiss, masturbate, caress each other in slow abandon until they perceive the presence of the man. The orgy pauses. The crowd clears and the woman on the table turns over to present her backside to the man who opens his robe in return, his large penis ready to enter her. She begins fellating the phallus of a skinny youth as the man sodomizes her. The group then couple in abandon.

Meredith paused to watch the film, smiling to himself at the excess on screen, before letting his eyes wander.

To his right, in the middle block, lounged a boy in his early twenties. Meredith homed in on him.

On screen the woman groans as the skinny youth ejaculates on her face. The man does likewise, his semen covering her back in a torrent. The group respond in a frenzy, the other men baptizing the woman in a monsoon of ejaculate.

He sat next to the boy, spread his legs to brush his thigh. The boy turned. Meredith looked him in the eye whilst fumbling for his lighter.

"Pardon," he said.

The boy nodded slowly, then provided a light.

In the sulfurous flash of the flame Meredith knew he was the one. The boy had a perfect complexion: olive-skinned, a light corona of stubble adhering to the fine, neoclassical lines of the face, the hair jet black, magnificently sculpted over the scalp. His eyes, Meredith saw in the instant of the flame, were brown, an unusual shade between gold and bronze. His lips were full, rich, ruby.

Meredith felt the heat in his groin explode through his system, causing him to look away, shocked by the fallout from the chemical charge that passed between them. The boy continued to hold his gaze.

On screen the image skipped as a new film replaced the previous one and Meredith was glad of the distraction.

A close-up of a mouth, open wide.

The camera pulls back to reveal a man, naked except for a leather harness, strapped to a chair. A tall dominatrix, her black hair matching her cat suit, masked, nails his scrotum to a piece of wood. In the background two old men bugger a child.

A boy or a girl? Meredith could not be sure.

Next to the pederasts is a woman, her feet and hands chained to the wall, her body systematically invaded with sexual devices wielded by a woman of indeterminate age.

A title slowly superimposes itself over the tableau: Crucified By His Cock.

Meredith chuckled at the pretension, then dared to look back at the boy, who was still gazing intently at him, a trace of a smile on those inviting lips.

On screen the masochist screams.

Behind the intensity of the boy's expression lay a deadness that, had he been more aware and less drunk on the sexual pulse pounding through his body, he would have noticed, but the charge between them was so strong his judgement was impaired. He'd been through enough encounters to see the danger signals but his instinctual warning was lost in the riptide of deep desire. All he perceived was the object of his passion.

The boy stood, squeezed Meredith's knee, moved toward the exit sign.

He was halfway across the auditorium before Meredith gathered his wits to follow. He dropped the cigarette and walked after him, nearly tripping in his eagerness to do so.

The boy went through the left exit. Gathering his composure, he followed.

The exit doors led to a narrow corridor. To the right was a bar with a few patrons. Meredith didn't take any notice, as the boy was heading in the opposite direction. Meredith moved quickly. He could not lose him. Not now.

Curving to the left, the corridor paralleled the auditorium. Both walls and carpet were deep red. Small orange spotlights cast pools of tangerine on the floor. Every fifteen feet a palm that had seen better days resided in a red pot.

The boy stopped and turned, smiling with satisfaction as he spied the writer was in pursuit.

Meredith stopped dead. Something was not right. The adrenalated pursuit had cleared out his system, the warning signs flashing.

No.

Dread gripped him, desire and fear in conflict.

He stumbled as he turned, heading back in the direction he'd come.

Meredith ran, the sense of threat increasing with every step. As he rounded the curve, approaching the bar area, his heart fluttered, a steel band tightening around his chest. He collided with the wall, clutching at his torso.

Oh God, I'm having a heart attack.

Then he was filled with a vision of the boy's eyes. Inviting, placid, offering peace. He gasped.

The image persisted as his breath came in tight gasps. Then he sensed a presence behind him, felt a hand on his shoulder transferring a sense of emotion unlike any other. He turned, falling into the boy's arms. Their tongues automatically entwined and he stroked the boy's crotch, which felt full and heavy. After a moment the boy pulled away, yet it was not a rebuff. He smiled, squeezing Meredith's crotch in return, began to unbutton his jeans, turning to face the wall.

Finally, he was in.

Moving gently, Meredith pulled the boy toward him, devoting his attention to the hymn of his thrusts. From the auditorium came a faint sound of applause mixed with screams.

The boy's heat excited him further and he knew he could not last long. Tension in his groin rose like water filling a lock and the threshold was breached far quicker than he expected. Then, behind the bodily heat came a numbing coldness, a chill so sharp it cut into his cerebral cortex, disrupting the wave pattern of lust instinct for a split second that expanded into eternity. He opened his eyes and panicked.

Before him was the Void. Total, unforgiving, relentless. To ejaculate into such a place struck him with primal terror, the horror of the Void absolute. Surely, to give an offering to such a place would not be enough; he would be consumed without a trace. If he had sought the darkness before he had done so in error. Now he wanted no part of it.

Then it was gone.

Meredith withdrew as his cock jerked spastically, spitting his seed onto the humus lining the palm's pot. He grunted. The boy stood still. For an instant the image of the void returned, then was gone as quickly as it had arisen. He felt suddenly sick, as if a cold ethereal hand grasped his scrotum, passing through the skin to penetrate his bowels. The boy turned to face him.

The smile was still on those ruby lips, but the light that had resided in his eyes was gone.

Meredith, dazed, was pushed gently to his knees: the boy's erection appeared in front of his sweat-washed eyes. He opened his mouth. The offering stretched him to the limit. His eyes shut, the boy pushed into his throat, slapping him as he did so to force open his eyes.

"Look at me," the boy said, his voice only a fraction above a whisper. "This is my body, this is my blood. Drink in remembrance of me."

He withdrew, spraying the writer.

The world went white.

Meredith lay there for an uncertain time. Were minutes seconds, or the other way around? He had no idea, no sense of proportion. Eventually he wiped the residue from his face, pulled himself upright, and moved toward the bar area, the sensation of a frozen hand performing a five-finger exercise in his guts. Sweat crowned his brow.

Three people were at the bar. The woman behind the counter ignored him as she carefully wiped a glass. She was familiar. Where had he seen her? Her hair was the color of rotting wheat, but he couldn't find the jigsaw piece to complete the picture. Two men were in front, one seated on a high stool. He turned to Meredith as the writer stumbled past at a snail-like pace. He, too, was familiar, causing further confusion in Meredith's unfocussed mind. As he inched by he noticed the man's fly was open, his penis hanging off the stool rim, puncture marks in the phallus manifested as stigmata. Where had he seen him?

(Screams)

Nails through flesh . . .

Thinking clearly required too much effort. Despite throwing up before entering the cinema he still felt drunk; the alcohol still in his system had him cornered, was ready to lay him out in the third round.

He shuffled into the street. The two thousand yards to the *pensione* took an eternity to cover.

Of course, the Three Weird Sisters were outside the impoverished Spanish-style hotel, its edges crumbling with age, the walls tattooed with a patina of carbon. Miss Piggy laughed at him as he careened by with the precision of a seasoned drunk. He tried to snarl "fuck you," but it came out as "fug tu," his speech slurring with every step. He'd never felt so tired.

As he came through the entrance of the *pensione*, the concierge looked up for an instant, then resumed watching the TV set behind the counter. The Englishman's condition was nothing new; the old man had seen it many times. Nothing mattered to him anymore, hadn't since the passing of his wife, yet he flinched when the guest kicked open the door to his room, realizing the fool had collapsed onto the creaking bed and wasn't going to close it. He forced himself from the comfort of his armchair to trot down the hallway, pulling the door closed without looking in on the prone figure of *il morto*. He'd watched the process take place before—once had been enough—and if it took place behind closed doors, even if they were his own, he could convince himself it didn't exist. The world was changing in strange ways and denial was his only defense. But the sex zombies, the emotionally dead, posed no threat to him. They stuck to their own kind, their bodies rotting as they performed their dance of empty desire. The old concierge grunted to himself, fully aware of his own mortality; he was not long for this world and wanted to live out his last few days as peacefully as possible. Let them inherit the earth.

Several minutes later he heard the bed creak through the thin wall. It would be the last noise to come from the room for some time.

Inside, despite the unbearable weight of exhaustion pushing down upon him, Meredith managed to raise himself from the mattress to discard his clothes and crawl between the dirty sheets.

It had begun.

The road lay before him, bright in the sexual flush of a newly aroused sun: a future of limited possibilities, restricted variations of the sex act, for their bodies were not strong. A barren future, predictable, life-negating, not life-affirming, sterile in its simplicity. Yet what faced Meredith did not appall. He welcomed it with open arms and mouth, and it in return welcomed him. Not with arms but with a multitude of genitalia and orifices: big ones, small ones, every taste, color, texture. A pornucopia of organs transformed from the frustrated parameters of the human state to that of a new flesh. Flesh, nerve endings, and blood that now coursed with a life—and death—of their own; a transmutational entity so powerful the host would atrophy within months.

In truth the transformation had begun long ago. A summation of desires misaligned, of emotions discarded,

left to fracture in the cold expanse of a life misdi-
rected.

Meredith lay between the dream and the desire, comfortable between the sheets of change. Somewhere in his
cortex memories skipped like daguerreotypes, flickered,
jerked, then faded. Fragmented scenes from his childhood, soft-edged with an innocence long lost, revolving
one last time. He frowned, then smiled serenely in his
sleep of the damned as the dream took shape, wiping
the screen of the old, tired images, replacing them with
visions of the future. The future inside his body.

Time would be short, but what a time. The fact there
would be no laughter, no light, no love didn't matter
anymore. If indeed they had once truly mattered, they
seemed now nothing more than trivial concerns, of little
consequence to the wider scheme of death within life.
That was all behind him. It was easier this way, lack
of choice soothing in its streamlined shape. And in the
dream a line from a song crept unbidden to provide a
momentary soundtrack: Don't dream it, be it.

He slept on, safe in the knowledge his Sisters outside
were spreading their gospel to the heathens. All over the
world it would eventually be the same: one Church, one
Body, one Belief.

The Church would welcome fresh converts that night
and there would be new films to watch, new stories to
tell, Meredith's amongst them. In the name of the Father
and the Son the congregation would sing silent praises to
the Gods of Flesh and Fluids.

He slept like a newborn baby, his shallow breath rising and falling in a psalm to the rhythm of the deathly
desire.

SWEETIE

G. Wayne Miller

G. Wayne Miller works for the Providence Journal *and has written several nonfiction books which require enormous amounts of research. In his "spare" time he finds the discipline to have written a novel,* Thunder Rise, *and a growing body of short stories which are so smoothly written, you don't notice the barbs and sharp edges until it's far too late. A story by Miller often has a vein of dark humor running along its pale underside, and this one is no exception. He lives in Pascoag, Rhode Island with his wife, Alexis, and their two daughters.*

Tony's driving fast.

Tony's grinding his teeth.

Tony can't get all this divorce crap out of his mind. It's killing him. Just sucking the energy straight from his body. Messing up his job. Screwing up his finances. It's gotten so bad lately it feels like his head's going to explode.

He remembers yesterday, that incredible hassle at the IGA. All he wanted was iron pills, to fortify his body. You'd think that would've been simple, wouldn't you? A great big store like that with a medicine aisle half a hundred feet long. But no. We're temporarily out of iron pills, the pipsqueak clerk said. Sorry, sir. But you can't pull fast ones on Tony. Tony knew, all right: the little pipsqueak was lying. The little pipsqueak was hiding them from him, no doubt on orders from the bitch, who was conspiring against him in extremely creative ways lately. That's what Tony told the police when they came to calm things down, that it was all part of the conspiracy. That's what he made sure they wrote into their report.

Tony keeps driving. He's getting all worked up again. The bitch . . . one of these days, she's going to get hers.

Jesus fuck Mary!

There's something in the road! It's blocking the way! It's like it materialized out of thin air.

Tony hits the brakes.

Jesus. Damn near hit it.

Tony takes a huge breath. His temples are pounding and he's trying to get a grip. What the hell is it? He squints. Looks like some kind of blanket, some kind of duffel bag or gunnysack. Maybe a sleeping bag, all ratty and torn.

Tony gets out of the car, a Hyundai. Instinct tells him to look up and down the road and so he does. You'd think he was some kind of common criminal. Jesus, what divorce will do to a guy. He pats his underarm, to make sure his pistol's still there. You never know what's around the next corner.

But everything's cool. No one in either direction. No houses. No other cars. Nothing but trees and fields and a long stone wall running up one side of this two-lane blacktop that dissects the Connecticut countryside.

Tony walks around to the front of his car. It's a blanket, all right. One of those Army surplus jobs. What the hell's a blanket doing in the road? What's in the blanket? There's definitely something in it. Something the size of an animal.

Oh Christ, he thinks. Some asshole's dumped his dead dog out here in the middle of nowhere. These hicks will pull shit like that. Why the hell did he ever move out here, anyway? Because of her, of course. Because of Louise, the bitch.

Except it's not a dog, as he discovers when he unwraps it.

It's a baby.

A baby girl.

A dead baby girl.

And not a scratch on her precious little body. Not a cut or a bruise or a single drop of blood. He looks at her carefully, not at all repulsed by what he sees. How could he be? What a pretty young thing. Her eyes are open and blue as sky. Her hair is blonde, her skin as white and flawless as a pearl in a jewelry-store window. Not a stitch of clothing on, not even a diaper or a frilly little pink bonnet.

Should he touch her? Something inside of him wants to. Just once. Now, while nobody's looking. That would be all right, wouldn't it? If her father had happened upon her, that would be the first thing he'd do, wouldn't it? Not just touch, but pick her up and give her a great big hug?

He won't go that far. But he will let his finger brush her cheek. Nothing wrong with that.

What's this?

Her skin is warm. Dear God, he thinks, maybe she's still alive. Maybe all she needs is an emergency room. Maybe just a couple of jolts with the paddles and then a ventilator and some heavy-duty drugs to pick her up. Tony feels frantically for a pulse, but he can't find one anywhere. And she's not breathing. He's sure of that. He took a CPR course back in college. He's forgotten some of it, but not the part about how to tell when someone's stopped breathing.

No, Sweetie's dead.

Say what?

Where'd that come from, that name? Just popped into his head, the way words sometimes will. But it fits, he thinks. That's what's so darn crazy. Sweetie fits. Poor little Sweetie, lying all by herself so dead in the road.

"Christ, now what?" Tony says.

He's already decided he can't leave her here. Can't just continue on to work as if nothing's happened. That wouldn't be fair to Sweetie. That would be heartless and cruel, something a ghetto person would do, not someone of his character.

Tony gathers Sweetie into his arms and places her on the seat next to him. The blanket's dirty but it's all he has. He wraps it around her. Never know when you'll run into some goddamn busybody, even on a lonely country road. He buckles the seatbelt around Sweetie and puts his Hyundai into drive.

Where to? Now there's a question.

It's too late for the hospital. That much is clear. Sweetie's dead. Sweetie's dead. The thought keeps going through Tony's head, over and over and over and making him so sad. Tears fill his eyes. It's going to be tough to drive.

The police station.

Of course, he thinks. I'll take her to the cops.

But almost immediately, doubt fills his mind. When I got to the front desk, he asks himself, what would I say? That I'm on my way to work, Officer, and I just thought I'd turn in this dead baby? Can you list it in lost and found?

No way. Tony's no fool. He's a certified public accountant. He knows about the authorities. He knows what they'll do. They'll have two options. First, they could charge him with a crime—and wouldn't murder and kidnapping be a good place to start? Something along those lines. After a hearing at which no bail would be set, it'd be off to the pen.

The other option would be the forensic unit. See if he's competent to stand trial. See if he needs rubber walls for, say, the rest of his life. Tony can see it now, how everything would unfold. Louise's lawyer would get wind of things, and he'd trip all over himself getting to court, and he'd be telling the judge about how, Your Honor, Mr. Anthony Simeone is impotent, is incapable of biologically fathering a child, which is why my client has filed the divorce petition she has, and, well, certainly Your Honor can see how this played into Mr. Simeone's sick mind when he killed this poor innocent child. If you look at the record, Your Honor, you'll note this man was nearly arrested after an altercation involving iron pills at the IGA. Yes, Your Honor, you heard correctly: *iron pills*, they usually go for about five bucks a bottle. You'll especially note that he has recently been hospitalized for nervous exhaustion, which followed several years of pharmaceutical treatment for an underlying depression. And while the hospitalization was at General Hospital, may I draw your attention to the fact that his admission was to Ward Seven? That he was discharged with a prescription for haloperidol—which isn't exactly aspirin, Your Honor.

All lies, of course, especially talk of any chronic underlying depression, but who can trust judges? Who ever gets out of institutions? They'd stick needles in him and cart him away and Sweetie . . . poor Sweetie . . .

What would become of Sweetie?

No loving, caring parents left her there in the road. Any idiot could see that. Someone wanted to be rid of poor Sweetie. Some teenage welfare whore, probably, strung out on drugs and not a clue as to who the father might be. Tony can't let her go back to a situation like that. Things being what they are, there's every chance some liberal judge would give that mother a second chance. If not, the state would get her. That would be worse. Tony catches the evening news. Tony knows about foster homes and shelters. No. Tony can't let any of that happen.

Tony pulls into his driveway.

For the first time since being served with papers, Tony is thankful for the bitch. At least she's moved out. True, it was into that fuckhead Peter Downing's place, but those two shacking up was only a matter of time, anyway. Better to get *that* messy detail out of the way. And Tony has the house, at least for now. Tony can be alone, which is all he wants lately.

Tony hits the switch to the overhead. The garage opens. Tony drives in and closes the door behind him. He uncovers Sweetie. Must be hot under that blanket. He lifts her in his arms. Her skin is very warm. He hopes it's not a fever. When Tony was a kid, he got St. Joseph's aspirin. They don't sell it anymore. They sell St. Joseph's *acetaminophen*.

How the world's changed, Tony thinks as they go in.

He sets Sweetie down on the couch and dials the phone. As it's ringing, he closes the front drapes.

"Rosalyn," Tony says when his call's answered.

"Tony," says his secretary.

"I'm not having a good day. The bitch's at it again."

"I understand."

"Anything that needs my attention over there?"

"Nothing that can't wait until tomorrow."

"Good. I'll see you first thing in the morning."

"Hang in there, Tony," Rosalyn says. "Remember: it's always darkest before dawn."

Tony hangs up and takes the phone off the hook. No interruptions today, which is barely eight hours old and already momentous beyond all contemplation. He looks over at Sweetie. Is it his imagination or has she shifted position? Not halfway across the couch or anything dramatic like that, but maybe a teensy-weensy inch or two? As if she were trying to get into the kitchen? As if she might be hungry?

Of course you're hungry, he thinks. I'd be hungry, too, Sweetie, if I'd been lying in the middle of a road like that.

Tony rummages through his cabinets, but the best he can find is instant oatmeal. It's cinnamon and spice, one of the bitch's favorites. It'll have to do. Tony mixes up a bowl and as it sits on the stove, cooling to baby temperature, he wonders how he will feed her.

But he doesn't wonder for long.

He's remembering Louise. For years, the bitch had tried to get pregnant. They'd gone to fertility specialists, even tried a treatment in Acapulco, all without luck. Artificial insemination had worked. On the first try, the bitch had gotten pregnant. All the way into the third trimester, there were no complications. The Simeones could breathe easier. At least easy enough to buy a crib, a highchair, sleepers and bonnets in pink and blue. They'd painted the spare bedroom. They'd put up curtains. And in her eighth month, Louise Simeone had miscarried. Miscarried and blamed it on his Xanax, which he'd only ever taken once or twice years and years ago, he swore. Six months later, she'd filed for divorce.

Well! So the bitch was good for something, after all. The crib and high chair are still down cellar. He saw them just last week, when he stowed away the assault rifle and ammunition he procured in case things turn too crazy. Tony gets the chair, brings it into the kitchen, and settles Sweetie into it.

"There, now," he says, bending her knees. It's not easy, bending her knees. Like all her joints, they are very stiff. It's never good, Tony thinks, for babies to lie in the road.

"For you, Sweetie," he says. "Have to have your nourishment if you want to grow up big and strong."

He tries spooning some oatmeal into her mouth. But Sweetie doesn't eat.

"Sweetie's probably tired," he says. "Sweetie needs her rest. You wait here while Daddy sets up your crib."

The crib is still in its box but it goes together without a hitch. Tony's always been a handy sort of guy. He hangs the Fisher-Price mobile the bitch got during her shower. He slips a sheet over the mattress. He shakes the dust out of the curtains and sprays a generous amount of Lysol. You never can tell about germs. Never can be too careful.

Every hour, Tony checks on Sweetie. Crib death, he thinks, is such a tragic thing. Sweetie sleeps, even if Tony can't. At midnight, when he's sure she's down for the night, he leaves in his Hyundai. He finds a convenience store that's open and buys Gerber baby food and a box of Pampers diapers and a bottle of fish oil gelatins that are on sale.

The next morning, Tony tries a bottle of warm milk. Sweetie won't take it. Sweetie's looking under the weather today. No color and very dry lips and skin. Tony gives her her bath. He towels her dry, spreads baby oil all over her body, powders her, and gets her diaper on. He dresses her in pajamas and a pink bonnet.

"Daddy's got to go out," he says. Sweetie's on the floor in front of the TV. The TV is on Channel 2, public television. Kermit the Frog is singing a funny song.

"Sweetie be good," Tony says. "Don't get into any mischief. Daddy will be home soon."

Tony makes an effort at work but he's only going through the motions. Rosalyn makes a few cracks about the bitch. Tony mentions the fact that it's the Friday before the long Fourth of July weekend. They laugh. Tony leaves before lunch. Since the stock market crash, things have been marginal at Simeone & Smith. A year ago, Roger Smith left to go sell insurance. Since then, it's been only Tony and Rosalyn and a part-time clerk.

By Saturday afternoon, the smell is god-awful. Tony keeps bathing Sweetie, but it isn't doing any good. Powder's not helping, either. Tony's worried. Sweetie seems to have developed some sort of terrible rash. Must be this July weather, so sticky and hot. The skin is broken in several spots and what appear to be blisters have popped up on her ankles, wrists, cheeks, the back of her neck.

"Poor Sweetie," he says as he rocks her by the TV. "Poor, poor Sweetie."

Tony's thoughts are racing now. Before Sweetie, the minutes crawled. Now time's speeded up. Right now, it's racing like a rocket. Sweetie desperately needs a doctor but Tony doesn't have one, at least not a G.P. or anyone like that. He'd have to take her to a walk-in clinic or a hospital. Tony knows what they'd do. They'd take Sweetie behind some curtain and then start asking him all sorts of prying questions. They'd want to know who Sweetie's mother was, the name of her pediatrician, the number of her insurance. And while one of them was getting to the bottom of all that, another of them would be placing a nine-one-one call.

Tony's got mammalian diving reflex on his mind.

Last winter, there were articles about it in the paper. In children, he read, it's especially well developed. The younger, the better. There are cases on record of kids falling through ice and lasting an hour or more. On kids, cold water seems to have a preservative effect. Why shouldn't it have curative powers as well? That's nothing but simple logic. This lousy heat wave they're in. It just seems to bring everyone down. Fans don't help and Tony's central air conditioning is on the blink. Water, he thinks. Cool, clear water. *Ice* water.

He's experiencing divine inspiration.

"I won't be gone long," he says to Sweetie as he pockets his keys. "Daddy's going to make everything OK."

The pet shop is three-quarters of an hour away. Thank God it's well-stocked. Thank God they take MasterCard and their little telephone verification machine is on the blink. He'd hate to have to use heavy force, although a man like him must be prepared for anything, and he is. Tony buys their biggest pump, their biggest filter, a fancy hood, 200 feet of clear plastic tubing, and their biggest tank, a 100-gallon job. The tank barely fits in the car. Tony has to move the front seats all the way forward to get it in.

It's almost dark by the time he gets back. Sweetie's where he left her, in front of a fan.

"Daddy won't be long now, Sweetie," he says.

Tony goes down cellar. He has a workshop down there. He has a second refrigerator. He moves a sturdy old dresser next to it. He puts the aquarium on the dresser and hooks up the filter and pump. With his half-inch Black and Decker, he drills a series of holes through the refrigerator walls. He threads several lengths of tubing through the holes and connects the ends to the pump to complete the circuit. He seals the holes with silicone adhesive and gets a garden hose ready.

"That's my Sweetie," he says when he places her inside the tank. She fits easily.

Tony starts filling the tank. There's only one problem.

Sweetie floats.

The water's rising and she's going up with it. That'll never do. Sweetie has to be submerged. With his free

hand, he holds her under. Her lips flutter and air bubbles
come out of her mouth. Tony lets go. Sweetie bobs to
the surface. Boy, is this ever tough. Tony shuts off the
hose and ponders the situation. Soon, it dawns on him.
Hammers. That's what he needs, hammers to weigh her
down. And he has hammers. Hammers galore! He gets
his three heaviest. They do the trick. Sweetie's underwater now. He fills to the top and starts the pump. He
checks for leaks. There are none. Yes, Tony's always
been handy. Tony was an Eagle Scout. Tony's father
was an automobile mechanic, the best there was.

"Such a beautiful baby," he says as he looks into the
tank. "Such a beautiful Sweetie. Daddy's taking good
care of you now. Nothing in the world to worry about
now."

That night, he takes his bed apart. He reassembles it
next to Sweetie's tank. He puts the overhead light on.
It casts a purplish tint. Very flattering to Sweetie. The
sound of the pump lulls Tony to sleep. For the first time
in weeks, he doesn't wake until well after dawn.

Sunday is such a pleasant day. Just relaxed and quiet
and finally cool. For breakfast, he has his usual V-8
juice, oat bran, lecithin, and fourteen vitamin pills. He
spends a couple of hours oiling his assault rifle and
resharpening his survival knives. Then he takes Sweetie
out, but she's still not interested in a bottle. That's OK.
Whatever Sweetie wants.

On Monday, Tony's up at six. The temperature inside
Sweetie's tank is thirty-eight degrees. Perfect. Sweetie's
doing just fine. Everything's going to work out all right,
after all. Tony is in a celebratory mood. It's the Fourth
of July and Daddy's with his little girl. This calls for
champagne. He buys a bottle when the store opens at
eight. He chases each glass with a 1,000-mg. Vitamin
C pill. By eleven, the bottle's gone. He buys another.

When Sweetie graduates from high school, he thinks,
I'll give her a bottle of her own. That, and a brand-
new car. A red Miata would be nice, if they're still
making them.

* * *

On Tuesday he stops by the office. Nothing much is doing. He leaves before noon. When he gets home, there's a car in the drive. A fancy blue Saab. Jesus fuck Mary! It's her! The bitch! What the hell's she want? Why didn't she call? And where is she, anyway? She's not in her car. She's not in the yard. She must be inside. Tony runs to the door and goes in.

Louise is in the kitchen. The phone is still in her hand. She looks like she's suddenly taken ill. Her face is ashen and she is shaking so badly Tony can feel it through the soles of his feet, halfway across the floor.

"The police are on their way," is all she says.

What does that mean, Tony wonders. Then it hits him. Oh Jesus. She's found Sweetie. Must have been rummaging around down cellar for some of her old clothes or the TV she left behind. Must have let herself in with her key. Why didn't he have the locks changed, the way he kept intending to? Why has he been so stupid? Why didn't he know the bitch was bound to mess things up? How could he have been so careless?

Instinctively, his right hand creeps under his jacket. Thank God he's packing his pistol. This could get nasty.

"You didn't . . . *touch* her, did you?" Tony says. His voice is hysterical. He's all tight again. "You didn't *break the glass*, did you? Answer me, Louise. Answer me!"

He steps toward her. She screams. She brushes past him. She runs out the door. He doesn't care. His only concern is Sweetie. The harm that bitch might have done. An image of Sweetie on the concrete floor explodes across his mind; he sees broken glass and a giant pool of water. How that would hurt! What shape that would leave his dear Sweetie in!

But nothing's been touched. The pump's still running. The tank's intact. Sweetie's happy and content, just like when he left her. He pries the hood off and reaches in for her.

"Oh, Sweetie," he says.

He starts to cry. Everything suddenly has changed. Tony understands that. Tony's very sensitive like that.

Funny, isn't it, the way the mind works?

You'd think a guy would have blotted almost everything about his ex from the old memory bank, but quite the opposite's been true for Tony. He remembers every little detail, the clothes she wore on such and such an evening, the salad dressing she prefers, her Social Security number, the name of her hairdresser, the inscription on her engagement ring, her favorite characters on her favorite show, *Saturday Night Live*. He remembers the perfume she was wearing the night they met. He remembers their first phone conversation, their first date, the name of the place where they spent their honeymoon: Dante's Retreat, located in one of the prettiest, most out-of-the-way parts of the whole Northeast.

"Pocono Pines," he says to the long-distance information operator. "Dante's Retreat."

He listens, hangs up, dials.

"And do you still have water beds?" he says. "Good. What about air conditioning? Super! Great! One more question: is it central air or individual units? Outstanding!"

Individual units, he thinks. I could loop a coil through it and back to Sweetie as easy as pie.

"Yes, I *would* like to reserve a room," he says. "Near an ice machine, if possible, please. The name's Smith. Mr. and Mrs. Warren Smith. We'll be staying at least a week."

Before he closes the trunk, he opens the lid of the cooler. The ice is packed carefully around Sweetie. She's got her Raggedy Ann. She's got her blankie.

"We can't stay," he says, "because mean and nasty people are coming to try and take you away. Daddy could never allow that to happen to his precious Sweetie. Not in a million years."

It's not only Sweetie who's in the trunk. He's got his power drill and toolbox and some leftover plastic tubing and his assault rifle and knives and ammunition. He smiles, thinking about how he bought the rifle hot and purchased the ammunition a little here, a little there, to make it all but impossible to trace back to him. Those bastards with their computers—Tony Simeone can play their game! Yessiree Bob!

He closes the trunk. He gets in his car. He double-checks his wallet to make sure he has the MasterCard. He double-checks his revolver. He starts the engine. He backs out of the drive. He turns left on River Road. As he starts over the crest of the hill, he hears sirens. In his rearview, he catches a glimpse of flashing red lights. Cruisers. There must be six or seven of them. They're all turning into his drive.

"You just close your eyes now and rest, Sweetie," he says. "We've got a very long drive ahead of us."

ROMANCE UNLIMITED

James S. Dorr

The next story, by James S. Dorr, has a bit of an odd history. I originally received "Romance Unlimited" as a submission for the initial volume of Borderlands. *I read it, liked it, but wasn't sure it was appropriate for the anthology series. I put it in the "maybe" stack—which represented less than 10% of the submissions I receive (2% are selected, the other 88% are sent back immediately after reading them)—and let it sit around for months. As my deadline approached, I received several stories which demanded inclusion in Volume 1, thereby ruling out most of my "maybe" submissions. I sent back "Romance Unlimited" along with the rest, but something interesting happened: I couldn't get the damned story out of my mind. Months went by, more than a year, and I was reading for* Borderlands 2, *when I received another story from James S. Dorr. I rejected it, but I somehow remembered/connected his name to the "maybe" story. I scribbled a note on the bottom of the rejection slip, telling him his previous submission was so memorable that I should buy it after all. Surprisingly, it was still available (well, perhaps not so surprising—most editors lack the perspicacity of the not-so-humble writer of this intro) and here it is. Dorr has sold to many SF, fantasy, and horror markets and is also a semi-pro musician, playing in a recorder consort called* Aufblitzentanzetruppe. *Play on, Jim.*

"Ugh!" Karen thought, half out loud. She almost dropped the latest issue of *Romance Unlimited* in her haste to turn to a new page. The article's title, "How I

257

Wormed My Way into My Man's Heart by Taking Him Fishing," had started out on a promising tone, but she had not expected that it would turn out to be about *real* worms. The thought of actually picking up one of the slimy things, even if it was the hook of one's lover-to-be that one was baiting, was enough to give any slightly . . . um . . . large-boned, independent, twenty-six-year-old redhead the shivers.

In Karen MacIver's case, in fact, that was putting it mildly. She still remembered the summer her brother had terrorized her, when she was little, by putting the filthy things in her bed. She placed the magazine carefully on her bedside table, her hand still trembling, and went to the kitchenette to make cocoa. She told herself the pungent, hot liquid would calm her nerves, but in her heart she knew the real reason she wanted to fix it. She loved the flavor.

But did she love cocoa more than she burned for the love of a man?

She had to chuckle. *Romance Unlimited* was always asking its readers questions of that sort. But it did more than just ask questions—it also gave answers. In this case she knew from a previous issue that it was not the cocoa itself that was at fault. At least not exactly. The magazine told her that she could have anything she wanted, and have love as well, provided only that she shed the extra pounds eating and drinking would put on her figure.

Put that way, the course of her life always seemed so simple. That was one reason *Romance Unlimited* was her favorite publication.

And yet it was always coming up with nasty surprises—like this month's article on fishing.

That was like life, though. Nasty surprises. The bad with the good. The whistle of steam told Karen her water had started to boil. She tore open a packet of instant Swiss Miss, the kind with the little marshmallow pieces already added, and shook it into her favorite mug. After a quick stir, she took the aromatic mixture with her to her bedroom and picked up the magazine again.

* * *

It never really occurred to Karen that she might be lonely—after all, vicarious love can sometimes be better than even the real thing—until she arrived at work the next morning. She took off her coat and hung it as usual, then went to her desk to see what needed immediate typing. She kept her mind on her work until it was nearly coffee break time, then looked up to see Sherri, one of her best friends at the office, standing over her.

"Have you heard about the new man yet?" Sherri asked her.

"What do you mean?"

"They've got a new executive in the department upstairs. One of those on-the-way-up Yuppie types from what I hear. The gossip has it he's fresh out of business school—and a real hunk. Used to play football."

Suddenly, for some not quite explicable reason, Karen wondered if he ever fished. She laughed out loud in spite of herself—now she remembered. The magazine story the night before. She found herself thinking that football types usually did not go in for sports like fishing, sports performed best when one was alone. She wondered, though, if . . .

"Karen, are you all right?"

She wondered why she was even interested in just another office rumor, just like the gossip that made the rounds whenever there was a hiring or firing. "I'm sorry, Sherri, I guess I'm just tired. I must have gotten to bed too late last night."

"I'll bet you *were* up late. You're blushing, Karen." Sherri giggled, then continued. "Anyhow, his name is supposed to be Jeffrey Parnham and . . ."

"Come on, Sherri. I need some coffee—and maybe a Danish. Or do you think that maybe the cocoa machine's been fixed yet?"

Still she did wonder. Sherri had gone on to other topics until it was time to return to their desks, but there was something about the sound of the name, Jeffrey Parnham. She mouthed the syllables under her breath and they rolled on her tongue. *Jeffrey—Jeff—Parnham.*

And Sherri had said that he was a hunk.

But then the boss came in with extra typing and she had to take her lunch at her desk before she was able to get out from under it. By mid-afternoon, however, the pace had slowed somewhat. She thought again about Jeffrey Parnham. She had an idea.

Beatrice, in personnel, still owed her a favor.

She looked around, feeling slightly silly, then reached for her phone and dialed the extension. She whispered her questions, so no one but Beatrice would hear, and discovered not only that Parnham was an outgoing man whose hobbies suggested a love for the city, but also that he was, as yet, unmarried.

And still she wondered—why did she, all of a sudden, regret that second Danish she had decided to have with her cocoa that morning?

What would *Romance Unlimited* say?

What the current issue suggested, she learned that evening after she got back to her apartment, was that she should try to stick to coffee and sugar-free sweetener, whether the office cocoa machine was working or not. It also suggested she lay off the Danish, and not even *think* about beverages after dinner at home. She swallowed hard. She leafed through the pages in the hope that she might come across something to restore her courage.

She looked at the pictures. The small print underneath, she noticed, always said "posed by professional model." And yet she knew better. These were people just like she was—ordinary, back-home type people, except that maybe they weighed a few pounds less.

Except that, maybe, they did not eat Danish—or even drink cocoa with marshmallow pieces.

She went to bed hungry, her mouth dry with thirst. She had trouble sleeping. At mid-morning break time at work the next day, she stuck to black coffee without even artificial enhancement. And yet, she kept thinking, the men and women who posed for the pictures in *Romance Unlimited* were still just people, the same as she was.

And then she saw Jeffrey. The boss came down with the new man in tow and even introduced him to Karen. And he *was* a real hunk.

When quitting time came, Karen took a taxi back to her apartment. The bus was too slow. She felt weak, shaky, sick to her stomach. She knew she was suffering withdrawal symptoms from cocoa and sugar. *Romance Unlimited* had to provide an alternative way.

After all, models or not, some of the people in the pictures *had* to drink cocoa. She knew it was true— when she had been introduced to Jeffrey she had not known what to say. She blurted the question without even thinking.

"Do you drink cocoa?"

He looked surprised, but then he nodded.

"Swiss Miss 'Extra Rich'—with marshmallow pieces already included?"

"Sometimes," he said, but then the boss had dragged him away to introduce him to somebody else.

His voice had been mellow, like dark, sweet chocolate. And he drank cocoa.

And Jeffrey Parnham was more than a hunk. He could have stepped out of one of the pictures in *Romance Unlimited*.

Even the cover.

She grabbed the magazine and desperately flipped through its pages. Only a few pounds, she thought— from the cocoa. It was not as though she was actually *fat*. But Jeffrey drank cocoa. There had to be something. A different method.

She flipped to the advertisements in back and saw the twin headline: *EAT AND DRINK ANYTHING YOU WANT AND POUNDS DISAPPEAR! IT'S EASY WITH PATENTED "WATE-OFF" JELLY!*

She read the small print, tore out the coupon, and wrote a check. The stuff was expensive, but if it worked half as well as the advertisement promised, it should be well worth it. In her excitement, she even forgot her bedtime cocoa, rushing after dinner, instead, to stand in front of the full-length mirror next to her closet. She took her clothes off, inspecting her body—her stomach, her thighs—her . . . um . . . chest was fine—and she dreamed that night of the slimness she would find when she looked in the mirror again, after she had successfully finished the "Wate-Off" treatment.

She mailed the coupon on her way to work the next morning, and then continued her normal routine. The days went by slowly, as they always did. One of the typists was having a baby, and then the cocoa machine broke again, but by the time it was fixed this time, Karen had begun to decide she really could get along with just coffee.

And then, when another week had passed, another typist was sick with the flu. Winter would be coming soon—the work piled up faster and she began to have lunch at her desk on a regular basis. And then, the next Friday, only an hour or two before quitting, Jeffrey appeared. He carried some papers.

"Ms. MacIver?" he asked.

"I . . ." Karen was speechless. She felt herself blushing.

"I . . . uh . . . know it's an imposition on Friday"— he dropped the papers onto her desk—"but this is a rush job and my regular secretary is swamped already. If you would, you could just leave it in your 'out' basket when you're finished."

Karen nodded. She realized she was glad she was sitting, so Jeffrey could not see what she looked like from the waist down. She tried to say something—something pleasant to let him know that she would be happy to do his typing—but the best that she could come up with was a vacantly contented stare. And by the time she had accomplished even that much, Jeffrey was already out in the hallway.

But he had spoken to her—a second time—with his voice that sounded as deep and rich as cocoa. Even if it was only business. She picked up the papers and typed the presentation copies that he needed without even noticing when it was five. When she finished the work, she put it in the basket as he had asked her to do, and did not realize, until she was waiting at her stop for a late bus home, that she had been singing under her breath.

When she got to her apartment, she picked up the mail. The first thing she saw was the latest issue of *Romance Unlimited*: cover story, "Independence, or Just Plain Shyness? How I Learned that the Men I Worked With Could Sometimes Be Just As Timid as Me." Fat chance, she thought, as she sorted further—she winced when she realized the phrase she had used. Then she saw the slip that told her that she had a package waiting at the apartment custodian's office.

That night she skipped her cocoa again and stood nude in front of her full-length mirror. Like so many things in *Romance Unlimited*, what she found when she unwrapped the package was not exactly what she had been led to believe it would be. For one thing, the "Wate-Off" was not a "jelly"—not precisely—but more like a lumpy, sour-smelling cream. Nevertheless, she read the directions and smeared a liberal portion on, as the small print put it, "the afflicted part or parts" of her body.

Ads, she thought, as she turned the light out and crawled into bed, should contain a disclaimer the same as *Romance Unlimited*'s pictures. "Composed by professional copywriters." The same with directions—she felt rather foolish, but, as they instructed, she lay on her back and pulled the covers up to her chin. She felt a pleasantly warm sensation come over her stomach and upper thighs and she nodded off quickly.

When she woke up, she did not feel as rested as she usually did in the morning. Still, in a different way, she felt *good*. She rushed to the mirror—because she had not wanted the Wate-Off to stain her pajamas, she had slept nude—and, while her skin appeared somewhat puckered, what she saw *did* look a little bit slimmer.

And yet, when she turned back and looked at her bed, she found once again that what one read in *Romance Unlimited* was not always exactly what it at first seemed to be. Whatever weight she might have lost had not, as the ad promised, quite "disappeared."

She looked at the sheets, catching her breath. She reached to touch one of the hundreds of deathly white, ball-like particles spread on the bed where she had been lying. She drew her hand back—quickly. What she had touched was soft and slimy.

She looked at herself again in the mirror, and burst out laughing. She had not lost much—perhaps just a few ounces—but obviously anything lost so quickly would not simply float away into the air. She thought of the warmth she remembered feeling the night before. Somehow, in some way, she must have *sweated* the stuff off her body.

She crumpled the sheets up to throw away, then looked in the mirror again while she dressed and decided that, for one morning anyway, she might skip breakfast. The little particles left in her bed had looked, in an uncomfortable way, just a bit too familiar.

It was not until she was on the bus to work that she remembered what marshmallow pieces looked like in cocoa.

She threw two more sets of sheets away before it occurred to her that she could just spread newspapers out to catch whatever melted off her while she was sleeping. She assumed that was what happened—that the fat, or whatever it was, just melted off and formed into balls—but it was not as if it really mattered. What did matter was that "Wate-Off" worked.

The weeks went by and, little by little, she started to reach the slimness she wanted. She also noticed, as time went on, that Jeffrey came down to her desk more often. This latter, of course, could have something to do with the fact that she was an accurate typist—one of the best, as even the other girls sometimes told her. But one time he caught her, filing some papers, her figure in full view.

The thing is, he smiled.

She remembered that smile—it warmed her way home, like steaming hot chocolate, despite the increasing cold of the weather. And then the December issue of *Romance Unlimited* came, with its feature article, "How I Survived the Holiday Season Despite the Decline of Workplace Sexism." She made an effort to stop being shy and to smile back the next time.

And then the Christmas season arrived, and with it the year-end office party. And Jeffrey cornered her next to the bar.

"Ms. MacIver," he said. "Uh . . . may I call you Karen?" She saw he was blushing, although, of course, she realized it could have something to do with the fact that he appeared to have already had several cocktails.

"Uh . . . uh . . . Mr. Parnham?" She tried to say more. She could not speak. She nodded quickly. She made sure she smiled.

"Uh, Karen, the thing I wanted to ask is—I've seen your work and you're very good. And some of the other junior executives have invited me on a ski trip the week after New Year's, but, as it happens, uh, it'll be couples. But, uh, the thing is I don't have a date yet . . ."

She felt her smile freeze.

"Uh . . . I mean . . . separate dormitories, of course." She saw him turn beet red—it was not the cocktails. "I . . . uh . . . why don't I ask again Monday? Monday morning at work. Okay?"

She nodded blankly, her mind taking in only half of what he said. Jeffrey—Jeff—had invited her *skiing*. And that meant ski pants. Tight. Form fitting . . .

"Uh . . . Monday, then. Okay?"

She nodded again. A decision on Monday.

She tried to keep smiling as he turned and left her. She tried to look as if nothing had happened when she asked her office friend, Sherri, to help find her coat so she could go home.

* * *

Saturday morning she looked at her figure in the mirror. Almost, she thought. Just an ounce or two more. But in *just* the right places.

Saturday afternoon she went shopping and bought herself three pairs of bright green ski pants. She had another night—Sunday, she knew, she would need to spend making her final decision on whether to accept Jeffrey's offer. When she came back, she found the new issue of *Romance Unlimited* in her mailbox.

She opened the magazine—shuddered when she read the title of the first story. "How I Realized I'd Found the Right Time to Hook My Man and Reel Him to Me." She closed it quickly, trying to avoid thinking about an earlier story—one about fishing—how long ago? She tried her best to avoid remembering the time when her brother, that horrible summer when she had been little . . .

She cooked her dinner and afterward, for a special treat, she fixed herself a cup of Swiss Miss. She did not drink it as much as before, and she never had the kind with marshmallows, partly because the virtues of "Wate-Off" included helping suppress the desire.

Or rather, perhaps—the thought suddenly struck her— because it replaced one desire with another . . .

She put down her cocoa, almost spilling it. She had *never* had thoughts even half that explicit before. She went to her bedroom, spread the newspapers over her bed, and took her clothes off in front of the mirror. She reached for the Wate-Off and opened the lid.

The jar, she realized, was almost empty, but that was fine. One way or the other, this should be the last time she would need it. She concentrated on the inner parts of her thighs—a bit on her hips, curving in toward the center—her stomach was okay. She felt the warmth starting to make her tingle as she climbed slowly into her bed, pulled up the covers, and switched off the light.

She went to sleep quickly, but this time she dreamed.

She dreamed that the tingling warmth was increasing, kneading her flesh, as if a man's fingers were stroking her body. She dreamed of a man's hands—Jeffrey's—Jeff's hands moving over the hips, caressing her thighs, then slowly working their way up and inward.

She felt the heat become more intense.

She felt that she could no longer stand it.

She woke in the darkness—*the heat, the tingling, the kneading were still there*. She reached for the lamp and kicked off her covers.

And started to scream.

She remembered her brother—the worms in her bed. The lower part of her body was covered with maggot-like worms, eating, gorging themselves in the lamp's glow. She watched as first one, then another exploded, filled beyond fullness, into white, marshmallow-cocoa-sized pieces, even as new ones hatched out of the jelly. Her screams grew louder.

But then, as she brushed them off in her panic, she remembered the feeling she had had in her dream, of hands on her body. It was not unpleasant.

She thought of the article she had not yet read, about hooks and reels, and her mind became calm. She thought about why *Romance Unlimited* had always been her favorite magazine, whether or not the things found in it were always exactly what they at first seemed.

She looked at her body, surrounded by whiteness.

She turned the light back off, then gritted her teeth and reached with both hands into the mass of still squirming maggots. She reapplied them, working by feel, over her thighs and the curve of her hips and, when she was finished, she pulled up the covers.

She would inspect herself in the mirror when morning came. She would try on her ski pants, even if she knew already that they would fit her precisely the way that they were designed to. She would think about shyness in men.

She would think about bait.

And Monday, on the bus to her office, she would be sure she had read every word that *Romance Unlimited* had to say on the subject of fishing.

SLIPPING

David B. Silva

I've been a big fan of David Silva's writing from the very first story I ever read by him. "The Calling," his story in Borderlands 1, *was the lead-off story in that volume because I subscribe to the old notion that an anthology has to start off as strong as possible. Apparently a lot of people agreed with me. "The Calling" has been selected for reprint in several* Year's Best *anthologies, and at this writing has garnered HWA's Bram Stoker Award. A tough act to follow, but Silva sent me the following story for the book you hold in your hands, and friends, I gotta tell you, I was stunned. "Slipping" is what superior writing is all about: plot, characterization, style, and that rare ability to make us* feel.

Okay, okay, enough from me. Sit back and be impressed.

1

"It's hard to tell the difference sometimes. You spend all day and half the night editing the final version of an ad, then you go home, crash for a few hours, and start all over again the next morning. Every once in a while I have to remind myself what day it is and where I live. And there's always the danger, I suppose, that if you're not careful, you might drift a little too far from the reality loop. It's happened to some of the best of them."

Raymond Hewitt

2

For a moment, before he became fully aware of his surroundings, Raymond Hewitt, age thirty-two, didn't know where he was. He had been sitting in the La-Z-Boy in the living room of his apartment, watching *Nightline*, and nibbling at a leftover chicken burrito from last night's dinner. But now, he realized suddenly, he was standing in his bathroom.

The light was on above the mirror. He stared at himself, dressed only in his pajama bottoms, the toothbrush in his hand. There was a thin line of toothpaste sitting on the bristles, and his mouth was dry. He hadn't started to brush yet. But . . .

But what am I doing in here?

A sliver of grayish light slipped through the open bathroom door. He glanced down the hallway at the living room, where the television was off now. There was a plate sitting on the end table next to the La-Z-Boy. Even from here, he could see it was empty, except for a fork and a crumpled napkin. The chicken burrito was gone. He had finished it, he supposed, though he couldn't recall having done so.

What happened here, Raymond, my friend?

"I don't know."

He looked again at his reflection in the mirror, at the puzzled expression staring back at him, then brought the toothbrush mechanically to his mouth. What had happened, he decided, was simple: he hadn't been paying attention. He had finished the burrito, turned off the television, and changed into his pajamas without paying attention to what he was doing. It had been like driving on automatic. Entering the on-ramp, thinking about how you're going to get everything done by tomorrow's production meeting, then suddenly finding yourself a block away from home with no recollection of the miles in between.

Either that . . . or he had misplaced a little piece of himself tonight. Stashed it away in the same hollow place where he kept the bitterness of his separation from Sherrie and his every-other-weekend visitations with Robin. Somewhere out of mind, where the memories were kept dull and painless.

One of those, Ray decided as he climbed into bed. He pulled the bedsheets up under his chin and covered his eyes with his left arm.

It would be another twenty minutes before the Sand Man would accompany him down a long, spiral stairway into the pure black peacefulness of slumber. In the morning, he would struggle to pull himself out of that dark, safe sleep, and by the time he was fully awake, the episode of the night before would be long forgotten.

3

"I'm going to miss it," Bev told him late the next night.

Ray switched his briefcase to his other hand, and checked his Rolex. It was five to midnight. A light rain had fallen sometime after dinner, and the streets mirrored the soft shimmer of the surrounding city lights. It seemed later than it was. In fact, Ray told himself, it seemed almost as if the night had settled in to stay. "No you won't. We've got five minutes before the last train leaves."

He took her by the arm, and together they hurried across Fourth Street and started down the tunnel entrance to the Midtown Station. If there had been someone else on the street, they might have been mistaken for a young married couple heading home after a late-night dinner with friends (a late *sup*, as they liked to say on the Hollywood side of the business). But that would have been a mistaken assumption. Bev had hired on with Baylor & Baylor Advertising a little less than a month ago, after a national ad campaign at another agency had won her a Clio, and CEO Chet Baylor had lured her away with an offer of bigger bucks and more creative freedom. She had been lured right into Ray's office, to work on a campaign for a small independent film called *Timescape*. A get-your-toes-wet project while she learned her way around the agency.

At the bottom of the steps, Bev switched her purse from one shoulder to the other, and brushed a wisp of hair back from her forehead. "I still don't understand why they're front-loading this movie. It's not that bad."

"Ours is not to reason why."

"God, you're cynical."

"Not a cynic, a realist," Ray said easily. "It's a horror flick, not *Gone With The Wind*. Two weeks after it opens, it'll close. And two months after that it'll be in every video store across the country. Doesn't matter how good we do our job, we aren't going to make *Timescape* into a box-office hit. They know that. As long as we can max the theater gross they'll be happy. Video sales'll take care of the rest."

"Seems like a waste. I've seen Oscar winners that were worse."

As they arrived at the platform, Ray checked his watch again. Midnight, straight up. It had been ten or fifteen minutes since the last train had come through, though it felt as if it might have been days. A cool breeze carried out of the tunnels, howling softly and faraway. The train was running late, and they were the only two people waiting. He couldn't recall that having ever happened before, being alone in the station.

"Why is it so quiet?" Bev asked. "We miss something?"

"Maybe the system's down."

Overhead, the information monitor ran through a blurb for the symphony: The Skylight Center. Saturday night at 8:00 P.M. General admission $15.00. Ray watched until it went into the Arrival/Departure Schedule. "Nope. Looks like it's just a few minutes late."

"Where is everyone?"

He placed his briefcase on the floor between them, and glanced about the empty station. Someone had spray-painted a symbol in day-glow orange across the face of a billboard of a local FM station. It looked a little like an hourglass on its side, with a man buried in the sand to his knees. A sleeve of newspaper swirled out of one of the tunnels. Ray cleared his throat. "It's midnight," he said with a shrug. "There's never much of a crowd this time of night."

She seemed to relax a bit. "You have your daughter this weekend?"

"Supposed to, but Sherrie took her down to Florida on some sort of business trip. They're doing Disney World and Epcot while they're down there."

"So what's your weekend look like?"

"I don't know." He watched the sleeve of newspaper drop back to the tracks. "Maybe I'll spend some time at the office tomorrow."

"Another look at *Timescape*?"

"Yeah, if you don't mind?"

"No, of course not," she said, and he could see she really was comfortable with the idea. "I suppose I should have brought this up earlier, though . . ."

"What's that?"

"I was wondering what you thought of the IPMs."

"For *Timescape*?"

She nodded, a little less comfortably now.

"What about 'em?" He looked past her, down the tunnel beyond the long line of tracks leading off into the darkness, and was struck by the myriad of images they had put together for the ad, each one flashing on, then off again, as if its afterimage were burned permanently into his retinas.

"I'm feeling a little uneasy with the pacing."

"Too slow?"

"No, too fast."

He looked at her now, surprised. "We've got to quick-cut it. There isn't a fifteen-second run in the whole damn film we can bring up. What else are we supposed to do with it?"

"No, I understand that. It's just that we've got— what?—better than forty cuts in the thirty-second lead?"

"Forty-seven."

"It's too fast, Ray."

"Not if you're targeting the MTV crowd. The world's a faster place than when we were kids. People don't have the patience anymore to sit back and wait for us to make our point. They want everything to be a roller coaster ride."

"You know that's not true."

"Truer than you think." He checked his watch again. 12:06 A.M. Except for their conversation, the platform area had fallen into an even deeper hush. But now, approaching by way of the South Tunnel, the sound of the next train came clicking along at a reassuring rhythm.

"About time," Bev said with a smile.

Ray looked at her, thinking how lovely she looked, even under the weak fluorescent lights of a late Friday night. Her outfit was all business: the gray jacket, single-breasted with padded shoulders and dropped-notch lapels; the skirt pleated in the front with angled pockets and a wide waistband. All business at a glance. But you couldn't look at her without seeing the woman. She was thin, elegant lines and small breasts. She could smile at you, reflect serious, or throw a tantrum without ever making you feel uneasy about her. And her eyes— they could stare mysteriously in your direction with never a hint of . . .

(*CUT TO*)

. . . what was going on behind them.

"Don't work too hard this weekend," she was saying.

Ray closed his eyes, then looked again.

The train had arrived. He had closed his eyes and opened them, and the train had arrived out of the black midnight of the tunnel. Bev was standing just inside the doorway now, holding on to a stainless steel rail with one hand, looking tired from the long day's work but hiding most of the exhaustion behind a polite smile.

"Bev?"

"See you Monday, Ray." She brushed the hair back from her eyes, waved, and the doors closed, like a wall coming down between them.

The subway train began to roll forward, lurching a time or two before it finally found its stride. It skimmed down the short span of rails, making a sound something like the wind swirling around the tops of the skyscrapers, then sailed off into the mouth of the North Tunnel.

Mystified, Ray watched it disappear. Something strange had just happened. He wasn't sure exactly what it was, but for a moment it had felt as if time had somehow skipped a beat. He checked his watch again. 12:08 A.M. A full two minutes had passed. The train had pulled into the station, the doors had opened, Bev had climbed aboard. All that had somehow happened without him.

He stood there a moment or two longer, feeling strangely out of place, and finally, after the platform had fallen back into its uneasy silence, he climbed the stairs again. On the street, there was a chill in the late-night air. The rain had stopped. The sky had opened to a spattering of dim stars. He tucked his briefcase under one arm, and walked with both hands jammed into his pants pockets to keep them warm. It seemed unusually peaceful beneath the sparse patches of night sky. He crossed Washington against a red light, only distantly aware of what he was doing.

By the time he arrived at his apartment on Sixty-Second Street, his thoughts—which had never been far from that picture of Bev standing inside the subway train—had drifted back to the night before, when he had suddenly found himself in the bathroom, confused and feeling as if he had just come out of anesthesia.

The lock clicked into place, and he leaned heavily against the inside of the apartment door. The cast of a streetlight seeped through the living room curtains and cut a path across the floor toward the end table next to the La-Z-Boy. The plate was still sitting there, with its fork and its crumpled napkin. The chicken burrito was missing, though.

Because you ate it, don't you remember?

No, he didn't.

And that was the problem, wasn't it?

It seemed lately he had begun to forget a number of things.

4

Bev beat him to the office Monday morning. After checking his messages—there was only one, a panic call from the B.M. Myers folks who were having second thoughts about their new dog food campaign—Ray wandered into the editing room and found her sitting in the dark, running through the *Timescape* ad.

"Morning."

She waved, back-handed, without looking up from the projector. "Just a sec."

"No hurry." He closed the door, and as the room settled instantly back into its comfortable darkness, he was taken back to Friday night again. It was something he had nearly put out of his mind over the weekend, but suddenly he was there again, on the platform, looking down the long, dark tunnel, wondering when the train would come in. He had been haunted all that night by a strange, unexplainable sense of detachment, and finally on the edge of sleep, had decided that something precious had begun to slip through his fingers. He had wondered—quite legitimately at the time, he thought—if maybe he hadn't begun to lose a little piece of his mind.

Which piece would that be, Ray old boy? A couple million neurons, perhaps?

Perhaps, he thought now, solemnly.

Someone had left a conference chair next to the door. Ray pulled it away from the wall and sat down. He stared vacantly at the soft green light emitted by the projector. He found it, along with the rhythmic clicking of the sprockets and the Monday morning chill that had collected in the room over the weekend, momentarily meditative, and allowed his mind to wander off again.

Sherrie had called from Florida Sunday night. They were having a good time, she said, though Robin was a little cranky from a long day at Epcot. Everything else was doing fine, even the business part of the trip. They still intended to be back the afternoon of the twenty-fifth as planned, she said. Then she had put Robin on the line. "Hi, Daddy! We're on the other side of the country. We went to Epcot today and on Tuesday we're spending the whole day at Disney World, and there's a swimming pool where we're staying!"

"Sounds like you're having a pretty good time."

"Yeah. It'd be better if you were here, though," she said matter-of-factly. "But I understand. Most of the time, you and Mommy don't like it when you're around each other."

That's not true, he thought. *At least not entirely. Sometimes we just forget what it was like a long, long time ago.*

Now, as he was sitting in the chair, silently watching Bev run through the thirty-second tape, four, maybe five times altogether, he realized he had forgotten most of the bad times. The happiest times—when they had first met and started dating, and in the early years of their marriage—those were the times he recalled most clearly now. How had he ever lost sight of those?

The rat-tat-tat of the sprockets ended abruptly and the silence brought Ray back from his thoughts. He looked across the room at Bev as she swung her chair around. In the faint green light her face was half-hidden in shadow, but it appeared as if she were lost in thoughts of her own.

"Okay, no secrets between co-workers," Ray said. "What's eating you about this thing?"

"It's too fast," she said evenly. She sounded every bit the woman who had won a Clio, though the degree of concern in her voice surprised him somewhat.

"That's still bothering you?"

"It's still bothering me."

"You're worrying needlessly," he said. He leaned back on the legs of his chair and flipped on the light switch next to the door. The room brightened immediately, and for a reason he could not explain, it seemed as if something nearby had suddenly stopped moving.

"I don't think so. This one is going to crater on us if we're not careful."

"If it craters, it won't be because of the IPMs," he said. He had come across a black-and-white, quick-cut Nike spot during a Bears/49ers game over the weekend and that ad had convinced him that they had made the right decision for the *Timescape* campaign. It was a gritty, emotional series of shots that had left him feeling pumped up and powerful, the same kinds of feelings they had set out to convey for *Timescape*.

She turned back to the projector, staring silently at the white screen. "I'm not so sure, Ray."

"It's the perfect vehicle for this movie. We take the thrills and all the action, splice them together in a thirty-second run . . . and as long as we leave viewers feeling excited, it doesn't matter how much of it they absorb. It's the *feeling* we're trying to convey here. That's what'll get them in the theater on Friday night."

"I suppose," she said with a degree of resignation. "But?"

"But . . . don't you ever feel it?"

"Feel *what*?"

"How fast everything seems to be moving?"

He leaned forward, staring at her, thinking: *You feel it, too? That sense that a tight spring has suddenly let loose and everything's becoming unraveled? You feel that?* But that wasn't what she was talking about. She was talking about the rat race and how fast the days sometimes go and how confusing the world can be with all its changes. And he was talking about something much more personal than that. He was talking about closing your eyes while watching *Nightline* and opening them again and finding yourself somewhere else, doing some*thing* else.

"I guess I do," he said.

"Doesn't it ever scare you?"

"I don't think about it much."

She turned back to the projector again, and Ray felt the muscles in his neck relax, as if the air had been let out of them. She seemed momentarily occupied by the screen, then . . .

(*CUT TO*)

. . . placed the menu down on the table and looked up at him. "Sorry I was late," Bev said.

He heard a *clinking* sound and followed it across the room to a middle-aged man who was touching wineglasses with a much younger, and appreciably more attractive woman. They were sitting at a small table in the corner, with a flowered trellis behind them. The woman giggled.

"Chet dropped by. He said you were busy on the phone but he wanted us to know that the company got the Timex account. It's ours for the asking, Ray."

A waiter brushed past him like a breeze, kicking up a swirl of hair on the back of his head. He combed it back, and looked up at the man, who was carrying a silver tray on the palm of one hand. There were three or four other tables in the area, covered in white-lace cloths, centered with candles and fresh bouquets of flowers. Through a latticed divider, he could see the soft glow of sunlight slipping in past a curtained window. It was still daylight out.

"Ray?"

He looked down at the menu in his hands, feeling as if he had just opened his eyes after an accident and was still shaking the cobwebs out of his mind. They were at Fitzgerald's. It said so across the top of the menu. And they were having lunch, he supposed. They often lunched at Fitzgerald's.

"Are you okay?"

"Huh?"

"You look pale."

"No, I'm fine," he lied. Across the room, another waiter appeared from behind a pair of swinging doors. He weaved his way through the maze of tables, half of which were empty, and disappeared through an archway into another room of the restaurant. "What time is it?"

"One-fifteen," Bev said. "We've still got forty-five minutes."

One-fifteen.

My God.

Ray closed his menu, and stared across the table at her. She was wearing a pearl gray, loose-fitting blazer over an attractive silk crepe de chine blouse and a slim, elegant skirt. It was the same day as it had been this morning, he realized. Those were the same clothes she had been wearing in the projection room. Only now . . .

"Are you sure you're all right?"

"Just hungry," he said, looking down at his menu again. "So how much do we get to play with?"

"Pardon?"

"The Timex account."

"Two million for the first go around. If they like what we deliver, five mil a year for a three-year run."

"Sounds good," he said absently. An empty, gurgling sensation had begun to roil in his stomach. Not, surprisingly, out of hunger, as he would have expected—he hadn't eaten breakfast this morning and last night's dinner had been nothing more than a couple of bites from a reheated tuna casserole—but from a slight sense of nausea. He slipped a hand below the table and loosened his belt a notch. "When do we start?"

"There's a meeting this afternoon with Chet and Boswick and the production people."

"What time?"

"Three," Bev said.

"Good," he said. "Look, could you excuse me for a moment?"

"Of course."

"I'll be right back."

In the restroom, he leaned heavily over the sink, both hands braced against the porcelain, head bowed. A light sweat had broken out over his forehead, though the sensation of nausea had passed now. He glanced up at his reflection in the mirror, at the man who was quietly becoming a stranger.

What was happening to him?

5

By the time Ray arrived home that night, the apartment was draped in thick shadow. He dropped his briefcase on the entryway tile, next to the door, and thanked sweet Jesus he had made it through the rest of the day without closing his eyes and suddenly finding himself somewhere else. He moved down the hall, pausing a moment to look at the end table next to the La-Z-Boy. It had become an unconscious habit the past several nights, to stop there and reassure himself that the plate and the napkin and the fork had all been put away and everything was in its place now, the way he last remembered it.

On his way past the phone in the kitchen, he slipped the receiver off its cradle, then pulled a chair out from the table, sat down, and began to dial the push-buttons with the thumb of one hand. It rang four times before she answered it.

"Mom?"

"Raymond," she said delightedly. "What a wonderful surprise."

"How are you, Mom?"

"I'm fine, of course."

"And Dad?"

"Your father's watching his football game. He's in heaven. You want to talk to him?"

"No, that's all right. I forgot it was Monday night." He had spent much of the afternoon retracing the last few days of his life, and when they had led him nowhere in particular, he had traced the days back even further, all the way back to his childhood, in fact. Thirty-two years of days, all behind him now, and . . . and they were beginning to pass even faster now, he had decided.

"Mom?"

"What is it, Raymond?"

"I know this is going to sound like a strange question, but . . . what's it like . . . growing old?"

There was a thoughtful silence on the other end of the

line. Then, in that soft voice that someone who didn't know her might mistake for frailty, she said, "It sneaks up on you, Raymond. Like an early winter. One day it's autumn and you're picking wild berries and baking pies, the next day it's snowing and picking berries seems like something you used to do a long, long time ago."

"Is it true, that old wives' tale about time going by faster the older you get?"

"It certainly feels like it."

Yes, he thought unhappily, it certainly does. He ran a hand through his hair, and by the time he hung up the phone, the words on the other end had become distant and unimportant. He had heard what he had called to hear. However distasteful it felt.

It was getting late.

Later than you think, my friend.

He glanced down the hallway again, at the pale-gray light slipping in through the curtains, and thought about trying to reach Sherrie in Florida. He wasn't even sure where she was staying, but she had given him a number, he thought, and he had written it down somewhere.

But then what was he going to say?

You better hurry back if you ever want to see me again. I'm not sure I'll be here much longer.

No. Not that. This: *stay where you are, Sherrie. You and Robin stay right there in Florida. I won't be able to see you, but as long as you're there and not here, I'll know I haven't lost anything more than a week. I'll know that much.*

No. Better not to call at all, he decided, burying his head . . .

(*CUT TO*)

. . . in his hands.

"A hard night?"

He heard her voice, and knew immediately it was a voice that shouldn't be there, not in his apartment at this time of night, uninvited. It was almost more than he could do, but he forced his hands away from his face. Bev was sitting across from him on the other side of the . . . desk. They were sitting in his office at Baylor & Baylor. She smiled cautiously, with a look of mild concern.

"Ray?"

"What time is it?" he asked, though the exact time didn't matter, did it? There was sunlight pouring in through the window behind him, and that was all he needed to know. It was daylight out.

"A quarter to ten."

Twelve hours, or nearly that much.

My God.

He stared down at the coat sleeves of his business suit, and realized he had changed clothes since a moment ago—or last night, or a week ago, or however long it had been. And he had shaved and washed up, spent a night alone in bed, and climbed out of that bed early, had breakfast, and hurried into the office, all of that, and maybe not just once, maybe half-a-dozen times by now.

"What day is it?"

"Tuesday."

"Thank God."

"Are you all right?"

"I don't know. I've been . . ."

"What?"

Losing time, he was tempted to say, but it was an easier thing to think than speak. Therefore, instead, he asked a question he thought might lead into something he had been kicking around recently: "Did you ever see the movie *Sybil*?"

"Sally Field? About the woman with all those different personalities?"

"Yes."

"It was a good movie."

"Yes. But remember what happened when another personality had stepped in? She couldn't remember things. It was as if she had gone to sleep in the middle of making dinner and then suddenly she would wake up again and she would be somewhere else—at work, maybe—and it would be a different day and she would be wearing different clothes."

"But she thought that's the way it was for everyone. I remember that. It was creepy."

Not as creepy as the real thing.

He couldn't ask his next question while looking at her, so he swung his chair around, and stared out the window at the mirror-glassed high-rise across the avenue from his office. The sun was above the building, shining in his face at an odd angle; otherwise he wouldn't have been surprised if he had actually been able to see himself on the other side. It had happened before, on a clear winter day, in the early afternoon hours. Not this time, though, and he supposed that was all for the best because it might have been too much, seeing himself where he knew he shouldn't be.

"Have you ever noticed anything unusual about me, Bev? Times when I wasn't myself? Not just bad days, but days—or maybe only hours—when I seemed like someone you hardly knew?"

At first, she let loose with a barely audible giggle, no more than that, then followed it with something that sounded vaguely like an attempt to swallow the rest of her laughter. It had occurred to her, no doubt, in that short mini-second of a moment, that the question had been a serious one. "Ray, you're one of the most consistent men I've ever met."

"Consistent?"

"I've only known you for a few weeks, but yes, I'd say consistent. I know what to expect when we work together. I don't have to worry about temper tantrums or sudden outbreaks of egomania from you. We can differ on things and still respect each other's opinions—no hurt feelings."

Wrong straw, he thought. You're grasping at the wrong straw. No Sybil here. This isn't about multiple personalities, it's about one personality. One badly frightened personality quickly losing touch with himself.

"Ray, about the IPMs on *Timescape* . . ."

"You were right," he said in a whisper. "I think I'm beginning to understand that now. The world's spinning

faster than when we were kids, when all you needed
to sell breakfast cereal was some animated kid saying,
'I want my Malt-O-Meal.' Now . . . well, things are a
little more complicated, aren't they?"

"They don't have to be."

"Don't they? I wonder how we slow them down, make
them . . .

(*CUT TO*)

" . . . comprehendible?"

Oh Christ.

6

The room was pitch-black here and it took a moment
for his eyes to adjust to the sudden darkness. Out of
the shadows came a sound, a *clickety-clicking* that he
recognized as the sound of a projector, and he slowly
put it together in his mind. He . . . they were in the
projection room now.

"What did you say?" Bev asked.

"Uh . . . nothing."

"It works better now, don't you think?"

"What does?"

She glanced over her shoulder, her expression partially masked by the shadows, but even in the dark he could
see the trace of a smile as if she thought he were joking
with her. "Hey, I know you didn't want to do this, at
least not initially."

The Timescape *spot. She's talking about the* Timescape
spot.

"But you were right," he said calmly. He sat forward
in the chair, feeling an arrhythmic hammering in his
chest. He wondered if his heart were beating faster,
trying to keep up with the seconds, minutes, hours that
were flashing by. And it felt as if just by wondering,
his heart skipped another half-beat. "It does work better
now."

"I'm glad you think so."

"Bev?"

"What?"

"I need to tell you something. It's going to sound insane, absolutely Atascadero out-of-my-mind insane. But I need you to listen, because I'm not even sure how much of it I'm going to get out." And he told her about the first time it had happened in his apartment late at night, and the second time in the subway station, and the third time when he had suddenly been at the restaurant with her, and it all seemed to blur together like a grayish-black nightmare that had only just begun. "Five minutes ago," he said finally, "we were in my office, and I was staring out the window wondering what you meant by *consistent*."

Except for a soft intake of air, she was perfectly motionless in the darkness, not saying a word, not giving off a hint of what thoughts were going through her mind at that moment.

"Bev?"

"I don't know what to say."

"You think I'm crazy, don't you?"

"No, of course not." She had draped an arm over the back of her chair as he had shared his story with her, and now she swung the chair all the way around, face-to-face with him, as if she wanted to be able to read his expression in the dull, greenish-white glow of the projector. "Do you know what time it is now?"

"No."

"It's nearly five o'clock. The conversation we had in your office was this morning, almost seven hours ago."

"Oh sweet Jesus."

"Ray, we had a quick lunch at Mattie's, spent two or three hours in a head-banger over what to do to placate the folks at B.M. Myers, did a conference call with Jim Mathews at Timex, and have been hiding out in here for at least a couple of hours now. We've been together the whole time."

"But I don't remember any of that."

"Not a minute?"

"Not since this morning when you told me things don't have to be complicated." He leaned back to flip on the light switch, because it was *her* face that was hidden in shadow now and he didn't like the idea of not knowing what she might be hiding. Instantly, the room went from dark to . . .

(*CUT TO*)

. . . light, and he found himself back at his apartment again, sitting in the kitchen. A slight tremor waffled through his body. He closed his eyes, took a deep breath, and tried to hold himself together. How long was this going to go on?

"Ray?"

The sound of the woman's voice swam up from somewhere nearby. He opened his eyes again, feeling the muscles in the back of his neck tighten. The telephone was off the hook and lying in his lap. He raised it to his ear, listened.

"Ray?"

It was Sherrie's voice.

"Are you still there?"

"Sherrie?" He felt his throat narrow ever so slightly, and fought back a sob that was trying to force its way out. "Don't hang up! Please, for God's sake, don't hang up on me."

"I'm not hanging up; I just got on. Are you all right?"

"Yes. No . . . not really. Hell, I don't know anymore." He sank back in the chair until his body felt as if it had melted into the soft, padded leather. "Where are you?"

"At home. We got in about an hour ago. There was a delay taking off from Orlando, almost three hours. I thought if you didn't mind . . ."

Home?

" . . . I'd keep Robin until tomorrow."

"What day is it?" he asked.

"Saturday."

He stared down the hallway toward the living room. The curtains were drawn, but he could tell it was dark out. If the sun were up there would be a soft, golden-yellow glow washing in around the edges. Instead, he could barely make out the dark lines of the La-Z-Boy and the couch.

"What time is it?"

"A little after ten. Ray, did I wake you?"

"No, no, you didn't wake me. But I want you to . . ."
(*CUT TO*)

" . . . come over as soon as you—"

Too late.

The receiver was gone.

He stared numbly at his empty hand, first curling it into a fist, then prying it open again, grateful that he could *feel* the mechanics of the motion. But the phone . . . it was gone now. So was the table, where he had been sitting. And the refrigerator, the stove, the plastic simulated wood-grained canister set on the counter. All of it was gone. Across the room from him, in its place, he found the familiar face of a newscaster on the television screen, and the couch up against the wall, and the ceiling-to-floor curtains open. He was in the living room now.

Through the window, he could see where an orange-brown haze had settled over the cityscape. It was evening, he decided. City colors were always muddier in the evening.

That was something he had never noticed before his separation from Sherrie two short months ago. But the day he had moved his last box of clothes out of the house, he had come here, and standing in the entryway he had looked out this same window. The world had been a dirty place that day. Dirtier than he had ever imagined it could be. It hadn't gotten any cleaner since then.

Sherrie, he thought. *I was on the telephone, talking to Sherrie.*

And what he had to do now was get her back on the phone again, get her to come over so she could stand right next to him, maybe even hold on to his hand when he closed his eyes and woke up somewhere else, some*time* else. Maybe then she could tell him what had happened, if he were crazy, or if (as he had come to fear) the world had suddenly begun to spin a little faster while he was busy looking back at their marriage—hoping,

praying, *needing* things to be the way they used to be.
There is *no going back. There's only going forward.*

He pulled himself out of the La-Z-Boy, all his weight
on the arms, and before he had fully balanced himself,
there was a knock at the front door.

"Ray, are you in there?"

It was Bev.

He felt his way along the hallway, his legs inexplic-
ably weary. It was not an easy task to keep himself
balanced. That's because your gravity's changing, he
thought crazily. He pulled open the door and leaned
heavily against its edge.

Bev stared at him in silence, her eyes bright with
surprise. "Jesus, Ray, what's the matter with you? You
look awful."

He glanced down and was madly amused to find
himself dressed in a bathrobe and socks. The robe was
open. He had an old pair of boxer shorts on underneath
and a T-shirt with a stain that looked like dried egg. "I'm
sorry," he said as he closed the robe and tightened the
sash around his waist.

"Are you okay?"

"I . . . I . . . don't know."

"You haven't been in all week. I've been trying to
get you on the phone. Don't you ever answer the damn
thing?"

"I do . . . I was . . ." He turned, and pointed weakly
toward the kitchen. "I was just talking to Sherrie a minute ago."

"Has she been to see you lately?"

Lately? He realized he wanted to ask her what time
it was, but hours didn't matter anymore. It was days
and weeks and maybe even months that concerned him
now. *Lately? When was that?* "I'm . . . not sure. What
day is it?"

"You keep asking me that. Every time I talk to you,
you ask me what day it is."

"Well?"

"Thursday, Ray. It's Thursday."

His body slumped heavily against the door . . .

(*CUT TO*)

. . . and he heard the phone ringing.

Wherever he was, it was dark now. There was the luminescent glow of a clock face nearby—9:56 P.M.— and a sliver of light coming from somewhere behind him. It divided the darkness into two uneven sections: one on his right, which seemed to exist only a foot or two beyond him; the other, which seemed to stretch across an open area, through a doorway and beyond. He pulled himself up to one elbow, realizing suddenly that this was his bedroom and he had been sleeping.

The phone rang again.

He found the receiver and brought it to his ear without a word.

"Ray?"

"Yeah."

"It's Sherrie."

He closed his eyes, and in the complete darkness could feel his hands trembling, as if they belonged to a boy about to pin his first corsage to the bosom of a girl's dress. The last time he had seen her had been just before she had left for Florida with Robin. They had met for lunch in a little cafe off Market Street called Demercurio's, and talked about how things were going, her in her life, him in his. They had always been on good speaking terms, even as the strain of their two careers had sometimes raised their voices. It had been a pleasant conversation that time out, and yes—though he hadn't said so at the time—he had allowed himself the vague hope that sometime down the road he would be able to move his things back home again. It was a hope he wanted to share with her even now, but he couldn't seem to get it clear in his head just how he should go about saying so.

"Ray?"

She had changed her hair style since their separation, cut it short in the front and brushed it away from her face, bringing out the soft, slender contours of her cheeks, the bright innocent hazel of her eyes. She had changed other things as well. Started wearing bigger,

bolder earrings like the pair with the black onyx stones.
And she had used her own credit card to pay for their
lunch at Demercurio's. But the thing that hurt the most
was this: she had changed from an unhappy woman to
a happy woman. He had watched it happen.

"We're never getting back together again, are we?"
he asked hoarsely.

"You need help, Ray. You can't keep locking out the
world."

"*Are* we?"

There was a pause—he had to give her that—a moment
of consideration before she actually answered him. Then
she said it: "No."

He closed his eyes . . .

(*CUT TO*)

. . . and began to cry.

"Don't cry, Daddy."

*I have to cry. It's started now and I don't think it's
ever going to stop.*

He took his hands away from his face, and she was
there, standing in front of him . . . his little girl.

"Robin?"

"I didn't mean to make you sad," she said. Sherrie
was standing directly behind her, with her hands on
Robin's shoulders as if she were trying to make certain his daughter didn't get too close. For her own
protection, no doubt. Daddy hadn't been himself lately.

He became aware of the tall ceiling overhead, of the
three rows of tables, of another small group of people
huddled together at the other end of the room. This was
a place he had never been before.

"Where are we?"

"It's called Oak Ridge," Sherrie said. "It's a treatment
facility."

"Oak Ridge." He liked the sound it made. "Ohh—
kkk—rrr—idge."

On the table in front of him, he noticed the cafeteria
trays. Sherrie and Robin apparently hadn't been hungry.
They had hardly touched their food: a little milk from

an open carton, half a serving of applesauce gone, and
a few bites out of a hamburger that must have been
Robin's. His own tray was empty, though he couldn't
remember what he had had to eat. Then he started to cry
again.

"We've got to leave now, Ray."

"You just got here."

"We've been here all afternoon," Sherrie said. She
had a look in her eyes as if her heart were breaking,
and he thought she might join him in his tears, but
she didn't. "We'll come back again next Sunday. I
promise."

"Promise?"

"Yes."

"I love . . ."

(*CUT TO*)

" . . . you," he said. Though he was somewhere else
by the time he had finished the words. It was a small
room. Two beds. A stale, unventilated smell in the air.
He glanced around . . .

(*CUT TO*)

 . . . him.

A different place.

Robin was there now, holding his hand.

"You haven't been shaving, Daddy."

He stared at her. God, she was beautiful.

"You should shave."

"I'm . . ."

(*CUT TO*)

" . . . sorry," he said.

Somewhere new—no, the cafeteria this time—and
Bev was there. She was wearing the saddest face he had
ever seen her wear. "*Timescape* opened with a weekend
take of nearly seven million," she was saying. "They're
happy folks at the production company."

"*Time* . . ."

(*CUT TO*)

" . . . *scape*?" he asked, and found himself sitting in
a wheelchair outside on a flagstone patio, overlooking
a grassy knoll.

Sherrie was with him, holding his hand the same way Robin had held it, as if she were afraid she might lose him completely if she let go.

"It's a beautiful day, isn't it?" she said.

"Please don't go away . . ."

(*CUT TO*)

7

"I've got to talk fast because I don't know how long I might be here. A few seconds? A minute? Maybe an hour? Sometimes it's hard to tell the difference between here and that other *place. They can fool you if you don't watch them. One's right. One's wrong. It's confusing. Every once in a while I have to remind myself what day it is and where I live. And there's always the danger, I suppose, that if I'm not careful, I might drift a little too far from the reality loop. It's happened, I've heard, to some of the best of them."*

Raymond Hewitt

ABOUT THE EDITOR

Thomas F. Monteleone has been a professional writer since 1972. He has published more than 90 short stories in numerous magazines and anthologies. His notorious column of opinion and entertainment, "The Mothers And Fathers Italian Association," currently appears in *Mystery Scene* magazine. He is the editor of two anthologies prior to the creation of the *Borderlands* series. Of his eighteen novels, recent titles include *Fantasma, Lyrica, The Magnificent Gallery,* and *The Blood of the Lamb* (1992). His two collections of his short stories are *Dark Stars and Other Illuminations* and *Fearful Symmetries.* He is also one of the guiding lights of Borderlands Press, a publishing house he founded in 1990 to publish limited and other special editions.

He likes baseball, computers, British ales and stouts, comic books, getting lots of mail every day, all kinds of music, driving his sports car on country roads, and women who laugh at his jokes. He lives in Baltimore, is forty-five years old, and still dashingly handsome.